# ENDLESS

CLARITY COAST OMEGAVERSE

DEVYN SINCLAIR

Cover by Mayflower Studio

*For the ocean, forever my home away from home...*

# AUTHOR'S NOTE

Dear Readers,

*Endless* is not a book that's meant to be dark. However, as with most of my books, there are some sensitive themes and situations. If you feel like this could be a problem for you, please protect yourself. No work of fiction is worth your mental health.

The full list of content warnings is available on my website, or through the QR code below.

Devyn Sinclair

## CHAPTER ONE

### ISOLDE

"I cannot fucking believe I let you guys talk me into this," I called across the room to my two best friends, currently two tiny pictures on my phone.

"It's called being supportive," Trinity said. "Not to mention I could get in serious trouble for doing it at all. So, you're welcome."

I grumbled something about her being supportive of nothing but my *ass* as I tried to shove the suitcase closed. But it didn't want to. In fact, it seemed to be refusing to close in an attempt to not get on the plane.

Me too, suitcase. Me. Fucking. Too.

"But you're coming back for good, right?" The second voice asked. Softer and sweeter than Trinity's. Because Ocean was about as soft and sweet as they came. "Like, once you're back, you're going to call a moving company and actually be home?"

Not looking at the camera, I glanced around the bare bones bedroom I'd lived in for the last year. It's not like I was particularly attached to this place. I wasn't. But being home was complicated, and I honestly didn't know how I'd feel once I was there.

And the clusterfuck that was going to happen after I got off the plane wouldn't help.

"I don't know," I admitted. "Maybe?"

"Come on, Iz," she begged. "We miss you. It sucks that you're on the other side of the country, and don't pretend you like it. We all know you don't. Beau can suck an egg. He doesn't get to chase you off."

A snorting, cackling sound came through the phone, and Trinity covered her face to hide the mimosa now coming through her nose. "Suck an egg? Really?"

In spite of myself, I smiled. "Be nice, Rin. Ocean's not going to tell my ex to go fuck himself."

No, that was my job. If I could muster up the courage to do it instead of hauling ass across the country and hiding. Their little plan was going to help. Supposedly. Personally, I had my doubts.

Plans made while drunk and sad didn't tend to work out well for me. But it was too late to turn back now. The deposit was paid, the questionnaire was filled out, and even though I had my doubts—and absolutely *no* interest in men *or* Alphas—showing up to my sister's wedding extravaganza alone, with my ex as the best man?

Not a fucking option.

Which was why the St. James pack was meeting me when I got off the plane today. So they could pretend to be with me. First for my parents' anniversary party and being thrown into the deep end with people I hadn't seen in a year, and then everything else.

I shook my head and tried to shut the suitcase again, putting all my weight on it and going slowly.

"You're second guessing again," Trinity said.

"Of course I am." I forced the words out between my teeth. "Hiring a pack of escorts to take me to my sister's wedding and pretend to be my... I don't even know what for *three full weeks* is frankly not high on the list of 'best decisions Isolde Allen has made.'"

Ocean tilted her head. "Is there actually a list?"

"No," I sighed. "Well, not one that's written down. It's a mental list. Two lists. This is on the worst decision list."

"What else is on there?"

Trinity snorted into her glass again. "Dating Beau in the first place?"

I ignored her. "That, and this. Pretty much it." Finally, I shoved the bunched up shirt in the way of the zipper *just* far enough for the suitcase to close. "*Victory!*"

"Good. Now get your ass to the airport. You have hunks to meet."

I glared at my friend, who was getting cut off from champagne even if I had to reach through the phone to do it. "Don't start."

Trinity leaned forward, her eyes startlingly clear and serious. "No, Iz, *you* don't start. Beau and his too-tan ass don't deserve you. What you deserve is to walk into that anniversary party tonight with your head held high and hot men surrounding you to prove what an idiot he is for choosing to let you go.

"So stop acting like you're committing some hideous crime by doing it. You're not taking advantage of them. This is their job and they enjoy it. And if you happen to get some excellent dick along the way, so be it."

I flopped back on the bed. "You had me until the last bit. I'm not paying them to have sex with me. I don't want sex. I don't want anyone. I just want to be alone."

"You haven't seen them yet," Trinity muttered.

My friend interviewed the secretive pack for her magazine. An exclusive feature on the elite pack of anonymous escorts to the rich and famous. Somehow, no one had figured out who they actually were. But she knew now, and when I'd called my friends drunk and crying about being lonely and *dreading* seeing Beau again, Trinity broke every rule in the book and sent me their number. Told me to buck up and ask them to be my escort.

I did.

For whatever reason, they said yes.

It took most of my savings, but money was just money and I could make more. I couldn't take back the shame of facing my ex alone. Did that make me weak? Maybe. But as much as my stomach twisted at the idea of hiring them, there was an undercurrent of relief too.

I wouldn't be alone.

Trinity and Ocean coached me through the call, on video through my computer, listening to my—admittedly teary—request, and then helped me fill out the questionnaire the pack sent.

The incredibly detailed questionnaire, which lightly covered things like basic family and favorite color. And more sexual questions than I'd ever read in my life.

And because I was drunk and sad and more than a little desperate, I answered honestly. So now this pack of strangers knew everything about me, including how I imagined being fucked, and I knew nothing about them.

I didn't think they would even give me their real names.

"I don't need them for sex," I finally said. "I need them so I can look people in the eye when I'm there and Beau has his arm around his *fiancée*. That's it."

Trinity shrugged. "I'm just saying. There are worse things than shacking up with smoking hot Alphas for a few weeks. You're paying them anyway. Might as well get all the benefits."

I tried to cover my flinch, but didn't hide it fast enough.

"Rin." Ocean scolded. "Really?"

"Sorry. Seems like the champagne has more of a hold on my mouth than I thought."

"It's okay. I need to get going anyway if I'm going to make my flight."

"And we want that," Ocean said with a smile. "We'll see you tonight?"

"Yes, ma'am. Trinity, try not to be too drunk to party?"

She winked. "Nah, I'm saving the real thing for you, babe."

I rolled my eyes as I ended the call, wincing again at the memories. What Trinity said wasn't too far off what Beau had said after unceremoniously dumping me. Within weeks, he'd been promoted, and was dating someone else at the company who was beneath him. He said he was already paying her, might as well take advantage since he hadn't been getting any with me.

Putting on my standard travel clothes—leggings and a plain t-shirt so I had to do as little as possible at airport security—and putting on scent canceller, I made sure I had everything I needed before leaving the house. I wouldn't be back for at least a month, hence shoving my entire life into a hardshell suitcase.

At the very least, the plane was comfortable. My parents insisted on bumping me to first class. They gave me champagne, and I took it to calm my nerves. Because even if it would be fine, I was still meeting the St. James pack at the airport so we could go straight to my family's estate like we were together, and my stomach was in *knots*.

I choked a laugh, making the Beta businessman next to me look over like I was a naughty child. But the comparison wasn't lost on me. My stomach was in knots, and I was going to meet a pack full of Alphas, who likely had very large knots, if this was what they did for a living.

By the time the plane was making its final descent, the napkin that came with the champagne was in tatters across my lap and seat, my hands gripping the armrests tight enough to whiten my knuckles.

It wasn't too late to turn around, right?

As soon as we touched down I flipped my phone on and texts started coming through.

MOM

Please let me know when you land. We're so excited to see you!

OCEAN

It's going to be okay, Iz. We're not going to let Beau ruin this for anyone. Especially you.

TRINITY

Sorry for the asshole comment. But I stand by the sentiment. Can't wait for you to get here with your eye candy!

UNKNOWN

We've arrived and will be waiting at baggage claim.

The last text was only a few minutes ago. My stomach tumbled with nerves. What if they weren't as nice as Trinity said they were? What if they were awful and I just roped myself into spending three weeks with men I couldn't stand? What if they smelled bad?

I pressed my head back into the seat as we taxied, cursing scents. If it weren't for scents, I probably wouldn't be here in the first place. Alphas and their fucking instincts.

Normally, I loved being an Omega. But in the last year it hadn't exactly served me well. I pulled my thoughts out of the spiral they liked to fall down and typed out a response.

ISOLDE

Just landed. Will be there soon.

Time to face the music. I stopped in the bathroom on the way to baggage claim, and I looked about as good as someone could after being on a plane for five hours. But I ran a brush through my hair and put on a little lip gloss. I didn't lie to my friends—I wasn't paying these men to have sex with me. But I still cared enough to make a good impression.

Or at least not make a *bad* impression.

Joining the crush of people heading toward baggage claim, I ignored the butterflies in my stomach. Which definitely had everything to do with the party tonight and seeing Beau. Not meeting this pack.

Nope.

Definitely not.

The array of drivers and family holding up signs came into view as I rode down the escalator.

To the left, I saw a sign with my name on it, held by a built redhead. Behind him, there were other men, standing together and talking.

*Fuck.*

Trinity was right.

They were hot.

My one saving grace was that they didn't know what I looked like either, so I had a chance to stare at them openly. I was far from the only one doing that. They stood out in a good way. In an *incredible* way.

I walked toward them, and as I entered their space, each of them looked at me. The bubble of their scents rolled over me, one after another. So good. Holy crap.

Omegas couldn't scent match outside of heat, but these were definitely some of the best smelling Alphas I'd ever come across.

"Umm, hi," I said.

The redhead froze for a second, gaze roving over me before he smiled, eyes crinkling at the corners. His eyes were blue, and I got lost in them for a second. Spending time with them for three weeks? Getting to just stare at them and scent them?

I was so fucked.

Like he could read my mind, he smiled deeper. "You must be Isolde."

## CHAPTER TWO

JOEL

Vaughn scrolled through the questionnaire as we drove to the airport, reviewing. "Three weeks? You sure about this, Joel?"

It wasn't the first time they'd asked if I was sure. A fair question, given we usually didn't take jobs longer than a single event. A weekend at most. Three weeks was unheard of, and yet...

"Yeah. I'm sure."

Strangest phone call of my life, but I had a feeling. Deep down, I couldn't say no to her. The woman on the phone had been crying. Pretending not to cry, but crying while she explained what she needed.

Vaughn chuckled again. "I like this comment. I missed it the first time."

"Which one?" Cade asked.

"Before the sexual preferences. 'I'm filling this out, but you don't need to read it. I'm not hiring you for sex, so get it out of your heads. I'm done with men for the foreseeable future.'"

We all laughed a little. Not that we were bothered by it. If a client didn't want that, it was fine. We were there for what they needed, not the other way around. If she didn't want sex, there wouldn't be sex.

But I wasn't about to pretend that part—and many other parts—of the questionnaire hadn't caught our attention.

"Everyone got your identities ready to go?" I asked.

"Yes, sir." Hawk gave me a mock salute.

Usually it didn't matter. The jobs were so short that picking a name and a career was all that was needed. But for this we needed to be real. There couldn't be slip-ups. Another reason we didn't usually do events that involved client's families.

Apparently I was breaking all the rules now.

Our suitcases were in the back of the car, ready to go to Isolde's parents' house. I didn't know anyone who planned three weeks of things leading up to a wedding, but then again, not many people living on Clarity Coast were normal. The wealthy, the eccentric, and the artists.

I guessed this family was the former.

Rowan pulled the SUV into the parking garage and I grabbed the little sign with her name. "Ready?"

"Sure thing, boss," Hawk said with a smirk.

I shook my head but couldn't stop the smile. Pulling out my phone, I texted the number Isolde gave us.

JOEL

We've arrived and will be waiting at baggage claim.

We gathered near the escalator and waited. Her flight would be arriving any minute now.

"Anyone want to quiz me?" Hawk asked.

Rowan raised a single eyebrow. "Quiz you?"

"On the fake identity."

"Yes," Cade laid the sarcasm on thick. "Because when our client comes down the escalator and walks up to us we want to be reviewing the details of your fake identity."

My phone buzzed.

ISOLDE

Just landed. Will be there soon.

"She landed."

"Did you manage to bump all your classes?" Vaughn asked Cade.

He shook his head. "No. But she made it seem like there would be some days where we weren't needed. I can fit them in around this."

Hawk crossed his arms. "Just don't let Isolde see your rope bag."

"Based on the questionnaire, Isolde might very much want to see Cade's rope bag," I said.

Under the very long lists of interests we included, rope, bondage, and a host of other things were checked off. But the shibari classes Cade taught weren't a part of his persona, and since she didn't want sex, it wasn't going to come up.

Rowan stretched. "It was a good list."

It was.

A damn good list.

But we weren't looking for something permanent. Our dream of an Omega had died. Been there, done that, watched the ship sail into the fucking sunset.

After matchmakers, dates, well-meaning friends and family didn't find us one, it wasn't likely. It hurt, the empty nest in our home pulsing like a bruise. But with jobs like this, we all got to fulfill the pieces of our instincts that longed to protect and care for someone. It wasn't enough, but it was the best we had, and it hurt less when we set the terms.

This arrangement was better for everyone involved.

Vaughn nudged my shoulder with his. "Incoming."

I looked up and did a double take. The woman in front of us was stunningly beautiful. Fiery red hair that was slightly messy, like she'd just woken up. Or used a bed in a more *fun* way. Leggings which clung like a second skin, showing lush hips that could only mean an ass that was worth worshipping.

Her teeth worried her lower lip like she was nervous as she approached.

And then it hit me.

Her *scent*.

The first thing I smelled were roses, but it wasn't just that. Something deeper and even more floral, with a darker undertone of sex and secrets.

*Omega*.

Every instinct I had flared to life, and every thought of our dream being dead evaporated like morning mist. I smiled at her, but inside I was straining to break free and haul her into my arms and just fucking breathe. The way Vaughn stood rigid beside me told me enough.

This little Omega was our scent match.

Our client.

The woman we were going to pretend to be in love with for three weeks.

A woman who made it clear she wanted absolutely nothing to do with sex—or us—outside of the arrangement.

Who had no idea what was happening to us, because for Omegas, scent matches only manifested during heat.

She had no idea that she walked up to the five of us and turned our entire lives upside down with a single breath.

And fuck me, all I wanted to do was drop to my knees between her legs and be a throne for her to sit on like a queen.

"Umm, hi."

"You must be Isolde." How I managed to keep my voice from shaking, or myself from purring, I had no idea.

"Yeah," she laughed nervously. "That's me."

I held out a hand. "I'm Joel."

Vaughn's head whipped toward me when I told her my real name, and I sensed the shock going through my pack, but I couldn't lie to her. No matter what happened, I wasn't going to spend the next three weeks pretending to be someone I wasn't while this Omega was with us. She was *ours*.

So fucking rare.

And we couldn't even tell her. Not without scaring her away and trampling all over the very clear boundary she set.

We would have to show her.

Her hand was so small in mine, soft and warm. "It's good to meet you."

I just managed to get myself together enough to move aside so the others could introduce themselves. On their faces I saw the same awe. Except for Cade, who looked at the four of us like we'd each just grown a second head.

We all used our real names.

The blush on her cheeks while she shook each hand was intoxicating. So she wasn't entirely immune.

Good.

That was good.

Hawk turned away from Isolde and asked quietly, "What the fuck are we going to do?"

"I have absolutely no idea."

Rowan's hand came down on my shoulder, voice equally low. "We're going to go to this party and do our job. It's going to be a hell of a lot easier to act like we're together. And after? Then we figure it out."

We didn't need a discussion to be on the same page.

She wasn't a client.

She wasn't a job.

She was absolutely everything.

Isolde Allen was our Omega, and we had three weeks to prove it.

## CHAPTER THREE

### ISOLDE

Joel stepped aside so the others could reach me, and I felt like I shrank under the intensity of their eyes on me. The scent of bourbon and cardamom lingered in my nose from Joel's closeness, quickly morphing into a gentle sweetness. Orange and vanilla. Fucking hell, this Alpha smelled like a creamsicle.

Tall and blonde, he reached out and took my hand in both of his. "It's very nice to meet you, Isolde. I'm Vaughn."

"Vaughn," I repeated, blinking. He was gorgeous, hair a little long and shaggy, but just enough. Like you could sink your fingers into it and *grip*. And his scent didn't make him any less lickable.

I wasn't interested in anything, of course, but I was still an Omega.

And I had eyes that worked.

One side of his mouth tipped up as he watched me, like he could see every thought on my face. He probably could—I was a terrible liar.

Tall, dark, and handsome was next. Tattoos covered both arms. I spotted musical motifs before his face caught me. Harsh but beautiful, with lips that were almost a crime. No one could look at those lips and *not* imagine what they felt like. Hair that hung just above his shoulders and curled around his face.

I was going to kill Trinity tonight.

"Can I hug you?" He asked.

Managing a smile, I cleared my throat. "Since we're all going to pretend to be together in a few hours, yeah, that's okay."

He laughed, wrapping me up in both strength and sweetness. *Fuck*. I inhaled without even thinking about it. His scent was almost sweeter than mine. Like sugar cookies. The big, fat, soft ones with frosting nearly as thick.

"I'm Elliot," he murmured with his arms still around me. "But everyone calls me Hawk."

"Why?"

"Probably a story for another time," the man next to him said. His scent said Beta, but the calm power he exuded made me do a double take. There were some Alphas that couldn't hold the kind of presence he clung to without even trying.

The tiniest of smirks and warming of his eyes was all it took to transform him. Suddenly he was playful, and I had whiplash. "Do I get a hug too? I'm Cade."

"Yeah."

The spicy scent of woodsmoke surrounded me. Like a bonfire on the beach. Sandalwood and peppercorn. Soft vanilla. Rich darkness. Calm power. And he was a Beta.

Not like any Beta I'd ever met before.

Then again, none of them were like what I'd met before.

Lastly, the largest of them stepped forward. Sea salt and coconut. Sunshine and the sea. His scent felt like home, because it was so much of what I grew up with. One warm smile, and I was smiling back, my nerves easing. "Rowan," he said.

I chewed on my lower lip as I looked at the five of them, silence stretching out between us.

The alarm of the baggage claim starting pulled me out of my daze. "Right. I just need to get my bag."

"Of course," Cade said. "We'll help you."

"It's okay. It's just the one bag."

His lips twitched like he was fighting a smile. "We're about to tell your family that we're together and make them believe it. I think it's okay if we grab your bag. Just tell us which one it is."

Then he winked.

He actually winked.

I never knew a wink contained magic that could create butterflies in someone's stomach, but here we were.

"Um, it's a big hardshell. Teal and sparkly. You can't really miss it." My cheeks heated.

A few minutes ago, I was determined not to care what they thought of me. It was a business arrangement. But I very much cared what they thought of me now, and a sparkly suitcase was what Beau would have called childish.

"I think I see it," Hawk said with a grin. "Let me grab it."

There it was, in all its glittery glory, and Rowan nodded. "Good call. It's so much easier when you can pick it out of the sea of black bags."

I stared at him for a second. "Thank you."

Hawk rolled it back to us, and I wrapped my arms around myself. As good as they smelled, and as hot as they were, it was still a bit awkward. "So... what happens now?"

"We have all our things with us," Joel said. "We can head straight to the estate from here. The drive will be long enough to talk about everything."

Everything. Meaning our arrangement.

The worst decision I'd ever made.

Or the best one.

I couldn't tell yet.

"Yeah, okay. I'll need some time to get ready once we get there, anyway."

Vaughn gestured toward the airport doors, hand falling to the small of my back as we crossed the busy streets to the parking garage.

Sweetness and orange. God, this wasn't fair. No wonder they did this for a living. They were sex on a stick. Women of every designation probably fell all over them. If I looked like that, I might be an escort too.

I hadn't changed my mind about the sex, tempting as it was. I was better off alone. I couldn't take the heartbreak all over again if another person—or pack—decided I wasn't worth it.

They led me to a giant dark SUV with tinted windows. Joel and Cade spoke quietly behind us, but I couldn't hear what they said. I pulled out my phone to respond to some of the other texts I had so I wouldn't just be... silent.

I sent the message to my group chat with Trinity and Ocean.

ISOLDE

I'm here. I'm with them. You were right, Rin. They're hot AF. This is also *awkward* AF.

TRINITY

Why? Because you want to bang them?

ISOLDE

Or because I'm about to get into a car with five complete strangers who know everything about me and smell incredible?

I could practically hear her laughing.

TRINITY

Sounds like a personal problem to me.

OCEAN

Well, I guess it's a good thing though? You won't mind spending the time with them.

ISOLDE

True.

But seriously.

This was a bad idea.

TRINITY

The best ones always are.

"Where would you like to sit, Isolde?" Cade's voice dragged my eyes from the screen. It was low and just a little rough. The kind of voice you imagined hearing in places that were shadowed and intimate.

I swallowed.

"I'm not sure. Wherever it's easiest to talk, I guess?"

Hawk pulled open the side door and smiled. "I'll take the back. Cade, you're with me. Isolde, why don't you sit in the middle row with Vaughn. You'll be able to see everyone."

With a grateful nod, I obeyed. This was overwhelming enough as it was, and I was secretly glad not to have to spend the hour-long drive turned around in the front seat just to see them.

Cade turned and grabbed my hand to help me into the car, and the gentle strength there froze me. He helped me without even thinking about it. Like it was a given. The same way Rowan was loading my bag into the back. Like it was an automatic thing.

I guess it was, since I was paying them to do it.

The butterflies in my stomach turned sour.

I needed to be careful. If I wasn't, I would start wishing someone would do this for me without me paying for it. This wasn't something to get used to.

*Enjoy it while it lasts, Isolde.*

Everyone piled into the car, and Rowan pulled away. Suddenly hands were around me, and I startled at Vaughn's closeness. "Seatbelt," he murmured before fastening it for me.

"Right."

One side of his mouth curved into a smile. Fuck, he had dimples.

"I'm sorry," I said, clearing my throat. "I know this is weird."

"Nothing weird about not wanting to face family alone at an event like this," Rowan said. "It's perfectly normal."

"But," Joel said, turning in his seat. "We do need to talk about a few things on the way. So it can all go smoothly."

I nodded, squeezing my hands between my knees. Talking I could do. Answering or asking questions I could do. I needed a direction, not to flounder around like a fish out of water. "Sure."

"Starting with the basics. We know you have boundaries as far as our physical relationship." Did I imagine some hesitance in his voice there? Was I making it up? "However, there will need to be some contact if you want everyone to believe we're together. What's okay and what's not? Are we allowed to kiss you?"

My entire body exploded into embarrassed flames. So much heat so quickly that I felt sweat prick at my temples and neck. Kissing them?

It was hard not to get caught up in the image of Vaughn sliding across the small space between us, cupping the back of my head, and kissing me like my life depended on it.

A small sound from behind me drew my eyes to the back seat, but Hawk and Cade looked normal.

"Yeah," I said, voice rasping. "That's okay. I'm not exactly good at it or anything. But you can touch me. Whatever you need to make it look real. Just no sex."

Rowan's eyes locked on mine in the rear-view mirror. I read the question there. What was making me so adamant about that?

Surely every other client was trying to tear their clothes off the minute they got them alone. So why not?

But I wasn't about to go into the horror that was Beau and me. They didn't need to hear it, and I didn't want to relive it. Once we were at the estate, they were sure to get the picture after everyone and their mother treated me like I was a diseased member of the herd that should be put down out of pity.

Vaughn took my hand, and I jumped. He smiled. "Just practicing. If you startle every time one of us takes your hand, it won't look real." Slowly, he ran his thumb over the back of my hand.

"Oh."

It was a wholly inadequate response to the way his hand made me feel. Shaky, heart pounding, the whole nine yards.

Damn it, I should have made sure to use my vibrator before this trip to take the edge off. One thing I didn't bring with me. Go fucking figure.

"You mentioned you were a graphic designer but are now a bartender?"

"I'm not exactly sure what I am now," I told them. "I bartended when I moved to the east coast, but everyone's trying to get me to move back. And I kind of miss it. But I don't know what I'd do if I moved back."

"Fair enough," Cade said. "But is there anything you'd like us to tell people if they ask?"

I shook my head. "No. If anything, I'm in between jobs. Locations. I don't know."

"For the next few weeks, we're consultants with our own firm." Joel turned and handed me a tablet. It showed the consulting firm that held the same name as the charge on my bank account.

"You can do almost anything as a consultant," Hawk said, grinning when I looked back at him. "People generally don't ask questions. And if they do, it's our real company, so it's not a lie."

Anxiety welled up in my chest. What was I going to do when this was all over? Pretend like I'd been broken up with a second time? Hope nobody would ask questions when they weren't around anymore?

I really didn't think this through.

"So that's what I say? Cause they'll ask." I glance back at Hawk. "Not sure they'll believe it with the tattoos."

"Don't worry," he said, leaning forward close enough for me to get a dose of his sweet scent. Hell, the entire car was filled with rotating breaths of fucking incredible aromas. "I clean up well."

Of that, I had no doubt.

Rowan looked at me in the rearview again. "Can I ask you something, Isolde?"

I nodded.

"Your scent." The rich baritone of his voice ran over me, and I stifled the shiver it gave. "What is it? A little of roses, but the other floral part? I can't seem to identify it."

A laugh bubbled out of me. "Don't worry, most people can't. Hell, it took my own family a while to actually figure it out. It's magnolia."

"The tree?"

"Yes. Not super common."

"I recognize it now. It's fascinating," Cade murmured. "Floral, but with those shades of honey and rose and... *sex*."

He didn't look away when I turned to him. If anything, there was blatant interest on his face and in his eyes. "Thank you, I guess."

"You're very welcome."

The silence stretched out as we stared at each other, that quiet power he held building a little more. Joel came to the rescue. Otherwise, I didn't know that I'd be able to break the contact myself.

"Can you walk us through what to expect tonight and the next couple of weeks? We're good at going with the flow, but anything is helpful."

I cleared my throat, suddenly realizing Vaughn still held my hand. He'd never let it go. "Yeah. I can do that. I'd rather you not get eaten by the wolves."

They all chuckled, and I started talking about what the lion's den we were all walking into. "First couple of days are busy, then it slows down. My parents' anniversary party tonight, and then the fittings for the bridal party tomorrow. They're having everyone hang out for a couple days before they go home and everything slows down."

And once it slowed down? It would be me and them and a whole lot of time. With the way they looked and all their scents? I would need a backbone of steel to get through it.

Too bad my backbone was historically made of rubber.

Go me.

## CHAPTER FOUR

### ISOLDE

I wished I had another cocktail napkin to rip into pieces. The signs for Clarity Coast had my heart pounding, even though it would be fine. It was going to be fine.

If I kept telling myself it would be fine, I hoped my brain and body would believe it instead of feeling like I was walking into a firing squad.

And not because of my family or friends. But because seeing Beau made me feel out of control. I should be able to walk in there with my head held high because I didn't do anything wrong. Instead, the thought of seeing him made me want to curl in on myself and hide.

At the same time, the first glimpse of the ocean made me breathe out a sigh of relief. The airport was near the ocean too, but it was hard to see it until you were here. At least from the highway.

It sparkled in the afternoon sun, stretching out into infinite blue. I could just barely see the cliffs that edged our estate in the distance, and my entire being settled. If there was anything I missed moving away from here, it was the sea. It wasn't the same anywhere else.

I woke up every day of my childhood with the song of waves in my ears. I rarely went a day without sand in between my toes. The beach was one of my favorite places, sitting on the sand and just gazing out at something so much bigger than yourself.

Of course, that was as far as it went. No swimming for me, but I was still comforted being near the water.

After I told the guys about everything we were doing—which was frankly too much—we lapsed into a comfortable silence with music on quietly in the background. I was so much more relaxed. I didn't know if it was because they put me at ease or because I liked being home, but I felt better than I had when I got in the car, and that was the important thing.

Rowan pulled off the highway where the GPS told him to, following the roads through the strange combination of the glitzy and the artsy to where the big houses were. The kind you saw on television and thought 'no one could ever live there.'

I glanced up at the cliffs and did a double take. A house stood on the top now. It wasn't there before. I think I might have known someone bought the property, but I pushed it from my mind because it made me sad. The view from those cliffs had always been my favorite, so not getting to climb the switchback path and sit there for sunset hurt my heart.

It was okay. I could still do that on the beach.

I changed while I was gone. Couldn't expect everything to freeze in time when you were the one who ran away.

The long drive up to our gates unfolded in front of us.

Vaughn let out a low whistle. "Been around here, but never been up close to this one."

"It's nice," I admitted.

Who was I kidding? It was way, way more than nice. My stepfather was one of the most sought-after entertainment lawyers in the country, and my mother was an interior designer whose work graced the cover of magazines. The only reason she didn't have her own TV show was that she didn't want one. I knew for a fact she had producers banging down her door and begging on a regular basis.

The security guard at the gate leaned into the window, looking at Rowan skeptically. "Name?"

"It's me, George. Isolde."

His eyes skipped into the backseat and onto my face. Then he smiled. "It's nice to see you, Miss Allen. I know your family is looking forward to having you home."

"Thank you. Can you put this car on the open access list? I'll make sure to get you everyone's names."

"Of course."

Stepping back, he waved us through. There were already cars

along the road, and several pulled up on the gravel driveway in front of the house. All the guests wouldn't be here for a couple of hours, but I swallowed anyway. Showtime.

As soon as the car stopped, I went for the door, and a hand fell on my shoulder. "No." Cade's hand stayed there, gently holding me in place me as Joel exited the car and opened the door for me.

"I can open my own doors."

"Yes, you can," Joel said. "But you won't. Not with us around." He helped me down from the taller height of the SUV.

"Why?"

With a hand on my hip, Joel pulled me to the side, guiding my back against the warm metal of the SUV's side. "Why what?"

"Why can't I open my own doors?"

His laugh rasped over my skin, voice impossibly deep. Those slate-blue eyes focused on mine. "You might not want the entire package offered to you, Isolde. But we're here to do more than just put on a show in front of your family."

All I could do was blink. If they weren't here to do that, what were they here to do?

He leaned closer. Close enough to overwhelm me with the rich, sharp scent of bourbon and that depth of spice. So close I could feel his breath on my neck. It was hard to remember that I *didn't* want the entire package when he was this close.

"We're here to take care of you, Isolde. As many... needs as you'll allow us to take care of. Whether that's standing with you in front of your family and offering support, no matter the reason, or opening your car door for you."

I let out a shuddering breath and swallowed, trying desperately to find words when my mouth was suddenly dry. "Still, I've been opening my own doors for a while now. It's okay if I do it."

Joel's eyes crinkled with a smile again. "Sorry, beautiful. Comes with the deal. No opening your own doors. Not while we're around. If it makes you feel better to think it's all a part of the ruse, go ahead." He leaned closer, my breath going still in my chest when his lips brushed over mine in a non-kiss. Nothing more than contact.

Contact that made me feel more than I had in years.

"But it's going to happen anyway," he said.

"What is?" I couldn't even think with him so close, his scent in my nose.

His laugh vibrated against me. "Us taking care of you. Better get used to it."

I looked up at him when he pulled back, unsure of the look in his eyes. Or the rest of them, now congregated behind Joel, blocking us from anyone's sight.

"Is that my baby?" A voice called, followed by crunching on gravel.

My mother's words pulled me back to my senses. "Yeah, Mom," I said.

Joel took a step back, creating physical distance, but his eyes never left my face. Not even as my mother barreled through the five of them and pulled me into a hug. It didn't matter that she was wearing a pale blue pantsuit and heels that could kill her on the gravel, she was here anyway.

"Hey, Mom. Happy Anniversary."

"If I knew a wedding and a silly party would make you come back, I would have made Warren propose to Ellie earlier. Then maybe you would have come home."

I hugged her back. "Planes exist," I whispered lightly. "You could have come to see me."

Pulling back, she waved a hand. "You know I'm not built for the cold."

There were many times I informed her that the northeastern coast wasn't *only* cold, but it didn't really matter. This was her home, and she was comfortable. I couldn't imagine my mother in the tiny apartment I rented above a laundromat and a takeout Chinese place. It was better she didn't know about that particular detail.

I might have oversold my living situation, knowing she would never see it firsthand.

"And this must be your lovely pack," she said, looking around at the men surrounding me. "I have to admit, I was a little surprised when Isolde told us she was bringing a pack home. We had no idea she was even seeing anyone."

Rowan stepped forward and shook my mother's hand, towering over her even in her heels. "It's incredibly nice to meet you, Mrs. Caruso. We've been looking forward to it. I'm Rowan."

I watched as they all introduced themselves and were perfectly charming. Not like me, stuck to the side of the SUV like I was a bug that got smashed there on the highway.

Cade took my hands and wove our fingers together like it was the most natural thing in the world. And it most definitely did *not* send warmth shooting straight through me.

My mother led the way into the house. "Well, come inside. Geoffrey will take your bags to the suite, so don't worry about that. I'm sure Henry will want to meet you as well."

"The suite?" I asked. "What do you mean?"

"Oh, I'm putting all of you in the guest suite on the south side. It has a pack bedroom. I thought it might be more convenient."

My mouth dropped open, my entire body freezing. "But you—"

"I what?" She raised an eyebrow.

"You don't let unmarried or unbonded people stay in the same room. Suite. Whatever."

Mom rolled her eyes. "You make me sound like I'm an uptight prude or something."

I looked at her hair, curled into an updo so tight it looked like it was slicked to her head, and gave her a face that said *really*? Whenever Beau came here, he had to stay in a separate room.

"Well, that may have been the case before," she said. "But not anymore. You'll have the suite. Ellie and Warren are staying together too. I'm not such a bore that I'm going to keep my daughter away from a pack. Especially not one like this."

Hawk choked back a laugh, and the others glared at him. But I was still figuring out how this was going to work. Part of this plan was the fact that I wasn't going to be sleeping in the same place as them. AKA, no temptation.

When I had no idea who they were and what they looked like, I wasn't concerned. Now? I was going to need *several* walls between myself and them if I expected my body not to betray me.

"There she is." Henry strode out into the foyer from the direction of his office.

I smiled. "Hi, Dad."

He was my stepdad, but it never felt that way. I didn't know my real father well enough to even remember him. The only thing I still had of my biological father was his last name.

Henry was Ellie's biological father, but he never treated us differently.

"How are you doing?" He asked quietly, pulling me in for a hug.

"Surviving. *Really* looking forward to tonight."

Dad laughed. I'd never been a big party person to begin with—at least not this type of party—and he'd never been Beau's biggest fan. So he knew I was thinking about pulling the fire alarm and heading to the beach just to get out of it.

"Henry, stop monopolizing her and meet her men."

We did the rounds of introductions again, but this time, Hawk pulled me against him and wrapped his arms around me. Possessively, around my shoulders and across my chest, so his body lined up with mine, his cheek pressed against my temple. I got lost in the sweetness of his frosting scent.

"You guys must be tired from the trip," Dad said. "We'll let you get settled and ready before I thoroughly interrogate you."

They all laughed and Joel smiled. "Looking forward to it, sir."

"Sir?" Dad looked at me. "I like them."

I smiled and hoped it looked real. "Me too."

Rowan took a step forward. "Lead the way."

This was happening. We were all staying in one suite. A suite I knew only had one giant bed.

I was so, so, *so* fucked.

## CHAPTER FIVE

CADE

I watched Isolde lead us through a house that could easily be used as the set of a film. Our house was lovely, and not too far from here, but this was an entirely different level. Which made sense. Adelaide Allen Caruso was known across the *world* for her design skills.

Something you couldn't really appreciate unless you saw the details up close.

It was impossible not to look at Isolde as she walked—all of her. From the curves those leggings hugged to the slight hunch in her shoulders that told me she was uncomfortable. I'd never wanted to be a piece of spandex so badly. Especially now that I knew what was happening.

Isolde smelled incredible. Something intangible that made me want to draw her closer and dig beneath the surface to figure out what made her tick. What made her *moan*.

Not to mention that fucking list she gave us told me she wanted exactly what I could give her.

As soon as we stepped out of the airport and Vaughn had Isolde far enough ahead of us, I turned on Joel. "What the fuck is going on with all of you?"

His expression rested somewhere between terror and awe. "She's ours."

I stopped walking, nearly tripping over my feet. "What did you just say?"

"She's *ours*, Cade. She's our match. Scenting her feels like a battering ram in the gut."

Not for the first time, I wished my designation was different. Isolde smelled so fucking good, but I couldn't ever feel what Joel described. I'd never know what it was like to know with utter certainty someone was meant for me, no matter how much I wanted it.

"You're sure?"

"He's sure," Rowan said from behind me. "It's true."

I looked again at the small Omega. Her bright red hair tousled like she'd taken a turn at the mile high club. Her unsure smile. Her fucking *incredible* scent.

One thing was certain: I'd never scented anyone like her before. It did hit me differently. Maybe there was something my soul recognized too, and I wanted it. Even if I couldn't, it wouldn't matter. If she belonged to my pack, she belonged to me. End of story.

No one in my pack had ever cared that I was a Beta. We belonged together as surely as the woman in front of us belonged.

Rowan's hand came down on my shoulder. "She's yours too."

I pressed my lips together, rolling my shoulders back. "Thanks."

"Now we just have to figure out a way to tell her that doesn't make her run," Joel said quietly. "Something happened to her. Clearly."

This I could work with. We needed a plan, and I was good at making plans. Figuring out puzzles, too. Isolde was a puzzle. Relief flowed through me as I walked the rest of the way to the car. "We'll figure it out."

Now, as we followed her through the house, I reviewed what I knew about her. Sure, the client questionnaire told us a lot, but it was basic information. Things you might find on a dating profile or a job interview. It didn't tell us about her soul or who she was when no one was watching.

It didn't tell me why she seemed so nervous about being here, in a home with a family who clearly loved her. It didn't tell me why the idea of staying in the same room as us made her panic.

All it made me want to do was get my ropes and tie her up so I could pleasure her until she gave me true answers. And maybe let me replace whatever thoughts made her shoulders cave in like that.

My phone chimed in my pocket. The pack group text.

JOEL

I'm refundinq her money immediately. Any objections?

That made sense. As far as we were concerned, Isolde wasn't a client. She was ours. We weren't going to take her money while we were courting her and trying to figure out how to tell her who she was to us.

Ahead of me, Hawk checked his phone and typed a response.

HAWK

You don't think she'll notice? I don't care, I just don't want to blow the play early.

JOEL

I don't think she'll notice. She seems overwhelmed, and while she's here, we'll be taking care of things.

I typed my response.

CADE

No arguments from me.

The others gave a quick thumbs up in the chat.

"It's right here," Isolde said, gesturing to a set of tall double doors. Intricately carved wood that somehow didn't seem out of place.

She pushed one open, and we followed her inside.

It was basically an entire house. A kitchen, living room, and covered veranda that overlooked the back of the estate and down to the ocean.

A man in a dark suit was rolling our suitcases into what must be the pack bedroom. The one that made her nervous. "Thank you, Geoffrey," she said.

"Of course, Miss Allen. It's good to have you home."

She went out onto the veranda and leaned against the marble railing. I recognized the pose. Her head dropped, shoulders rising and falling. She was overwhelmed. This, I could handle.

I held out a hand to the others, telling them not to follow before I joined her. It was a risk to touch her, but Vaughn was right. She couldn't jump every time we made contact if she wanted this to work.

And we wanted to keep touching her long after this.

I let my hands gently land on her hips before placing them on the railing on either side of her, lining our bodies up together. "You okay?"

"Of course."

Laughing once, I covered her hands with mine, seeing how far she'd let me push. Isolde stiffened, but she didn't pull away. So I intertwined our fingers before wrapping her arms around herself so I was hugging her too. "Take a breath for me."

"I'm breathing."

"Isolde." I let my voice drop into a place of command. She might not understand that she needed it, but I did. "Take a breath."

She did, body expanding in my hold. The softness of her against me was so damn tempting, I couldn't resist leaning down to press a kiss to her neck. "You seem overwhelmed."

"That's an understatement."

"Why?"

She huffed out a breath. "It doesn't matter. I'll be fine."

Turning her in my arms, I pushed her back against the railing and met her eyes. Green, but soft. On the grayer side. Like moss on stone. Utterly fucking captivating.

Her scent whirled around us, and I held back my smile. The little Omega was far more affected by us than she let on. The entire car ride I inhaled breath after breath of it, and I'd been about five seconds from pulling her into the back seat and testing her commitment to abstinence when we pulled into the driveway.

"Do you know why we do what we do?" I asked.

She raised one eyebrow. "Money?"

"It helps," I acknowledged with a grin. "But no, not entirely."

"Then why?"

"Because each of us knows what it's like to go through something alone, and desperately need someone to be there with you. Especially if someone is going to judge you. The fear climbs up your spine and your throat and it feels like your lungs are so full of rocks you can't take a full breath.

"And all you want is someone to stand in that space with you. We like taking care of people."

Isolde looked at me skeptically. "You're telling me that all of you do this because you want to help people and not because you're all really fucking hot and can have sex for money?" Her voice lowered on the last words, like there was anyone around who could hear her.

I smiled. "There's actually a lot less sex involved than you might think. But I'm glad to know you think we're hot."

Her cheeks turned a delicious shade of pink. I wanted to see that pink on every inch of her body. Preferably while bound and squirming in my ropes.

"I want to make something clear," I said gently, gripping her hips. "You came to us, and we said yes. That doesn't mean we just show up and pretend to be with you while ignoring who you are and what you need. Sorry if that's what you thought was going to happen."

A whole new kind of fear bloomed on her face. "I'm not interested—"

I lifted my hand to her cheek, silencing her. "I know. We know."

"So..."

Our bodies were already lined up. I just closed the distance, pressing mine into hers just enough to feel her gasp. I smothered my own reaction. She could claim she wasn't interested all she wanted—we would happily wait.

"So, you called us. And people rarely call us because it's easy and things are going well. We're here to help you. Let us in. Let us take care of you while we're here."

I watched her eyes gloss over with tears and how she tried to blink them away. "I don't know how to do that. I didn't... expect that. I just can't be alone. Not when—"

She caught herself before she admitted the truth, but I waited, letting the silence draw out. She needed to be the one to fill it.

Isolde hadn't told us *why* she wanted us here. Joel said she had cried when she called, begging us to help her for this three week stretch. But as to why? She'd given no clues.

"I promise you. Whatever it is, we can handle it. And we're not going to judge you for it."

She swallowed, and I followed the movement with my gaze. The longer I stood here pressed against her, the harder it was to keep myself in control. But I had no doubt she was mine. No other Omega had ever captivated me like this. Her scent, her eyes, the way she *breathed*.

*Mine.*

Her teeth worried her bottom lip, and she looked away before she finally spoke. "My ex is the best man. He dumped me out of the blue a year ago. Now he's engaged, and I didn't want to be the sad, lonely Omega who everyone looked at with pity. Like I wasn't good enough, even if it's true."

Anger flared through me. No fucking wonder she was overwhelmed. This was her home, and it didn't fucking feel *safe* for her. I wasn't surprised she tried to keep the idea of sex and happiness at arm's length—she'd been hurt. Her heart butchered. And now she was going to see that heartbreak paraded in front of her for the next three weeks.

"How long were you together?"

"Four years."

*Fuck*. That was a long time to recover from. Her words were a pained whisper, and my own burned in my chest. "Do you want him back?"

Please say no. *Please* say no.

Isolde shook her head. I felt dizzy with the pure gratefulness that dropped through me. Waiting for her was one thing. Helping her win back an ex who clearly didn't deserve her was another.

"No, I don't. I just don't want everyone to stare and wonder what's wrong with me. Or give me their condolences. Or tell me this should be my wedding and not Ellie's."

Shifting my hand from her cheek to the back of her neck, I pulled her closer. "Thank you for telling me. Do you mind if I it share with the others?"

"That's fine. I know it's pathetic, not being able to face an ex. It's not like I'm pining for him. I just—"

I closed the remaining distance between us again and dropped my lips onto hers. Fully this time. Isolde froze, stiff against me, before she absolutely *melted*. She tasted as sweet as her scent, hands coming up to brace against my shoulders like she wasn't sure if she wanted to shove me away or haul me closer.

The plush softness of her lips under mine, her body under my hands... I was a goner. Tightening my grip on her neck, I deepened the kiss, tracing her lips with my tongue, savoring the little gasp that let me in.

Isolde tasted so fucking sweet. Would she taste like this everywhere?

She let go. I felt the moment it changed. Her lips and tongue turning from hesitant to desperate, hands finally pulling me closer. *Yes*.

Fuck, I wanted to kiss her forever, and I couldn't.

Pulling back, I pressed my forehead against hers. "Not wanting to face someone who ripped your heart out isn't pathetic. Far from it. And we're not going to let anyone look at you with a shred of pity, Isolde. The only thing your ex is going to see is the fucking radiant Omega he left behind, and he'll regret the day he did. I've only known you for an hour and I already know he doesn't have a *clue* what he lost."

The hope in her eyes was painful. All I wanted to do was kiss her again so I could take that pain away. Push her up against one of these columns and show her how good it could be.

"Clearly we're interrupting something," a voice said from behind us.

I turned, seeing a familiar face, and suddenly this adventure made a lot more sense.

## CHAPTER SIX

### ISOLDE

"Clearly we're interrupting something." Trinity's head hung around the corner of the door inside, Ocean right behind her. My friend took in the way Cade had me pressed against the railing, and her eyes glowed with what looked like victory.

I flushed with heat.

It wasn't what she thought.

Sure, he kissed me.

Yes, his hands on me made me feel things I hadn't felt *ever*.

And yes, the way he offered their help made me want to bask in that warmth.

But it wasn't what they thought.

Even though I kissed him back.

Cade's eyes left mine, turning to see my friends, and he huffed out a laugh. "Trinity. I suppose we should have made the connection sooner."

She winced. "Not too mad, are you?"

"No." He glanced back at me and smiled. "Probably should be, but not mad at all."

"Good." She marched across the veranda and grabbed my hand, pulling me away from his body. I already missed the warmth of him and the dark scent that had wrapped around me and made me feel *safe* when it had started to feel impossible. "We have to get Isolde ready now. But don't worry, you'll get her back later."

A flicker of a smile played on his lips. "We'll make sure to stay out of your way."

Trinity towed me inside the house and into the bedroom I hadn't set foot in yet. The other guys were in the living room area, watching with amusement as I was captured.

"So they know it was you."

"Luckily they don't seem too upset," Trinity said, closing the door behind Ocean. "I'm more interested in why you were tangled up with one of them when you said there was no way you were having sex with them."

I reached out and pulled Ocean into a hug. She shook with silent laughter. "She's been like this all day."

"She's like this all the time."

Trinity put her hands on her hips. "Excuse me, I'm standing right here."

Hugging her too, I finally found my suitcase among the group of them and pulled it over to the walk-in closet. I ignored the bed. That was a bridge I would cross when I got to it.

"And I'm not sure what you saw, Rin. But I wasn't being fucked on the veranda. No one's going to believe we're together if they never touch me."

"Yeah, but no one was watching you."

"You two walked in, didn't you?"

Ocean giggled. "Yeah, but we know the secret."

I flipped the suitcase over on the ground and started pulling things out and putting them away. I wasn't going to live out of a suitcase for three full weeks. Besides, if I was moving back here, it's not like I would have to shove it all back into the case.

They both grabbed things too, getting my suitcase unpacked in minutes. My makeup put on the vanity in the closet, and the dresses hung up.

Trinity looked at the dresses. "Which one are you wearing tonight?"

I sat down at the vanity and pointed to the black dress on the hanger. "That one."

"No."

"What?"

"Back me up, O. She can't wear that."

Turning, I looked between my friends. "What's wrong with that dress?"

Ocean smiled. "Nothing. It's pretty."

"But?"

"But," she winced. "It's not exciting."

"I'm not looking for excitement. I'm looking to fly under the radar."

Trinity rolled her eyes. "If you actually wanted to fly under the radar, you wouldn't have shown up with a pack that looks like sex on a stick. Everyone's going to be looking at you anyway, so you can't walk in there looking like you're attending your own funeral."

"Rin," I choked on a laugh. "It won't look like that."

"You're right. It won't. Because I thought this might happen." She strode out of the room without a backward glance, leaving Ocean and I to stare at each other.

"What did she do?"

Ocean laughed and shook her head. "I honestly have no idea."

My friends were already dressed. Ocean wore a flowy dress in a color that reflected her name, covered with a dark cardigan. She looked pretty, but I recognized when she tried to cover herself up.

While my family was supportive, Ocean's wasn't. She'd never been good enough for them in any way. Interests, personality, body. Anything. So while she was fucking gorgeous, her curves and size made her uncomfortable. Rin and I tried to get her into things which would show her off, but there was only so much we could do.

"How are you?"

"I'm fine. I have a really beautiful hybrid I'm working on. It should bloom in a few days. I can't wait to see how it turned out. But I'm more worried about you right now."

Taking a deep breath, I met my own eyes in the mirror. "I'll be all right."

Twenty minutes ago, I might not have said the same. Cade's insistence they were here to take care of me meant more than he could know. Now the thought of walking into the ballroom and seeing Beau with Angela on his arm felt slightly less horrifying.

Slightly.

"I knew I needed to be prepared." Trinity swept in with a slinky, silky, pile of emerald green fabric draped over her arm.

She held it up, showing the simple but stunning dress. Asymmetrical hem that would show off more than a little leg, spaghetti straps, and a gently cowled neckline. It was gorgeous. It was also completely unlined, and there was no way I could wear the bras I had with me.

And like hell was I going braless around these five men. I was only so strong, and whatever my commitment to resistance, I didn't need my nipples showing in front of Beau.

"I don't have underwear for that dress, Rin."

"Do you need it?"

"You really want me possibly sporting headlights at my sister's party? In front of my ex?"

She sighed like I was ruining her fun. "I'd rather you sport headlights for the five servings of *fucking edible* in the living room right now. But fine. I'll take care of that, too."

"I'm *not* borrowing your bra."

Rin shook her head. "You won't have to. I'll get one delivered."

Ocean covered her mouth to hide her laughter, but her eyes sparkled. She might be quieter, but my friend was fully on board.

"You can't just have underwear delivered like a pizza."

Trinity scoffed. "Fucking watch me."

"Are you having a blood sugar high?" I asked. "A low?"

All that earned me was a glare.

In seconds, Trinity swiped on her phone, typed a few things, and showed me the order confirmation for a black strapless bra from one of the luxury boutiques in town. I rolled my eyes. "And I really don't need a bra that costs that much."

"We both know you can afford it, Iz. But this one is my treat."

Swallowing, I looked away and started unpacking my makeup. I did just fine. My parents had a trust for me, but it wasn't something I could access until I turned thirty-five. I was far from rich, and far from ordering lingerie that cost a full shift's tips.

They made the same rule for my sister. My parents didn't want us to rely on it, so they made sure to keep it out of reach past the point when we were supposed to be able to fend for ourselves. And I could. I was.

Bartending—especially when I showed more skin—paid my bills, but I was no longer rolling in cash. And no one really knew about it, either. Which was why my very expensive purchase sitting outside ready to escort me was a bad idea.

My family would help me if they knew. I hadn't told them. A year ago I wouldn't have said I was a prideful person, but being dumped and leaving my job only to find myself living in a building my mother would consider condemned and bartending six days a week to make ends meet changed that.

I couldn't quite wrap my head around the change in my circumstances myself, let alone face the horror, pity, and charity of my family. That was another thing I wanted to do out here. Interviews. Surely I could get an interview somewhere that wasn't Tate Marketing.

If Beau hadn't poisoned the well with everyone who could possibly use a graphic designer.

"Isolde?"

I startled, meeting Ocean's eyes in the vanity mirror. "Yeah?"

She smiled faintly. "You've been staring at your blush like it murdered someone for about three minutes."

"Well, you know how blush can be. Have to keep an eye on it."

My friends laughed, and then an awkward quiet settled over us. I finally put the blush down. It hadn't hurt anyone.

Ocean sat on the comfy bench on the other side of the closet. The place was big enough to be its own boutique, it was a good thing it had seating. "Are you really okay, Iz?

"I'll be fine."

"That's not what I asked."

Pressing my lips together so hard they disappeared, I looked anywhere but at her. Here, in person, it was harder to avoid the heart of these questions.

"No," I finally said. "Not really. But it doesn't matter. This is all about Ellie. I can get through it and figure my shit out later."

Stepping up behind me, Trinity put her hands on my shoulders. "You know we love you, right? We're going to make sure you're okay, no matter what."

"I know."

Her phone chimed. "Oh, good. Ronnie is here. And the bra delivery will be here in a few."

"It's been like ten minutes."

"It's a bra," she called over her shoulder on her way to the door. "Not like they have to spend time browsing."

I shook my head, unable to contain my laughter.

Ocean smirked, finally looking more relaxed. "Regretting everything yet?"

"Oh, you have no idea." The giggles wouldn't stop now that I'd let them out. "Who the fuck is Ronnie?"

## CHAPTER SEVEN

VAUGHN

"Well, that clears up a few things." I sat heavily on one of the couches, pretending not to be jealous that Cade just kissed the hell out of our Omega.

He told us the real reason we're here. It made sense. More sense than someone wanting company for the wedding extravaganza about to take place.

"She won't admit it, but I think he did a number on her," Cade said. "We need to be careful."

A growl rolled out of me. Of course I would be careful of her. The ex? Not so much.

Laughter filtered through the doors to the enormous closet. I could pick hers out among the three. Like my entire being was now attuned to her. The room already smelled like her and she'd only barely walked through it. The next three weeks would be delicious torture.

"How do we approach this?" I finally asked. "Because I can't just walk away when this is over."

Rowan sat forward, elbows on his knees. "I'm honestly not sure yet. Maybe after tonight, when we can actually spend a little more time with her, we'll get an idea. I don't feel like we can formulate a plan yet."

"Agreed." Joel ran a hand over his face.

I smirked, meeting Cade's eyes. He knew what I was thinking. Tonight, when we were all sharing a giant bed. I looked forward to seeing how Isolde dealt with that. We would never cross a line she didn't want, but it didn't mean I couldn't think about it.

Hawk stood, wandering around the couches to stare out the windows. He rarely stood still when he had a choice. "I don't like lying to her."

"We're not lying," I said.

He turned to look at me, a frown on his face. "It kind of feels like we are."

"If we tell her now, she'll run," Cade said. "She's determined not to want anyone."

I crossed my arms. "I think that kiss says otherwise."

His grin spoke volumes. "I said she's *determined* not to want anyone. Not that she doesn't. This ex of hers fucked with her head. It's a defense mechanism. She doesn't want to be hurt again or feel what he made her feel again, so she's choosing to shut down first."

Joel sank deeper into the plush couch. There wasn't any part of this house which wasn't sheer luxury. Even just running my hand over the cushion felt expensive.

We'd always been curious about this place. It was visible from our house, and obviously gorgeous. Being inside it was a whole different ball game.

But I liked our house better, new as it was. We had plenty of luxury, and it was designed for our needs. Now I could think about how Isolde might fit into that picture, and I liked it. The nest nestled between the empty Omega suite and the rest of the house. Imagining that—

I stopped the thoughts. First, we needed to make sure she knew, and that she wanted us. We needed her to want us.

"If she asks us, don't lie," Joel said. "About anything. If she has an idea, or wants to know, we hide nothing. However, in this case, I think a little caution is necessary." He looked at Hawk. "For the record, I don't like it either. But I hate the idea of losing her more."

Hawk shoved his hands in the pockets of his black jeans and looked down at his feet. "Can't argue there."

The closet door opened and Trinity Crawford came striding out like the powerhouse she was. We agreed to do a confidential interview with her because she had a track record of good interviews with people of every background, including sex workers. The last thing we wanted was an interviewer who spoke with us and then wrote an article trashing who we were and what we did.

But I wasn't sure what we were anymore. Like hell was I going to continue taking clients if Isolde was in our lives. I couldn't. Maybe the others could, but I doubted it.

It was like lightning striking. The place it struck would never be the same as it once was. She consumed my every thought, and we'd only just met her.

Trinity gave a little wave as she walked to the door and opened it for a woman with wildly curly hair wrapped up in a scarf, and a big black rolling case nearly as big as Isolde's suitcase.

I should have been furious at the Omega for breaking the incredibly strict non-disclosure agreement we made her sign, but I wasn't. Because her actions gave us Isolde. And her risking that for her friend told me mountains. Both about who she was as a person, and what she thought her friend needed.

How little she knew.

"Can one of you go back to the front door? Iz is getting a delivery, and I need to help Ronnie get set up."

"Sure," I stood, wanting to stretch my legs. "Who am I looking for?"

Trinity glanced at her phone. "Says his name is Daryl." That was all she gave me before disappearing back into the closet.

I looked around at my packmates. "I guess I'm going to see Daryl."

The Caruso mansion sprawled. Thankfully, I paid attention on the way in, but even then, it felt like I was wandering in a palace. People were here and there, moving with quick determination. Probably getting things ready for the party, which is what we needed to do as well.

I blew out a breath when I saw the front door. Now to get back to the suite without getting lost. The front steps were wide, cascading down in front of the mansion into the gravel drive, which was slowly and steadily filling with cars and people.

"You're going to have to remind me of your name."

The voice came from my left. Isolde's stepfather stood there, smoking a cigar. I turned to him and held out my hand again. "Vaughn, Mr. Caruso."

He clasped my hand with his free one and gestured with his cigar. "Call me Henry. Mr. Caruso feels like I'm at work."

"All right, Henry."

He looked at me, gaze sharp. "Have you known Isolde long? She never told us about you."

This was something I needed to handle delicately. No lying.

"Not too long, no. But we were more than willing to come and support her for this."

There was a knowing look in his eyes. So he understood what was going on with my Omega. Good to know. I didn't plan on being polite to her ex, which would have been harder if he were the golden boy to her parents.

"Well, in that case, I hope to get to know you better while you're here."

I nodded and glanced toward the driveway, noting the car pulling up that was distinctly out of place in the sea of glossy vehicles.

No part of what I said next was a lie, either. "I know we just met, sir, but I want you to know I care very much about your daughter."

Henry took a puff on his cigar, watching me. Then he smiled. "Good."

The beat-up car stopped in front of the steps, and a guy stepped out. I nodded to Henry and went down to meet him. "You're Daryl?"

"Yeah." He held out the bag, small, glittering pink, with *Cheria* stamped on the side. My eyebrows rose without realizing it. *Cheria* was a lingerie store nearby. Not just lingerie, but the stuff that was the stuff of fucking dreams. Impractical, expensive, and hot. Isolde ordered something?

Fuck me. As if being near her scent wouldn't be hard enough—and make *me* hard—knowing she had on something naughty beneath whatever dress she wore would make it ten times harder.

"I'll take it."

Daryl smiled, the expression hitting me right in the chest. "I looked in there. Good for you. Jealous."

Every ounce of politeness dropped from my body. I stepped into his space. I had a good foot on him, and I used every inch. "Do you regularly violate the privacy of your deliveries? Or just the women?"

"I—What?" He paled.

"You heard exactly what I said."

"It's just a bra, man. Not that serious."

My teeth ground together. I couldn't punch this guy in the face no matter how much I wanted to. I didn't have that claim to Isolde yet, and her stepfather stood right behind me. "What a woman orders, whether it's a bra or not, is none of your *fucking. Business.* Am I clear?"

He scoffed. "Whatever."

Snatching the bag, I pushed him up against the car. "You're lucky I have better things to do than kick your ass today. Now get the fuck out of here and try not to be a fucking creep."

"I'm just dropping it off." He held up his hands. "Not like she'll ever know."

I shook my head and backed up. It wasn't that hard, but I wasn't going to get myself into deep shit today because of an asshole who didn't understand the meaning of privacy or the slippery slope that came with little violations.

Men like that started small, and if they got away with it, they pushed further.

Trying not to crumple the sparkling bag, I watched him until he disappeared out of the gate, and when I turned, Henry watched *me*.

We were far enough apart that I doubted he'd heard the exchange, but between the bag and the energy rolling off me, he got the gist. He nodded once. I nodded back.

The guys looked at me when I came back, and Rowan stood immediately. "Don't go in there like that."

"Like what?"

All he did was look at me.

"Fine." I took a breath, trying to release the tension. It wasn't something I was used to. Even the *thought* of someone hurting Isolde or violating her privacy made me see red. He was right.

Rowan stepped aside. "Better."

I knocked on the closet door and waited, listening to the trickle of voices. Trinity opened it so quickly I had to duck out of the way. She laughed. "Sorry, Vaughn."

"Here you go."

"Thank you."

I looked past her into the huge closet and froze. Isolde sat in front of the vanity, bright lights on her face while her makeup was being done. The silky robe fell around her shoulders, exposing too much skin, and *fuck* it was hard to look away. Her scent floated out like a beacon. I felt like one of those cartoon characters following a visible line of scent to find a prize.

Trinity followed my gaze and smirked. "See something you like?"

Isolde's eyes rose and met mine in the mirror. We weren't going to lie to her, so I simply said, "Yes."

"Better start getting ready," Trinity nodded back outside. "She'll be done soon."

"Trinity," I whispered before the door closed. "Report the driver."

She frowned. "Why?"

"Because he looked in the bag, fucking congratulated me, and said he was jealous."

The smile that grew on her face was one I *never* wanted to be on the wrong end of. "I'll take care of it."

She closed the door, and I kept standing there. Couldn't quite get my feet to move. She was so *close*.

"Vaughn, you can take a turn in the bathroom to get dressed."

"Right."

Hawk, now in a suit, smiled. I just shook my head. "Like you're not thinking the same damn thing."

"Oh, I am."

It took almost no time to change. We were nearly always in suits for our clients. I could probably put one on blindfolded. Thankfully, by the time we'd all changed and stood in the living area waiting, the doors to the closet opened, and Trinity announced, "She's ready!"

Isolde rolled her eyes at the grand reveal, but none of us did. Green silk, creamy skin, curves. Fiery hair and glossy lips. Eyes dark enough to make my body heat.

And, of course, her scent washed over us like a wave of exquisite sugar that sent all my blood racing south. It felt like salvation and tasted like forever.

Holy.

Fucking.

Shit.

## CHAPTER EIGHT

### ISOLDE

Turned out Ronnie was a friend of Rin's. She brought her in to do my hair and makeup, brushing aside any mention of cost.

Ronnie, or Veronica, was a dream. Sweet as pie and made me up better than I ever could. When she finished, I barely felt like myself. I felt like a woman who could walk into the grand ballroom on the other side of the house and still hold my head high.

"Thank you so much."

"My pleasure," she said. "Make him wish he'd never fucked up."

I grinned.

Yes.

I would do just that.

Ocean and Trinity deemed my shoes acceptable. So I was a few inches taller, and despite my resistance, the dress fit me perfectly, and it looked *good*.

"Fine," I told her. "You win. This is better."

"I know." She strode over to the doors and grabbed the handles. "Now let's show you off. She's ready!"

I rolled my eyes as I walked out of the closet. There wasn't a reason to show off for the men I was paying to be with me, even if they were...

All my thoughts evaporated.

My mouth went dry.

All five men stood in the living room in perfectly tailored suits. Hawk was right. They cleaned up *good,* and they hadn't been bad before.

I didn't know what it was about a man in a suit that turned me into a puddle, but wow. And all five of them stared at me like I was the center of the universe. Like they wanted to tear me apart and put me back together. Like they wanted to *consume* me.

Four years with Beau, and I couldn't think of a single time he'd looked at me like this.

So five of them?

The weight of their eyes was almost too much.

Rowan stepped forward and reached for my hand. I gave it to him, watching in a daze as he lifted it, kissing the back of my hand. "You look beautiful, Isolde."

"Thank you." I sounded like I'd just crawled across the desert without water the way my throat rasped.

Without releasing me, he turned and threaded my arm through his. "Shall we?"

"Yeah. Um," I glanced away from them, because if I didn't, I wouldn't stop staring. "You guys look great."

"No one will be looking at us," Vaughn said.

I glanced up at him. The darkness of his suit emphasized his light coloring and the sheer broadness of his shoulders. He looked at me like he'd looked at me through the closet door. Like I was more than anything.

They were very, *very* good at their jobs.

Managing a smile, I took a breath. "You guys know how to make a girl feel good. I'm not surprised you're so good at what you do."

Vaughn's eyes shuttered, and I couldn't explain the flash of hurt there before he looked toward the door where Trinity and Ocean were already slipping out and heading for the party. "We should get going."

"Of course." Something in my chest didn't feel right. But I wasn't sure why saying that would be an issue? It was clear from their interview with Rin they valued their reputation and prided themselves on a good experience. Wasn't it a compliment?

With my arm in Rowan's, I led them through the house to the other side. Guests already milled around the public areas, champagne in hand. Not many yet, but already I saw people glancing at me with polite smiles before looking away and quickly going back to their conversations. Like I couldn't see them talking about me.

Suddenly, the confidence I'd felt in the closet wasn't as strong. I paused at the entrance of the ballroom. People floated here and there, and it would only get more crowded. My parents knew a lot of people, and there would be plenty here hoping to charm them because of who they were.

I hadn't been here in a year. Who knew what Beau had told them? What did everyone in Clarity think of me? Even my parents weren't powerful enough to stop all rumors. Even though Beau was the one to dump me like four years together was nothing, I was the one who looked guilty. I ran. I hid. I didn't let all of silly Clarity society see me standing tall afterward, and I knew how this town worked.

If you weren't smiling for everyone to see, something was wrong. You had something to hide. My fingers tightened on Rowan's sleeve.

"Do you have more lip gloss?" He asked.

"What?"

I had to look up at him. Rowan was tall. The tallest of them, just barely clearing Vaughn's height. The light scent of sea salt curled filled the air, relaxing me. The coconut hit a second later. Standing next to Rowan was like standing on the beach in the sun.

He searched my face with a smile. "Do you have more lip gloss? Because I'm about to ruin yours."

Leaning down, he captured my mouth with his in a possessive kiss that had people gasping around us. I couldn't think. Couldn't breathe.

Rowan's hand slid up my spine, warming my bare back where my dress exposed my skin. The vibration of a growl rolled from him to me a second before he kissed me deeper, and I couldn't bring myself to care that we stood in the middle of a crowd. The way he kissed me made everything else turn to mist.

Kissing this Alpha felt like coming home in a way I couldn't put my finger on, and all I wanted was more. At the same time my brain screamed alarm bells at me. I needed to pull away from him. The temptation to fall into them was already so high, I couldn't let myself. It wasn't real, and if I let myself pretend it was, my heart would break all over again.

I couldn't survive that.

Rowan broke the kiss but didn't pull away. This close, I saw the warmth in his eyes. Brown that shifted to nearly amber in the afternoon light, and beyond that, a playfulness in them. "Something else for them to talk about," he whispered.

Worrying my teeth into my lip, I tried to steady myself. Because even in his arms, knowing he wouldn't let me fall, I felt like I was walking on loose sand. "I'm not sure that's better. They're still talking."

"I don't know. I think kissing you makes everything better."

He straightened us both before he could see how red I was turning. People looked at us behind their hands and their champagne glasses, but Rowan ignored them, pulling me further into the party.

"*Izzy!*" A flying blur of white came flying at me. Rowan barely let go in time for Ellie to barrel into me and wrap me in a hug. "Oh my god, I'm so happy you're here. Mom made me promise I wouldn't crash your suite, so I've been waiting."

I laughed. "Hey."

"It feels like it's been forever."

"I talked to you yesterday, Ellie." I met Hawk's eyes over her shoulder. He was smiling, watching the interaction with interest.

"I know, but it's not the same. Come on. You need a drink." She towed me away from the guys. I glanced over my shoulder to see Warren, Ellie's fiancé, introducing himself to the pack. Joel nodded in my direction. They would be fine.

Ellie pulled me to the bar. "Can we talk about how I've been talking to you every week and you never mentioned a pack? *Ever*?"

"I wasn't sure where it was going. What was the point of anyone getting excited if it's not going to last?"

"And now? They're here with you. That's a good sign, right?"

I lifted my shoulders and let them fall. "I guess so."

"White wine, please. Same for her." Ellie narrowed her eyes. "Why are you so reluctant? If you didn't like them, you wouldn't have brought them with you into the center of attention."

The bartender placed the glass of wine in front of me, and I spun it on the bar. "I don't want to get ahead of myself, Ellie. It's still new, and you know that time isn't always a factor. I just want to be sure."

"If you think it's not going well, you need your head checked. I saw that kiss, and I saw the way the rest of them looked at you. I don't even know their names and I'm convinced they're in love with you."

I choked on my wine. "They are *not* in love with me."

"Bullshit," she muttered. "If you're not engaged by the time the wedding gets here, I'll be shocked. And besides, wouldn't you want the pack you're seeing to be in love with you?"

*Danger*. My mind pulsed with the word. Too much resistance

and this whole thing fell apart. "Oh my god. Have you been talking to Rin? Cause I think you guys are having the same shared delusion."

"What delusions are we having?" Rin appeared as if summoned. "As long as the delusions are hot, I'm fine with that. Ellie, your mother is looking for you. Something about needing hostess support?"

My sister sighed and took the biggest sip of wine in history. "She means she wants me to help butter people up, even though this isn't my party, because some of them will be at the wedding. My favorite. My feet are already killing me. I might need to steal some flats before tonight is over."

Disappearing into the crowd, I leaned against the bar. She and I couldn't be more different. We barely even looked alike, with her blonde hair and tan skin. I couldn't get a tan if I camped *on* the fucking sun.

"Okay," Rin said after she ordered her drink. "You have to help me out."

"How?"

She lowered her voice so there was no chance of being overheard. "I know you said no fucking the escorts. But I'm begging. You. Please. For me."

I took a sip of my drink, watching people begin to dance. "You're free to go get some. You're at a party attached to a wedding. Events *known* for creating bad decisions and one-night stands."

She huffs. "I would. Believe me. I can't."

"Why not?"

"My pussy is out of commission."

I stared at her until she relented.

"I have a yeast infection."

"Shit."

Rin grabbed her drink off the bar. "Par for the course. Gotta love it." She grimaced and drank.

Trinity's diabetes made her more susceptible, and even though she was almost religious in taking care of herself, sometimes nature just happened. Like going into rut or heat, some things were inevitable.

Didn't mean we had to like it, though.

Cade came up on her other side and ordered a drink, glancing between us. "Everything okay?"

I smiled. "Just encouraging Rin to go mingle and find some… company."

The bartender set a glass down in front of Cade, and Trinity grabbed it, downing the drink in one go. "Thank you. That was delicious."

All Cade did was chuckle. "One of these days, Trinity, someone's going to put you in your place, and I can't wait to see it."

"What the fuck is that supposed to mean?"

Cade's eyes were on me before he briefly looked at her and smiled. "It means he'll be the one who can handle you, and he—or they—will be the only ones you let do it."

Her eyes went wide, mouth dropping open. The way he said it was all teasing, but I started to laugh at her expression. "You can't even pretend that's not true, Rin." My best friend loved to stir up shit, and the pack or man that managed to tame her would be a sight to behold.

Rolling her eyes, she lifted her own drink and flipped her hair over her shoulder. But even now, she was trying hard not to smile. "Guess I better go start riling up Alphas." Then she lowered her voice. "The pussy's out of commission, but they don't have to know that."

She disappeared into the crowd before I could say anything, and I stepped closer to Cade. "You didn't tell me you liked to play with fire."

"I can handle a little fire."

"People always say my hair's on fire. You going to put me in my place?" I asked with a laugh, covering what I actually thought about that.

The words weren't something you should like. It wasn't *okay*, but when Cade said it, I knew he didn't mean it as shoving a woman into the kitchen and ordering her to make a sandwich. It wasn't nearly the same. And the idea of this pack taking control and leading, allowing me to fulfill the role of Omega with ease?

Kind of hot.

"Is that something you want?" Cade asked softly. He wasn't looking at me directly, eyes focused on the thin strap of my dress like he imagined what it would be like to push it off my shoulder.

I smiled into my wine glass, shivering. This pack was something else. And I didn't have an answer for him. A laugh caught my attention, floating over the crowd, and it rooted me to the spot. Beau.

Looking over my shoulder, I spotted him and Angela in the

receiving line, speaking to my sister. She glanced at me for the briefest of seconds, smile tight. Beau didn't notice.

It hurt to look at him. Not because I wanted him back. I didn't. But because it still didn't make sense to me. I'd been limping along this whole time without closure. It was just... sudden.

I thought we'd been fine. We hadn't been having sex that often, but we were both busy. And then, shortly after my heat, he said it was over. I didn't like to think about that heat. It wasn't my favorite memory.

The thing that hurt the most was that Angela looked like me. Or a better version of me. Coppery red hair curled around her shoulder and she somehow managed to pull off a red dress at the same time—something that wasn't easy.

It just felt like he'd traded me in for a new model and it hadn't hurt him at all. Maybe that was what bothered me. We were together for four years. We were happy. I thought we were happy. So did leaving me mean absolutely nothing?

Having someone mean everything to you and then see it wasn't mutual—that apparently you meant less than nothing to them—wasn't a feeling I'd ever wanted to understand.

And never wanted to feel it again.

"That's him?"

I startled at Joel's voice. He stood near me now. They all did, arrayed subtly out so we all weren't bunched together.

"Yeah." I stepped away from the bar so I wasn't in the way anymore. "That's him. In the flesh."

Rowan shrugged. "Not what I imagined the asshole to look like."

I blinked at him, and I caught a flicker of something deeper in his gaze. The feeling that what he showed on the surface wasn't nearly everything. Of course it wasn't. This was all for show.

So why did I desperately want to peel back those layers and find out what he was hiding? Just like after the kiss, the air spun out between us, going electric. I needed to get my shit together.

"Isolde, there you are." My mother appeared in front of me and grabbed my hand. Cade just barely rescued my wine from my other hand as she towed me across the ballroom. "Sorry to be so abrupt. Marie can't stay and she wanted to see you."

One of my mother's friends and business partners. "Really?"

"Yeah."

I held back my sigh. Clearly that wasn't the truth, but Mom would get to it when she got to it. "Oh, it looks like she left already."

"Mom, if you want to talk to me, you can just say you want to talk to me. You don't have to make stuff up."

"Yes," she said. "But why do I get the feeling if I tell you I want to talk to you that you'll find an excuse to stay with those handsome men and dodge my questions?"

*Because you're right.* "I have no idea."

She sighed and touched my arm. "I want to make sure you're okay."

"Why wouldn't I be?"

Mom gave me a look I absolutely deserved. I left so quickly I gave my family whiplash. They barely heard the news before I was out of the city. I couldn't look at anything without feeling like I was going to lose my mind. Every place in Clarity Coast had memories attached, and so many were of Beau. They were happy, and then all of a sudden it was like my entire world was covered in sadness and pain that couldn't wash off. I couldn't *breathe*.

"I'm fine, Mom. Promise."

"It just seems sudden, with this pack. I've asked you about meeting anyone, and you said no."

I flexed my fingers, resisting the urge to run them through my hair and ruin the gorgeous waves Ronnie managed to give me. "Yeah, I know. But everything with Beau was so public. After that, I wanted some space just to get to know them without anyone looking at us."

We weren't paparazzi famous. But we didn't have to be. Society in Clarity Coast, and an hour north in Sunset City, everyone knew everyone. Beau and I had been a golden couple. Two big families coming together by chance because of work. It was—should have been—a fairytale.

"Well," she said softly, "*they* are certainly looking at you."

I didn't have to look back to where we came from to know she meant my guys.

My heart stuttered at that thought. *My* guys.

"I hope you like them," I said honestly.

"I'm sure I will. If they'll be around for everything, it'll be nice to get to know them."

"They will be," I said.

Pulling me into a hug, she sighed. "I just want you to be happy, Isolde." My eyes pricked with tears because I could hear the emotion in her voice. "I know this really isn't the place, but I can't think about anything else."

"I'm trying."

"I know." She pulled back, blinking quickly to clear the tears. "I know you are. And whatever you need to do to be happy is fine with me. I just hope we can be a part of it."

Shame washed up and over me. My family was going to fall in love with them, and when the whole charade was over, they were going to be devastated. "For sure." The words felt like dust in my mouth.

"Okay." She brushed invisible lint off my shoulders and arranged my hair. "I need to get back to it. Everyone's here for me and Henry, after all. But the family and the wedding party are having breakfast tomorrow. We'd love to see all of you."

"I'll tell them."

"Mom... I really am sorry." Apologies for running had already happened, but I still felt the need to say it. Especially since I wasn't telling her the whole truth.

She touched my arm again. "I know. And you don't have to keep saying it. It's long forgotten. We're just happy you're home."

When she walked away, she wasn't just my mother. She was Adelaide Allen Caruso, host of the party. She'd always been better at that part of it than me. I could play the game, but I didn't *love* the game. My family loved it, and despite me not quite matching, they loved me anyway.

I saw Ocean standing near the windows, looking out at her namesake, and chose to be grateful. My family had their faults, and none of us were perfect, but they loved me. Not everyone could say the same.

People were beginning to notice me standing alone, so I started across the room, back to my guys and my wine. Someone turned so quickly I had to duck out of the way not to get hit.

The scent of lemongrass and eucalyptus. Blonde hair. Blue eyes. A smirk I couldn't forget even though I desperately wanted to. And at his side, a smile sharp as knives.

Beau had found me.

## CHAPTER NINE

ISOLDE

Beau's smirk turned into a smug smile. "Hello, Isolde. Good to see you."

I straightened my spine. "Hello, Beau."

"You remember Angela?"

I glanced down at the hand she had wrapped around his arm. The diamond on her finger glittered. "Of course."

"It's *so* wonderful to see you again," she said, the words kind enough. But they weren't. We weren't friends, and never had been. Angela had never been a fan of mine while Beau and I were together —in the few times we interacted at all—and now I knew why. I couldn't even muster the energy to care. But I felt the eyes in the room turning toward us, hungry for a fight. An altercation. Any kind of gossip at all.

A cloud of sugar wrapped around me. Almost frosting. The softness of that first bite and the moan that came after. Hawk's arms wrapped around my shoulders and chest, just like he'd done in the foyer earlier. His whole body pressed up against my back, offering me both solidity and heat.

He leaned down and pressed a kiss against my neck, drawing his lips up to my ear. "You okay, baby girl?"

The words were soft enough that only the two of us, Beau, and Angela, could hear. It was a fucking good thing Trinity made me get that bra, because goosebumps raced across my entire body, tightening *everything*. I couldn't breathe deep enough to speak, overwhelmed by scent and sensation. When he kissed my hair I closed my eyes and leaned into it. Not because of Beau, but because it was impossible to do anything else.

Beau cleared his throat, and I felt Hawk grin. "Sorry," he said to Beau and Angela. "Can't seem to keep my hands off her."

Beau stared at the two of us, and the look on his face made me want to smile. I held it back. Barely. He was furious. Though why he thought he had any right to be angry was beyond me.

Releasing me just enough to tuck me into his side, Hawk reached out a hand. "Elliot Diaz. My friends call me Hawk."

For a long second, Beau stared at the hand like it was an alien thing. Or a fish that had washed up on the beach. Finally, he shook Hawk's hand. "Beau Jefferson. This is my fiancée, Angela."

"Good to meet you both," Hawk said. His fingers drew circles on my hip where his hand rested, and *fuck* it felt like the entire universe had narrowed to that single spot. I didn't want the dress between my skin and his fingers. I wanted to feel them on me.

"You're with him?" Angela asked me. I'd been so distracted by Hawk that I hadn't noticed the shock on her face.

Hawk looked down at me, drawing me into his gaze. True intensity rested there. Dark fire so deep that I questioned everything. Were they really this good? Because the singular attention was doing... *something* to me, and it was a riptide. Pulling me along so quickly I didn't have time to swim or breathe. I knew the sensation well.

"She is," he said softly. "Well, my pack and I. She's our Omega."

My stomach tumbled into freefall.

For the briefest second I imagined it being real and pulled back. The vision was too perfect, and it would crack me to want it.

Nope.

No.

They deserved awards for their fucking acting.

But god, I wanted to be someone's Omega.

"Your *pack*?" Angela gaped.

Hawk ignored the way she asked, like the idea of me having a pack was so beyond the pale it was ridiculous. "Yep. Over there."

He nodded back toward the bar, where the other four congregated near the windows. Just like at the airport, they stood out. Mouthwatering eye candy. And since I was paying for the view, I would look at them.

"Well, Hawk," Beau cleared his throat. "Since—"

"It's Elliot."

Beau blinked. "I'm sorry?"

"My name. It's Elliot."

I smothered the laughter bubbling up in my chest. A clear line in the sand. His friends called him Hawk, and Beau was *not* his friend.

"Right." Beau seemed unsure, and I savored the look of confusion on his face, bitchy as it might be. No one ever stood up to Beau Jefferson. He charmed his way through life and assumed everyone would fall in line. I barely knew anything about the men who were with me, but I already knew they weren't the type to simply surrender.

"Well, like I was going to say, I'm sure we'll see a lot of each other in the next couple of weeks, since I'm in the wedding party."

"You will," Hawk confirmed. "If you'll excuse me, Isolde needs a new drink."

He pulled me with him, walking me back across the party. Now that our backs were to Beau, I let my smile shine through. "That was hysterical."

"I don't like the way either of them looked at you."

I shrugged. "Not unexpected. Just thankful for the rescue."

Stopping before we reached the group, he turned me to him. "Any time, baby girl."

My head tilted, disguising the same rolling chills moving over my skin. "Baby girl?"

"Too much?" Hawk's eyes sparkled.

I didn't have an answer for that. "Just curious."

"About?"

My mouth opened and closed. None of the questions flashing in my mind were things I could say out loud in a crowded room, no matter how quietly I asked them.

Hawk leaned in again. "If you're asking if I like to be called *daddy*, then the answer is no, not really. But that doesn't mean I don't like taking care of someone or giving them exactly what they need. No matter what that is."

"I don't need to be taken care of."

The softest growl. "Don't you?"

"No." But my voice held no conviction.

Smiling into my skin, Hawk kissed below my ear. "I don't believe you."

"What about you?" I felt dizzy. Somehow I was clinging to the lapels of his jacket despite not remembering reaching for him. "What do you need? Is this something *you* like? Or just an act for your clients?"

"Mmm." The low sound vibrated through me. "I don't think you're ready to talk about what I need, Isolde."

"Why not?"

"Because you told us you didn't want anything to do with us. Or sex. It's purely the arrangement you want. So we're here to take care of you and what you need. Don't worry about us."

I couldn't explain why my heart dropped in my chest or why I suddenly felt the bitter tang of disappointment on my tongue.

"I'm... sorry."

"Why?"

"I don't know."

Confusion swirled around me. I didn't want them to feel like that. They were already so good to me, I didn't want to feel like an asshole who only cared about herself, no matter if I was paying them to do this.

He straightened just enough to brush a kiss to my temple. My body leaned into him like I wasn't controlling it. "If you don't want me to call you baby girl, I won't, Isolde. I don't want to make you feel uncomfortable. Thought I'd give it a try."

One side of his mouth tipped up, and I caught a single moment of vulnerability in his eyes. There and gone in a flash.

"Remember, this is all about you."

I reached out and took his hand. "I didn't say I don't want it. I—I'm not used to that. I'm not sure how I feel about it. But..."

"But?"

"But," I swallowed and looked away. "I didn't hate it."

"Good to know. Though I'm not sure not hating something is good enough to keep using it."

I looked up, getting caught in his gaze. "I... don't stop yet."

Hawk's smile slowly deepened, and he pulled me closer by our joined hands, dropping his lips to mine, kissing me far too briefly. "All right," he paused for another kiss. "Baby girl."

My stomach tumbled into free fall. *Not hating it* was the barest truth. Everything in my mind and body *loved* it.

"Okay, okay," Vaughn said, stepping into our space. "Stop monopolizing our Omega."

We both laughed, and Hawk tucked me against his side once more. "Can't help it. She's too tempting."

Vaughn focused on me. "You okay after that?"

"Yeah. I liked watching *Elliot* hand Beau his own ass on a platter."

"And I will happily do it as many times as I can over the next three weeks."

"Likewise," Vaughn said.

I looked away, embarrassment welling up. "Thank you."

Rowan's voice came from my immediate left. "Our pleasure."

He was fucking quiet for someone so large. I jumped, and his hand smoothed down my spine. "Sorry," he whispered.

"You're so quiet." I laughed. "My mother would like all of us to join family breakfast tomorrow, if that's okay."

"Whatever you need."

The scent of the three of them so close was overwhelming, and I was...

Fuck me. Was I *perfuming*?

Cade appeared with my glass of wine. But it was new, based on how full it was and the cool condensation gathering on it. Ocean still stood near the windows. I needed to talk about some shit, and my best friends were the only ones I could do it with. "I'm going to talk to Ocean for a bit."

I didn't let them answer. As soon as I was out of their sphere, I breathed out a sigh. This was such a bad fucking idea. I was in over my head, and I knew it.

"Hey, O," I whispered, stepping up beside her. "Feel like going for a walk?"

"*God*, yes."

Glancing around, I found Trinity talking to a rapt audience of three men. She smiled, telling some kind of story before she noticed me looking.

"*We're going outside.*" I mouthed the words and gestured between Ocean and myself. She nodded.

Ocean still had her drink in her hand, though it didn't seem like she actually wanted it. We walked down the wide stone steps over to one of the lawns that stretched out. I left my shoes at the edge of the grass, wanting to feel it on my feet.

"How are you?" I asked. "Really." The answer she'd given me earlier didn't quite ring true.

"I'm okay."

"Is that the real answer, or is that the one you think I want to hear?"

She smiled. "It's real. I'm... fine. Not great, not awful. But I'm just here. I'm glad that you're back. It'll be nice to have a second excuse to get out of the house. Not that you're an excuse."

"No, I get it." Other than her greenhouse, where she worked on breeding flowers, her office was in her house. Frankly, it was a miracle her family let her have a business at all, but since it was at home, they supposed she could do *something* with her time.

"So why are you out here with me instead of inside with them?"

I sighed and tossed back half the wine. Great choice? Probably not. But at this point, I felt like I needed to have my edges softened. Not get so drunk I was sloppy, but my whole spine and body were wound tight around these men. "They're too much, O."

"How so?"

"Have you *seen* them?"

She snickered. "Yes. You're lucky."

"Am I?" Confusion swirled through me again. "It was so easy to say I wasn't going to fall into bed with them. But now that I'm here, they're so fucking tempting, but I *can't*. And then they say things that make me think—" I blew out a breath. "This has been the longest day in the history of the world. It feels like I've known them forever and not a few hours."

"Why can't you?"

Ocean's words interrupted my thoughts. I'd been so lost in them I was zoning out. "What?"

"You said you can't. Why can't you?"

"What kind of hypocrite would I be if I did that? After what Beau said? I'm not like him. I don't take advantage of people."

We had wandered around on the grass in a circle, so I took the last sip of my drink and left the glass next to my shoes. Ocean left hers too.

"Of course you're not like him. I don't see why that means you have to hold back."

"O—"

"No," she said, her voice uncharacteristically firm. "Beau said what he said because he's a fucking asshole. What kind of man talks about the woman he's going to marry like that? He said it to hurt you, and you won't convince me otherwise.

"This?" She pointed to the house. "Nothing about this is the same. Yeah, you paid them money. But you're paying them *for this*. You're not paying them to clean your house and then asking them to fuck you, Iz."

"But—" I pressed my hands to my stomach, fighting the swirling anxiety. "I don't—" It was like I couldn't get a full sentence out. "It's only three weeks. What happens when it's over?"

"Then you had a good time for three weeks with five *excruciatingly* hot men who treat you better than your ex ever would have. I refuse to see how that's a bad thing. If it's the fact that you're paying them that's bothering you, I'll pay for it."

That made me snort with laughter. "You're not paying for my escorts."

"I will if I have to. I have plenty of money, and you know I rarely get to use it. If you need this in order to let go and have some fun, tell me. I'll send you the cost right now."

I looked at her. There was no joking or hint of sarcasm on her face. "You're serious?"

"Yes."

"Why?"

She sighed and crossed her arms. "I told you I'm fine, and I am. But I'm not blind, Iz. You're not happy. I know what that looks like."

Going to drag my hands over my face, I stopped just short of ruining my makeup. "They smell so good, O. Like *so* good. And I swear it feels natural with them. And that's terrifying."

"Why?" It was her turn to ask.

"Because look at my track record. Beau asked me out, and within a month, I was..." I shook my head, frustrated at what now felt like the worst kind of naivete. "I was so head over heels for him. And then I spent four years only to be tossed aside. If I fell for him that fast, I can't know I won't fall for them, and it's not even *real*."

Ocean smiled. "You know it's bad when I say the same thing as Trinity. But I think you should. Have some fun. Let yourself loose. There's nothing wrong with this. And having Beau watch you get treated like a queen while he's with his knock-off Isolde Barbie is the best revenge I can think of."

Like I couldn't help it, I looked back at the house. Hawk watched me from one of the doors, leaning against the frame like he had no cares in the world. "O, the way they look at me feels real. How am I supposed to just let go and pretend we have something and then get over it?"

She shrugged. "So let it be real. You have three weeks. Why the fuck not?"

My mouth opened and closed again. There were about a hundred different reasons I could list about *why not*. But they were all me. Every reason came down to me. *I* was scared. *I* didn't want to get hurt. *I* didn't know if I could handle their acting.

But could I?

All the thoughts which had snuck in today—loving their scents, their kisses, Hawk's hand on my hip, him calling me 'baby girl'—I wanted it. Their actions and words felt effortless, and leaning into them felt effortless too.

"I'll think about it," I finally said.

"Good."

I would think about it. But the one thing still stopping me was the deepest fear: what if they showed me exactly how happy I could be?

Because either way, after Ellie's wedding, I would once again be alone.

# CHAPTER TEN

## ROWAN

Stepping up beside Hawk, I watched our Omega with her friend. They were talking about something that affected her, and I selfishly wished I were closer so I could hear. Anyone could see they were both fully engaged, and I couldn't seem to keep my eyes off Isolde for more than a couple of minutes.

"How was he?"

"The ex?"

"Yeah."

Hawk snorted. "He didn't say anything too dickish while I was there, but you know the type. His fiancée was almost worse. She acted like Isolde being with us was shocking and horrifying."

"Mm."

Blowing out a breath, he turned and leaned more fully against the frame so he could see me. "I called her 'baby girl.'"

My eyebrows rose into my hairline. "Not your normal term of endearment."

"It slipped out, and it felt so fucking *right*. This is going to hurt." He shook his head.

Watching the way the late afternoon sun glinted off Isolde's hair, I couldn't look away. She was like a living flame. Fuck me. I wanted to walk out there and kiss her again. Those moments kissing her felt like an eternity, and even more confirmation she was mine.

"It won't hurt," I said. "She's ours, and she's going to feel it. Hell, she already does."

"Omegas—"

I rolled my eyes. "Yes, I know. Omegas don't form scent matches outside of heat. That doesn't mean they don't feel anything. You can't tell me looking at her that she doesn't sense it. She does, but she doesn't understand what it is."

"And that Alpha hurt her," Hawk growled. "It was the reason I had to go over there. I saw the look on her face and I literally *could not* stop myself."

"Know the feeling," I said. My body was rooted to this spot by sheer will alone.

I wanted to walk over to her and kiss her until she was nothing but a mess. I wanted to ruin her makeup and see her completely undone. I wanted—

"So you're another one of the pack?"

Hawk pushed off the doorframe to stand at his full height. "Speak of the devil," he muttered.

I turned and found myself looking down at Isolde's ex. His fiancée was nowhere to be found. I had a good six inches on his height, and I shouldn't have enjoyed him having to look up at me as much as I did.

"Rowan St. James." I offered him my hand, and when he shook it, I squeezed it harder than was strictly necessary. He tried to cover his wince.

"We're all a little surprised to see you here with Isolde," he said, looking between the two of us.

"Why?"

Sliding his hands into the pocket of his suit—which was clearly expensive for the sake of it, considering it didn't fit him well—Beau shrugged. "You know, she's..."

Hawk and I waited for him to finish.

When he didn't continue, Hawk looked at him. "Is there an end to that sentence?"

"Don't pretend you don't know."

"Actually, we have no idea. Please enlighten us."

His jaw ticked, and he glanced past us to where Isolde stood with Ocean. I moved, blocking his view. "She's cold," he finally said. "Boring. Hardly ever comes, so she barely wants to fuck. She's great other than that, but there's only so much you can take. Five of you? It must be torture."

Rage flowed through me. I locked it down, grinding my teeth so hard my jaw ached. Cold? The last thing my Omega was, was *cold*. As far as coming? Sex wasn't all about orgasms. If she had trouble, I'd gladly spend the time learning how to make her body beg. And if that wasn't enough, I'd throw my entire soul into making her feel good, no matter if she did or didn't find release.

Sex wasn't fucking easy. It was a skill. You had to practice, and you had to *listen*. You had to observe and learn how to read people even if they weren't speaking. Which clearly, Beau hadn't, because if he noticed the way Hawk and I were wound up, he'd be on the other side of the room by now.

I clapped him on the shoulder and put on my most charming smile. "Sounds like a personal problem. But hey, if you have trouble pleasing a woman, that's your business. If you'll excuse me."

Turning, I left him standing in the dust. And no matter how slowly we needed to take things with Isolde, I needed to touch her. Right the fuck now. I needed to inhale her scent, so sweet it was almost honey. Nectar. Ambrosia.

She still stood barefoot on the grass with her friend, and Ocean saw me first, eyes going wide.

Isolde looked over her shoulder. "Everything okay?"

I didn't bother to speak, slipping a hand behind her neck and pulling her to me, turning her so she was flush against my body before I kissed her, long and slow.

She tasted so fucking good.

Her lips parted beneath mine, a tiny moan turning into a whine. Isolde's hands slid up my chest, wrapping around my neck like we'd been doing this forever and not only since this morning.

"What are you doing?" She murmured the words against my lips.

"Proving a point." I slid my hand up into her hair, gripping it so I could deepen the kiss. I wanted to tell her everything I liked and everything I craved. Because all I could think about were her answers to those questions.

Hair pulling? *I've always loved it. Can't explain it. But no one really does it right. No big deal.*

She moaned again when my fingers tugged at the strands, perfume swirling around us. I was glad we were outside. That fucker didn't deserve to breathe the same air as her, let alone taste her scent.

I broke the kiss, afraid I would take it too far in front of so many people, and we tried to catch our breath. She smiled as she searched my face. "What point?"

My mouth firmed into a line. "Is he still watching?"

One glance at the house, and her eyes narrowed. Clearly Beau still stood there. "What did he say?"

"I'd rather not repeat it."

"Please?"

I dropped my hands down her body to her hips, still holding her close, ever the picture of the perfect couple. "He said you were cold and barely came, so it couldn't possibly be fun for the five of us. I didn't want to punch someone at your parents' party, so I came out here to prove him wrong."

Blood drained from her face. Isolde was already fair skinned, and now she looked *white*. "He said that?"

"Unfortunately."

"I—" she cleared her throat. "I do have trouble sometimes. It's hard to turn my brain off, and I'm always thinking about the other person and how I look and smell and—"

I kissed her again to stop her panicking. "I didn't come out here to ask you about it or for you to justify what your body needs. Everyone is different, and if your partner doesn't care enough to learn about your pleasure, that's his loss. All it does is prove what a fool he is, and make me pity his fiancée."

"He's not wrong though."

"Isn't he?" I watched her carefully. "Is it that you can't come, or that *he* couldn't make you come?"

Isolde bit her lower lip, cheeks turning pink. That one little movement told me everything I needed to know. My Omega wasn't cold. All she needed was someone willing to learn her pleasure and do the work to fucking earn it.

"I'm sorry, Ocean," I said over her head. "Didn't mean to steal her from you."

"That's okay. I don't mind."

It actually looked like she didn't. If anything, she looked happy I had Isolde in my arms.

A low, resonant sound echoed through the air. A bell. "That's dinner," Isolde said. "Or food, I guess. I don't think they're having everyone sit down to eat."

"Are you hungry?"

Instead of answering, her body answered for her, stomach growling. "I think I was so anxious that I forgot to eat," she whispered.

"Then let's go eat," I said. "And I vote you only eat things that are hot. Right in front of Beau."

Isolde laughed and took my arm. That sound was everything, and I would do everything I could to keep hearing it for the rest of my life.

## CHAPTER ELEVEN

ISOLDE

The rest of the party passed in a blur. The guys brought me food and made sure I was on the opposite side of the room from Beau at all times. It was like having my own private security team.

Every time it looked like he was getting closer, one of them would pretend like we were making our way to speak to someone else. And we did. Old acquaintances who were far too curious about me and the new pack. Old enemies too.

Now the sun had fully set and I was fading. My feet hurt from putting my shoes back on and balancing on the torture devices that were high heels for hours.

Ocean had already left, rushing out of the party when her Aunt and Uncle decided to leave. Rin was drunk enough I would put her in the spare bedroom, and everyone else...

I didn't give a fuck about anyone else at this point.

Geoffrey stood at the door to the ballroom. "Will you please make sure Trinity gets to one of the guest suites, please? I don't want her driving."

"Of course, Miss Allen."

"Thanks."

Joel appeared at my side. "Are you all right?"

I smiled at him, unsure of everything at the moment. "I'm fine, but I'm tired. My feet hurt. I think I'm going to get ready and go to bed early. I'm still used to the time on the other coast, so it's later for me."

"We'll come with you."

"That's okay. You guys enjoy the party."

A low chuckle skimmed across my skin. "What would there be to enjoy about the party without you here?"

"Not having to keep me away from my ex."

Joel raised his hand, and one by one they appeared. Emotion pricked my eyes, so I looked away from them and out into the rest of the house. It wasn't a big thing. I was tired and overwhelmed from seeing Beau and my family and *them*. I wasn't really tearing up about them being willing to leave a party for me. Was I?

The number of times I took a car home alone because Beau wanted to stay somewhere longer than I did...

Gentle fingers brushed my lower back, guiding me out of the room and into the subtle quiet of the rest of the mansion. I could hear the waves in the distance, and the tightness between my shoulders eased.

I hadn't realized just how much I missed that sound.

We reached our suite, the whole thing lit with warm, low lighting. A slew of blankets and pillows had been stacked on and next to the bed. Whether Mom had told the staff to give us extras or it was Geoffrey being kind, I appreciated it.

Joel's hand still rested on my lower back. "I feel like I stepped on a landmine back there. Did I?"

"A landmine?"

"Us leaving with you. Or were the tears from something else?"

Fuck. They noticed that. I wasn't used to being so... *observed*. It was unnerving as much as it was validating.

"It's nothing." They didn't need to hear my trauma about it. That's not what I was paying them for.

He caught my arm before I stepped away and guided me back to him, tilting my face up to his with a single finger. I closed my eyes and breathed him in. I'd never been a bourbon girl, but the Alpha made me want to start. "If it bothers you, it's not nothing."

"I'm just not used to—you really want to hear this?"

"I do." He didn't look away at all. The others were close by and they could hear us too.

I swallowed. "I'm not used to anyone changing their plans for me. If I duck out of a party early, I'm usually doing it alone. Not that I've been to many parties this last year," I mumbled the last bit. The wild weekends at the bar where I worked could be considered parties, I guess, but I left those alone too.

"Beau didn't leave with you." It wasn't a question.

I fought my wince. "Not usually, no."

All five men were quiet.

Too fucking quiet.

"I'm going to change," I said softly, and Joel let me slip away from him and into the closet. Good thing I decided to bring my cute pajamas. Even with nothing happening, I wasn't prepared for these men to see me in ratty sweats and a t-shirt so thin it was starting to get holes.

Instead, I put on a silky pair of shorts and a tank top. They had little cartoon clouds on them. Not my sexiest look, but not the worst, either.

I stepped out of the closet to find more chaos than when I left, with luggage everywhere.

"Do you mind if we share the closet with you?" Rowan asked.

"Of course. Sorry I hogged it."

He stared at me, eyes roving over the pajamas I wore. But there wasn't any judgment or derision on his face. There was... heat. Rowan cleared his throat. "That's not what I meant. If you want your own space, it's okay."

"Oh."

Avoiding the rest of their gazes, I went to the stacks of pillows and grabbed some, claiming a corner on the edge of the bed near the windows. There were more than enough pillows to do what I needed, so I began to line them up in a rectangle, blocking off the little chunk of the bed from the rest of it.

"Isolde?" Hawk's voice caught my attention. I turned to look and froze. Low-slung black sweats and nothing else. The tattoos he had ran down both arms, but more than that. They flowed over his shoulders and down his sides, disappearing into those same sweatpants.

The tattoos framed his abs and the rest of his chest, his hair a little messy like he'd run his fingers through it while he changed. My mind didn't need any more invitation—it filled my mind with images of the two of us. Me licking those abs as I fell to my knees. Those tattooed arms holding me down and moving me wherever he wanted.

Fuck.

I swallowed. "Yeah?"

He smirked like he knew exactly what I'd been thinking. "I know you didn't expect to be in the same room with us, but I promise we're not going to touch you if you don't want us to."

The pillows. I hadn't thought they might think I didn't trust them. What I didn't say was that the pillows weren't for them. They were for me. I didn't trust myself this close to them, and I hadn't decided what I wanted to do about the discussion Ocean and I had.

"I know."

He smiled. "Just making sure."

The rest of them took turns going in and out of the closet and the bathroom, and I was treated to five bodies that were on the verge of me saying *fuck it*.

I slipped into the bathroom and brushed my teeth, not fully prepared for the sight of all five of them sprawled across the giant bed. Hawk was the closest to my little nest.

"You guys okay for the lights?"

Murmurs of agreement drove me to the light switch, and I practically dove into the bed, nestling beneath blankets and cuddling into too many pillows. I closed my eyes, but they were so *close*. I could still smell them, tempting me closer. I could hear their breath.

"Isolde," came the whisper. Cade's voice. "Will you tell us how you met Beau?"

Here in the dark, it didn't feel as vulnerable, and the comfort of finally being in bed and relaxed loosened my tongue. "We worked together. Tate Marketing. It's the biggest marketing firm on this side of the country."

"We know of it," Vaughn said. "They do good work."

"They do. I got a job there for graphic design, and I got it myself. Not because of my parents or anyone else. Beau is one of their ad executives. I mean, he is now. He was a junior account manager when we met and he was..." I sighed. "He was charming."

Way too charming. Maybe that had been a sign?

"The lunch room. I had been craving a blueberry muffin, and they were out. But Beau was in line in front of me and had taken the last one. He saw the look on my face and gave it to me.

"It was our thing after that. The next day I found a blueberry muffin on my desk, and he kept bringing them to me. We became friends, and not long after that..." I shrugged even though they couldn't see me.

"It came together so easily. I just said to Ocean today, I think I fell in love with him in a month. And things were good. I thought we were happy. Or at least happy enough. Then one day it was all gone. I know things don't happen out of the blue, so I missed something. I just wish whatever I missed hadn't taken four years."

I turned on my back and stared at the ceiling. Now that the dam was open, I couldn't stop. "I just didn't see it coming. We lived together. He came home one weekend, he'd been out with friends, and told me it was over. That I needed to take my stuff and get out by the end of the next week. He wouldn't tell me why. Hell, he wouldn't say *anything* else to me. After he left again, I got what I could, and I was gone before he came back that night. Only took what I couldn't live without. And by the end of the week, I was across the country, doing the last tasks at my job remotely. *He'd* been promoted. I just..."

My breath caught, and a familiar ache filled my chest. More because of my confusion and lack of closure than grieving anything to do with Beau. Which made it worse. Shouldn't I be sadder? "I couldn't face all the questions and all the pity. Instead, I ran and made everyone think I had something to hide."

A harsh laugh. Vaughn. "I doubt that."

"It's true," I said. "The people here only know and care about what they see. And because I didn't dress up and go out holding my head held high, I'm—" I lifted my hand and let it drop back onto my stomach. "It doesn't matter. But that's why I couldn't be here alone."

Slowly, a hand touched my ankle. I jumped, but it didn't move any more than that. It wasn't a touch to break boundaries, it was a touch for comfort.

"I'm sorry," Joel said, thumb brushing against my skin. "He didn't deserve you."

I wanted to say thank you, but I couldn't. My throat choked on the words. Too much emotion pulling me in every direction. Instead, I tucked myself down into the pillows and closed my eyes, falling asleep to the gentle rhythm of that one single touch.

## CHAPTER TWELVE

### HAWK

It was one thing to wake up hard. It was an entirely different thing to wake up hard after your dreams starred a redheaded Omega you wanted to drag underneath you and pleasure until she lost her voice.

I shifted, noting the heaviness of my body. Man, I must have slept hard to feel like this. *Wait.*

Sweet and deep floral scent that was too strong for where said Omega was sleeping. Suddenly, I was fully awake. *My* body wasn't heavy.

One peek was all I needed to grin like a damn fool. Isolde was on top of me. One leg slung over my hips, head on my chest, hand curled around my ribs. The pillow wall she'd so diligently put together was a mess.

This felt incredible. This felt *right.*

Her leg was so close to touching my cock, I was tempted to shift her just enough. But I didn't. All I did was lift my arm and hold her closer. The story she told last night broke me. The pain in her voice? I didn't see myself getting through all three of these weeks without laying hands on her ex.

I stroked my hand gently up and down her spine, which made her cuddle closer. Fuck, she was cute. I wanted her cute. I wanted her sexy. I wanted her *mine.*

Her lungs expanded beneath my hand, and she moved. I felt the moment she realized where she was. Her whole body froze, moving her head to look up at me, horror in her eyes. "I'm so sorry," she whispered.

"I'm not."

"But—"

I moved, rolling us together away from my packmates and into her pillows. Now I could *feel* her beneath me. So fucking soft. I barely held my hips in check from rocking and my groan from escaping.

"Isolde." My voice was a breath of a breath so we didn't wake anyone else. "I am in no way upset by waking up with a beautiful Omega draped over me. Actually, it ranks pretty high in my favorite mornings."

Her pale skin flushed. This close, I could see the gentle freckles sprinkled over her nose and cheeks.

We moved together, pulled like magnets, but I held myself in check. We weren't in public, and as much as I wanted to kiss the hell out of *my* Omega, I wasn't going to do something to push her away. I was already on top of her. If she wanted to kiss me, she needed to be the one to close the distance.

"You guys are so good at this," she whispered.

"Good at what?"

"Pretending. Making me feel like someone worth... anything. I can see why you're the best."

I looked down at her, unable to keep my gaze off her lips. In the morning light, her hair was a delicious shade of red spread across the pillows. Hopefully soon I'd see it messier. And I could make her see her own worth, because it was *all* I could see. "What makes you think we're pretending?"

Isolde's breath caught, an expression somewhere between arousal and fear on her face. "Because that's your job?"

"Our job isn't to pretend shit." I leaned down and whispered the words into her neck before dragging my mouth up to her ear. "Our job is to make you realize exactly how incredible you are. To show you that you're worth so much more than what that asshole made you believe. I have pretended with others, yes. But Isolde Allen, I am not pretending with you."

Pulling back, I saw her doubt. The little wrinkle on her forehead that betrayed her confusion. I could hang Beau up by his balls for the damage he'd done to this woman. She believed they were *happy*, and he threw her out like trash.

Something told me there was more to the story, and I fully intended on finding out. But this moment was about my Omega, and I wasn't letting her leave this bed with doubt, even if she didn't yet know the truth. So I took the risk and shifted my body higher, lining our hips up perfectly so she could feel all of me.

Just my sweats and her skimpy pajamas between us. "Does this feel pretend to you?"

She blushed as bright as her hair and wiggled out from under me. I let her go, noticing the shadow of hard nipples through the silky pajama top.

"We need to get ready for breakfast," she said. Her voice was a little rough.

She disappeared into the closet and Cade turned over. "You need to be careful."

"There's being careful and there's being *too* careful. We agreed not to lie to her, so I'm not fucking lying to her. I want her to figure it out. I want her to realize this isn't a game."

"I want that too. Just don't push too hard too fast."

Fair point.

We got ready, Isolde managing to hide from us until we were ready to go. The black, flowing dress she wore looked incredible, but the color didn't suit her. Last night in the green she practically *glowed*. Now, while beautiful, the spark was missing.

I took her hand as she led us out the veranda doors instead of through the house. On one of the lawns extending down to the beach, a white, open-sided tent rested, a long table underneath already filled with people.

There was enough space for us, but I noticed as we approached, Beau and Angela sat with the group. "What are they doing here?"

"He's the best man," Isolde reminded me. "He'll be here the whole time. Well, at least when the rest of the wedding party is."

"Perfect," I growled.

"I know, I'm sorry. Protecting me from him is going to get old."

I pulled her to a stop and glanced at Cade. He read my mind and stepped in behind her. We were close enough for people to see, but not hear. "I don't give a shit if I have to protect you from him every second of every day, Isolde. I wish he weren't here for your sake. He doesn't make you feel safe, and I hate that. This is your home. You deserve to feel comfortable."

Her mouth popped open in shock. I could so easily lean in and bite that lower lip. Pull her into a kiss that would make her believe me. Every time I had to pull myself back from kissing her, it got harder.

Lifting my hand like a man possessed, I ran my thumb along her lower lip. Isolde's pupils dilated, and a wave of sweet perfume swirled around the three of us. Cade's eyes closed as it hit him. I needed to step away before I did anything more.

"Oh," was all Isolde said.

"We are here for *you*," I told her. "What *you* need. Not him and not anyone else, okay?"

"Okay." A shy smile.

"Morning," Mrs. Allen called from down the table as we approached.

Isolde waved, and I pulled out a chair for her a few seats down from being directly across from Beau and Angela. Joel and Rowan took those a little too gleefully.

"Morning, Isolde," Beau said.

"Good morning." She froze for a second, covering it well as she made herself comfortable in her chair. "That bracelet is lovely, Angela."

The other redhead looked up like she was startled that Isolde even spoke to her, and Beau watched the two of them like a snake. Vicious. Dangerous. "Oh. Thank you. Beau gave it to me. He's thoughtful that way." She leaned into the man, bumping his arm with hers. He barely looked at her, his eyes focused on Isolde.

I sat down beside Isolde and looked at the bracelet. A simple silver chain with what looked like a purple stone graced Angela's wrist.

"You like the bracelet, baby girl?" I hadn't used the term in bed this morning because I thought it might have overwhelmed her too much. But here? Here I wanted to remind her.

She sucked in a breath and reached for her glass of water. "It's mine."

"I'm sorry, what?"

"Remember I said I only took what I couldn't live without? The bracelet is mine. He must have taken it from the jewelry I left and given it to her."

I moved to stand and her hand landed on my arm. "Don't. It's just a bracelet."

"It's fucking disrespectful is what it is."

"Please." She moved her hand to grip mine. "Don't. But thank you for wanting to."

I lifted her hand and kissed the back of it, never looking away. "That's not something you have to thank me for."

"We're leaving after breakfast for the fittings, Iz," her sister called from the other end of the table. "You good with that?"

"Sure."

Warren, her fiancé, looked at the rest of us. "We have fittings as well, but after, we'll find something for the rest of us to do. I'm sure Mr. Allen wants a chance to interrogate you."

We laughed, and Rowan lifted a glass. "I think we can handle that."

Conversation ebbed and flowed, but I heard none of it. I was too focused on the way Beau stared at Isolde. For someone who'd tossed her aside, he certainly seemed invested. And now that I saw him like this, the way he approached me and Rowan last night seemed strange. Like he was trying to get us to abandon her too.

What was his deal?

"Hawk?"

Startling, I looked over at Isolde. She stood next to me, hand on my shoulder.

"You okay?"

I placed a hand over hers. "I'm good."

"We're going to the dress fitting. I'll see you later."

Winking, I kissed her hand again. "Have fun, baby girl."

The shade of pink on her cheeks was my new favorite color. I wanted to paint whole rooms with it just to show her how gorgeous it was. She glanced back once as she followed her mother, sister, and the other bridesmaids.

And for the first time, the look on her face was something like hope.

## CHAPTER THIRTEEN

ISOLDE

"You have to tell us *something*," Ellie said from inside the dressing room.

My fitting was already complete, and I was back in my sundress, waiting for her to put her wedding dress on. Ellie was a Beta, and so was Warren. They were adorable, happy, and I couldn't wait to see them get married. I loved Warren, aside from his poor choice of best friends.

Then again, other than ending our relationship out of the blue, Beau hadn't really done anything *wrong*. He never treated me badly or did any of the things you hear stories about. Sure, he liked to stay at parties after I left, and he apparently was cheap enough to reuse jewelry, but did that make him a bad person and friend?

As much as I wished I could say yes, the answer was no.

"What do you want to know?"

My mother just laughed where she sat across the room. Thankfully, the other bridesmaids were finishing up their own fittings, leaving the three of us alone.

"I think," Mom said, "we'll be happy with anything. All we know is that you told us you'd be bringing people with you, then showed up yesterday with a pack of gorgeous men. We have questions."

And I didn't have answers. Because I had my own questions,

along with my quickly-crumbling resolve not to fall into their arms and enjoy the time with them.

"How did you meet?" Ellie asked.

"Trinity introduced us," I said truthfully. "She met them through work somehow."

Mom glanced up from the magazine she flipped through. I spotted one of the houses she'd designed on the cover. "So they're from here?"

"Yeah. They've been going back and forth." Not true, but of the things I wasn't saying, it was small.

"Where do they live?"

*Shit.* "I actually haven't been to their house yet, but they live in Clarity."

"I'm surprised we haven't run into them, then."

I laughed. "They live in Clarity, but I don't think they're going to the kind of parties you do, Mom."

The curtain in the dressing room slid aside, and Ellie came out, followed by the seamstress. She stood on the little pedestal, looking radiant. "It's gorgeous, El."

"Thank you. As long as I don't do anything drastic, the final fitting won't need anything."

Her dress was a ball gown, with a full skirt like a cake topper. Off the shoulder neckline and so many sparkling beads she shimmered under the lights of the shop. On the actual day when the wedding was outside? She would glitter.

"I'm glad you're happy," I told her. "Really."

She turned, giant skirt swishing. "I am happy. I wish you were happy too."

Regardless of what the St. James pack and I did together, being here with everyone and the hold on my mind and heart loosening, I felt better. I shouldn't have stayed away so long. "I think I'm getting there."

One of her friends peeked into the room and shrieked. The whole place was filled with exclamations and laughter, and I just smiled. This was nice.

Mom came over and sat next to me. "I'll hide over here with you."

"Good call."

"You seem lighter than when we talk on the phone."

Shaking my head, I watched Ellie twirl in her gown while a

friend filmed it. "Have you ever done something, and you didn't realize how much it affected you until later?"

"Pretty sure that's part of being alive," Mom said. "We can't see what's right in front of us until it's shoved into focus or far too late."

"I didn't realize how alone I was." I looked over at her. "And it seems silly that I didn't notice it. But now..."

She reached over and took my hand out of my lap. "Sometimes we have to do something for ourselves. Even if it doesn't make sense, and even if it doesn't work out the way we hoped. Whatever happens now, you needed that time, Isolde. We missed you, and we're so happy you're back, but this wasn't the place for you to heal. Maybe now it will be."

I blinked away tears. "Thank you."

"Now," she straightened, and I smiled at the shift. Mom was in planner mode. "Do you have plans with those handsome men? Or can you help me today?"

"What are you doing?"

"What am I *not* doing? Finalizing flowers and place settings. Ellie gave me all the details she doesn't care about. I'll have you back in time for the bonfire tonight."

"Bonfire?"

Mom smiled. "Warren's idea. Something for the bridal party to do all together before they disperse. Until the actual bachelor and bachelorette parties, of course. Figured it could be fun."

A bonfire was a *great* idea. I hadn't had a chance to set foot on the beach yet. And spending time with Mom might help me clear my head. "I can help. The guys will be fine. Tell me what you need."

I completely forgot what spending a day with my mother while she was in full planner mode was like. A sight to behold, but exhausting. By the time her driver pulled back up in front of the mansion and the sun was blazing a path to the horizon, the only thing I wanted was to relax on the beach in front of the bonfire.

But we'd taken care of necessary details. Not everything, but enough that my mother felt infinitely less stressed, and I wouldn't feel bad about lying low for the next week while there weren't any 'official' wedding events.

The suite was empty, so I flopped back onto the freshly made bed, closing my eyes for a second. I was out of practice being around people.

My phone chirped, and I fished it out of my purse.

OCEAN

Did you decide?

ISOLDE

No.

OCEAN

And what's stopping you?

ISOLDE

Nothing's changed since yesterday, O.

OCEAN

Exactly. Nothing's changed, and you didn't have any good reasons yesterday either.

Rowan had pulled me away and kissed the hell out of me before Ocean and I had finished talking about it. But I was still afraid. And more than that, I'd said what I wanted and what I was going to do. If I changed my mind, what person did that make me?

ISOLDE

If I change my mind after a day, doesn't that mean I'm weak? I'm not so sex crazed that I can't last without dick for three weeks.

OCEAN

Oh, for fuck's sake.

The phone rang a second later. "Hello?"

"Hold on, I'm bringing Rin in."

A second later, Trinity answered. "Sorry, I didn't text you this morning when I left. I got distracted by this new article I'm working on. Thanks for putting me in the guest suite."

"No problem," I said with a laugh. "But I'm not the one who actually called you."

"No. I did," Ocean nearly growled. "Because when *I* think it's time for tough love, you know something's wrong."

All three of us went silent. Ocean rarely ever raised her voice. She was soft-spoken by nature, and the way her family treated her only made it worse. She had a powerhouse inside of her, but it took coaxing to bring it out.

"I didn't realize my sex life called for tough love," I joked.

"Well, it does," she said. "Not just your sex life. You're going to be quiet for a second and listen, Iz. Hell, I'm on the verge of driving down there and smacking it into you."

"Ocean," Rin laughed. "What's going on?"

The hitch in her breath told me something else was wrong, but I didn't say anything. This wasn't the time to deflect things back on her. I would ask later.

"Iz, I know why you felt like you needed to leave. I understood it, even if I hated it. I get needing time to recover from something. And I understand the nerves you have about jumping into something so fresh when it's not 'real.'" Her voice put quotes around the word. "And if you don't actually want to fuck the pack, then don't. But if that's your decision, let it be because that's what you *want* and not because you're afraid of yourself or what'll happen when it's over.

"You have a *choice*." Her voice broke. "You can do whatever you want, and I'm tired of watching you fight yourself because you're scared and Beau made you think you're not worth what you want."

My mouth dropped open. I'd never heard Ocean talk like this. Ever. "O, are you okay?"

"This isn't about me."

"I know," I said gently. "But that doesn't mean I don't care."

She huffed out a breath. "I'm fine. Just do me a favor and stop prioritizing the shit in your brain that doesn't matter and do something that makes you feel good."

"I'll try."

What she said was entirely true. I did feel that way. I did feel...

"I'll try to think about just me."

"Good," Ocean's voice sounded normal now. "I'm glad. Let me know what you decide. I have to go."

She hung up without letting us say goodbye, leaving Trinity and me hovering in the silence.

"What the hell was that about?" Rin asked. "Other than you. You know what I mean."

I did. "No idea. She seemed good yesterday. Normal. Can you try to find out?"

"Yeah," she said. "I will. And Iz?"

"Mm?"

"She's right."

"Yeah." My throat felt thick. "I know."

"Talk to you later."

The phone went dead in my hand, and I stared at the ceiling. It was one thing to know something about yourself, and another thing to have someone tell you. I curled onto my side, trying to ease the tightness in my chest.

It was shame.

Shame that I'd let myself cling to Beau so desperately that him doing what he'd done had destroyed me. Shame that I was so afraid of myself and my own judgment I felt paralyzed. Shame that I felt... worthless.

The shitty thing about realizations was that even if you had one, it didn't make the feelings go away. I was still terrified. But Ocean saying *'you have a* choice,' like she didn't, gave me enough of a push to try.

Setting my phone aside, I went into the closet to change into my bathing suit and something simpler. I love dresses, but for this I needed to feel like me.

Here went nothing.

## CHAPTER FOURTEEN

ISOLDE

Orange, yellow, and pink lit up the sky like someone took paint and smeared it across the surface. Windswept clouds catching the colorful light and reflecting it back. The surface of the sea mirrored all that brightness, a smudged and gorgeous copy of all the dying beauty, disappearing into infinity.

My bare feet touched the sand, and I sighed, all the tension leaving my body. Ocean breeze carried the scent of salt and sun, the gentle, rhythmic sound of the waves lifting all the heaviness on my chest and shoulders.

This is what I missed the most. Just this. Standing in the face of something so *huge* and feeling like it saw you. Like you breathed, and it breathed back.

The fire was at the north end of our beach, near the cliffs. The bases were worn away into arches and caves that were as gorgeous to explore as they were terrifying at high tide. But I loved them. The hours I'd spent hiding from everyone and just enjoying the ocean were more than I'd ever admit.

I took my time walking down the beach. The guys were already there. Rowan and Vaughn towered over everyone else. After spending the day away from them, I wasn't sure how they would greet me. Or how they would respond to what I would ask.

*Isolde Allen, I am not pretending with you.*

What the hell did that mean? I hadn't let myself think about it.

But now that I was opening myself up to possibilities, I couldn't *not* think about it.

I had a blue bikini on under the shorts and shirt I wore. Even in summer the air took on a chill after sunset. Hence the thin shirt. That, and I wanted something to cover my skin while I was deciding. If they touched me too much, I would make the decision based on that alone.

Trinity would tell me it meant my body had already decided. Ocean would tell me it was smart to keep small checks and balances. Me? I didn't know. I was diving in head first and had no idea how it would turn out. We would have a conversation at some point tonight, and then...

Ellie saw me coming and waved, running down the beach to meet me and nearly tackling me into the sand. "Took you long enough, slowpoke."

I laughed, slinging her arm over my shoulders. She was already well on her way to getting drunk. "I was helping Mom. With stuff for *your* wedding."

"I know," she sighed. "But you still took forever."

Warren waited, amused smile on his face, hands in the pockets of his board shorts. I shook my head as we approached. "Gotta keep better track of her."

"There's never a time when I'm not," he said, his eyes only on Ellie.

My sister looked at me. "Want a drink?"

"I'm gonna say hi to the guys first."

She giggled. "I get you. Let *them* get the drinks. Smart."

I handed her to Warren and watched him pull her close, lifting her off her feet before kissing her. For a long time I thought Ellie would be happiest with a pack until Warren came along. He worshipped the ground she walked on, complementing her vibrance with his steadiness. They truly were good for each other, and it showed.

Eyes were already on me. Through the wavering, heated air above the reaching flames, Rowan stared at me. Vaughn too. My feet started moving before I decided, and this felt different, because I was approaching them with entirely different intentions.

Vaughn caught me first. He swept me up the way Warren had Ellie, purr rolling through both of us. I froze. It was the first time any of them had purred for me.

How long had it been since I felt an Alpha's purr?

Far too fucking long.

I relaxed, choosing to lean into the feeling and not fight it. Vaughn kissed my cheek. "Missed you today."

"It was exhausting."

"Want a drink?"

"Honestly? Not really. I want to relax, but I'm not sure getting drunk is what I'm feeling right now."

Rowan stepped up next to us. "I can help with that."

"Oh?"

He pulled a little case out of his pocket. "A hobby of mine."

The case held hand-wrapped joints that were so neat they could have been professional. My eyes widened. "Really?"

"Why so surprised?"

"I don't know. I just didn't get the feeling you were a stoner."

Rowan's laugh echoed across the beach. "I'm not. I like it, but it's not an every day or all the time thing. My sister deals with chronic pain, and my dad had cancer. I started growing to help them out. Turns out I enjoy it. I have edibles too, but I think you might need something that kicks in faster."

"Is your dad...?"

"He's gone."

I winced. "I'm sorry."

Rowan handed me one of the small joints. "Don't be. He had a great life, and he was ready. Does me growing bother you?"

"No," an inelegant snort fell out of me. I covered my mouth and nose with my hand. They heard it anyway, though they didn't say anything. "I grew up here, remember? Most people were doing things harder than weed." And there were far worse things.

Vaughn lit the joint for me, and as soon as I'd taken one breath, Hawk stole it from me.

"*Hey.*" I tried to steal it back.

"Don't want to share, baby girl?"

I shivered, and it had nothing to do with the cool breeze off the water. "No, I'll share."

He took a drag and handed it back to me. "Did you have fun today?"

"If by fun, you mean tasting more food than is entirely reasonable and checking every boutique in Clarity for *exactly* the right vases for centerpieces, then yes. But it was nice to hang out with my mom."

Hawk took me to the sand, pulling me down and arranging me

between his legs. Close enough to the fire to feel its warmth as the sun faded, and not close enough to get burned. His scent wrapped around me along with his arms. "I'm glad you had fun."

Someone sat down next to us. Joel, smiling, with a beer in his hand. They were all dressed casually, and they looked *good*. I let myself look. Shirts stretching over muscles and enough scruff along their jaws I wanted to reach out and touch. Joel had freckles like me, and the waning sun lit up his hair the way it did mine, bright as the fire.

But—

"Where's Cade?"

"He'll be back soon," Vaughn said, hitting the sand in front of me, his back to the bonfire. "He had to go teach a class, but it should be over by now."

"What does he teach?"

Vaughn glanced around, checking where the others were. Ellie's bridesmaids and Warren's groomsmen mingled around the fire, but none were close enough to hear our conversation. I didn't see Beau or Angela, thankfully.

"He teaches a lot of things," Vaughn said. "But mainly shibari."

A deep shudder rolled through me, and it didn't go unnoticed. "We know you're familiar because of your questionnaire," Hawk murmured in my ear.

"He teaches it?" Imagining Cade working with people, tying them up, the image was so hot I had to take a deep breath. And fight off the sudden flare of jealousy. I didn't want his hands on someone else, especially since I knew so much of shibari and rope play was done without clothing to help with friction.

Hawk's chuckle warmed me up, and he started to purr too. Fuck. My head rolled back on his shoulder, and he held me tighter. "We all have things we do when we're not doing *this*. Cade actually owns the place and teaches kink. How to do things safely."

"I didn't—" I swallowed. "I didn't know there was anything like that in Clarity."

Joel leaned forward, stroking a hand down my bare leg. "It's the perfect place for it. Rich people are kinky as fuck, and in Clarity? So is everyone else. No clubs, but Sunset City has plenty of those, if you want them."

Breathing in another lungful of smoke, I snuggled down further into Hawk. A low sound in his throat, and suddenly he was turning my head back to capture my lips with his. Naturally. Easily.

Even with Beau, it hadn't felt like this.

Fear rose up in me, and I tried to push it down. What if I got addicted to them? What if it hurt to let them go?

What if I shut the fuck up and enjoyed Alphas and a Beta who wanted to show me something more?

One more breath of smoke. It was starting to help me relax. Weed was never one of those things that made me feel out of control. I didn't get paranoid and I didn't lose my mind. Instead, I felt *good*. Relaxed. It lifted my fears and loosened me. Made me who I knew I could be.

I just needed to figure out how to do it sober too, and something told me these men might be the ones to show me how.

"I have a question for all of you, but I..." I offered the joint to Hawk again. He took it and pulled in a long breath. "I don't want anyone else to hear, and I'm nervous you'll judge me for it."

Joel jerked his head at Rowan, and he joined us. The others scooted closer. Circling me, keeping close enough that anyone else at this fire would simply see a pack enjoying each other's company and nothing more.

"We're listening." Vaughn pulled my feet into his lap, sand gently scratching my skin as he ran his hands over my bare legs.

Nerves swirled in my gut. I stared into the flames, figuring out how to word it. Hawk squeezed me gently. "Isolde?"

"I—" I cleared my throat. "I might have changed my mind. But I made such a big deal out of saying no that I feel silly. It was more about me than you, but I don't want you to think I'm... I don't know."

Rowan looked at me like he could see through me. "Changed your mind about what?"

My whole body went hot. I dropped my voice to a whisper. "Sex."

Hawk froze against me, and a second later his purr vibrated so hard through me I wondered if he did that between my legs if he could get me off. "You thought we would judge you for that?"

"Not the actual sex, no. But for being so fucking adamant about not having it, and then changing my mind."

Joel leaned forward. "It's more common than you might think."

"Really?"

"Really." He grinned. "The idea of having sex with strangers isn't normal for most people, and when you're reaching out to someone, or a pack, to help you through something emotional, sex isn't as important. But now you're here. You're safe. And you're comfortable. If it's something you want?" Joel shook his head. "Fuck, Isolde, we want you."

"Why?" I blurted the word out without any thought, and they laughed.

Hawk put the joint back between my lips. "What possible reason would there be not to want you, baby girl?"

I didn't have an answer to that.

Vaughn pulled out his phone. "In that case, I have some things I want to ask you about."

"Oh?"

He smirked. "For someone who wasn't interested, you were *very* thorough when you filled everything out."

"I was also drunk, so there's that."

"Then you were probably honest," Rowan said with a smile, his own joint hanging from his fingers. "If I'd known you were going to tell us this, I wouldn't have given you that." He gestured to my hand.

I whined. "You're not going to leave me hanging because I'm a little high, are you?"

"Leave you hanging?" Hawk whispered. "Never. Make sure you're clearly able to consent? Absolutely."

Vaughn's face was lit by his phone screen. "How much of this have you done? Or tried?"

"Almost nothing."

"Because you didn't want to? Or because you didn't have the opportunity?"

I rolled my eyes. "Because getting Beau to do something that wasn't the same five moves wasn't worth my time, and before that, I didn't know shit."

Joel kept his expression carefully blank. "Were the five moves any good?"

"They were... passable."

He choked on his beer. "Passable?"

"I got there most of the time." Not true. "Some of the time. It wasn't mind blowing."

Hawk growled. "*Some of the time* isn't a phrase you should ever use when describing getting off."

"When you have a hard time getting there it is. It wasn't always his fault. Sometimes it's hard."

"You're right," he whispered, running his hands up my ribs. "Sometimes coming is hard. You know what's not? Caring about someone enough to make sure they're satisfied even if there's no orgasm involved."

I shook my head. "You guys say that like it's the most natural thing in the world. Have you met most men?"

Vaughn leaned forward and slid his phone into my hand. "Yes, we have, which is why we're nothing like them. Now tell me what things on the list actually interest you."

The screen was almost too bright in the near darkness, but I saw all my answers typed out next to the questions, and the long list of checkboxes for interest. That list was based on all the things *they* were interested in or willing to do.

My eyes skipped down the list, catching on things.

*Blowjobs.*

*Bondage—rope, metal, hands, miscellaneous.*

*Breath play.*

*Consensual non-consent.*

*Hair pulling.*

*Primal Play.*

*Cock warming.*

*Cock swaddling.*

*Pain.*

*Praise.*

*Primal.*

*Somnophilia.*

*Spanking.*

And those were only some of the things listed. It was too much.

I swallowed. "I didn't lie. On the list. Whatever it says there is what I'm interested in."

Across the fire, I saw Beau arrive with Angela looking far too mussed. She still had the fucking bracelet on her hand, and that hurt more than the idea that she and Beau were just having sex. That didn't hurt at all, and I smiled.

Vaughn followed my gaze. "Why are you smiling at them?"

Taking a deep drag on the joint before putting it out, I blew it out into the velvet sky. "Because they were just having sex from the looks of her hair, and I feel nothing about it. She can have him."

Hawk's purr sprang to life beneath me, and Rowan took Vaughn's phone from my hand, but kept holding mine. "Okay, Isolde. Tell us exactly what you want."

The edges of my mind were blurring in a good way. I felt like I could *breathe*. The crackle of fire and the sound of the sea and everyone's chatter and laughter. This was good. "I know it's not real," I said quietly, shaking my head. "But it's been a long time since I've had fun. Any kind of fun, honestly. And with that many things I haven't tried on the list, it could be a good idea to—holy fuck, I'm rambling."

They all laughed, the sound warming me from the inside.

"Let me help you out, baby girl," Hawk whispered in my ear. "Are you saying that you want us to help you explore things you've never tried before, while at the same time fucking you at every possible opportunity for the next few weeks?"

My whole body shuddered, arousal, longing, and need twisting through me like a living thing. "Yes," I said, closing my eyes and surrendering to the truth and also to all my fear. "Yes, that's what I want."

Joel lifted his beer in a toast. "Then that's all you have to say."

## CHAPTER FIFTEEN

CADE

I dropped my rope bag off at our house before heading back to the Caruso estate, and my phone chirped as I was parking the car.

VAUGHN

Down on the beach for the bonfire. You're going to want to get here as soon as possible.

CADE

Why?

VAUGHN

You'll see.

Forcing my growl into a sigh, I shut the car door harder than was necessary. I wasn't in the mood for vague games. My first lesson had gone well, but the group beginners class hadn't. An Alpha who knew next to nothing kept trying to interrupt and correct things that didn't need to be corrected, confusing the other people in the class.

And because I was a Beta, I couldn't tell him to sit down and shut the fuck up the way I really wanted to. Not that I couldn't have taken him, but the man's instincts would override mine every time.

He wouldn't be invited back to the center. Before I left, I made sure to put him on all of our 'no,' lists. It wasn't something I relished, but if someone wasn't willing to learn how to do things safely, they had no place coming to classes where people did.

Regardless, I'd keep an eye out for his name in the community. He seemed like someone who'd stick around and try to impress people with his non-existent knowledge. If he tried, I could step in and gently let people know not to mess with him.

So restless energy moved under my skin. I could do with a good session in the gym. No doubt the mansion had one, though I wasn't sure where it was.

CADE

Unless it's urgent, I'm going to the gym to blow off some steam.

He answered immediately.

VAUGHN

You might be able to blow off some steam in a different way if you get your ass down here.

My eyebrows rose. That was interesting.

I changed direction from going back to our suite to heading out the back. The fire was visible from the house, with plenty of people around it. Music played from somewhere, and a few couples and packs in the bridal party danced on one side. On the other, my pack-mates surrounded Isolde, who cuddled with Hawk like she was born to be in his arms. Miles of pale skin was visible with the length of those shorts and the way her thin shirt tugged off her shoulder. She looked *lighter*. Happier.

Rowan spotted me and came to meet me before she saw me. "What's going on?"

"Isolde changed her mind."

"About?"

He smirked. "Sex."

All my attention shifted to the beautiful Omega in my pack-mate's arms. "Really?"

"Yeah. Still nervous as hell about something, and she very clearly said she knows this," he gestured to all of us, "isn't real. But as far as everything else? All bets are off."

"Fuck." I shook my head. Relief poured through me. Not touching her the way I—we—wanted had already been difficult, and it had barely been two days. Weeks would have been torture.

"We haven't had a chance to talk without her, but I'm game to treat her like she's ours. Show her what that's like. Then, after the wedding, we tell her. By then, she'll know we're not just saying it because she's a client or because she thinks she's paying us."

"Fine with me."

I couldn't stay away from her anymore. Joining them, Isolde looked up and saw me, a smile coming to her face. "There you are."

"Here I am."

"I missed you." She scrambled out of Hawk's arms to stand and throw hers around my neck. A deep sigh left her when I pulled her close, like I was exactly what she needed.

Fuck, a man could get used to that.

The sweetness of her scent mixed with a lower, darker fragrance, and I chuckled. "I see you've discovered Rowan's hobby."

"I did. But he didn't corrupt me. You think I grew up in Clarity Coast and didn't get high?" Then she grinned, rising up on her toes so our lips were barely an inch apart. "Don't worry, though. I'm not *that* high."

"They told me what you said. Is it true?"

"That I want you all to fuck me into next week? Yes."

I tilted my head, studying her face. She was more open, but correct. She wasn't so high she didn't have control of her body or senses. "What changed your mind?"

"Ocean. Trinity. Myself realizing just how fucking sad I've been. So I'm choosing something different. I don't fucking trust myself, but it's okay, because I think I can trust the five of you. Whatever happens, I'll deal with it."

"What would happen?"

Isolde laid her head on my chest and looked out at the sea. "I fell for him in a month, and you treat me so much better. I might fall for you, too. It's okay, I know this is your job. You don't have to worry about me. I'll figure that part out later."

Smiling into her hair, I looked at the rest of them. They knew, even without being close enough to hear. I couldn't wait for our little Omega to fall for us. Because it was already too late. She was ours, we were falling for her, and we had no plans to let her go.

"Look at me, Isolde."

She did, with no hesitation. Fuck, this Omega had no idea what she did to me with one simple movement. I already imagined her obeying other commands and falling apart under my hands. Couldn't fucking wait until I could touch all of her.

Her lips were under mine before she could ask me anything. I was starving, and she was the only thing which would satisfy me. She tasted like cannabis and sunshine and that sweetness which was only her.

Isolde kissed me back.

So unlike the first time I kissed her, she wrapped herself around me, blooming like a fucking flower. It was like she couldn't get close enough to me, and I needed to consume all of her. Why the fuck did I take my rope home? It wasn't far. I could run over and grab it, but I didn't want to take my hands off my Omega.

"Get a room," a voice called, followed by laughter.

When I turned, I found Beau glaring at us, clearly pissed.

"Don't worry, we'll use it later," Vaughn called.

All I did was smile before turning back to Isolde and kissing her again, this time curling my fingers into her hair to keep her still before I took her mouth with all the savagery I felt.

"You have no idea what you've done by unleashing us, angel."

She giggled, and I swore in that moment I would never forget the sound or take it for granted. "I'm no angel."

"Oh, you are," I said, leaning in to kiss her neck. Across her shoulder to where her shirt sagged and bared her skin. "Better be careful. We're the devils who will drag you down and dirty that halo. We may not have corrupted you yet, but it doesn't mean we won't."

Her teeth sank into her bottom lip, and I groaned. I fucking loved it when she did that. With her lips swelling from my kisses the movement made her that much more appealing.

"Corruption sounds kind of fun."

"It will be."

Rowan stole her away from me, carrying a laughing Isolde into the shallows of the water. I sat down in the sand next to Vaughn, accepting the joint he held out.

"Glad you didn't go to the gym?"

"Fuck you."

He chuckled, watching the same thing I was—Isolde and Rowan, feeling the rightness that came with knowing she was ours and we could actually *show* her. I passed the joint back so he could take a hit.

"I might still have to go to the gym if I don't want to pounce on her like a wild animal."

"Or," he handed me what was left of the joint between his fingers. "You can stay for a bit and watch our Omega."

"Watching is Hawk's thing," I teased.

Too fucking true. But even now, I couldn't take my eyes off her. With the sun now below the horizon and the flickering firelight so close, I could barely see her and Rowan in the shallow waves.

Vaughn made a face, and I leaned back into the sand, blowing bad smoke rings into the sky. His voice was quiet. "I think with Isolde, watching might become everyone's thing."

## CHAPTER SIXTEEN

ISOLDE

My feet splashed into the water where Rowan put me down. I gasped. It wasn't cold, but still a little jarring.

"I should take you out deeper so we can mess around right in front of them."

"Not too deep," I whispered. "I can't swim."

"You can't *swim*?" He sounded horrified. "You grew up with the beach right here and no one taught you?"

I studied the sky at the horizon, color draining down into gorgeous blues. "I mean, there were offers. I just never wanted to."

"Why not?"

My head lolled back on his shoulder. Or as close to his shoulder as my short ass could get. My whole body felt floaty and amazing. "Does there have to be a reason?"

"No, but there usually is."

"Got pulled into a riptide when I was little. After that I just stayed on the beach. I love the beach. The sounds and the way it smells. You remind me of it. Why ruin something I love with fear?"

Rowan hummed, his hands slowly moving over my ribs and down to my hips. Back up to my shoulders and my neck. Just touching me. Because I said yes.

"Did you bring me over here just to stand in the water?"

"No."

I thought about the list. It was long enough that all five of them couldn't be into *everything* there. That would be...

Heat streaked through me.

"What things on the list belong to you?" Was my voice thinner than before?

"I like a little bit of everything, Isolde."

"But what's your favorite?"

One hand came up and circled my throat, pulling me back against his chest. His other arm pressed low on my hips so our bodies were flush together. I felt him against my back, hard, and very much not pretend.

"My favorite? I don't know if you're ready for that."

"Try me."

The hand at my hips slid up beneath my shirt. "First, I need to know if I can touch you."

"You've been touching me."

"Isolde." I loved my name growled from his lips. "Tell me."

I nodded, gasping. "Yes. I'm not out of control. Please, touch me."

We faced toward the horizon, no one in our view. Since Rowan was the biggest, the only thing anyone would see was his back as he held me. But his fingers slipped beneath the waistband of my shorts, and then my bathing suit. It wasn't until he slipped one long finger between my legs that I realized how wet I was. How far my mind was ahead of my body.

"I didn't lie when I said I like a bit of everything," he bent his head to whisper the warm words in my ear while he toyed with me, fingers exploring, stroking *around* my clit without touching me there. The hand at my throat squeezed gently. "I like pleasure and I like pain. I like seeing tears well up while you're trying to take all of my cock down your throat. I like watching you come over and over again, whether that's on a tongue, fingers, cock, or vibrator."

Now he did touch me. Barely. Keeping my body desperately tense. My nipples hardened so much you could see them through both the shirt and swimsuit. Perfume whirled around us, stronger as Rowan slid a finger inside me. I jerked against him and it did nothing. He held me where he wanted me, going so fucking, deliciously slow.

He kept using the word *you*, like he'd already done these things to me. It painted images in my mind. I couldn't get enough, hanging on every word.

"I like taking you two at a time, feeling you stuffed so fucking tight you're about to break. But you want to know my favorite?"

"Yes," I begged, not sure if it was for the words or for him to go faster. "*Please.*"

"My favorite is your absolute, unconditional surrender."

I blinked. "That's it?"

He chuckled. "You think it's easy?"

"I just didn't think it would be submission."

Rowan slid a second thick finger into me at the same time he squeezed my throat. "I didn't say submission. I said surrender."

"What's the difference?"

"Unconditional surrender means that, within whatever limits we set, you take what I give you."

My breath caught, desire swirling low in my gut, though it was nowhere near enough to get me there.

He kept going. "So if I decide I want to spank you for an hour, that's what I'll do. If I want you on your knees beside my chair holding my drink, you will. If I want to spend an entire day exploring you with my tongue, or fuck your throat every hour, or put you on display for the rest of the pack," the heel of his palm ground down into my clit. "Whatever I think or desire, that's what happens."

I panted the words in shallow gasps. "Does unconditional surrender mean no safeword?"

Rowan's low growl had every hair standing on end. "You will always have a safeword, and anyone who tells you that you don't need one should be strung up by their thumbs and castrated."

"Good to know." I sank further into his hold, savoring the feeling of his fingers and the way he paused to circle and tease my swollen clit. But it wasn't enough. "Rowan?"

"Mmm, yes, Omega?"

"When I mentioned it's hard for me, I wasn't kidding." A different heat rolled through me, staining my cheeks and spreading up my chest. "This feels really good, I promise. It's just that I can't quite..." Pressing my lips together, I tried to relax. But now that I was in my head, I didn't know if I'd be able to get back to that place. Not in public.

The hand at my throat held me still while Rowan gently pulled out of me, still teasing my clit before lifting those fingers to his mouth and sucking them clean. The sound that came from him made my vision go blank with desire. Fuck, why couldn't this be easier?

"Maybe we should go back to the suite, where there are fewer eyes and ears, and you can let everything go when we make you scream."

"We?"

"If you're okay with it."

All I saw behind my eyes were visions of tangled limbs and hands, shared breath and close bodies and *yes*. "Yup. Very fine with that."

He turned me around, keeping our bodies flush. "How would you like to get out of here?"

"What do you mean?"

Rowan drew his hands down my arms. I hoped he didn't notice the goosebumps that followed. Just a simple touch from them and I was losing it. "Do you want to walk out of here with us? Do you want me to carry you? Do you want me to throw you over my shoulder and show your asshole of an ex how much we want you?"

My mouth went dry. I shouldn't want to shove it in his face. Years of living here in a world where appearances meant everything taught me I should be better than that. But fuck it. I wanted him to know exactly what he lost, even if it wasn't real.

"You choose," I said, knowing exactly what would happen.

Rowan crouched and brought his arms around my legs, hoisting me over his shoulder while laughter bubbled out of me. The joint he gave me wasn't too strong. I was pleasantly relaxed, but this high wouldn't last long. Still, I loved the feeling of dizzy flying.

"Let's go," Rowan said to the others, laughing.

"We're going to get that room now," Vaughn said to Beau. I couldn't see him from this angle—the only thing I could see was Rowan's glorious ass—but his expression was probably priceless.

We hit the grass, and Rowan began to jog, jostling me. "Okay, that's going to make me way too dizzy," I laughed.

One tug on my legs, and I slid over Rowan's shoulder only for him to catch me in his arms. "We're far enough away. No need to manhandle you now."

"What if I like being manhandled?"

His mouth came down on mine. Fuck, he tasted so good. The sweet rawness of coconut and that nearly intangible flavor of salt on the wind. I whined, melting deeper into his arms before I got dizzy all over again. Rowan dropped me on the bed.

All five of them stood there, staring down at me with hunger in their eyes. Bottomless, fathomless hunger. Was I blind enough that I hadn't seen it before? Or had they hidden it? Was it even real?

I shook my head to clear it. Whether or not all of this was real, you couldn't fake the lust rolling off them. There was no way. They wanted me, even if it was just for now.

Nerves built up, and I looked between them. Finally, I focused on Rowan. "Remember when I said I couldn't turn my brain off?"

"We'll help with that." Joel went to the bank of switches on the wall and dimmed the lights. Not all the way, but I no longer felt like a spotlight was on me.

Rowan knelt at the side of the bed, tugging me with his hands to sit in front of him. "I'll admit this isn't the sexiest conversation, but I'm not taking chances. I'm not fucking you tonight. None of us are."

My shoulders fell, and he caught me by the arms. "Not because I don't want to, but because we're going to have a conversation about sex, substances, and what you're okay with if you've had something like one of my treats." He winked. "But that conversation has to happen while you're entirely sober."

I wasn't as high as I'd been, but he wasn't wrong. I wasn't sober. "And the rest of it?"

He locked eyes with me. "Did you come to the bonfire wanting this? Wanting us? Or did you decide after?"

"Before," I said. "I was planning on it. All the joint did was relax me enough to actually ask."

"In that case," he murmured, rising up on his knees and catching my lips with his. "I—we—plan on touching you. *Everywhere.* Kissing you. Also everywhere. Learning exactly what makes you come and making you drown in pleasure even if it doesn't happen. Does any of that sound like too much?"

I shook my head. "No. I want all of that. Tried pretending I didn't, and it didn't work."

Vaughn slid onto the bed behind me, dropping his lips to the skin of my shoulder before lifting my shirt up and *off.* I felt him pull his off too, and we were skin on skin. "Why?"

The way he dragged his mouth up my neck made all the words disappear out of my head. The only thing in the entire universe was where his hands grazed my ribs, lips below my ear, Rowan's hands on my hips, getting rid of my shorts and leaving me in nothing but my royal blue bikini.

"Why what?"

"I'm guessing he's asking why you tried to resist." Hawk's voice drew my gaze to him and the fact that he lost his shirt. So had the others. Just like last night in bed when I couldn't even focus because they were close and they looked like *that*.

"That's not fun."

Cade was the one to lift me out from between them and spread me out on the bed. A necklace dangled from him, the charm I couldn't see brushing between my breasts. I felt rings on his fingers where he held my wrists, stretching them over my head and rendering me helpless beneath him.

*Oh, fuck.*

Blue eyes pinned me in place, and he smiled. "I can see you didn't lie."

"I might have."

"Is that so?" He leaned down and kissed the edge of my bathing suit, so close I got a hit of his scent. Sandalwood, vanilla, and a touch of smoke like the fire. "Then why did you drown me in perfume the second I pinned your hands? Arch your back and close your eyes like it's everything you've *craved*."

That single word carved itself into me. I did crave this. So much more than I'd had and experienced. I wanted it all, and I was so sick of feeling guilty and sad and like I wasn't enough.

"You gonna keep lying, princess?"

"Princess and not angel?"

He smirked. "Definitely not treating you like an angel tonight. But a princess gets both what she wants *and* what she needs. Now are you going to keep lying?"

"No," I gasped, arching again just to feel him. "No."

A hand slid across my stomach and up over my breasts, slowly finding the ties to my suit. I didn't look away from Cade while it was pulled off, watching the heat build in his gaze before he took in the rest of me. "Fuck, Isolde."

He broke, kissing me hard enough to bruise. *Yes*. More than just them and what they liked and wanted, I craved their marks on me. I ached for all of it.

I moaned into Cade's mouth, the delicious feeling of being able to let go slowly coming back. I needed to be overwhelmed and taken past the point where my brain could dig in its heels and question if I was good enough or any of the other bullshit it invented. I needed to feel—

A gasp and a whine slipped out, captured by Cade's mouth. There it was. At the core of it, I still felt like I belonged to Beau. Not in a literal sense, but because he threw me away. His fingerprints were all over me, and I didn't want it anymore. No more thinking about him. No more trying to avoid everything that made me remember. I just wanted it to be over, and they were already helping.

Hot tears pressed against my eyes. These men barely knew me, and they'd already shown me so much more than he had in four years.

"Woah," Cade pulled back, seeing the gloss in my eyes. "You okay?"

"I'm good." A choked laugh. "I'm so good. Promise."

Strong arms tugged me away from Cade, and I was suddenly arranged against a *very* naked Hawk. Those tattoos ran all the way down the legs that now bracketed mine, his cock long and hard against my back. Such fucking sweetness in his scent I could bathe in it forever.

He untied the strings of my bikini and tossed it aside, leaving me bare in front of them. "You mind if I hold you, baby girl? I like to watch. I want to see and feel you get off with their mouths between your legs."

"Not the best view," I told him.

"I don't know. I think it's pretty great." He slid his hands up my stomach, lifting my breasts in his palms. "Looking down your body and seeing your clit peek out? Feel these gorgeous tits of yours? Fucking fantastic."

Vaughn appeared beside us, bending to take one nipple into his mouth. Joel's mouth was suddenly on the other, and I couldn't keep my eyes open. Hawk's fingers crept down, brushing over my clit. All I could do was moan, my voice rendered useless by mouths and fingers.

"You never told us why," Vaughn said. "I think we're pretty irresistible."

"Not something for right now."

Rowan moved between my legs, pulling me toward him and down Hawk's chest before glancing up. "Help me out, Hawk."

"Wha—"

Hawk pulled my legs over his so I was spread wide and captured my hands, folding them with his. Behind my back. "These are mine now."

Placing one kiss low on my stomach, Rowan consumed me. Lips

and tongue, fucking deep into me before coming back to my clit to tease and touch and suck.

"He's going to figure out what you like," Hawk whispered. "Practice makes perfect, baby girl."

"I like it all. It's all great. Super great."

Beside me, Joel laughed and turned my head to his for a kiss. "All you have to do is say yes or no, Isolde. If something's bringing you closer, say yes. If it's not, say no. Can you do that?"

I nodded once.

Rowan's tongue curled under my clit, making my hips jerk towards him, trying to chase the sensation. "Yes. *Fuck*, yes."

"Mmm." He did it again. And again. And again. "You taste better than I imagined."

Thinking about him imagining this drew heat straight into my body and made me wetter. Rowan just laughed. "Cade, her pussy just flooded. You need to try it."

"Yes, I do."

He traded places with Rowan, never looking away from my eyes as he drew his tongue up my center and sealed his mouth over me, sucking harder than I'd ever felt in my life. I said yes. I don't know how many times I said it.

I said no too. But it all felt good. They took turns, each of their mouths trying different things to drive me crazy while Hawk held me open. I drowned in pleasure, skin slick with sweat, no breath in my lungs. But I still hadn't come.

"I'm sorry," I managed to say, though my voice was raw. "It's amazing, but I don't think it's going to happen."

Rowan had taken his place between my legs again. He smiled, drawing small circles with his fingers. "If it doesn't, I want you to know I won't be disappointed. But I'd like to try again."

I wanted an orgasm so fucking badly, and I couldn't seem to get there. Maybe I was broken. I thought I might be better at letting go during my heat, but I'd never had a chance to find out. "If you're sure."

"I am sure, if you are."

"Why wouldn't I be?"

He kissed my clit. "Because if you say yes, I'm going to force an orgasm out of this gorgeous cunt, and I won't hold back in order to do it."

This was just a glimpse of what he told me on the beach. Total and complete surrender. We weren't there yet, but he was asking me to trust him and give him this. Let him try. "Yes."

Rowan slid one finger inside me slowly, and that was the only thing slow. His mouth came down on me and he used his tongue exactly the way he'd learned to, adding another finger, finding that spot that Beau had never managed to though he claimed he tried, and thrusting *right. Fucking. There.*

Mouths on breasts. Hands on my skin. Hawk's purr beneath me and the hardness of his cock. So much. Too much. I sagged into them, sinking beneath their control and trust, and let everything go.

The shimmering beginnings of an orgasm sparkled to life, and I didn't think about it. If I thought about it, I would wonder if Rowan's arm was getting tired or if his jaw was sore from fucking me with his tongue, and I would lose it.

"Please," I gasped. There was no other way to ask for the help I needed.

Cade's voice was there, next to me. When did he get there? I loved the sound of his voice. No doubt and no hesitation. "Don't open your eyes," he commanded. "Keep them closed and listen."

I did. His voice got closer.

"I can still taste you," Cade said. "See?"

He kissed me, our flavors blending together in heady harmony. Oh god, I wanted to taste *them*.

Cade devoured my mouth, claiming me, making sure all of my focus was on him. Pleasure seeped through my bones, rising in a golden cloud to hover around me. So delicate and so *close*.

"Hold your breath," Cade commanded. "Don't take a breath until I tell you, understand?"

I sucked in a breath and held it. My own pulse pounded in my ears, Rowan's fingers pounded into me, my hips now rising to meet him. My breath ran short. Cade hadn't said anything. My eyes flew open to find him watching me. "Don't you fucking breathe, Isolde."

But...

His hand landed at my throat, pressing with the barest pressure. "Trust me, princess."

I fought the instinct to haul in air, body desperate for more than I was giving it. No thoughts, only the need for air and rising pleasure—

"Breathe."

Air and life flooded my lungs. Everything slammed into me at full brightness and volume despite the dimness of the room, body so relieved to breathe that it released everything.

The orgasm crashed over me like a tidal wave. All-consuming. Everywhere. Like drowning while I could breathe. My body writhed like it had a mind of its own, trying to find an outlet for all that euphoria to break through, and it found none.

I don't know if I'd ever had an orgasm like this. It came in waves, leaving me spent and wrecked on the shore, sprawled out on top of them.

My whole body felt limp and shaky when Rowan took me from Hawk, spreading me out in the pillows and cradling me to him. I closed my eyes and tried to catch my breath while sinking into that perfect place of peace that so often followed pleasure.

One thing was sure. Resisting was pointless, and I wasn't doing it anymore.

## CHAPTER SEVENTEEN

### ROWAN

Isolde's breath came in hard gasps as I laid her across my chest. Her hair and skin damp with sweat, and it made her scent that much sweeter. Richer. Flowers and sex. It made me want to fuck her on a bed of petals to see how it compared to her.

I wasn't shocked she was out of breath and trembling. We essentially edged her for an hour, even though we weren't trying to edge her. Her body loved pleasure, and the fact that she had a hard time finishing wasn't exclusive to her. Plenty of women had trouble. But she was ours, and I knew we could help her get there more easily.

Sometimes it wasn't a physical thing. Sometimes it was mental, and I felt like that was at the core of Isolde's struggle. She didn't feel safe in her pleasure, and if I could change that, I would.

"You still alive?" I asked her.

"Barely."

Laughs rolled through all of us. Vaughn laid down behind her, stroking a hand down her back. "You're incredible."

Isolde snorted into my skin. "Says one of the men who just helped me instead of giving up because my body doesn't work right."

I rolled her beneath me, savoring every inch of skin I felt against mine. It was a damn good thing I still had my shorts on, or this would be a far more painful temptation. "Your body works just fine," I said. "And if you think we didn't enjoy ourselves, you're wrong."

She looked up at me, eyes still blown wide with the remnants of pleasure and her high. The hope in her eyes pained me, and I wanted to kill whoever put the doubt in her head. In this case, I was pretty sure I knew.

Licking her lips, Isolde's eyes traveled over my face. She looked over at Vaughn and past him to whoever was behind us. "What about you?"

"What about us?"

"You didn't..." her cheeks turned bright red to match her hair. "You didn't finish."

I grinned, dropping a kiss directly to the center of her chest. "Don't get me wrong, I can't wait to fuck you every way possible, Isolde. But I'm a big boy. If I need to come that badly, I can make it happen, and anyone who tells you there's a quid pro quo for sex isn't worth your time."

A shade of doubt passed over her face. "Is that how you really feel? Or is it how you feel because I'm paying you?"

I bit my tongue from spilling every single secret we had. It would come soon enough. "It's the way I feel. Period."

Vaughn leaned close. "Time to tell us the truth about why you resisted."

Isolde lifted her hands to my arms, touching my skin like she wasn't sure I was real. "I promise you don't want to know."

"I don't ask questions I don't want to know the answer to."

She blew out a long, slow breath. "Okay fine. After Beau dumped me, he started dating Angela. Like he couldn't *wait* to move on to someone new. She worked with us. Didn't know her well, but she never seemed to like me. After his promotion, she was in his line of direct report. I still had friends at the company, though most of them have moved on to new jobs now. One of them heard Beau talking to another coworker, asking why he'd jumped in so fast with Angela. Beau said he was already paying her, so he might as well take advantage since he hadn't been getting any with me." Her eyes flicked to anything but us, trying to avoid meeting our gaze. "I didn't want to be alone, but I also didn't want to be like him."

Glancing over at Vaughn, he saw and nodded once before slipping an arm between Isolde and me to steal her away. I needed to get up and move, and like hell was I going to let her think it was because of her admission. No, it was because the man who'd broken her confidence was such an utter piece of shit I needed to walk it off.

Not to mention I didn't believe him suddenly going to someone new *at the same company* after the breakup.

"Did he cheat on you?" Cade asked, voice dark with promise, and following my same line of thinking.

"Not that I know of. There weren't any signs of it."

That was a good thing at least, but I still needed to move and get this restless energy out of my system.

Vaughn pulled her to his chest, and she snuggled into him before I moved, making way for Joel to take my place and provide her with warmth.

"You're nothing like him," I told her as I paced across the space. "Nothing."

"I know," she murmured. Sleep colored her tone. In the dim light of the bedroom, we all looked at each other. She was fading in the face of such an intense orgasm. I hoped we could keep giving her exactly that. Pleasure and showing her what she was worth.

Everything.

It felt like we all held our breath until she fell asleep in Vaughn's arms, with him purring and stroking a single hand down her spine. I jerked my head across the room. All the others came, but Vaughn shook his head. He wasn't leaving her, and he already knew.

Even in the next room, we kept our voices down. "Do we tell her?"

"I want to," Cade said. "But I don't think she's there yet. She needs to let go of the idea that we're doing this for money."

I shook my head. "How will she let go of it if we don't *tell her* we're not doing it for money?"

"If you're Isolde," Joel said. "Your confidence and everything you thought you knew has been shattered. You've basically been living in exile. Then you come back and take a risk with a pack like us, and you realize it's so much worse than you thought it was. And just when you decide to do something for yourself? A pack sweeps in and claims you as theirs with no fucking proof." He shook his head. "She's vulnerable, and we can't take advantage of that. If we force her hand in any way, she'll always have doubts. It needs to come from her. Even if it kills me."

"I hate that you're right." Hawk scrubbed his hands over his face. "Fucking hate it. But you are. As soon as we can, I want to tell her.

Just in a way that doesn't make her think we're using her or we're just paying lip service to a client."

"We're done, right?" The words tumbled out of me. "I don't think I could stomach taking more clients now that she exists."

Joel smirked. "Yeah. We're done. We'll figure out the money later."

"Would be nice to actually show my face online," Hawk said. He had an insane following for him and his music, but he'd always been faceless. Someone could potentially recognize his tattoos, but people were less observant than they claimed to be, and without a face to a name, it was easy for him to fly under the radar.

I pointed at him. "If you commit to it, we're all going to hold you to it. Going after music for real."

A faint smile. "I can do that."

Joel looked between the four of us. "We've got a few days before the next wedding thing. Let's take the time and show her who we are now that we're not limited. Lay everything we can on the table. After that?"

There was only one answer to that question. After that, we would do everything in our power to make this Omega ours.

## CHAPTER EIGHTEEN

ISOLDE

I loved the feeling of a purr. The way it resonated through my chest and relaxed me. It made me feel so completely safe, and I missed that feeling.

How long had it been? Longer than I'd let myself admit.

Here in this shadowy, half-awake place, I could give in to the horror of realizing I'd clung to something mediocre *at best* for so long, and I had been too naïve to see how badly I was treated. Because...

I didn't know. Was I afraid of being alone? Was I so convinced we were happy I just lived in the clouds? Even if I wanted to know, in the end it didn't matter. All that mattered was that I wasn't in that place anymore, and that there was an Alpha lying behind me, purring.

Turning over, I reached for whoever it was, wrapping my arms around their neck before even opening my eyes. A rough, rich purr and the delicate scent of cardamom mixed with what was left of what they'd done to me. Traces of my scent on him.

That was so fucking hot.

"I swear I can hear you thinking," Joel said. "Are you all right?"

"I'm good." My body felt heavy and sated. I could probably go back to sleep if I wanted to, but I didn't. The day stretched in front of us, along with a conversation I very much wanted to have. "Your purr is going to send me back to sleep."

He chuckled. "Does that mean I should stop?"

"No." My eyes flew open to find him grinning. "Don't. Please."

"Good morning." He kissed my forehead, still purring like he was an engine. "Sleep okay?"

"Like the dead, honestly."

One hand slid down my side under the blankets until he could curl it around my thigh and pull my leg over his body. "It was my job to tell you there's breakfast on the veranda and we want to eat with you. But now that you're awake, and naked, I don't want to let you out of this bed."

I pressed my forehead into his chest. Joel cradled me closer, holding me against him, and I savored the feeling of being *held*. Sometimes this was all I wanted. Just to touch and be touched and feel like I wasn't so alone. "I like this."

"Fuck breakfast," he said. "Let's stay here."

"You would?"

Another kiss, this time on the top of my head where I was tucked against him. "I have a gorgeous, naked Omega in my arms. No food in the world is more tempting than that."

My stomach swooped, a whine breaking out of me. Fuck *everything*. I was going to soak up every minute of this kind of attention. At the very least, it would show me what I deserved and nothing less.

I would have committed to the plan of staying in bed, but my stomach had other plans. It growled, louder than his purr. "Well, that's embarrassing."

"Let's get you fed," he said with a laugh. "If you want to come back and cuddle after, we can."

Sitting up, I looked down at myself. "I need a shower."

"Hurry, or we'll want to join you."

Joel, sitting in the middle of the bed, shirtless, with blankets bunched around his hips, was mouthwatering. "Yeah." I swallowed. "That would be... bad."

Laughter followed me into the bathroom. But not laughter at me. If someone asked me, I couldn't say how I knew the difference, but I did. I didn't take long, pulling on another bathing suit and a sheer, shimmery cover-up. I didn't know what we were doing today, and I wasn't getting dressed more if I didn't have to.

A table on the veranda held an entire spread of breakfast food, though a glance at my phone told me it was almost noon. I looked at them, trying to ignore the way their eyes skimmed over my body, because if I did, I wouldn't be eating. "You did this?"

Cade jumped up and pulled out a chair in the center of the table for me. "Well, we told Geoffrey and helped as much as he'd let us, which wasn't as much as we would have liked."

A magnolia blossom sat on the plate in front of me. It wasn't the season for them, but it looked fresh. The entire estate was covered with the trees. Hell, they were all over Clarity, even before we moved to this house. Sometimes my mom joked that I looked around while I was still in the womb and chose my scent for that reason. "This is beautiful, thank you."

My stomach rumbled again. I reached for the plate stacked with waffles. Because *fuck* yes, waffles sounded incredible. Too much syrup and butter later, I moaned with the first bite. The food was something I missed. My parents always hired incredible chefs.

Rowan coughed to cover a laugh. "I never thought I'd be jealous of a fucking waffle."

"Why?" I asked, not even taking my attention from the deliciousness in front of me.

"Because it's every man's dream to hear that sound when someone puts you in their mouth."

My head snapped up, and Rowan just watched me, taking a sip of his coffee with a straight face.

Oh.

"Noted," I mumbled around my next bite, my face going hot.

"Any regrets from last night?" Rowan asked.

"Is that a trick question?"

Cade shook his head. "No."

"Not a single regret," I told them. "And whatever you want to ask me, let's do that now, because I don't want to put anything off in the moment. I just want things to happen naturally."

Joel began folding the sleeves of his shirt up to his elbows. "We're not going to talk you to death. Just ask if there's anything you *don't* want us to do. Especially if you're under the influence. We'll still check in with you, of course, but before we start bending you over tables, we want to be on the same page."

I almost choked, reaching for the glass of water by my plate. The image of being bent over this table was so vivid, it overtook everything. One of them pushing my sparkly dress up and moving my bathing suit to the side while they finally fucked me. It wasn't a wide table. If they put me over it far enough, one could stand behind me while one in front—

"What did you say?"

The tick of Hawk's mouth told me I'd been zoning out to thoughts of them absolutely railing me. "I asked if you have any limits beyond those you already outlined."

"No." I took another sip of water. "I was pretty thorough. No permanent damage, no scars, no tickling, no degradation. Other than that, what's on the list is good for me. But I still want to know which things belong to you. Rowan's I know."

"It's a bigger list than just our preferences," Vaughn said. "But I'll tell you all about mine when you come with me to the beach after you finish breakfast."

"What are we doing?"

"Teaching you to swim."

My body went cold. I swallowed. "That's okay. We don't have to."

Vaughn's face went serious. He stood and came around the table, going to one knee beside me. Cade pushed his chair back to make room. "Rowan mentioned it in passing this morning. If I'm overstepping, I apologize. But I promise I'm not going to let anything happen to you. We don't have to do any lessons, but I'd like to be in the water with you. And if it's too much, we'll stop."

Nothing but earnest truth showed on his face. He wanted this. It wasn't a trick to humiliate me or get me to do something silly, he just wanted me. "Okay," I said softly. "I can try."

"Thank you."

"But you're putting the sunscreen on me," I warned him. "Or Ellie will kill you because one of her bridesmaids looks like the worst kind of contrasting reds because I fry like I'm an ant someone is burning under a magnifying glass."

Standing and leaning down, Vaughn kissed me. He tasted so *good*. I smiled into the kiss. Rowan didn't have to worry. If they all tasted the way they smelled, I would definitely moan when I put them in my mouth.

Vaughn spoke against my lips. "Putting sunscreen on you will be no hardship, Isolde. I might have to do it more than once, just to make sure you're fully protected. And I know we don't usually put on sunscreen beneath clothes, but we should be extra safe."

When he pulled away my body followed him, silently asking for more. I forced myself to stay sitting and finish my waffles, because if I was going in the water, the last thing I needed was to be nervous *and* hungry.

Cade leaned back in his chair and set his arm across the back of mine like it was the most natural thing in the world. His fingers brushed the bare skin of my shoulder, which felt more like electric shocks. In a good way. "Yesterday while you were out we got a chance to talk to Warren," he said. "Seems like a decent guy."

"He is."

"Then why is he friends with someone like your ex?"

I froze. Literally the same question had come from me, from Trinity, from Ocean, from everyone. I still didn't know the answer, but I suspected it was a lack of information. "I don't know. But like I told you, Beau is charming. He probably told everyone the breakup was my fault, or that it went differently than it did. Taste in friends aside, he's really great, and I'm happy he and Ellie found each other."

"I'd like to set him straight on a few things," Hawk muttered under his breath before downing what little was left of his orange juice.

"I wish."

Hawk's eyes found mine, filled with heat. All I could think about was the feeling of him behind me, long and hard, while he held me still for everyone else. "I can take him aside and tell him the truth. It would be my pleasure."

"I don't want to make this whole thing about me. It's already focused on me enough. I don't need to throw a bomb into the middle of the bridal party. Besides, for all I know Warren knows the truth and just decided to stay out of it. I wouldn't blame him for not touching this mess."

He didn't look happy about it, but he nodded. "Say the word, baby girl. I will make sure he knows exactly the kind of person his best man is. A man who would kick a woman out of his home and steal her jewelry for his new fiancée."

Did Angela know the bracelet was mine? I hoped she didn't. But I had hoped a lot of things about Beau, and as it turned out, not a single one of them was true. Why should this be any different?

Suddenly I didn't have an appetite anymore.

"I'm finished. I need to grab a couple of things before we head down to the beach."

"Geoffrey gave me some towels this morning, and I have sunscreen." Vaughn pointed to a bag sitting at the top of the Veranda steps.

My eyebrows rose. "You're prepared."

"When I know what I want, I make it happen." The way he was looking at me made me doubt it was the sunscreen he was talking about. Butterflies fluttered around in my stomach, and for the first time in what felt like forever, they weren't nerves, but anticipation.

## CHAPTER NINETEEN

ISOLDE

Vaughn dropped the bag on the ground, spread out a huge beach towel, and grinned. We were all the way at the end of the beach, where the bonfire had been, and further, near the cliffs. The shade was perfect in the heat of the summer sun, and there was a smaller chance of me burning to a crisp.

"Time for sunscreen?" He shook the bottle in his hand. One of the spray-on kinds.

"You're enjoying this far too much."

"I don't think so." He prowled toward me, shirt already gone, body on full display. "I think you're not used to having someone appreciate you, let alone savor you."

He stopped in front of me, and I had to look up at him. "Why do you all say things like that? I mean, I get it. It's a part of the whole... experience, I guess. But I'm no one to you."

"Isolde." My name was low and soft on his lips. I couldn't puzzle out why there was so much pain in it.

"You talk like I matter."

One hand reached out and pulled my body to his. The sunscreen fell to the sand as he wrapped me up, hands dragging over my skin like he wanted to feel everything at once. "You *do* matter," he whispered.

"Why? I'm—"

"Because you're a fucking person," he said, holding me flush to his body. "You're beautiful, and I won't lie, I searched your work. You're fucking talented. You're kind when you don't need to be. You care about your friends and family. It took me no time at all to see those things, and even if not one of them was true, you're still a person, Isolde. You matter."

Vaughn threaded his fingers into my hair and pulled my head back to kiss me. Hard. Orange and ice cream and sweetness. A trace of syrup from breakfast. He didn't let me back away, teasing my mouth open beneath his until he had all of me. Stole my breath. Consumed my voice. Pinned me to the spot and kissed me until I was nothing but a blank slate to believe his words.

He kept my head arched back, drawing the words up my neck. "If I hear you say you don't matter again, or question your worth, I'm giving you to Cade and Joel. They'll spank it out of you if they have to."

"What?" My mouth dropped open.

A lazy smirk pulled at his lips. "'*I shouldn't want to think about this, but I have, and do. All the fucking time.*' Isn't that what you said about spanking on your questionnaire?"

"You memorized it?"

"Not quite." He released me to retrieve the sunscreen. "But almost. I've certainly looked at enough. Off." One tug of my sparkly cover-up had it floating down onto the sand. They had all seen me naked, but this felt different. "Turn around."

I obeyed, still caught on the fact that he knew my words by heart. "You said you'd tell me which ones belong to you."

The loud sound of the spray made me jump, and the coolness made me shiver. Vaughn ran his hands over my shoulders and down my back, continuing down my legs. "Do you have any guesses?"

The fingers brushing between my thighs had my mind going blank. How was I supposed to talk when he touched me like he was about to fuck me, not drag me into the ocean? There were so many things... "It could be anything."

He rubbed the sunscreen into my legs, large hands curling around my legs and finding every bit of skin. Fingers dipped beneath the edge of my bikini bottom, enough to make me close my eyes and revel in the heat, but not quite enough to be scandalous.

"It could be anything, but it's not." He was close again, body brushing against my back. Instead of spraying on my skin, he sprayed it into his hands and used both of them, slowly smoothing over my hips and stomach and upward in a massage far too delicious for the beach.

"You like," I had to pause to catch my breath. "You like impact play?" They had plenty of questions about floggers and whips. I'd never experienced that, and it wasn't at the top of my list, but I would try anything once.

Within reason.

"Mmm." He hummed the sound into my neck, raising goosebumps on my skin even though it was hot out here. "No. None of us love that. It's fine, but it's not our favorite."

"Tell me," I breathed.

"Primal." The single word was a growl. Vaughn ran his hands over my breasts, neck, and shoulders, covering me with sunscreen while he spoke. "The running. The chasing. Pinning to the ground and *taking*. Giving in to your deepest, and sometimes darkest, instincts. Letting them take over and doing what feels *right*."

One hand rested on my chest, and he lifted it to my throat, just where Cade had gripped me last night. I leaned into him further. "Do you want me to chase you, Isolde?"

I remembered every vivid detail of when I filled out their questionnaire and the thoughts racing through my head. Imagining the adrenaline of running from someone while knowing they were ultimately going to catch me. Thinking about doing nothing but what my subconscious commanded, whether it was fight or flight or fuck or flee.

My whole body shivered with the thought.

I over thought everything. In the same way that Rowan's description of surrender appealed to me, so did this in an entirely different way.

"Yes," I finally whispered. "I want that."

"Fuck," he murmured into my hair, pulling me back so I could feel how hard he was. "Do you want to plan it out?"

"Or?"

Vaughn bit my neck, not quite hard enough to bruise, soothing the pain away with his tongue. "Or I just take you. Let you loose and tell you to run. You don't have to decide now, or at all. Think about it and let me know."

A heavy breath fell out of me like he'd just released a hold on my lungs. "Okay."

"Now, let's get in the water." He was back to his normal, smiling self like he hadn't just growled in my ear that he wanted to hunt me and fuck me.

"Not too late to go back inside."

One eyebrow cocked. "Do you trust me?"

"I just told you I wanted you to chase me, which takes like a thousand times more trust, so yes."

"But you're not afraid of that." Vaughn held his hand out for mine. "I've got you."

His touch was gentle, guiding me into the water. Further than Rowan had. Further than I'd been into the actual ocean in years. Nerves sprang to life, and I froze with the water swirling around my thighs.

Vaughn stepped close and held me. "I've got you, sweetheart."

I closed my eyes and pressed my forehead to his chest. Breathed in his scent. Let it calm me. I was going to need to buy stock in creamsicles after this because I didn't think I would ever have enough.

He drew me deeper. Until the water rose around my chest. Terror flowed under my skin, waiting for the moment when the water would rip me away and hold me under. Try to kill me in the way only a giant, faceless thing could.

But nothing happened. Vaughn's arms still wrapped around me, and other than the swell and fall of the waves, there wasn't any current.

"Still with me?"

"I think so."

Vaughn gripped my ribs and lifted me, bracing my knees on his hips. The water held me too. I felt weightless. Powerful. And this Alpha looked up at me like I was the sun, not the one in the sky.

"Did it happen here?"

"No. I mean, yes, but not this beach. A few miles south. One of the public ones, and it happened so fast. A lifeguard saw me go under, and that's why I'm still here. But he almost didn't make it."

Slowly, he lowered me closer, nearly close enough for our lips to touch. "I'm glad you're still here."

"Me too."

It was easy to be here in the water with him, like he held all the water back and gave my soul space away from the fear. But it hovered at the edges, and I knew if I were on my own I wouldn't make it out this far. Being with him I liked. Learning to swim? I wasn't sure I was ready.

"Do you have to teach me?"

"I'd like to, but it doesn't have to be today."

I rolled my eyes. "Trust me, I don't think you'll like teaching me."

"Actually I would. It's what I do most of the time anyway." He smiled, eyes lighting up in that way someone had when they truly loved something.

"You're a swim instructor?"

"Scuba, actually. But I do teach swimming lessons sometimes. I do some free diving, too."

Free diving. I'd heard of it, but not enough to know what it really was. "I'm not familiar."

Vaughn smirked. "It means I can hold my breath for a really long time and not come up for air."

He was *not* talking about diving. "Good to know."

"How long has it been since you've been in the water?"

I shrugged. "I go in pools and hot tubs, but it's been a while. Just in the shallows."

"Do you know how to float?" There was no judgment in his tone.

"Yeah. Haven't done that since I was a kid, though."

Rising up, he caught my lips with his, using the motion to ease me down further into the water. "Still trust me?"

All I could do was nod.

"Lie back. I'll have you the whole time. Promise."

I believed him.

Stretching my body out, I took a deep breath and let the water—and Vaughn—hold me. A wave splashed over my face, and the fear came roaring back. I thrashed, only to find Vaughn's arms beneath me. Holding me up. Making sure I wasn't going anywhere.

"I've got you," he said quietly, moving one hand under my head.

The world grew quieter with my ears under the water. I closed my eyes, choosing this moment to let go and trust. If now wasn't the time, when was?

I floated, inhaling the sea salt and tang of citrus from Vaughn. This was...

Wonderful.

Knowing someone was there to keep anything from happening let me ease into it. My body felt heavier even though it wasn't. And no fucking wonder. Had I ever had this simple feeling of safety with Beau?

No.

That was the answer. No matter how long we'd been together, I could now look back and see how I'd always kept an eye over one shoulder. Kept everything together with my own two hands. Kept *myself* safe.

Until I couldn't even do that.

Hot tears flooded my eyes, followed by grief so sharp I couldn't breathe. One slipped out from beneath my closed lids, and I heard Vaughn suck in a breath. "Isolde? Are you okay? Is it too much?"

"It's not that," I managed. "I'm... okay."

Vaughn floated me toward the shallows, lifting me out of the water and cradling me all the way to the towel he'd laid out. "You don't seem like you're okay."

Lying beside me, he kept me close. A hand on my hip, thumb teasing the edge of my bathing suit. He propped up his head on one hand.

The way his body stretched out next to mine, I couldn't help but look. A tattoo peeked out from his bathing suit, begging me to find out what it was, and the water dripping down his chest mesmerized me. I reached out and touched him, tracing lines down his wet skin, and Vaughn didn't stop me.

"Have you ever had a moment where you looked back and realized how foolish you'd been? The truth of everything just slams into you and you can't stop it? You have to face it, even if it's painful?"

He slid his hand up my side, finally brushing a soaked strand of hair behind my ear. "I think everyone's had a moment like that."

A laugh without any joy. "That's what the last few days have been like. On repeat. The five of you. You're not even with me, and you're showing me how badly I was treated and still thought I was happy. I thought I was loved." My voice cracked on the word. "And it hurts. Maybe more than it did before. Because I'm not grieving for him, I'm grieving for *me*. I did that. I stayed. I didn't realize that I was a placeholder in someone's life until they didn't want me. I feel so stupid."

Vaughn looked at me for a while, searching my face. Again, no judgment. It felt like he was looking for the right words.

"You are not stupid, foolish, or any of those words for believing someone who offered you the world with no intention of delivering it. That man is a fucking fool for ever thinking he could do better than you." He closed the distance between us. "His loss."

I kissed him like it was real. Like Vaughn was mine. Like the whole pack was mine and after Ellie's wedding we'd be going home together. And for this brief moment, it didn't hurt.

"Did he?" I asked when we broke apart for breath. "Did he offer me the world?"

"You were with him for four years, you lived with him, and without you telling him, I imagine you thought you would marry or bond with him eventually. Right?"

"Yeah."

"Then yes, he offered you that. You had no reason to believe it wouldn't happen, and then he cut you out like you were nothing but an inconvenience. He's a prick."

The words stung, but they were true.

Vaughn kissed me again, this time pushing me back onto the towel. I giggled, and he still managed to keep kissing me. He was hard again, barely anything between us. "I'm not going to let you fuck me on the beach in the middle of the day."

"That's why we have a perfectly good bed."

"For sleeping."

"Among other things."

I liked being under him and his weight. It settled me and reminded me of our conversation earlier. "I don't want to plan it," I said. "The chase."

Vaughn pulled back in surprise. "Really?"

"Just take me," I whispered.

A feral gleam entered his eyes. "If we're near water, will that bother you?"

"As long as it's not deep, it's fine."

"Good. I won't do anything beyond your limits, but you might have some bruises. Comes with the territory."

I bit my lip to keep from smiling too widely. "I don't mind."

"Don't tell me that," he growled. "Because primal bruises aren't the only ones I like. I'll mark you with my hands and teeth, sweetheart, so that everyone knows you're fucking *mine*."

A shudder rolled through me, and he felt it. God, I loved those words. The depth of that claim. I craved it more than I could put into words. "Just don't mark me somewhere that will show for the wedding. I doubt Ellie will want pictures of marks from me getting fucked."

Vaughn groaned, dropping his mouth to my skin. "If you don't want me to fuck you on this beach, you can't say things like that."

"What if I'm aiming to make you pick me up and carry me off to the suite again?"

"That can be arranged." Then he paused. "You need a safeword."

To stop if something went wrong. That made sense. I'd never done anything that needed one before, but I had a feeling that was going to change with more than just Vaughn. "How about banana?"

He chuckled. "Banana?"

"I don't think I'm going to be using that while you're chasing me. I can feel how big your banana is, but I promise I won't call it that while you're inside me."

Vaughn burst out laughing, the sound echoing off the nearby cliffs. "I promise that when I'm inside you, the last thing you're going to be able to think or talk about is fucking bananas."

"Silly Alpha. Bananas don't fuck."

"Isolde."

I grinned. "Vaughn."

"Feeling better?"

"Yeah."

Opening my mouth, I started to ask him if he was going to carry me away, and stopped. People were coming toward us on the beach. The entire bridal party, actually. Two of the guys were setting up a net, and I spotted balls of various shapes and sizes.

Warren was the one who came all the way to us. "You lovebirds busy, or can I steal Vaughn?"

"What are you stealing him for?" I asked.

"Just some friendly competition. Losing side gets to set up all the stuff for dinner on the beach."

"And the winning side?" Vaughn didn't look away from me.

Warren glanced backward. "Winners get control of the barbecue."

Vaughn cocked an eyebrow at me, asking the silent question. If I told him I wanted him to take me inside, he would do it. Without hesitation.

I opened my mouth.

"*Isolde*." Trinity's voice carried across the beach. "Get your fine ass out from underneath his fine ass and get yourself a drink."

Suddenly we were laughing together, and Vaughn kissed me one more time. "Later?"

"Later. But you better win."

He winked before pulling us both to our feet. "Yes, Ma'am."

## CHAPTER TWENTY

### ISOLDE

I pulled my cover-up back on and made my way up the beach to Trinity. She slung an arm around my shoulders and shoved a drink in my hand. "You have shitty timing," I told her.

"Why?"

"Did you not see where I was?"

She sighed. "Yeah. Pinned under the smoking hot guy you refuse to sleep with."

I took a sip of the cold, fruity drink she gave me and stared at her. Her face shifted from resigned to shocked, then from shocked to excited. "*No.*"

"No, what?"

"You slept with them?"

Shrugging, I glanced back to where the guys were in a huddle, apparently figuring out what they were going to play and the rules. Cade saw me looking and winked.

My knees wobbled.

"I think that depends on your definition of 'sleeping with,' but I'm not resisting anymore."

"Thank goodness." She raised her glass and clinked it against mine. "What did it?"

"You, Ocean, and me getting my head out of my ass."

"Amen to that."

Ellie and the rest of her bridesmaids were up on the ballroom terrace, watching the guys and laughing. "I didn't know you'd be here."

"Well, I came to kidnap you to do something fun, and Ellie found me and said I should stay. I called Ocean. If she can get away, she'll come. Want to go up there?"

Angela was in the group. On the edge of it, for sure, but still on the edge.

"Am I a coward if I don't really want to be around her?"

Trinity snorted into her drink. "No. I don't want to be around her either. I just wasn't sure if Ellie would want you there since you're in the bridal party."

A fair question. "I'll ask, but I think she'll be okay. We can sit under one of the umbrellas so I don't get torched. Vaughn helped me with sunscreen but I've already been in the water."

Behind us, the guys abandoned the net and started kicking a soccer ball around in the sand. Vaughn, still damp and shirtless, was the first one to steal the ball. Right away from Beau.

I smothered a grin as we walked back up to the house, feeling far lighter than I had when I'd gone down to the beach. I felt good. Settled.

"I'm going to run to the bathroom."

"Okay. I'll figure out where we're going to be."

Meeting Ellie's eyes, she came to me right away, smiling. "You looked like you were having fun."

"I was. I am. Just wanted to make sure you wouldn't be upset if I sat... not here." My eyes flicked toward Angela, and my sister laughed.

"No, I don't mind. I'd rather her not be here either, but Beau insisted, and since he's the best man, we felt like we had to."

"Seems like a theme," I muttered. "Everyone around Beau feels like they *had* to do something."

Ellie smirked. "Keep the claws out. I think you're going to need them. For the record, I will be stealing you away at some point before the wedding to do *something*, but other than that? I'm just glad you're here."

"Me too."

She peeked around me down toward the beach. "They keep looking over here. At you."

"Probably a coincidence."

"I highly doubt that." She left me there, and I went farther down the veranda to an umbrella and chaise chairs where we could relax.

On the beach, there were makeshift goals for the guys to score through, and it was clear the lines had been drawn. Warren and my pack against the rest of the guys. Shirts and skins. My team was skins, and I wasn't complaining about it.

Hawk kicked the ball through the goal and stretched his hands out wide like he was flying before turning and pointing right at me like he was dedicating the score to me.

Laughing quietly, I sipped the drink. This was good. Sweet. Probably too easy to get drunk on.

"It's good to see you like this."

I startled, turning to find Dad standing just behind the table. He came around and stood nearby, watching the game.

"Like what?"

One flicker of a smile. "With light in your eyes."

I froze, waiting.

Dad shook his head. "I don't know how to explain it, Iz. It was like something was just... extinguished in you. I'd never seen you like that when you finally called us back."

When I ran, I avoided their calls. When I could finally stop panicking and crying I'd given in and called them back. I'd made sure the wall behind me looked better than the apartment as a whole. It became the set dressing for all of their calls.

"And it hurt, because there wasn't anything we could do. I'm glad to see you better. That's all."

Was I?

I looked down at the beach, where the guys were still dominating the game. Joel kicked the ball around Beau over to Rowan. More than scoring, it seemed like their real goal was to keep the ball away from my ex. Even his own team didn't pass to him often, despite waving his arms and saying he was open. It made me smile.

*They* made me smile.

And that hurt too, because it wasn't real.

But Dad wasn't wrong. I was better.

"I think I am."

"Good." He looked over and smiled. "Dare I ask if we can expect to still see you after the wedding?"

I winced and looked away. It was deserved. Hurting my family had never been my intention, but it didn't change that I did. "Yeah," I said. "I think so. I—" I took a breath and stood, putting my drink to the side. "I'm really sorry, Dad. For leaving that way. I know I apologized, but it's different in person."

His brow furrowed. "Isolde, I'm not angry with you. Your mother and I want to make sure you're okay. If being away from here was what you needed, that's fine. We missed you, but we mostly wanted to make sure you were safe."

"I know."

Dad held out his arms and I stepped in, enjoying the hug. "If you want to find a shitty apartment to live in, I'm sure we can find one here in Clarity Coast. You don't have to go all the way across the country."

"You know about that?" I gasped. "I made sure to keep it hidden."

"Not very well," he chuckled. "And if you need money you can ask. Just because you have to wait for your trust doesn't mean we won't take care of you."

"Does Mom know?"

He shook his head. "She doesn't. If she had, she would have marched out there and dragged you back. You didn't want or need that. But I kept tabs on you."

All I could do was smile. If he'd told me this even a few days ago, I would have been furious. Now, I was glad. "Thank you. And I don't know if I'll want to live here, but I think I'm past the shitty apartment stage. I'll need to get a better job," I said with a laugh. "If anyone still wants to hire me after the way I left."

"Why wouldn't they?"

"I cut everything and almost everyone off pretty harshly. There's a year gap in my resume now where I worked at a bar, which wasn't that bad, actually. But I can see people giving me the side eye if I try to come back. Besides... you know."

Dad looked out at the ocean mildly. "If a single employer chooses not to hire you because of that rotten mayonnaise stain Warren somehow still calls a friend, I'll crush them like the insects they are."

I burst out laughing, drawing eyes from everywhere. "You can't do that."

"I can and I will. It's discrimination."

Unable to keep the smile off my face, I swatted him on the arm. "Well, let me figure out what I even want to do first before you start lobbing lawsuits up and down the coast, okay?"

"That, I can do." He gave me a mock salute and headed down to the beach. Given he was dressed in slacks and a button-down shirt, I didn't think he would join in on the game, but I would pay money to see my stepfather call Beau a rotten mayonnaise stain to his face.

A question bubbled behind my lips. "Dad?"

He turned at the bottom of the steps.

"You never liked him. Why didn't you say anything?" Part of me wanted to cry and demand why no one told me I was being tossed around like a rag doll. Another part of me wanted to think I wasn't alone in my delusion.

"I did."

"No, you didn't."

He took a step toward me and smiled sadly. "When you first met Beau, I said something. But you were happy, and I don't think it fully registered. After a while, I stopped because I didn't want the only thing for us to talk about was how I hated your boyfriend. So I tried to make it clear how I felt in other ways, hoping one day you would see what I saw. But I wish it hadn't been so painful for you."

I didn't stop him when he walked away this time.

All these emotions felt like the tides. They came in waves. Up and down. I felt good. Then the horror of my own blindness rose up and threatened to crush me.

Straightening my spine, I went back to and laid on the chaise. It happened. No amount of beating myself up would change the past.

As much as I wished, I wasn't a time traveler or a wizard. I couldn't snap my fingers and make myself less angry or devastated with myself, but I could choose not to wallow. At least for today.

Where the hell was Rin?

The house was big, but not big enough for her to take this long to get there and back. My phone was in our suite where I left it. I downed the last of my drink, enjoying the mild brain freeze in the heat before I went to grab it.

I put on the same shorts and shirt I'd had on last night before they tore them off me and checked my phone.

Trinity:

*Hey, I'm so sorry. Work called me in. They had an emergency. A real one, not a gossip one. Like drop everything and get your ass to the office. Not sure what it is, but I'll let you know! Sorry to bail like that.*

. . .

That didn't sound good. But at least she wasn't wandering around the halls lost. Not that she would, considering she'd been here so much while we grew up she practically lived here.

My bare feet padded on the marble floors, the whole house quiet around me. There was something soothing about knowing you were alone like this, but close to people. Very different from actually being alone.

The choice was what mattered.

A shadow filled the door to the now empty terrace. I saw the bridesmaids all heading down to the beach, but Beau was blocking the way out.

"Beau."

"Hey, Izzy-bear."

"You have a lot of fucking nerve calling me that, after everything."

He winced, gripping the back of his neck. "Yeah. I was hoping we could talk?"

"I don't want to talk to you."

"I know I didn't—"

"There you are," Joel said, sweeping past my ex, pulling me into his arms, and kissing me so indecently I was glad I'd put my shorts on. My bikini wasn't enough to cover my arousal, and perfume filled the surrounding air. "We won, and crushed it, so we convinced everyone to play volleyball."

I grinned. Something I was actually good at. "There's too many people to play volleyball."

"Shh," he kissed my forehead quickly. "We know, but we're going to do it anyway. Come on."

He grabbed my hand and tugged me past Beau before he could say another word. "You okay?"

"Yeah. Thanks for the rescue. He wants to talk, and I'm not interested."

Joel stopped long enough to sweep me off my feet. "Well, he's going to have to try harder than that. And when he does, you'll have a wall of bodies between you and him."

Heat touched my cheeks, but I didn't say anything. I loved someone having my back. "Does the rescue come with door-to-door service?"

"It does. That, and it's been long enough that I think you need a refresher on that sunscreen, right?"

"Right. Probably a good idea. Where did Vaughn put it?"

"Right here," Vaughn appeared right as Joel put me down, and suddenly I was surrounded by skin, muscle, and *scent*. "I think we can help with that, but you might have to lose the shirt."

My mouth dropped open. "You guys don't have to put it on me right now."

Cade turned me to him, fingers brushing the hem of my shirt. I nodded, and he tugged it off. "You said you don't want him back, right?"

"I'd want a cactus up the ass before I want him back."

Hawk coughed, covering his mouth, and Cade's eyes sparkled with amusement. "Does not wanting him back include not wanting to torture him?"

"Not necessarily."

Vaughn passed him the sunscreen, which Cade sprayed across my stomach and in a line up to my chest. "I'm glad. Because the five of us rubbing sunscreen into your perfect body is enough to make a dead man jealous."

I didn't know who pulled the shorts off me to leave me in just the bathing suit, and I didn't care. Cade's fingers slipping across my skin had my eyes closing. "Just don't make me indecent."

"Never," he vowed. Then his voice was closer. "Your indecency is only for us to see, princess."

It didn't matter how hot the sun was, I was hotter. "*Fuck*."

"I tried earlier, remember?" Vaughn asked. "We were interrupted."

"All right, all right." Ellie pushed through the pack to get to me. "Hands off my sister. We need her. And we're going to kick your ass."

None of them looked like they believed her, and I kept my face even. What they didn't know wouldn't hurt them until it was too late. She smirked, and I paused before following her. "Want to wager something?"

"If we win," Hawk said, "you sleep naked for the rest of the time we're here."

"Done," I said.

He stopped short, surprised I'd agreed so quickly. "And if we win, the next time we go somewhere, I get to open my own doors."

A laugh slipped out. "Fine, baby girl. If that's what you want."

It was a small bet, because I liked them doing things for me, but I still wanted to prove a point.

I joined the girls on the other side of the net. There were way,

*way* too many of us, but no one really cared. Ellie and I stayed at the front. My guys and Warren stayed there too, looking at us like we were their favorite meal.

All I did was smile.

Vaughn served it, and I jumped on pure muscle memory and instinct, spiking the ball straight into the sand.

## CHAPTER TWENTY-ONE

### VAUGHN

I lifted a sleeping Isolde off the chair and began to carry her down the beach toward our end of the house.

We'd earned the spanking we got during the volleyball games. Served us right—pun absolutely intended—for assuming we would be better. Then we found out Isolde played volleyball all the way through college and the only reason she didn't go further was because she chose to retire, not because she didn't have offers.

Shaking my head, I looked down at my sleepy Omega, hair windswept and sandy, lips parted just enough to make them kissable. I imagined them red and swollen from too many kisses, the way her mouth would look after I chased her, caught her, and made her mine.

The whole group had played games until we were starving. Then we ate, played some more, and it had become an impromptu party. No bonfire this time, but music and drinks. Some people went in the water. A bridesmaid who had a pack had gone inside with her guys. One of the groomsmen and his husband also left for some alone time.

We'd stayed, watching Isolde as she talked with her sister and Warren. Chatted with the other bridesmaids. Watched her open up like the flowers she smelled like and be in her element.

But a whole day of people and sun wore her out. It wasn't late, but she'd started drooping even though she hadn't been drinking.

A figure stood near the steps to our veranda. I smothered the growl in my chest and turned to the others behind me. "Someone take her, please."

Hawk lifted her out of my arms and into his. She barely stirred, snuggling into his chest. "What's up?"

I nodded over my shoulder. "He and I are going to have a chat."

"Be careful." Rowan put a hand on my shoulder as he passed.

It wasn't a warning for my safety, but for Isolde's. Don't make anything worse for her. That wasn't my intention.

But this asshole had already done enough in her life. She didn't need him skulking around in the shadows waiting to pounce and make her talk about things she didn't want to remember.

Isolde had us now, whether or not she believed it, and as her Alpha, my job was to protect her. So that's what I would do.

I stayed back until the others were inside, watching as they passed Beau. He didn't stop them and didn't speak, just watched. Clearly he'd been hoping she'd come back by herself.

One breath in, one breath out. "Remember, Vaughn, you can't kill him," I muttered to myself. Then I raised my voice. "Can I help you?"

Beau jumped like I'd fired a shotgun behind him. Fucker hadn't even noticed we weren't all with her. "Uh, yeah, I was hoping to talk to Isolde. Our conversation earlier was cut short."

"Our Omega is sleeping right now."

He snorted and shook his head. "Your Omega. I get it. You don't have to piss all over her to stake your claim. It just makes you look like assholes."

I stared at him, waiting for him to fill the silence. Guys like Beau didn't know how to be quiet. He shoved his hands in his pockets and looked around before back at me. "Are you just going to stand there?"

"Until you leave? Yes."

"I have every right to be here."

"You have a right to be on this property. You do not have a right to stand outside our rooms like a stalker. So fuck off."

"What the hell is your problem, man?" His face was too red. He'd been drinking, and his voice rose. "All I want to do is talk to the woman I was with for four years. That's not a fucking crime."

"No," I admitted. "It's not. But Isolde doesn't want to talk to you. Because you were together for four years and then you put her out on the curb like your weekly trash. So until *she* says she wants to have a conversation with you, I expect you to keep your distance. Be a good boy and don't speak unless you're spoken to."

Beau came at me, and I stood my ground. I wasn't going to hit him. If he wanted to hit me, that was fine, but it wouldn't work out well for him when my eye was black and he had to explain why.

"You think just because you're with her now you get to talk to me like that? You don't know *shit*."

"I know enough. You're drunk, Beau. Back off before you do something you regret."

He growled. "I'm more likely to do something *you'll* regret, and I will talk to Isolde any time I choose." Regardless of the words, he left, lurching across the big lawn through the magnolia trees and toward the main house.

No wonder this guy didn't have a pack. Pack bonds were inherent, but you also had to be open to that connection. Pack life was about sharing. Your life, your possessions, love, however it worked out for the people involved. If he was this possessive over someone he'd broken up with, I didn't think it would work well for him.

I waited until he was out of sight to go inside, smiling when I saw Isolde curled up in the middle of the giant bed with everyone else around her, watching, entranced. Like Isolde was a dragon egg at the center of our hoard.

Which she was.

The most precious thing imaginable.

"He's gone?" Joel asked.

"Yeah, but don't expect him to stay that way. There's something up with him. He really wants to talk to her. I can't imagine why. He was drunk."

Rowan growled softly. "I'm starting to put a picture together of this guy, and it's not a good one."

I didn't disagree. Something didn't fully add up. Isolde didn't want him back. She'd made that clear, and I had no reason to doubt her. Plus, she was a terrible liar.

But Beau?

He wasn't acting like a man who'd moved on. When Isolde wasn't looking, he watched her. What he'd said to Rowan and Hawk was an attempt to scare us off. Now he'd tried to corner her twice.

Whatever it was, it didn't sit well with me.

No matter what happened, with him or otherwise, we would be her shield.

Because it was about fucking time she had one.

## CHAPTER TWENTY-TWO

ISOLDE

Ellie leaned her head on my shoulder as we stood on the steps of the mansion watching everyone leaving, the staff helping to pack the cars. "I love all of them, but I won't lie, it'll be nice to have a break. Don't tell them."

I laughed. "I won't."

The bridal party would be back closer to the wedding. For the bachelor and bachelorette parties. I had no idea what we were doing for those, but I would worry about that later.

The guys were using the gym here in the house and going about a more normal routine now that we had a few down days. There was something nice about them doing normal things here. It felt settled, even if I didn't.

I woke up between Cade and Rowan, and it might be the best sleep I'd ever had. They made me feel safe on a level I didn't even understand, and I wasn't fully ready to examine that. So I slipped out from between them and fled, finding breakfast and my sister before they told me they were using the gym.

A clattering sound made Ellie and I turn. Angela pulled her suitcase out of the door roughly, in high heels despite it being ten in the morning. She looked furious. "Doesn't the staff normally help with the bags?" I asked Ellie under my breath.

"Usually. Maybe I left their room off the list for that and only put it down for cleaning."

I tried not to laugh and failed.

"Something funny?" Angela snapped, glaring at me. The giant diamond on her finger sparkled in the morning light, so big I was surprised she kept her balance in the heels.

"Ellie told me an excellent joke."

She left the suitcase where it was and stalked toward me. "I don't know what you're trying to do showing up here with that pack and trying to make Beau jealous, but you'll never get him back."

I stared at her. "I have no interest in having him back. He's all yours. As for showing up here, hi, I don't know if you've met my *sister*. You know, the one who's getting married? I would be here anyway, no matter who came with me."

Angela rolled her eyes. "Just stay away from him."

"My pleasure."

She stomped off, and I sighed, looking at Ellie. "You realize that you're going to see her for the rest of your life, right?"

"Shit." She grimaced. "I don't love that. But I do love Warren, and he's worth it. Besides, maybe Beau will pull the same shit with her."

As much as I disliked her, I didn't wish that on anyone. For now, it didn't matter. We'd have a blissful time without both of them here. "Want to go to CD later?"

"Hell yes I do. Just us girls? Or everyone?"

"Either way is fine. But if we take the guys..." I kept forgetting they were from here. So they probably already knew about the best ice cream shop in Clarity Coast, with the absolutely horrendous name that made it famous.

The Cream Dream put crack in their ice cream. Or that's what it felt like, because it was so good you could never get enough. In the evening, they turned into an adults-only store with treats shaped like dicks and vaginas, leaning into the pun on the word cream. It drew people from all over, and if you lived here, you just went with it.

"Iz?" Ellie waved a hand in front of my face. "Where did you go?"

"Sorry. I'm just not used to thinking about the fact that they're from here. They already know all about the name."

"Something tells me it won't stop them from using it to their advantage."

She was absolutely right, and I remembered Rowan's comment from the other morning. "I'll ask them if they want to go. Besides, I already know they love waffles."

Ellie turned to wave to one of her friends pulling out of the drive, and I headed inside. A hand snagged my wrist and pulled me into the coat closet. Lemon and eucalyptus tickled my nose. I whirled and shoved Beau backward. "Get your hands off me."

He held them up and stepped back, blocking the door. "I need to talk to you, and your guard dogs haven't let me."

"Because I told them not to. I have nothing to say to you, Beau."

"Will you just *listen* for once in your life?"

I blinked and took a step back. The words felt like a slap. "For once in my life? I listened to you for *four years*. I've listened to everything and you took that for granted. I've listened enough. Now get out of the way."

"I looked for you," he said, looking down at the floor and slipping his hands into his pockets. "No one would tell me where you were, and you had me blocked on everything. I... wanted to apologize. And talk things out."

"Did you fall down and hit your head? Broken up or not, I know you, Beau, and you have tells. You're lying. And I want to be clear about this. I don't care." I sighed. "We're done. You're with Angela, I'm with my pack. We can coexist, but I'd prefer to do that separately."

I went to step around him, and he grabbed me by the arms, pinning me to the door frame. "Men like that can't make you happy. I'm just looking out for you. You know better than to get involved with people like them."

"Like what?"

"Not like us. They can't give you everything you need. I don't want to see you living some small life."

A laugh burst out of me. "Are you serious right now? You're trying to tell me they're not good enough because they don't have enough *money*? You gave up every right to have an opinion on my life when you kicked me out of your house."

"Yeah," he snarled. "But I didn't actually expect you to *leave*."

The words took the wind out of my sails. "What?"

Beau sighed, stepping back to run his hands through his hair. "I never actually meant for you to leave. I thought you'd cry and beg me not to do it. I thought over that week we'd figure it out, and things would get better. I wasn't happy, and nothing was changing. So I did something to force us to change."

I stared at him, mouth falling open. "Do you know how insane that sounds? If you weren't happy, there's an easier solution than burning a relationship to the ground. It's called *talking*."

"I just told you I tried." His voice rose, echoing off the walls and masking the sound of the front door closing. We both froze, but heard nothing. "I wanted to explain, but you had evaporated like a fucking ghost."

Shaking my head, I tried to wrap my head around it. Frankly, this didn't make what he'd done hurt less. If anything, it made it hurt more because he hadn't trusted me enough to think I'd be fine with changing things up.

"Well, you certainly moved on quickly for someone who claims they wanted to save our relationship."

"I was lonely and grieving. Angela was kind, and... you didn't come back."

I nodded. "You're right. Thank you for telling me, I guess. Angela is waiting for you."

"We're not done."

"What else could you *possibly* have to say to me?"

He gripped my arms again. "I still care about you, Izzy-bear. Trust me. They're not good for you. But I am. I can fix this. I can make it right."

"Said the man with his ring on another woman's finger. You're just going to toss her aside like you did me? No. We are done." I grit my teeth. "Let. Me. Go."

"No. Not until you listen. Not until you give me another chance. You and I were made for each other. Blueberry muffins, right?"

I tried to move, but he was holding me too tightly. Panic clawed at my insides. "Beau, stop."

A hand landed in the center of Beau's chest, shoving him backward into the other side of the door frame. Hawk, still sweaty from the gym, towered over him. "She told you to let her go."

I slipped out of the closet, finding Ellie there with wide eyes. It clicked. She was the one who came inside the front door and heard us, then went to get the guys. *Thank you*, I mouthed.

"Get your hands off me," Beau snapped.

"Funny." I let the sarcasm drip before I turned back to face them. "That's what I said. You didn't listen. Why should he?"

Hawk looked over at me, dark eyes filled with fury. His head turned slowly back toward Beau. No one in the world wanted to be on the end of that look. "You were warned to stay away until she wanted to talk to you. The next time you touch *my* Omega without her consent, you will get a lot more than a hand to the chest. Do you understand me?"

Beau looked over at me, eyes unsure, seeing if I was going to intervene. Like hell.

"*Do you understand me?*" Hawk's voice cracked through the air like thunder.

My ex rose to the challenge. "You think you deserve her? You and your tattoos? She was mine first, so enjoy that. Everything you get, I've already had. You really think she could want you when she's had me?"

Hawk didn't rise to the bait, standing there and glaring at Beau. There was no comparison. The bite in Beau's words told me the truth—he didn't care about me. Not really. He'd gambled with our relationship and lost, and now that I was back with a pack who showered me with attention, his ego couldn't handle it.

Beau's face twisted into a smirk. "Enjoy watching her fall for me all over again, *Elliot*."

"I'm not a chew toy." Words I couldn't hold back. Tears rose even though I hated them. "You don't get to put me down and pick me up whenever you feel like it. And I don't care what your intention was, you *broke me*. Don't you get that?"

He opened his mouth, and I spoke before he could, the tears spilling over. "You don't get to have both. You don't get to cut me out of your life like I was a tumor you wanted to get rid of, and then have any say in what I do. And you certainly don't get to say shit like that about me because you're pissed I'm happy, and it's not with you. If you wanted us, you shouldn't have gambled with four years of our lives. Your fiancée is waiting for you outside. Get the fuck out of this house."

Anger flared in his eyes, and confusion. I wasn't the Isolde he knew. Who I became was a direct result of his actions. He threw me off a cliff and was pissed that I'd managed to climb back up. Like me having a life after him was a hit to his ego and I should live in some perpetual state of grief, pining for him for the rest of my days.

Like he could set me on a shelf and pick me back up whenever he liked.

My chest ached, pain pulsing there like a burning coal that wouldn't fucking fade. I wanted to cut it out of myself, but there was no way to do it. "The only reason I'm glad it happened this way is because I know now how much better life is without you. But truly? I wish I'd never met you."

Beau shoved Hawk away and stalked past me. "You'll never have as good as me, Isolde. I'll prove it to you. These men will never have enough or be enough. I was the best you'll ever have. You will crawl back to me, and when you do, we'll both enjoy it."

Hawk's growl split the air. "Step the fuck away from her or I will lay you out."

The front door opened, and Warren stepped inside. He looked at the four of us, sensing the tone in the room and seeing my tears. "Beau, your car is packed and Angela is already inside. Ready to go?"

He smiled. For a brief moment, I saw the Beau I thought I knew. The charming face he had for everyone until he didn't get his way. That was the thing about Beau. He always got his way and thought it would be the same now.

Not this time.

"Yeah. I'm ready." Beau clapped Warren on the shoulder. "See you soon, man."

Warren waved before looking back at us. "What the hell happened?"

"You and I are going to have a talk about him is what's about to happen," Ellie said, turning sharply and disappearing deeper into the house.

With one more glance at me, he followed after her. "Wait, El. Hold on."

Their voices faded into a blur down the hall. I stumbled back a step, the weight of the entire interaction crashing down on me. Horror and anger and regret. Tears flooded my eyes faster now. I swiped them away angrily. He'd already caused me too many tears.

Warmth and sweetness wrapped around me. Hawk pulled me to his chest and held me tight. I tried to stop the tears, and I couldn't. The pain in my chest made it hard to breathe—that intangible ache that only came with grief.

Hawk held me against him. "It's okay, baby girl. I'm sorry he was anywhere near you."

"It's not your fault." I sniffed and tried to make myself sound normal. "You couldn't have stopped it."

"I could have tried."

He tilted my face up to his, brushing away the tears with his thumbs. Closing the distance between us, he kissed me. Softly. Delicately. With all the gentleness and care Beau *had never* shown me.

And for the moment, I didn't question it. I didn't care that it wasn't real. All I wanted was to feel seen, loved, and understood.

Hawk's lips on mine gave me all of it and more.

Without breaking the kiss, he bent his knees and lifted me off the ground, wrapping my legs around his waist. I leaned my head on his shoulder while he carried me back to the suite, just breathing in the scent of sugar and frosting.

Turns out people were right when they said sugar could fix anything.

"Where is everyone?" I whispered.

"I was the one who could leave the fastest with Ellie. They should be back here now. Don't think for a second they didn't want to follow me, but Vaughn's face is too pretty to get fucked up because he fell off a treadmill."

A laugh slipped out in spite of myself.

His hands tightened on my spine. "Do you want to talk about it?"

I did, and I didn't. Beau didn't deserve more of my energy, and yet it was eating me up inside. All I wanted to do was turn my brain off for a while. Leaning up, I kissed Hawk's cheek. "Not yet. But I need to ask Rowan something."

Bumping his head into mine, he paused to open the door. "Then let's go find him, baby girl."

## CHAPTER TWENTY-THREE

### ISOLDE

Hawk wasn't wrong. The rest of the pack waited for us in the suite. Vaughn was missing, but I heard the shower in the bathroom. Cade and Rowan had damp hair, the former pacing back and forth across the room like a caged animal.

Cade came straight to us.

"I found Beau pinning her against a doorframe."

"Is he still alive?" Joel growled.

"Unfortunately."

I dropped my eyes to the floor, all those emotions rising up again. Hawk let me slide down his body until I hit the floor. Cade pulled me in and held me hard, his unyielding strength allowing me to relax.

"I was actually coming back to ask you guys if you wanted to go to Cream Dream with Ellie and Warren tonight when he cornered me. Since you like waffles."

"Our Omega, waffles, and some ice cream?" Vaughn strode out of the bathroom in nothing but a towel. "Sounds like fun."

"We'd love to," Cade said quietly.

Hawk stepped out from around where Cade held me. "Rowan, Isolde wanted you."

"Yeah?"

I nodded.

He rose from the couch and came over to us, Cade brushing his lips across mine before he let me go.

"When I asked you guys to show me different things," I blurted, "I don't know if all of us needed be together for them? If one of you goes first, will that be okay? I'm just—" I shook out my hands, trying to get the nerves, anxiety, and everything else out.

"That's perfectly fine, princess," Cade whispered, tucking a stray hair behind my ear. "One of the best parts of being a pack, actually. You don't have to be everything for everyone all the time. We have different strengths. If Rowan has what you need, then take it."

Then he smiled, though there was still hardness in his eyes. Barely kindled rage at Beau, which made me feel...

Fuck. It made me feel everything.

"I look forward to my turn," Cade said.

"Me too."

Rowan took my hand, and I led him back out of the suite, guiding him through the house to a section that didn't get used a lot. Mom and Dad lived in the other wing, and now that people were gone, we were pretty much alone. Hell, even when I lived here full time, almost no one used this library but me. It had a big window overlooking the ocean with a window seat that got soaked in sunlight every afternoon. Tons of books—including ones I'd collected. But mainly it was private and isolated.

I locked the door behind us, though I didn't think any of the staff would be wandering in here.

Rowan looked around, taking it in. His hair was still damp from the shower, the fabric of his white t-shirt sticking to his skin. Well-worn jeans clung to his ass and thighs, making my mouth water.

"This is nice," he said.

"I used to spend a lot of time here when I was younger."

He traced a finger along one of the shelves. "I can see why. But I'm not sure why we're here now."

"Maybe I just wanted to show you."

"Maybe. But I don't think so."

I wrapped my arms around myself. "I can't stop thinking about what you said. While we were on the beach. And after what just happened, I need to turn my brain off. I don't want to think about Beau or what an ass he is or how stupid I was to ever love him. All I want is to have some time where it's not consuming my every thought, and I don't know how to do it without help."

A nearly intangible change shivered through the air. Rowan's very *presence* grew larger as he stared at me. "I can help with that, but I'm going to ask you some questions."

"Okay." Neither of us had moved, but it felt like I was suddenly naked and on my knees.

He took a step closer, hands in his pockets, watching me. Every nuance and fidget, he saw. "What is your goal for this?"

"To turn my brain off."

His smile broke through. "I know. I mean are you looking for sex? Or are you looking for something else?"

"I didn't think it mattered. If it's surrender, it's what you want, right?"

"That is true." He took another step toward me. "But as with anything in a power exchange, there's no point in fulfilling a want if the other person isn't getting what they need."

My mouth opened and closed. I wet my lips, because everything had suddenly gone hot and dry. "I hadn't planned anything beyond asking you."

One of Rowan's hands slipped behind my neck. "The things on the list you filled out? They're fantasies. Ways to play and connect with each other. Things to try. That doesn't mean they don't require practice. So as much as I love the thought of taking you under command and keeping you there the whole day, playing to my every whim, you're not ready for that."

"The whole day?"

A low, rough purr rose in the space between us. "I'd love to do more than that. Take you to a place in your mind where you could disappear for days. Just you and me," his lips quirked, "and whatever I want. Again, you're not ready for that, and clearly we don't have the time. I already know your limits, so what is it you *need*, Isolde?"

Everything felt so heavy. All I needed was the weight gone. Beyond that, I felt like I couldn't even think. "I need someone else to be in control. I promise I'm not trying to be vague, but that's what it is. Pleasure is great. Sex is great. But what I need is... surrender."

"You need a safeword."

"Banana," I said instantly. "I already chose that one with Vaughn."

Rowan chuckled. "Banana. I like it." He stepped forward then, his other hand coming up my throat. My neck was now ringed by his fingers. There didn't need to be pressure there for me to freeze, every Omega instinct melting in the presence of an Alpha.

His eyes warmed, unspoken approval flowing out of them. I would have leaned into his touch if I could move at all.

"For the next two hours, you belong to me. You will make no decisions—not take a single step—without me telling you to do so. Your obedience will be instant, and without hesitation. You don't need permission to come, but you will tell me if you're going to. Because we're new at this, if you have a question and you can't see me or touch me, say 'question.' If you can touch me, tap me three times. Until the time is up, or you use your safeword, you're mine, do you understand?"

"Yes."

Heat flared in his gaze. "Good girl."

It was the only warning I got. Rowan spun me, pinning my back to his chest, his hands going to the buttons at the top of my dress. "I fucking love buttons. It's like you wore this just for me so I could unwrap you."

Heated kisses down my neck and across my shoulder when he pulled the dress down. Pleasure and more than that, I knew I didn't have to worry about what he wanted or what I wanted, because he was already taking care of it.

Rowan pushed the dress off my shoulders, allowing it to pool on the floor. A few seconds later, the rest of my clothes joined the dress, and he released me just to stare. My whole body flushed at the attention, and I had to resist the urge to cover myself. Not because I was embarrassed—they'd all already seen me naked—but because I wasn't used to being *seen* like this.

"You're fucking beautiful, you know that?" He took my chin gently between his fingers. "And not only because you're naked in front of me. You have a beautiful soul."

I opened my mouth to speak and closed it again. He hadn't told me to. Liquid heat poured over me in a wave.

"You may speak."

"How do you know I have a beautiful soul? You barely know me."

Rowan looked around the library, gaze settling on a green velvet armchair. He picked it up like it was a feather, placing it in front of the window, so whoever sat there could admire the view. "The same way I know your parents and sister love you. Or the way I knew the others were my pack as soon as we met. Sometimes you simply know something. Time has nothing to do with it. Step out of your dress."

I moved to the side, and he picked it up off the floor, draping it over the seat of the chair. Then he turned, a sparkle in his eyes. "Your turn. Undress me."

Up close, Rowan was overwhelming. More than a foot of height on me, with the freshly showered version of his scent bathing me in memories of sunlight and the sea. He helped me get his shirt up and over his head because I wasn't tall enough, and I dragged my fingers through the hair on his chest, feeling every smooth plane and muscled groove.

"I didn't tell you to explore me," he said, but the words were light. Amused. "But I like it. Feel free."

My fingers moved like they had a life of their own, tracing the line of his abs and downward, skimming over the lines that dipped beneath his jeans.

He wasn't wearing a belt. The button of his jeans was easy to undo, with Rowan rescuing his phone before I tugged them down. His boxer briefs too, hit the floor, and I realized this was the first time I'd seen any of them truly naked.

My eyes rose to his. That same amusement lurked there, wondering what I would do with the hard cock I'd just revealed. Long, straight, the tip already glistening with arousal. The hair on his body had been neatly trimmed. I watched as his hand curled around his shaft and stroked once. Again. A third time.

I was hypnotized by a dick, and I wasn't mad about it.

"Isolde?"

My head snapped up and found Rowan smiling.

"Go lean on the window seat. Bent over, using your elbows. I want to see that pretty pink cunt on display for me."

Words like that undid me. Until these men, I thought the only men who spoke like that only existed in books or my imagination. Beau had certainly never been able to turn my body into a sultry puddle with a single sentence. But that's what I was now. Wet, wanting, and happy to obey.

The sun wasn't bearing down on the window yet. It was just bright and pleasant. Outside, the tide was coming in, slowly creeping up the beach. I heard the sounds of Rowan moving behind me, but I made myself not look. He hadn't told me I could, and there was something glorious about having nothing to do but rest here and watch the sea.

No worries.

No responsibilities.

A knot of tension I'd barely noticed released between my shoulders.

His hands landed on my ass, smoothing over the skin. "Do you think if this skin got enough sun, you'd get freckles here too?"

"I never really thought about it."

His fingers gave a tiny, stinging slap in reprimand for speaking. "Widen your legs. I want your feet outside mine."

Obeying, I found his feet and widened my stance. It exposed me obscenely, and I couldn't even care. His hands were still on my skin, always moving, making me feel like I was the center of the goddamn universe.

He ran one of his knuckles between my legs and groaned. "Fuck me. I don't think I'll ever get tired of the way you taste."

There was no warning. His mouth was on me. Devouring me. Tongue thrusting deep inside me. It felt entirely different like this. Had I ever been eaten from behind? I didn't think so. It didn't have a right to feel this good.

Rowan moaned. "I want to see you in this position getting yourself off. Showing the five of us how you touch yourself, and then be there to clean up your cum with our tongues."

I dug my fingers into the cushion of the window seat, holding on because it felt like I was swirling through space. Free falling into Rowan's words. But it wasn't out of control. It was freedom. The ability to let go and know someone held the boundaries.

He held me against his mouth, fingers digging into my hips like he couldn't bring me close enough or plunge deep enough, never taste enough. Rowan's tongue dragged upward, straying to my ass, and he consumed that too, without reservation. "Have you been taken here? You can answer."

"Kind of. We tried it once and neither of us really liked it, so we never did it again."

Rowan bit me gently, slipping a finger deep, just like he had the other night. "Would you be willing to try again?"

I nodded, my head falling to the cushion. Yes, I was willing, because I already knew they would stop if I needed them to, and they would do whatever they could to make it feel incredible. "I need words, Omega."

"Yes. I would try it again."

"Good girl."

My whine was swallowed by the cushions. I couldn't keep my eyes open when his tongue *fucked* me like that. Fingers, lips, teeth, tongue. Rowan took his time, until my whole body felt bathed in sensation, my knees shaking every time he ran his tongue over my clit.

I moaned when he pulled back.

"Turn around, Isolde. Slowly. Your legs might be stiff."

In reality, they were somewhere between being too stiff and absolute jelly, which didn't make sense but didn't make it any less true.

I wasn't prepared for the sight of Rowan sitting in the chair—sprawling in it like a king—on top of my dress, like he was claiming me that way too while keeping the chair clean.

"Kneel down."

My knees obeyed before I could think the thought. I knew what he meant now about being taken to a place where this could last days. It would be like taking the longest, most delicious nap of my life.

Rowan leaned down, his face close to mine. "You wrote on your questionnaire that you enjoy blowjobs, and further. Is that true?"

When I hesitated he smiled and kissed my forehead. "If I'm asking you a question, you can always answer, little flower."

I preened at the nickname, my Omega nearly purring in contentment. If Omegas could purr. "Everything I wrote on there is the truth."

"Good. Because you're going to put your mouth on me now. Feel free to move when you wish to keep yourself comfortable, because you're not allowed to remove your mouth until I tell you to."

Reaching out, I tapped his knee three times before he pulled back. "What's your question?"

"Why not just tell me to? Why ask if I enjoy it?"

He smiled and reached for my hand, taking mine and wrapping it around his shaft while he spoke. "Give some men power like this, and they'd have you on your knees, using your mouth, whether or not you enjoyed it. And that's all they'd do."

A smirk that sent shivers down my spine. Rowan moved my hand while he spoke, showing me how to stroke and twist at once. "I'm not saying I'll only do things you fully enjoy. But there's a reason this is called an exchange. Both of us getting something out of it. Today, I'm choosing only things I know you'll enjoy, because I fully intend on making you come, so I'm building to it."

My lips formed a small 'o.' He saw my hesitance while at the same time still moving both our hands, his cock hot and hard beneath my palm. When I squeezed him, he let out a groan. "Careful, Isolde. You wanted to say something?"

"How did you know?"

I loved that smile and the way his eyes traced over me. They were lighter in the brightness, honeyed amber too sweet for the dominance rolling off him. "Your face says everything you're thinking. Tell me."

"I like them, but I'm not very good at them," I whispered.

"Is that what you think? Or is that what you've been told?"

"Both."

He leaned forward further, lips brushing my ear, breath making me shiver. Goosebumps raced over my skin, my nipples hardened, and I swore I felt pleasure straight down in my core with his words. "How could you possibly be bad at it when I'm going to tell you exactly what to do? When I sit back, you're going to put those sinful fucking lips around my cock and take as much of me as you can *comfortably*. Nothing else. If you understand, say 'yes, Alpha.'"

The air must have gone up like ten degrees because it was so much hotter in here than it had been before. "Yes, Alpha."

Rowan sat back, the mantle of power around him nearly visible. I just wanted to stare at him. Gorgeous. The ambient sunlight made his hair more gold than brown, painting the lines of his body in sharper contrasts I was having a hard time not leaning forward and licking them. And the cock my hand was still wrapped around?

Fuck me.

He raised one eyebrow, and I blinked. Right.

Rising up on my knees, I slid my mouth around him, his scent suddenly concentrated into a flavor so real my eyes rolled back in my head. I moaned on purpose, giving him the sound he'd wanted at breakfast, his face told me he knew it.

But he groaned—a pure sound of pleasure—that made me eager.

It was the reason I liked this even if I wasn't great at it. Giving someone pleasure made me happy. And the raw fire in his eyes told me everything I needed to know.

I obeyed his instructions, sliding down his length until I couldn't take more of him comfortably, and waited. There was still more of him. I was pretty sure I could take him all, but it would be a struggle.

One I already knew I'd enjoy.

Beau hadn't let me do this. It was always fast and quick. He said I wasn't the best, but no man said no to a woman's mouth. Now those words made me cringe. How the fuck did I ever think that was normal?

I waited, my palms on Rowan's thighs, waiting. I thought it might be awkward, but it wasn't. If I were kneeling on a pillow, I could do this for a while.

"Suck it for me, Isolde, nice and slow." His palm spread across the back of my head, holding it in place. "Don't move. Just suck."

I did, closing my eyes and drowning in the taste of him. Coconut and salt. The feeling of being filled. The world narrowed to me and him. Nothing else.

He guided me an inch deeper. Farther than was comfortable, but it was okay. "Can you stay here? Tap twice if you can. Be honest."

Two taps.

"Damn, Isolde," he breathed the words, thumb slowly caressing my head as he held me in place. I sucked harder, wanting to drive him crazy. This was fun, finding the tiniest of loopholes. He told me to suck his cock—he didn't tell me how hard to do it.

He laughed, like he knew what I was doing. Slowly, Rowan pumped his hips into my mouth, forcing the last inches of himself in, and easing back. Over and over again, pushing into my throat with an almost ruthless consistency.

I'd never had my throat fucked *slowly*. Every nerve was on fire, arousal swimming in my veins, and I was far closer to having an orgasm than when he'd had his tongue on me. This was exactly what I needed.

My eyes fluttered closed, and I relaxed further. I didn't want to move from this spot. I had a vision of lying in bed with him, his cock in my mouth, neither of us moving, and I had no reason for why it was making me so desperately wet.

Rowan shifted his hand to grip my hair, pulling hard, taking the time to let me feel that sensation and revel in it before pulling me off him. I almost whined. "If I don't get your beautiful ass up here, I'm going to finish, and I'm not done with you." Then his mouth quirked. "Though I think you'd like your mouth knotted on my cock, wouldn't you?"

A shudder shook me to the core. *Yes.*

He lifted me, and suddenly I was sinking down onto him, stretched and full, and oh my god, it had been so long since I'd been fucked with an actual dick I'd almost forgotten what it felt like.

"Hands on my shoulders," he said.

I was caught between questions and desire. So much I wanted to know and ask. Instead, I bit my lip, grabbed his shoulders, and sank all the way down onto his cock.

"You can move while I fuck you, little flower. Anything to help get off, except touch yourself. That's my job."

All the slow gentleness of being on my knees was gone. Rowan gripped my hips and pulled them down, thrusting up at the same time, taking me hard and fast. He said I could move, but there was absolutely no chance of that. This was a ride I never wanted to get off of. Get off? Sure. Get off him? No thank you.

Rowan was bigger than Beau. He filled me in a way the other man hadn't. Delicious friction swirled beneath my skin, the tendrils of true pleasure drawing tighter.

"How close are you? Give me a percentage."

My mind blanked. Percentage? "Sixty."

"Mmm." One hand grabbed my hair and pulled my head back, exposing my neck. That alone brought me another ten percent. "You like words. Let's see what we can do with them. What would I do if I had you at my mercy for days on end?" His low laugh dropped through me. Like this wasn't a hypothetical, it was a fucking plan. God, yes. Please.

"No clothes. Ever. Because we wouldn't be leaving the house, and I want to see your perfect body. Maybe find out if we can get some freckles on that ass of yours. Maybe I'd order you onto the bed, face down and ass up, and tell you to play with your clit. No coming, but giving yourself pleasure, and then just leave you there. Wondering if and when I was going to come and fuck this dripping pussy."

Rowan found my clit and moved his thumb back and forth. Consistent, delicious pressure along with those fingers in my hair and the movement of his cock and—

"Maybe I'd come fuck you and leave you wanting so we could do it all over again. Or maybe," he dragged me closer to growl in my ear, "I'd sit you on my face and eat you until *I* was satisfied, no matter how many orgasms you had. Maybe I'd fuck you and hold a vibrator against your clit and prove to you how many orgasms you're capable of giving me. Then knot your mouth when your cunt is too tired.

"You'd give me *everything*, Isolde. Nothing left. Every inch of your body and soul would be mine by the time I finished with you."

He moved again, grabbing my hips and tilting them, changing the angle. Oh fuck. Oh god. I dug my nails into his shoulders to hold on, moving like he told me to. Awkward and without rhythm, I found it. Matching what he'd done and shifting so the head of his cock hit right *there*.

Light flashed behind my eyes, orgasm slamming into me so hard I couldn't even breathe. I wasn't in control of my body, every movement pure instinct to make it last longer. Feel better. Give me one more taste of the delicious sharpness slicing me to pieces.

Rowan slid home, knot locking into place as he came, adding to the wave. It fit me perfectly. Exactly where I needed it to be. Everything shook, all my strength gone, stolen by pleasure.

I melted as it left me, letting my head fall to his shoulder. The hand in my hand fell to my spine. "It hasn't been two hours, but we're finished. No rules or commands. Just rest with me." Long, slow strokes of his hand up and down my back. "Did it help?"

"I'm sorry I didn't tell you it was coming. It was so fast. And yes. Thank you."

His purr only made me cling to him further. "I think I should be thanking you. And if it was the person we're not speaking about who told you that you were bad at giving head, he's a fucking liar."

"He didn't say *bad*, exactly, just not amazing. But no one says no to a blow job, so—"

"Can I ask you something?"

I turned my head on his shoulder, breathing in the crook of his neck. His scent was so rich here it was like a hit of the best high in the world. "Sure."

"Was he your first?"

My body stiffened, and Rowan's purr strengthened, along with the movement of his hand on my spine. "You don't have to answer."

"No, um, it's okay. Yes and no. I was with someone in high school, both of us just wanting to get it out of the way. But yes for most things." Shame pressed me down. "Maybe if he hadn't been I would have seen the truth earlier."

Rowan growled lightly in my ear. Not enough to disturb the peace he'd brought me, but a clear reprimand. "Isolde."

"It's true, though. You can't say it's not. Me being naïve put me here."

"Believe me," he whispered, "I understand the desire to figure out why the hell people do what they do. Or why we didn't see something about them. But pinning down the exact moment or decision you could have changed won't alter anything."

"I know. Can't seem to stop, though."

He turned his head and kissed my neck. "I'm sorry about everything you've gone through, but I'm happy you're here now."

"Why?"

"Besides the fact that you're naked and impaled on my knot?" I heard the smile in his voice. "Because if you weren't here, and none of this had ever happened, I think I'd miss you anyway."

My breath caught in my chest. I pulled back far enough to look into his eyes. There wasn't any trace of a lie or a joke. He was telling the truth. "That's nice of you to say."

Rowan's knot began to loosen, and I went to stand off him only to find his arms locking around me. "Don't move, Omega." The command was all but a bark.

"I thought we were done."

"I thought we were," he said, thrusting once with his hips. "But neither of us are ready for this to be over. I want your body locked to mine a while longer."

It was a statement, but he asked the question with his face. I wasn't under his control. I could say no. But I didn't want to. Being here with him felt so good I didn't want it to end.

"Yeah."

"Hold on to me, little flower. This will be hard and fast."

I wrapped my arms around his neck and let go, falling into the pleasure of being fucked again, until Rowan's knot expanded inside me once more, filling me to perfection, making sure there was nowhere else I could go.

And I wished it could be so much longer than we had.

## CHAPTER TWENTY-FOUR

### ISOLDE

Cream Dream was just beyond the biggest public beach in Clarity Coast, which meant it was busy on a good day. Being the middle of summer? It was packed with lines out the door. Especially since it was after hours and the X-rated treats were now being served.

Vaughn stared at the building like he was trying to figure it out. We were way back in the line, but it was nice out. The energy here was good. One thing about Clarity Coast, it felt like a community even if you hadn't been here for a while.

"You look like you're trying to make the building burst into flames," I said to Vaughn.

He grinned. "No, I'm trying to read the menu with all the sauces. Haven't been here in a while and I have a very specific flavor I want."

"What?"

"Well, I'm obviously going to get a vagina waffle." Then he leaned closer. "And I'm trying to see what combination I can put together to make it taste as much like you as possible."

Hawk laughed at my stunned silence, pulling my back against his chest and wrapping his arms around my shoulders the way he liked. "That's an excellent idea. Let me know if you figure it out, V. Since I haven't had the chance to taste you yet, baby girl, I need a clue."

I glanced around at the people in line in front and behind us, seeing if anyone had noticed. But not even Ellie and Warren had heard.

"You spent the afternoon with Rowan and you're still turning bright red."

"I'm not used to such..." I chose my words carefully. "Enthusiasm? When it comes to me and my scent."

He chuckled, the rich making my tummy do a flip. "If you want to make a waffle that tastes like me, feel free. I'd watch you eat it and memorize every second so I could remember it."

"Now, that wouldn't be fair. There are five of you."

"Then we'll just have to come back."

So simple. We'll come back. My head was so much clearer after this afternoon with Rowan, and I didn't have the energy to keep myself from falling into them or keep them at arm's length. Being held by them felt so good. Too good.

Ellie came forward and stole me away from Hawk. "You guys go entertain my fiancé for a minute."

Vaughn gave a cheeky salute. "Yes, ma'am."

All five men gave us a little space, and the line moved forward.

Ellie slipped her arm through mine. "You okay?" I asked.

"Fine."

I gave her a look, and she sighed. "I'm annoyed with Warren. We do not see eye to eye on Beau. I explained everything I saw, and told him everything I know, and he still thinks it was some kind of misunderstanding. He said he'll talk to Beau and put some sense into him, and I told him he could try, but it wouldn't work."

Fighting a wince, I looked out toward the ocean and the line of fire leading to the setting sun. "I don't blame him. It's hard to see people for who they truly are. Especially if you've known them for a really long time and are loyal. Trust me. I would know."

"But you're my *sister*."

"Which is why I appreciate you backing me up and going to get Hawk."

She laughed. "I didn't go for him specifically. Just skidded into the gym and said something about you needing help. Hawk was the first one to follow. But between you and me, I think they all wanted to. Beau would have shit his pants."

"I've asked them to try to keep things low key. This is all about you. I don't want the drama between me and him to mess up the wedding. But as far as Warren, I'm your sister. But Beau's been his friend far longer than he's known me."

"Yeah, well, without you, Warren would never have met me. He should be grateful."

I slapped a hand over my mouth to stop the laughter and failed completely.

Ellie stared at me. "Why is that funny?"

"It's not. I just... I never thought of it that way. This morning I said to Beau I wished I'd never met him, and it's hard not to feel that way. But I never thought about that. If Beau and I weren't a thing, none of us would be here. You wouldn't be getting married, and I'm not sorry about you getting to meet Warren. It's nice to have something good come out of all the bullshit."

"I could have met him some other way. You don't know that."

"True. Still, Ellie, I'm glad you're with him. You're good for each other."

My sister looked at her future husband and smiled. He saw and immediately smiled back. There was love in those looks, absolutely impossible to hide. "I'm glad too. Even when he pisses me the fuck off."

"Don't punish him too much for loyalty, even if it's misplaced. The only thing we can be sure of is that Beau will show his true colors eventually, and you'll be there to hold Warren together when he does."

We moved another few feet forward in line.

"El, if I ask you something, can you promise to tell me the truth?"

"Ominous, but yeah, of course."

I crossed my arms and kicked the sandy concrete. "Did you know?"

"Did I know what?"

"About Beau? Dad said he tried to tell me that he was bad news and I was so infatuated that I didn't hear him or listen. I'm trying to figure out how blind I really was to all of it." She opened her mouth but I keep going. "It feels like every day I learn just how much I thought was normal, and how much I excused, and how much I convinced myself I was happy. Was I just that poor girl everyone was smiling at and saying 'poor thing' behind my back?"

The horror on her face instantly makes me feel better. "Isolde, *no*. Did I love Beau while you were with him? No. But I didn't think this was who he was. Not at all. The way Warren talked about him, I thought they could have been twins. Later there were some times I thought you could have been happier, but it was your relationship and your business, so I figured you guys were just going through some shit like every couple does.

"But I had no idea. Neither did Mom. At least whenever she was around me. If I'd thought he was this much of a piece of shit during your relationship I would have told you. Hell, I probably would have hired a private investigator to prove it."

Part of the weight lifts off my shoulders. "Thank you. I've been wondering if everyone was just waiting for the other shoe to drop, and I honestly don't know if I could handle that."

Ellie wrapped her arms around me. "You know, I bet Dad knows some hitmen."

"*Ellie.*"

"What? Just because he's a lawyer he can't know shady people? Beau can disappear and no one ever has to know."

I glanced back at all the guys. "Yeah, that's a great idea, after Hawk very publicly threatened him this morning."

"Details."

"Stop," I laughed. "It's enough for him to fuck off. I don't need to kill him."

She sighed. "Fine. I'll settle for castration."

I didn't hate that idea.

"Okay," Warren stepped up beside Ellie and pulled her away from me. "Too much sister time."

Ellie scoffed. "She's been gone a year. There's no such thing as too much sister time." Then she patted his face. "Don't be jealous. You get me for the rest of our lives."

"That's true." He murmured the words against her lips. "I'm fucking lucky, aren't I?"

"Yes, you are."

They started making out. A few hoots and hollers from behind us in the line didn't even make a dent.

"What do you say? Should we give them a run for their money?"

The warm and buttery side of bourbon infused my senses a second before Joel wove his fingers between mine with both his hands, bending down to lean his chin on my shoulder.

I gasped in mock horror. "And risk someone cutting in line because we're not paying attention? Never."

He purred, holding me easily. Not desperately or possessively, like it was a natural thing to have me tucked into his side. Like he wouldn't have it any other way.

"Did you have fun with Rowan?" He asked quietly.

Perfume exploded around me, and he grinned. "I guess that answers my question."

"You haven't told me what yours are."

"My stuff on the list?"

"Mhmm."

Joel tugged me around so I was plastered against him, hands moving to knead my lower back slowly. "I think *almost* everything I like on there can be summed up with 'comfort.'"

I frowned. "I don't remember that being on the list."

"Not directly, no. Things like massages that lead to more. Sleepy sex. Or sex while one of us is sleeping." He winked. "Holding you on my lap, my cock deep inside you, teasing your clit until you shatter all over me, no matter how long it takes. Maybe we'll be watching a movie while we do that."

There wasn't quite enough air in my lungs. "I don't think I'd be paying much attention to the movie."

"No," Joel agreed. "The movie is just an excuse."

He guided me forward. We were getting close to the store now.

"But I like the soft and the comfortable. I like taking care of my Omega. I like taking my time."

"So pretty much the opposite of Vaughn?"

Joel's eyes twinkled. "Pretty much. See? You've got options."

I rolled his words through my head. "Do you have an Omega?"

"No, just you."

"Oh. You said you like taking care of your Omega. You meant me?"

A single finger tilted my chin upward as he dropped a kiss on my lips. That single kiss told me everything I needed to know about what Joel called *comfort*. Slow and easy, but *deep*. There was no less passion in this kiss than ones that were wild and feral. Pure intention that resonated through us. "You're mine," he said, smiling.

He didn't say the unspoken truth—that I was his for now. For this moment. With him looking at me like that? I could almost believe it.

From one breath to the next, I made myself a vow to not care. I was theirs. Just because it was only for a while didn't make it any less true. Why wouldn't I grab the opportunity with both hands?

My cautious mind screamed that grabbing them would be like

holding onto the third rail of a railroad track. Or getting struck by lightning.

The reckless part of me thought *what a way to go.*

I could flip back and forth as many times as I wanted, and it wouldn't change. So why worry? Worry was for the old me. All that worry and caution brought me was heartache and a year in hiding. Maybe this heartbreak would be easier to take if I dove in headfirst and took everything. Felt everything. Experienced everything.

My eyes dropped to Joel's mouth. "I'm yours," I whispered.

So much for not making out in the line. Joel kissed me again, and I couldn't give a shit who saw or who said anything. He gathered me up, drowning me in the spicy sweetness of his scent, marking me with his lips. Staking his claim. Telling me in the most carnal way how he intended to take care of me.

"What's this about sex while sleeping?" I murmured when he pulled away.

"I'm only human," he said mildly. "Sometimes I wake up and can't wait until morning, and my hand isn't enough. Only if you agreed first," he clarified. "But something tells me you might like it."

I narrowed my eyes, which made him laugh. Joel knew damn well I was interested. Because even drunk, reading that fucking list, the idea of waking up in the middle of being fucked was hot. Part of me wondered if it would be easier for me to come if my brain wasn't involved.

"And let me make one thing clear." He lowered his voice, thumb brushing my lower lip. "Just because I *prefer* comfort and ease doesn't mean I can't thoroughly ruin you, Omega."

My heart skipped a beat. Maybe two. Was I still standing upright? Were my eyes open? I couldn't really tell. The surge of arousal and need rendered me incapable of anything but staring at him.

New hands touched my waist. "You'll have to tell me what he said to you to make your scent get even sweeter, princess. I didn't think it was possible." Cade pressed gently against my back, pulling me with him. We were probably ten feet from the front door, the line moving faster now that we were closer.

I cleared my throat. "Don't know what you're talking about."

"That's too bad. Maybe Joel will tell me later."

But Joel shook his head. "A gentleman never arouses and tells."

Rowan clapped Joel on the shoulder. "If you ever become a gentleman, then maybe it will apply."

I realized they were all surrounding me, creating a barrier. "Did I have a wardrobe malfunction?"

Hawk barked a laugh. "What?"

"You're all..." I gestured to their circle.

Cade squeezed my hips. "A small attempt at containing your scent. It's so fucking tempting. We wanted to make it clear you're off limits. And besides, you didn't seem super comfortable with PDA."

They were shielding me. "Thank you."

Ellie watched me from Warren's arms when they broke apart, a knowing smile on her face. All I could do was smile back.

A pack in front of us came out of the small shop, and it was suddenly our turn. The overwhelming scent of sugar and batter infused the air. Not quite as sweet or buttery as Hawk's scent, but delicious.

Vaughn stepped up to the counter first, rubbing his hands together. "I need a vagina waffle and the sweetest, most floral flavor you have."

The woman behind the counter, a Beta who looked like she'd been running a marathon looked at everything in front of her. "Floral? Can't say we have much of that. Sorry. Fruity, yes. Floral, no."

"Fair enough." Vaughn glanced back at me, landing on my hair. "Let's go with raspberries and cream, then." His smirk told me enough. Red for my hair, cream for...

The woman, who wore a name tag that said *Tracy*, drizzled the waffle and handed it over.

Cade ordered blueberries. Rowan went with lemon tart. And I had no idea what I wanted.

I missed Joel and Hawk ordering, trying to decide what I wanted. All their scents were so appealing, but I found my mouth watering for my old favorite. Pineapple jam. It sounded weird as hell, but it was *delicious*. The sharp acidity cut through the sweeter batter Cream Dream used and made it perfect.

"Penis waffle with pineapple jam and the regular frosting."

I watched Tracy drizzle the *very intentionally white* frosting over the treat, desperately trying to keep a straight face since I could practically *feel* them laughing behind me.

We didn't stay in the shop to see Ellie and Warren ordered, instead spilling out onto the beach to wait for them.

"Fuck me." I looked over to find Vaughn face first into the waffle, eating straight out of the middle, the sight hotter than it had any right to be. "It's almost as good as you," he said. "Almost."

"Come here, baby girl." Hawk slung an arm around my chest and pulled me against him before pulling out his phone and pointing the camera at us. "Take a bite of the dick for the camera."

I laughed, color high on my cheeks as I looked at us on the screen. But I did it. Lifting the dick waffle, which was on a stick like a popsicle, I bit into the head of it right as Hawk licked through the center of his. He snapped pictures, and I couldn't stop laughing.

"Cunt waffles are incredible."

"Shh," I swatted his arm. "That's not what they're called. And someone could hear you."

He raised an eyebrow and nodded toward the fence surrounding the property. "No kids in here now, remember? Everyone here knows the word cunt and is thoroughly enjoying their waffles. Cock waffle is just as fun to say."

I stared up at his dark eyes, getting lost in the way he looked at me. What he said the morning I woke up on his chest came back to me. "Still not pretending?"

"I'll never pretend with you, Isolde. Promise." He kissed me, the rich chocolate of his waffle still on his lips. I tried to pull back and he wouldn't let me. "Not finished yet."

Laughter bubbled up through the kiss, making it nearly impossible to continue. He tried anyway, but we both ended up laughing.

"What did you get?" He asked. "I didn't hear."

"Pineapple jam."

"I've never had that."

I held the waffle out to him. "Man enough to take a bite of penis?"

"Bet your ass." Hawk bit into the waffle without hesitation. "That's really good, actually. Maybe my next cunt waffle will be that one."

I fought my smile and took a bite.

The rest of the world filtered in, and I realized Ellie and Warren were already out and eating, my sister looking at me like she didn't know who I was. "What?"

"Nothing." She cut me off before I could pester her. "I'll tell you later."

"You better."

I lost count of the innuendos thrown back and forth by the time the waffles were gone. Everything from taste to the fact that their faces were covered with toppings. Relentless, and my abs hurt from laughing.

True to the bet we made, I opened my own car door on the way there and back. But Joel gave me a hard look as I closed it. "No more."

"Because the world began to collapse when I opened my own door."

"You are perfectly capable of opening your own doors," Cade nodded in agreement. "But here's the real question. Why should you have to?"

I didn't have an answer for him, except for it being 'unnecessary.' If I pulled at that thread, it would go to the core of everything I was dealing with, which was that I didn't feel worthy. Of them, of having a door opened, of anything.

Cade lifted my hand and kissed the back of it. "It's not a bother. It's not an obligation. It's not something we're doing while internally rolling our eyes. If it truly, *truly* makes you uncomfortable, I don't want that. But if it's because you think you're making things easier for us, don't."

"You don't like things easy?" I teased.

But Cade didn't rise to the bait. He stepped into my space and pulled me to him, kissing my forehead with such tenderness it stole my breath. "Of course I do. Everyone loves easy things, princess. But someone who only looks for the easy way out, especially in something as small as this, is never worth your time."

I breathed him in, leaning into his hold, and he smiled into my skin. "Can I say something?"

"Thought you already did."

Soft laughter. "You don't want to let us do this because being taken care of makes you afraid. Letting your guard down means it can happen again. That you'll get hurt, and it will prove everything you already think is true."

My heart stuttered in my chest, like Cade had reached into my chest and pinpointed the heart of me. "Will you give us a chance to change your mind?"

I'd already started to, and with my vow earlier tonight, I had to let them in. I had to give them this chance. "Okay."

"Thank you."

He released me, my body unsure what to do now that he wasn't holding me. I swallowed. My knees were unsteady as I crossed the gravel drive to the house. Ellie waited by the front door, watching. "What were you going to tell me?" I asked.

"I've never seen you like that. That's all I wanted to say."

"Like what?"

Ellie searched my face. "So fucking happy, Iz. I may not have known what a piece of shit Beau was, but I know you're happier with them than you ever were with him. I hope you can feel it."

I glanced over my shoulder at the pack, chatting with Warren and giving the two of us space before they came inside. "I do," I finally said. "I really do."

## CHAPTER TWENTY-FIVE

### HAWK

I smiled at the photos on my phone. They were perfect. The one I'd managed to snap while I kissed Isolde was a photo I was going to keep forever. Once she knew who we were to her—and I refused to believe she wouldn't be with us after—I was having it fucking framed.

Said Omega was sleeping late. The others hadn't objected when I told them I wanted to spend the day with Isolde. Now I just had to see if she wanted to spend it with me. I had a plan, but I would change it in a second if that's what she wanted.

Crawling across the bed, I brushed her hair out of her face, making her stir. "Five more minutes," she mumbled.

"Five more minutes and it will be the afternoon."

Isolde's eyes flew open. "What?"

"Such a sleepy Omega," I teased. "Rowan and sugar wore you out."

"Why didn't anyone get me up?"

I eased myself down beside her. "You didn't even move when we got up, and you didn't have anywhere to be, so we didn't see the harm. You clearly needed it."

She sighed and stretched like a cat, clinging tighter to the pillow she was wrapped around. "I don't remember the last time I slept that well."

Because she felt safe. More than anything, Omegas needed comfort and safety. From what I knew of Isolde so far, she'd spent a long time not having those needs met. It didn't surprise me at all that her body would reclaim some needed rest.

"Where is everyone?"

"Off doing their own thing. I think Vaughn is surfing, Rowan went to check on his plants, Cade had some classes, and if Joel isn't here, he's probably at home doing some nerdy shit."

She smiled. "Nerdy shit?"

"The man loves his video games."

"So you don't?"

I grinned then. "No, I do."

Isolde snuggled closer to me. "And what do you do in your spare time?"

"Music. Well, kind of. You may have seen me before."

She trailed her fingers down my right arm, following the curving movement of the music staff that curled through all the rest of it. Then back up, until she reached the hawk inked across my shoulder, mid-flight. "I've seen you before...?" Her question hung in the air before her eyes went wide. "Wait, are you *that* guy?"

I smirked. "I don't know who you mean."

"I'm very comfortable. Don't make me get my phone to prove it."

"Yes, ma'am. Bossy Omega." I pulled her so our hips were flush, bodies only separated by that fucking pillow. "I am that guy."

"Shut the fuck up."

All I could do was laugh. By 'that guy,' Isolde meant the faceless musician who played electric guitar on social media. Covering popular songs more often than. I did plenty of my own music, but my following didn't know about that. "I never show my face, and even though my tattoos are recognizable, I'm not usually shirtless in public."

"You're so good," she whispered. "You don't want people to know who you are?"

"Eventually, yes."

It had always been the plan to pursue the real thing when we were finished doing this kind of job. Thanks to Isolde, this career was coming to an end earlier than I imagined, and I didn't mind a bit.

"If you've been here with me and nothing's posted, your fans are probably going feral right about now."

I shrugged. "I had some stuff scheduled, but it doesn't bother me either way. I do it for me and not them. It's fun, don't get me wrong, and I'm lucky to have the following I do, but I'm still going to live my life, no matter what anyone else has to say about it."

Isolde suddenly looked shy. "Will you play for me sometime?"

"Anytime you like." I couldn't help but purr. It was a reflex. Having my Omega this close to me made me so happy. *Complete.*

"So," Isolde yawned and stretched. "If they're all doing that, what are you doing here?"

"Hopefully spending the day with you."

"What did you have in mind?"

"Well," I reached out and sank my hand into her hair. I fucking loved her hair. "That depends on you."

"Sounds scary."

"Hopefully not," I chuckled. "You remember when I said I like to watch?"

She hid her face in the pillow. "I think it's going to be very difficult to forget that night, so yes."

"What would you say if I watched you? And after I watched you, we'd have some time alone." I twirled a piece of her hair around my finger, trying very hard not to imagine it wrapped around my cock.

Narrowing her eyes, Isolde studied me. "Watch me do what?"

"I have a photographer friend who's very good at what she does. Boudoir photos. You absolutely don't have to say yes if you're not comfortable with it, but I know for sure I'd enjoy watching you take them."

A little crease appeared between her eyes. "I'm not saying no, necessarily, but what would I do with photos like that?"

"Sometimes the experience is enough. I've been told they can be very empowering. And sometimes you need a reminder of exactly the badass you are."

"So this friend—"

I grabbed the pillow from between us and tossed it away, needing to feel more of her than just her legs. Rolling us, I put us where we'd been a few days ago, with my body pinning hers down. But now she was comfortable with it. Now I could kiss her and she wouldn't run away.

"This friend is just a friend," I said. "We've never slept together. She's taken some fully clothed photos of me before, and that's it."

Isolde's hands fluttered over my shoulders. "So what would the plan be? You watch me take photos and then we come back here?"

"She takes photos of you, and yes, I'll watch. You'll barely know

I'm there. And yes, I will absolutely be touching myself while I watch you. When she's done, she'll fuck off, and then I'll have my way with you right there. Because trust me, baby girl, I will not be able to wait until we get back here."

Her eyes went wide, pupils dilating with arousal. That fucking intoxicating scent of her perfume rose around the two of us. "She's willing to do that?"

"She is. Granted, I didn't give her the full details. But this is Clarity. Guarantee she's done weirder shit."

My Omega snorted a laugh. "Probably right."

Then her eyes dropped to my chest, and the shyness was back. I wanted to fuck it out of her. She didn't have to be shy about anything with us, and I knew it wasn't simply because she was shy. Isolde wasn't. It was that Beau made her question her desires without her even knowing, and it would take a while for her to see that asking for things wasn't wrong.

"Will you take some with me? Or is it weird if everyone isn't there?"

I kissed her, groaning when our lips met. Heaven. She was fucking heaven. "I'll take some with you if you want me to, but I also want it to be about you. Who you are."

"And so you can watch."

"And so I can watch."

She blushed pink. "I'll say yes, but there's one little problem."

"What's that?"

"You've already seen the extent of my sexy clothes. With the exception of that bra Trinity ordered on the day we got here, I don't have anything good for something like this, and I'm not taking pictures naked."

I grinned. "Would you take some naked if I were with you?"

Isolde's teeth sank into her lower lip. That spark of curiosity in her eyes got smothered so quickly. After this wedding was over, I would make sure it never died out. "Maybe."

"Good," I whispered. "I want to feel you naked against me again. And for the rest of it? Not a problem."

Rolling off her, I helped her to the edge of the bed. "How? I don't think I'm ready to wear communal lingerie if your friend has some she uses."

My laugh echoed off the walls of the suite, and I tucked her head under my chin. "No communal lingerie, baby girl. We'll just have to add a stop on the way to the studio. Now get dressed. Since you said yes, we need to get going. I'll meet you at the front door in ten minutes."

She stared at me, mouth open like she wasn't sure if she should protest or not. I smirked. "Keep your mouth open, baby girl, and I'll find a good use for it."

No pink this time. A furious red blush crawled over her face and neck, her mouth closing with a nearly audible snap.

I had to hold back my laughter as she ran to the closet.

## CHAPTER TWENTY-SIX

ISOLDE

I couldn't believe I was doing this.

Hawk's hand rested on my thigh while he drove. The back seat of their SUV was filled with *way too many* bags, each one with pale pink tissue paper sticking out of it.

*Cheria* had every piece of lingerie you could imagine, and I was halfway convinced we'd bought one of each. I'd told Hawk he didn't have to, but once he begged the sales woman for my sizes, he was like an unleashed tornado.

I pulled out my phone to calm my nerves about actually taking pictures like this, and texted Trinity first.

ISOLDE

Hey. You alive? Haven't heard from you since you disappeared.

A picture came through almost immediately. Trinity with her blonde hair in a messy bun, hair flying in every direction, and a silly expression on her face.

TRINITY

Proof of life! And yeah, sorry. Things have been crazy. The emergency was that somebody at the office died. A freak car accident. Thing is, they were one of our biggest people, so everyone's been scrambling to pick up the slack and make sure that stories don't get dropped in the middle. It's a mess.

I kind of got promoted though? Like not really, but I get to do some of these stories, and they're a bit more serious.

Damn. Trinity loved her job, reporting on the society scene in Clarity Coast and Sunset City, but she still wanted to do more. Sure, her profiles on people like the St. James pack were well received—I still had to ask them about that interview—and she had fun doing them.

It was the occasional boozy girl's night where she confessed she wanted a bit more substance. Not to leave the fun, glitzy part of the job behind, but expand it. She had killer interview skills. Why not use them to do stories on celebrities and society *and* the heavy hitters?

I hoped this would be that chance.

ISOLDE

That's great! I mean, not that someone died, but that you'll have the chance to do something more. If you need help or anything, let me know.

TRINITY

If I need a rescue from my own brain you'll be the first person I call.

Then I texted the thread with all three of us.

ISOLDE

I agreed to do something, and it might be a terrible idea.

OCEAN

Considering your last 'terrible idea' has turned out great so far, I'm going to withhold judgment until I hear it.

TRINITY

Yeah. What did you do? If it involves any of the handsome Alphas you're currently sharing a bed with, I doubt it's bad.

ISOLDE

One of them talked me into doing a boudoir photoshoot.

Talking me into it was a little generous. Hawk hadn't had to do much convincing once he told me exactly what he was thinking. But it was still nothing I would have come up with alone.

TRINITY

Holy FUCKING SHIT.

That's not a bad idea, that's incredible! I will need to see the photos immediately.

ISOLDE

Slow down, cowgirl. I actually have to take them first.

TRINITY

Details.

OCEAN

I'm with Rin in that I don't think it's a bad idea, but oh my god I cannot imagine doing that. I never could!

Trinity's text and mine came through at the exact same time.

TRINITY

Bullshit.

ISOLDE

Bullshit.

OCEAN

It is not bullshit. I barely want to take my clothes off, let alone take them off in front of a camera. Besides, this isn't about me. When are you doing this, Iz?

ISOLDE

We're on our way now. The man took me to Cheria and basically bought out the store.

TRINITY

Who is it?

ISOLDE

Hawk.

TRINITY

That Alpha is sex on a stick. Put your phone down and focus, Iz. We'll be waiting for an update later.

OCEAN

Have fun! 😘

Hawk squeezed my thigh. "You okay over there?"

"Yeah."

He chuckled, moving his hand to hold mine. "Very convincing."

"I have no idea how to take pictures, let alone take them in clothes that make me blush by just trying them on."

"That's one of the things people love about Janet. She has this way of making people comfortable even if they've never been in front of the camera before. I'll be there the whole time."

"Even if I can't see you?"

One glance at me and he smirked. "Especially then."

We pulled up to an unassuming building, and Hawk parked. I barely stopped myself from hopping out of the SUV, remembering the promise I made Cade. I waited until Hawk circled the car and opened the door for me.

His grin was blinding. "She can learn."

"Don't push it."

"Oh, I will push it, baby girl. Into you. Very soon. Go on in. I'll grab the bags."

My stomach was a jumble of nerves. Here went nothing.

As soon as I walked in the door, I stopped. The space was nothing like it looked from the outside. A cozy front area opened up into a bright, airy space where there were sets in different places. A wrought-iron bed, a bathtub, a window with floaty curtains, some pillows and blankets that looked very much like a nest.

"You must be Isolde." A woman sat behind the small front desk, dark hair, dark skin, and glasses. The scent of tangerines reached me. She was an Alpha, smiling at me. "Yeah, that's me."

She stood and came around. "It's great to meet you. Hawk seems absolutely taken with you."

"He's outside bringing in way too many bags of lingerie. Seriously. There's no way in hell we'll be able to use it all."

Janet laughed and gestured to the back. "Sounds like Hawk. We'll get you started on makeup and hair, and then we can decide on outfits. Ever done anything like this before?"

"Nope." I shook my head. "Not going to pretend I'm not nervous, either."

"Don't worry, that's totally normal." A brightly lit make-up station sat in a little hallway near the bathroom, with two more women. "This is Erin and Monica. They're my Beta and Omega, and they're going to take care of you."

The way she looked at them made me stop short. Janet looked at the two women the way the St. James pack looked at me. "It's nice to meet you."

I extended my hand and Erin took it. "Oh my god I love working with redheads. You're going to look so good when I'm done with you, none of your pack will be able to resist."

A laugh caught in my throat. "Some of them already have that problem."

"All of them," Hawk's voice echoed from the main entry. "We all have that problem. Janet, you want to take a look at this buffet to see what you can work with?"

Janet rolled her eyes, clearly amused. Then she leaned closer and put her hand on my shoulder. "Trust me when I say that the Alphas who go a little overboard always end up with the best photoshoots. You can be nervous, but we're going to make you look incredible." She strode away, and I heard her talking. "You really did bring the whole store with you, huh?"

Monica began brushing through my hair, and Erin stared at me. "Do I have something on my face?"

"Not yet. I'm deciding which way I want to go with you. Do you want something to drink? We've got tea, water, and soda. I think there's some lemonade in the fridge. Or I could—"

"Tea would be great," I said with a laugh, their earnestness breaking through the nerves. "Thank you."

"I'm thinking big waves and volume." Monica pushed her

fingers up through my hair, simulating the size. "Kind of old-school glamor. With this color it could be great. What do you think?"

I nodded. "Yeah, I love that. Good luck though. My hair hates curls. If you can get them to stick, you'll be a miracle worker." Even Ronnie hadn't gotten curls to stay for my parents' party. The blowout was incredible, but my hair loved to be straight.

She smirked. "That's exactly what I am."

Erin appeared with the tea, and they both went to work, chatting away. In the other room I heard the crinkle of tissue paper and low conversation as Janet and Hawk decided my wardrobe.

"Do you guys ever work with plus size clients?"

"Fuck yes we do," Monica said. "All the time. They're some of my favorites."

I smiled. "One of my best friends said she could never do this. Granted, I didn't think I could either, but if I can, I'd love for her to try it."

"We love our plus size girls," Janet said, appearing with Hawk. "If you can get her here, we'll make sure she has a good time."

"Noted."

Hawk crouched by my chair, taking my hand. The girls suddenly gave us some space. "How you doing, baby girl?"

"Better. I don't feel as nervous."

"Good. I'm not going to kiss you yet so I don't ruin your make-up." He kissed my temple instead. "That will come later."

The nerves in my stomach weren't from fear now, but anticipation.

"Fuck, Isolde, you can't perfume like that if you want me to last the whole shoot."

I raised an eyebrow. "This was your idea, *Alpha*. Keep it in your pants."

A low growl that went straight to my core. "Naughty Omega, calling me Alpha in that tone."

"You don't like it?"

"No, I like it far, far too much."

The girls finished my makeup—dewy skin with shimmering gold around my eyes—and my hair stayed in giant rollers that made me look like some horrific combination of a satellite and a flower.

"What do you think of these?" Janet asked.

Lingerie was laid out on the bed. Some I'd seen at the store, some I hadn't. All of it was beautiful, and pretty much all of it was nothing I'd ever worn before.

A gorgeous, sheer, emerald baby doll dress with matching underwear. Something that was vaguely bodysuit shaped with sapphire blue straps which would cover the important bits. A shimmering golden robe over a black bra and underwear set, which I had chosen. And finally, a black and silver corset. It didn't look like anything was paired with it.

Hawk wrapped me in his favorite pose, being careful not to disturb the curlers. "I think they're beautiful."

I smacked his hand around my waist. "Of course you do. You chose them." Then I turned around and looked up at him, whispering. "What am I supposed to do with all the rest of it? I know this isn't even close to the amount you bought."

"You keep it," he said. "You wear it. Hopefully for us. And I tear some of it off you with my teeth."

"That's too much, Hawk."

"No. It isn't." He turned me around. "Do you like them?"

"A couple are more... daring than I'd pick, but I'm willing to try."

Janet grinned. "Perfect. Rank them from the most comfortable to the least. We'll do that one last."

"Wouldn't it make sense to get it out of the way first?"

"Actually," she crossed the room and picked up her camera, glancing through the viewfinder. "The last photos of a session are nearly always the best because you learn what to do and you become more comfortable. If I put you in an outfit you're nervous about when you're already nervous, it will feel worse."

That made a lot of sense.

I ranked them. The robe first, the strappy thing last. "Where will you be?" I asked Hawk in a breathless whisper. "You really are going to watch, right? You're not going to take a coffee break?"

"I'm not going to take my eyes off you, baby girl. I'll even start where you can see me. But this is about you. Owning what a fucking stunning Omega you are."

I didn't tell him I only felt that way when they looked at me. Maybe this would help.

Erin gestured me over, and they helped me dress. The cool professionalism in their behavior made being in things I would only ever wear in my bedroom less awkward.

When Monica let my hair down into the huge, curling waves, my jaw dropped. "I didn't know my hair could look like that," I admitted.

"I'll text you all the products I used if you want to know."

"Yes, please."

The gold dress and black underwear were first, and oh god, it was just as awkward as I was afraid of. Monica and Erin disappeared, and Hawk stayed across the room, watching. I felt his eyes on me.

Janet took me over to one of the walls where a big, gilded mirror leaned against it. "I'm going to direct you how to pose for the first bit, okay? So you can get a feel for it."

"Oh my god, yes please."

"It's going to feel weird, but I'll show you the pictures so you can see I'm not blowing smoke up your ass."

I laughed, but I appreciated it.

She had me lie on the floor with my feet on the wall. The golden robe pooled around me, and Janet had me arch my back with my arms in different positions. She was right. It felt weird, and more than a little uncomfortable.

"Look this way?"

Looking toward the camera, my eyes caught on Hawk. He stood with his arms crossed, which made his tattooed biceps bulge in a way that was entirely distracting. But more than that, his eyes consumed me with *heat*. They traced down the arch of my back and all the way to my pointed toes and back to my face.

His eyes were already dark, but now, the way they burned, they seemed entirely black. I hadn't really understood why he liked watching, not to judge, but it had never done anything for me. But *being* watched like *that*?

Holy shit. It felt like sunlight pouring directly into my veins. So much easier to arch my back a little higher, lean into the pose, and keep my eyes on him.

"There it is. That's perfect," Janet said, snapping pictures. I barely heard her. My whole being was still held captive in Hawk's fiery gaze.

His face, so intense it nearly looked angry, barely changed. One little corner of his mouth sliding upward in a hint of a smile. It was really good I owned this lingerie, because with that smile, all of it would be ruined. I might have a hard time getting all the way there, but arousal wasn't a problem, and Hawk had me riled with a *look*.

Fuck me.

"Here." Janet came and sat cross-legged beside me, breaking the spell. "See?"

She turned the screen toward me, and all I could do was stare.

The woman on the camera couldn't possibly be me. She was... stunning. Voluptuous and sexy and confident. It was like splitting my brain in two, knowing I was the only one who she'd taken photos of, and still not being able to accept that the pictures were of me.

Janet laughed at my stunned silence. "Worth the discomfort?"

"Yeah. I'll say. But that's not me."

"That is you. It's all you. Want to see, Hawk?"

He still watched me, and had barely moved. "I promised Isolde I wouldn't take my eyes off her. Isn't that right, baby girl?"

Was there still oxygen in the room? I wasn't sure. "Yeah." My voice sounded like I'd run a hundred miles.

Hawk smirked. "Then I'll see the pictures later."

"Let's do some more by the mirror, but I've got some other poses I want to try."

"Okay," I straightened, finally believing I could do this. "Show me where you want me."

## CHAPTER TWENTY-SEVEN

### ISOLDE

I'd never taken so many pictures in my life.

Janet was absolutely right, the more we took, the easier it was, and by the time I was posing in the next outfit and on the bed with nothing but blue velvet ribbons covering me—barely—I was laughing and having a great time.

Somewhere in the middle, Hawk disappeared. Not entirely. I could still feel his eyes on me. It could have felt strange or creepy with anyone else. With him, it didn't. It felt like a whole new type of freedom. I was doing this for myself, and he gave me space to enjoy it while he enjoyed it too.

"Okay," Janet finally said. "Only one thing left to do, if you still want to take some pictures with Hawk."

"Yes. I do."

He appeared again from around a corner I'd barely noticed was there. "One condition, baby girl. You already know what it is."

I sighed and smiled at Janet. "He wants me to take everything off. Is that going to be weird?"

"Nope." She wasn't even looking at me, flipping through the last set of photos we took. "That's fine. Hawk, start in underwear and we'll progress from there. Isolde, sit on the end of the bed when you're finished undressing."

Hawk stripped out of his shirt. In the gentle light of the studio he already looked like a photo. A photo that I was allowed to touch. "You're staring."

I blushed and looked away only to find him in front of me making sure I *couldn't* look away. "I never said it was a bad thing."

So I still stared while he stripped out of his pants, suddenly remembering I was supposed to be naked too. I untangled myself from the gorgeous death trap of lingerie I was wearing and tossed it aside so the camera wouldn't catch it. I wasn't brave enough to just walk across the space fully naked.

"Sit," Janet said to him. "Isolde, kind of curl yourself around him from behind."

I did as she asked, and Hawk grabbed my legs, leaning back to look up at me. "Hi there."

"Hi." I couldn't stop the smile on my face. This was fun. He'd been right, and in spite of my nerves, I felt light. Happy.

We took pictures as we kissed, with my hands draping down his chest as I leaned over him. And when there were enough of those, we were on the bed and Hawk lost the clothes entirely.

"Although I really want you to fuck me," I whispered, "I want us to be alone for that."

"Don't worry." Hawk breathed the words against my cheek before nuzzling his head into my own. "No actual pictures of me fucking my perfect Omega."

I whined, barely noticing Janet. Hawk was the one moving us per her instructions. Even when she climbed on a ladder to take pictures from above, I felt like I was in a trance. Sweetness and cream. Frosting and sugar. I wanted to drown in his scent. Drown in him.

"You guys are great," Janet said with a laugh. "I'll have the pictures for you guys in a week or so."

It drew me out of my haze just enough. "We're done?"

"You're done. Stay put for a second and I'll get out of your hair. Hawk, you owe me one for this, and don't leave unless you're ready. The door's gonna lock behind you."

"Will do," he said.

"And change the sheets," she called over her shoulder.

My Alpha burst out laughing, but I couldn't. He was so close, and I hadn't had enough.

As soon as the door closed his mouth was on mine, rough and claiming. He growled, finding my hands and pinning them to the bed. "Do you have any idea how hard I've been for the last three hours?"

"It's been three hours?"

"Every fucking second. Delicious torture, watching you seduce that camera in lingerie I picked for you."

I'd been so wrapped up in his scent and the weight of his body on mine I'd hardly noticed the length of him pressed against me.

But I did now. And it felt different from when it was pressed against my back. Hawk raised himself far enough to shove my legs apart, and I saw him. A thick metal stud came through the head, glinting in the soft light. "You're pierced," I murmured.

"I am. Have you ever felt one?"

I shook my head.

"I think you and this piercing are going to be good friends, baby girl." He reached between us and dragged his thumb slowly over my clit, showing me how wet I was—how aroused and ready after hours being watched by him and bathing in his attention. Like the longest foreplay in the history of the world.

"Why?"

Hawk didn't answer with words. Only lined himself up with my body and entered me with one long, delicious thrust. Deep inside me, pleasure tingled, like his cock had found a secret button to push and make me moan.

"That's why," he finally said.

Every movement of his hips gave me more of that feeling, and it clicked in my horny, hazy mind. His piercing was the source of that pleasure. Tiny fireworks exploded behind my eyes. Sparks that spread.

"I—" My whole body shook. An orgasm approached. Probably the fastest I'd ever come in my life, if you didn't count the three hour edging session we'd just had.

"I see those thoughts in there," Hawk's voice teetered on the edge of an Alpha bark. "Don't think yourself out of pleasure, baby girl. Close your eyes and hold on to me. Nothing else, understand?"

There was no chance to respond. I wrapped my arms around his neck just in time.

Hawk fucked me. No other words. Ruthless and raw, pushing us both into the bed until the headboard slammed against the wall, marking the rising pleasure like a beating drum.

It came so fast I gasped, one second rising, the next second crashing over me so quickly I was no longer in control of myself. My body arched. My limbs shook. My voice came out ragged, begging for more, and he gave it to me.

Hawk gave me absolutely everything.

I was long past the orgasm, slipping down into the bliss of still feeling him, aftershocks shimmering in my bones, when he slid home and locked us together. I swore light flashed behind my eyes.

Hearing his moan nearly made me come all over again. "Just a little deeper. Even with my knot, you can take more." And he did press harder, deeper, knot bumping up against every piece of me that needed it. "You did so good."

For a minute we simply breathed each other in, his forehead resting against mine. Then he laughed softly. "The only thing I wish I'd done differently is eat your pussy first. I still haven't tasted you, and I'm jealous."

That made me smile. "It didn't seem like you could wait."

"I definitely, definitely couldn't. Not after seeing you in all those positions and poses. There wasn't a single one I don't want to fuck you in."

"I think you'll have to wait," I breathed, slowly wrapping my legs around his hips. "I can barely move right now, let alone do that again."

Smiling, he kissed me, deepening the way our lips met until he had me questioning my own statement. "We're going to work on that."

"In what way?"

"You're going to need more orgasm stamina for all the things we want to do to you, baby girl."

I rolled my eyes but pulled him closer, savoring the feeling of his weight on me. "I can barely get there as it is."

"Contrary to popular belief, orgasming is a skill, and you need practice. Maybe it will always be a little harder for you than someone else, but I'm guessing with some practice and some Alphas who are willing to practice *thoroughly and often*, it will get easier." His nose brushed mine. "If you want that, of course."

How could I say no to that? I didn't think there was anyone in the world who would say no to more orgasms. "Guess I'll need to practice a lot before the wedding."

Hawk nodded slowly, but he didn't seem thrilled by that statement. "Yeah. Before the wedding."

I chose not to focus on the idea that my lack of orgasms could be because Beau hadn't cared enough to really try. I'd come, but not nearly every time. Nope. Not thinking about that when I was fully blissed out.

A different question popped into my head. "When we first met, I asked you why people call you Hawk. Is there a reason the story couldn't be told right then?"

Chuckling, he pulled us onto our sides, my leg draped wantonly over his hip while his knot still stretched me full. "No. We just didn't want to linger in the airport. I did some falconry when I was a kid."

"Then why isn't your nickname 'falcon?'"

His large hand stroked over my hair, my whole body leaning into the touch like I was a cat lounging in the sun. "I worked with a hawk. People just call the training of birds of prey, in general, falconry now. But I quickly got the nickname 'hawk boy,' in school because I spent so much time doing it, and you know kids. They go for the easy nicknames. In high school I embraced it, dropped the 'boy,' and it stuck."

The soft ambient light of the studio revealed the truth of Hawk's eyes. As dark as they looked, they weren't black. Instead, they were the deepest of browns when you could really see them. I reached out and traced the lines of his face, marveling at them.

Was I sex drunk? I felt so relaxed and easy. It wasn't normal.

"Do you still do it?"

"No." He shook his head, taking my hand and moving it to his shoulder. "When my hawk passed, I didn't think I could raise another one. I still have him here, though."

The incredible tattoo of a bird in flight. I stroked the feathers on the wing, so lifelike I could almost feel them. "What was his name?"

"Signet."

"That's beautiful."

"Kind of like you."

Every Omega instinct I had came to life. I pressed closer. Buried my face in his neck. Clung to Hawk like he was the only thing rooting me to the earth. And he held me back just as fiercely.

His strong arms locked around me, Hawk murmuring softly in my ear. He called me baby girl. He told me what a good Omega I was. How beautiful I was.

My eyes closed, the aftermath of pleasure and the overwhelm of everything else making me tired enough to drift with him. Nothing bad would happen while I was here with Hawk. Nothing bad.

Nothing bad.

Nothing bad.

## CHAPTER TWENTY-EIGHT

### ISOLDE

The screeching of my phone jerked me awake. I felt like I was hungover the way my head spun, but it was light out, Alpha bodies were spread out around me, and that ungodly sound was still going.

Why the hell did I ever pick that ringtone?

Oh, right, because it was the only thing I could use to actually get myself out of bed on days when I had both late and early shifts at the bar. I needed to change it, because it was *awful*.

Joel rolled over and grabbed the phone from where it was plugged in at the edge of the bed. "It's Trinity."

I crawled over to him and took the phone, seeing it was still seven in the morning. Joel pulled me onto his bare chest while I answered. "You better have a damn good reason for calling me this early," I growled as much as an Omega could.

"Shit. I'm sorry. I didn't realize how early it was. Should I call back?"

"I'm already here. What's up? And have you slept?"

"Have I slept... a little? Probably not as much as is advisable, but who really gets the amount of sleep they need?"

"Rin." I dropped my head onto Joel's chest in exasperation. He rubbed his hands up and down my body. My clothes had disappeared last night, so we were skin on skin.

"You can lecture me later. First, I'm going a little insane and need a fucking break, and since you haven't been here in forever, I thought maybe we could revive ballgown bowling. Ocean's already in."

"Did you wake her up too?"

I could almost see her scowling through the phone. "Listen, you can't be this grumpy when you're waking up in the middle of sheer Alpha hotness, okay?"

"I beg to differ."

"Do you want to go bowling?"

We hadn't done that in years. Dressed up in ridiculous, cheap dresses, go to the bowling alley, and not give a shit about what anyone else thought. "I don't have a dress."

"Don't worry, I've got one for you. When I knew you were coming back I went to the thrift store and bought us all one for like five dollars each. So we don't have to keep them nice, and they're ridiculous in the best way."

"What time?"

"Seven? I'll come over at six to get ready. I still need to dig myself out from a bunch of work and I've got a deadline today, otherwise I'd come earlier."

I laughed. "Okay. I'm going back to sleep now."

"Sleep. Right."

"*Actual* sleep, Rin."

Her words were a sing-song. "Love you too."

The phone dropped onto the bed, call ended. I snuggled into my Alpha pillow and closed my eyes.

"What was that?"

"I'll tell you when I'm actually awake and not fake awake."

"You're faking it?"

"Yup."

Joel laughed softly and turned me so I was the little spoon, fully curling his large body against mine. I had no idea why I was so tired, but there was no way to fight it, and I sank into sleep again.

"Ball gown bowling sounds fun," Vaughn said. "Not this time because it's a girl's night, but I think suited up bowling would be fun too."

Them in suits was a sight I'd never get tired of, so yes. Absolutely.

"We did it after one of the dances in school and it became a tradition. But we haven't done it in years."

Yesterday, when I roused from my sex-induced nap in the photo studio, Hawk bundled me up into my clothes and took care of everything else. Cleaning up, loading all the rest of the *Cheria* bags, and throwing the sheets we'd used in the wash before bringing me home.

It hadn't felt like I used a lot of energy while I was in the middle of the shoot, but being looked at and posing so much took it out of me. There were sore places from the poses Janet had me hold.

Absolutely worth it.

I couldn't wait to see the pictures.

But last night we did nothing. Watched a movie with Ellie and Warren, and I'd fallen asleep in the middle of it, and apparently slept blissfully until Trinity's call this morning.

"Anyway, the dresses are from thrift stores so we don't feel bad if they get dirty or caught in the ball return and ripped."

"I'm glad you don't want to return our balls," Rowan said with a wink.

"Who says I don't?"

Cade laughed and crossed the room to me. "The way you're blushing." He caught me and kissed me soundly. "And I know I speak for everyone when I say we're *all* excited to see those pictures."

"It would have been fun with all of you."

"Maybe someday Janet will agree to doing one with all of us."

I smiled, a pulse of sadness moving through me. "Maybe."

A few minutes later my phone buzzed, Ocean and Trinity came in, and once again we were swept away into the closet. No real hair or makeup this time, just us.

I laughed when she pulled my dress out of the bag. "What on *earth* is that?"

"Glorious is what it is."

"Rin, I'm a *redhead*. I can't wear that!" The dress was a sunset orange. A shimmering layer covered it, making the fabric shift between yellow, orange, and flashes of purple. The neckline fell off the shoulders, with short, puffed sleeves straight out of a vintage movie. It wasn't awful, and the fabric was really pretty. If you didn't have red hair. I would look like one solid lump of color.

Laughing, Ocean pulled her dress out of the bag, making a face. "I think that's the point."

"We never went out of our way to look bad," I said.

Trinity snorted. "Like you could make anything look bad. I don't care what color your hair is, that's going to look stunning on you. Now put it on. We've got to get moving."

I raised an eyebrow. "In a hurry?"

"I wish I wasn't," she admitted. "But I uhh... sort of got promoted? Again?"

Ocean and I both looked at her. "What? When?"

"Why didn't you tell us?"

She stepped into her dress, which was an outrageous neon green satin with gold sequins. Probably a cast-off from one of the hundreds of movies that came down to Clarity to film. Private beaches were perfect to film on since there were no tourists, and the people who owned them had no problem taking the studios' money for practically no work. "Well, when Tracy got in the accident, she was working on a lot of stuff. Not only that, she was the features editor. They weren't going to fill the position, but it was obvious really fast that wasn't going to work. Evan read some of the stuff I was finishing up for her and gave it to me. I found out day before yesterday and I've barely come up for air."

My mouth dropped open as she ran out of steam. "Holy shit, that's amazing. Not that Tracy died, but that they gave it to you. Isn't that what you've wanted?"

"Yeah." She's quiet. "I mean, eventually. I thought I'd have time to write features without being put in charge of an entire department first, but yes."

I looked over at Ocean, and her face clearly shared my worry. "We don't have to go out tonight, Rin. If you need to catch up, that's totally fine. I'd like you to, you know, *sleep* at some point, but I don't want you to stress more."

"No." She shook her head. "Please. I can't stare at words for another second or I'm going to go mad. I want to do this. I just can't spend all night doing it."

"All right," Ocean said. "But just so you know, just cause you're a big time writer now doesn't mean we're taking it easy on you."

Trinity scoffed. "I don't need you to take it easy."

Ocean's dress was a sparkling white with one shoulder bare. I caught the hesitation in her eyes when she saw it, but honestly, of the three of us? The dress was something she could wear and pull off. "You look hot."

She rolled her eyes.

"I am one-hundred percent entirely serious. There are Alphas who would lose their shit over the way your ass looks in that dress."

"Thank you."

The words were soft, so I put a hand on her shoulder. "Are you okay? The other day—"

"I'm okay." A smile that didn't match her eyes. "Well, I'm not, but I also don't really want to talk about it. Let's go have fun bowling."

"If you need me, I'm here."

This time her smile actually reached her eyes. "I know."

I pulled on the dress and groaned when I saw the shoes. Gold heels that were just as tacky. If not more so. Colored jewels glued on the fake leather, like a craft store threw up on them. "I never thought I'd say I was *happy* to put on bowling shoes."

"You're welcome, Rin. Thank you so much for buying me shoes," Trinity said with a smirk, turning back from the mirror.

"I can't believe you're going to make me walk out there in front of them like this."

"You look hot," Ocean said. "Really. Besides, I don't think you could put anything on that would change the way they look at you."

"Because none of it's real," I muttered.

Rin snorted. "I'm calling bullshit so hard it's not even funny."

I glanced back toward the closet doors, like I could tell if they were pressed up against the other side listening, or that our voices would carry. "I'm paying them to be here. It was *your idea*."

"Yeah," she said. "But I had to interview them a lot for that piece. We talked about everything under the sun. They told me if they were going to let someone into their anonymous bubble, it needed to be raw and honest and not just paint them as cookie cutter people."

She wasn't wrong. The huge feature—which had ended up on the front page of her magazine—was incredible. It was the reason she'd convinced me to call them in the first place, despite her giving me their phone number breaking her NDA and possibly endangering her job. She'd painted them as polite, commanding, and intelligent. Caring and not simply men who would fuck you for money.

They were every one of those things.

But it didn't change the fact that we had an arrangement, and we were hurtling toward the expiration date, no matter if I wished we weren't.

"Meeting them and talking with them was the reason I knew

they'd be good for you. Because I'm telling you, when they talked about their clients, they spoke with polite distance. The way you speak about acquaintances or those 'friends' from work who you know but you'd never see in any other situation. When they spoke about them, not *once* did they look they way they do when they look at you."

"But—" I put my hands on my hips and leaned over, taking a breath because my chest felt fucking tight. "You didn't see them *with* a client. Maybe this..." I couldn't bring myself to say the words out loud. That maybe they were like this with everybody, because the idea *hurt*.

"Or maybe they want you, and you're letting Beau get in the way because you're scared of a repeat," Ocean said.

I glared at her, and she glared right back. I hated that she wasn't wrong. I was terrified of getting hurt again. Because as much as Beau's actions did hurt me, I already knew the St. James pack doing the same would destroy me in a way I would not recover from. So I had to keep my distance.

Had to.

A soft knock on the closet door saved me. I pulled it open and found Rowan staring down at me. His eyes followed the lines of the dress, and he smiled. "Your car is here."

"Thank you."

I made sure the girls were decent before I let the door fall the rest of the way open.

They grinned at me as I stepped out. "I know. It's something."

"I love it," Vaughn said. "You're like a shiny present for me to unwrap."

A flush stained my cheeks, and Ocean nudged me with her elbow like she was saying *I told you so.*

"Are you sure you don't want one of us to drive you?" Cade asked.

Trinity waved a hand. "The car's already here. We'll be fine." She looped her arms through both Ocean's and mine, any tension from the closet forgotten. "Now let's go bowl like absolute shit."

We laughed as she pulled us out of the room, but I couldn't help but notice every one of the Alpha's eyes remained on me until we were out of sight.

## CHAPTER TWENTY-NINE

ROWAN

The three Omegas left the room, and I shook my head with a smile. The dresses together were horrendous, but in a good way. Joel laughed quietly.

"If Trinity breaking her NDA hadn't brought us to Isolde, I would be pissed at her."

Me too.

The interview we did with the Omega reporter had business knocking down our door the last few months, but through our website. Where we were still anonymous. People didn't get our private number unless they knew us, or after they signed an NDA. I'd never been so glad someone broke their word—risking both their reputation and career. Would we ever have met Isolde otherwise? Unlikely. The thought made my heart hurt.

Vaughn put a hand on my shoulder and nodded toward the Veranda. I followed him. "What's up?"

"Willing to help me with something?"

"For the last time, I'm not going to help you bury a body," I said with a grin.

He snorted. "Funny."

"What is it?"

"The dress Isolde has on is cheap on purpose. So it can get messed up." I saw the gleam in his eye.

"You want to do the chase?"

"I'd like to try."

"What do you need?"

"Why only Rowan?" Hawk asked, leaning in the doorway. "I'd like to help Isolde have some fun."

Vaughn raised an eyebrow. "Are you all listening?"

"Obviously." Joel was the next one out the door. Vaughn winced. "Sorry. I just know it's not your thing."

Early on in our pack life, Joel had misunderstood Vaughn's interest in primal play for something darker. He'd walked in halfway through the conversation, and his Alpha reacted first. One black eye and a lot of apologies later, things had been fine. But Vaughn still tried to be subtle about it.

I knew it ate Joel up that he'd made that kind of mark on one of his packmates, but I was hopeful Vaughn would realize how sorry he was. Joel went straight to him, palming the back of his neck, faces close. The signal. We chose it a long time ago as the way for the others to know we weren't fucking around.

"I'll apologize as many times as you need me to. I'm the one who fucked up. There is nothing wrong with you or what you enjoy, and it's my biggest regret that I ever made you doubt it. Please don't hide."

Vaughn nodded, the tension in his shoulders easing. We hadn't had to address anything like this in a while, but we were human. We all had insecurities and fears, and while we were in such a tenuous place trying to figure things out with Isolde, it made sense that they would be at the surface.

"Besides, this is perfect. You promised Isolde you'd chase her, and I promised her I'd show her my brand of comfort. You'll do this tonight, and I'll do the rest tomorrow.

"Now," Joel stepped back. "How can we help?"

"I was thinking about using the beach past the cliff, and the caves. Low tide has almost perfect timing tonight. She has a safe word, and I'll make sure she remembers it, but I need help getting her there, preferably without tipping her off, and I need to make sure no one gets curious or decides they need a nighttime stroll on the beach in that direction."

Hawk chuckled. "Yeah. Wouldn't want Ellie and Warren getting in the middle of that."

A snarl grew in my chest. "Or Beau."

Vaughn's face went flat. "Is he back?"

"Not as for as I know, but fuckers like him tend to come out of the woodwork at the worst time."

"I'd like that," Hawk said, smile turning sharp. "Will give me an excuse to finish what he started last time."

"If he does show up, let's try not to get ourselves kicked out before the wedding," I said.

Cade smirks. "Something tells me no one would complain if *he* were the one kicked out."

"Isolde knows this is coming?" Joel asked.

"She knows it's coming. I asked her if she wanted to plan it out or just take her, and she asked for the latter. But I'll make sure she knows it's me before anything happens. But if any of you tell her to go meet me, I think it will tip her off."

I leaned back against one of the pillars. "I've got an idea for that. But I can help head off anyone coming from the house. Linger on the lawn or something."

Cade nodded and stepped forward. "I'll stay closer and within hearing distance in case you need me or in case something doesn't go to plan." He chuckled. "Not like I have rut to worry about."

"Thank you."

"It's getting harder not to just tell her," Hawk said. "Yesterday I mentioned having Alphas willing to practice..." He shook his head. "She made a point of saying we need to do things before the wedding. We need to tell her soon. I don't think I can make it all the way to the wedding without her knowing she's ours."

I nodded. "I agree. And I do think she's more open to it."

"The day after tomorrow. After the Bachelor and Bachelorette parties," Vaughn said quietly. "That leaves enough time before the wedding for us to leave if she wants us to, and not disrupt things. And it gives us a few more days to show her."

Show her how deep in we already were. Because we *were*. Isolde felt like a spot of sunlight. She lit things up wherever she went and made them more beautiful. Even when she struggled, she was so open, her Omega desperate to give her vulnerability to someone who would cherish it. Those moments in the library with her would stay with me forever.

Hawk ran a hand through his hair. "*How* do we tell her?"

"I think that's a problem for a different day," I said. "Because I need to think about it."

Joel nodded. “I agree.”

Looking at me, Vaughn raised his eyebrows. “You said you had an idea about how to get Isolde to the beach?”

“Yeah. And the first step is making sure she can’t find any of us when she gets back.”

## CHAPTER THIRTY

ISOLDE

My horrifying, sparkly shoes hung from the tips of my fingers as I walked back to the suite. The few hours we'd spent bowling were fun, but I was ready to take off this shining monstrosity and curl up with the guys.

My guys.

For however long I had them. I wanted them to peel me out of this dress, because they made me feel beautiful in anything, even when I wore nothing.

The house was quiet the way it used to be when I lived here because there were so few people here in the evening.

Trinity disappeared back into her vortex of work and no sleep, and Ocean went home, still unwilling to tell us what was wrong. But something was. I knew her well enough to know she was trying not to bother us, but I would figure it out eventually.

As I walked in, the suite was quiet too. No signs of life, or even the low hum of conversation. Where were they?

A piece of paper on the bed snagged my attention, handwriting scrawled on it.

*Isolde—*

*When you get back, come down to the beach. Let's look at that dress in the moonlight and see if it gets better.*

A little smiley face ended the note, with no name. So I wasn't sure which of them had left it.

I supposed it wouldn't hurt me to keep the dress on a little while longer. Soaking it in the ocean and ruining it with salt would be a fitting end for it. Rin had been right. It wasn't *that* bad. I felt like I'd stepped out of a prom photo from nearly forty years ago, but it wasn't terrible, even with the hair.

Take this dress, change the style a bit, and maybe I'd even risk wearing it for real.

I tossed my shoes aside and left the suite, savoring the grass, and then the sand, under my toes. The sun had set in a blaze of glory while we drove back, so dusk was darkening the beach with the last traces of light slipping from the sky and the moon already rising.

Tide was low, so much more beach was visible than usual, and it the water was slowly beginning to come in again. Near the cliffs, the rocks that jutted up like towers were completely exposed at the bottom. When I was young, you would find the best shells hidden in the pockets of those rocks. I tried to climb them a few times, but given they were nearly as tall as the cliff itself, I never got far.

Even my favorite part was visible. A hollowed out arch in one of the rocks, worn smooth from years of water washing in and out. You could swim down beneath it during high tide. Or at least that's what Ellie and Dad told me. I'd never done it myself.

But they weren't here either. From what I could tell, the beach was entirely empty. The moon peeked over the darkening horizon, pale light making the dress shimmer in a very different way. The purples in the iridescent overlay were bright over the orange. Like fire wrapped in ice. This, I liked. Give me a dress *this* color, and I'd wear it in a heartbeat.

I decided to walk down the beach anyway. Maybe they'd gotten tired and gone back inside or something, but since I was already here, I might as well stay. The soft sound of the rising water soothed something deep in me. I hadn't had a chance to be alone on the beach yet, just me and the water.

The shadows of the towering rocks painted me in darkness as I stepped behind them, heading to the other side. I'd walk down to the border of the private beach and then turn around.

I sensed movement though I didn't see it. An arm snaked around my waist, another over my mouth, pulling me against a hard chest and dragging me across the sand and against the stone face. The hand swallowed my scream. "I think it's time I unwrapped my present," a dark voice growled.

Orange and sweetness surrounded me, soothing the panic of being grabbed. *Vaughn.*

Our conversation echoed in my head. *Do you want me to chase you, Isolde?*

A low sound vibrated through me, somewhere between a growl and a purr. "You're too fucking tempting in a dress I can ruin with no consequences."

My whole body shuddered, and Vaughn shifted, turning me to the rock and pinning me there with his hips while he gathered my hands in one of his, making my mind go absolutely blank with need and the *visceral* knowledge that he had me and could do whatever he wanted.

And I wanted to let him.

"If you want me to let you go, tell me now," he growled. "If you don't, tell me your safeword."

I opened my mouth, and he tightened his hold.

"If you tell me your safeword, you need to know what it means. I'm going to chase you down, Isolde, and when I do, I'm going to take what I want from you. Fuck you any way I want. Fight back all you want. I can handle it. But you are *mine.* Even if you get away, I'll find you and take you all over again until *I* decide we're finished, understand? Now choose."

His fingers released my mouth. I could scream. I could tell him to release me and go back inside. But the whispers in my soul were louder than the tiny bit of anxiety and fear. I'd always wanted to try it, and I didn't know if I'd ever have another chance. What he said? I wanted it. Desperately. My voice sounded like I'd already been screaming. "Banana."

Vaughn's hand covered my mouth again, while his own mouth dragged up my neck to my ear. "Good girl. This dress isn't the only thing that will be ruined by the time I'm done with you."

I whined, arousal skimming over my skin like the tide rising. More than that, I felt what he'd described before—the deepest instincts I had coming to the surface, urging me to get away from the predator coming after me. To *flee*.

The hand over my mouth disappeared, instead gripping my hair and pulling my head back, exposing my neck. "Last chance to back out, Omega. When I let you go, I'll give you a head start." The softest of laughs. "Need to pretend it's fair."

There was no way I was backing out now, and more than that, my instincts were already taking over. His hand loosened in my hair, and I moved, twisting so sharply he had to let me go and shoving him while he was still off balance. I didn't wait to see if he fell—I was too busy running.

Past the rock and away from the house. The now-risen moon glinted off the water, and Vaughn's growl turned into laughter that made my hair stand on end.

I grabbed my skirt in my hands and pushed myself faster.

## CHAPTER THIRTY-ONE

VAUGHN

Isolde ran from me, and I smiled. Every instinct shifted, the darkness becoming clearer, sounds becoming sharper. Her sweet scent was like a beacon drawing me straight to her, as if I couldn't see her running straight down the beach.

The others were everywhere. Stationed so we weren't interrupted and Isolde didn't end up somewhere with other people. She was *mine.*

My cock was already hard beneath the jeans I wore. I'd left my shirt behind. It was only going to get in the way. Much like that frothy, bite-of-frosting dress I was going to rip off her.

I inhaled her scent, layered with anticipation and anxiety. The flowers in it smelled like they'd been crushed. Just a little too sweet, a little too far gone. Not rotten. A perfect blend for what we wanted. My mouth watered with the need to taste her, and I watched her stumble in the sand before reaching her feet.

She wasn't thinking, the prey instinct merely telling her to run without telling her she was still an easy target.

Time she learned.

Energy surged into my limbs, and I sprinted down the sand after her. That fucking dress glowed in the moonlight like a beacon, calling to me. Even if she'd had nothing on, the trail of scent she left behind her felt like it was on fire in my mind. I could follow her anywhere. *Would* follow her anywhere.

*Mine.*

The sand disappeared under my feet, years of spending days on the beach and running on sand giving me exactly the footing I needed. She wasn't fast enough.

One look behind her, and I felt the pulse of her panic. Heard her gasp as she realized just how close I was and tried to run faster. The fabric of the skirt tripped her, and I leapt.

I took her to the sand, rolling her underneath me in one movement. She fought. Hips bucking, nails scratching, groaning in the struggle as I pinned her to the earth with my full weight. "*Get the fuck off me*," she shoved my shoulders, but I didn't let them move.

I laughed, leaning down to inhale her neck. "I'm going to get the fuck off, that's for sure."

She moved, and I jerked back just in time, avoiding her head colliding with my nose. It made me grin. My Omega was a fighter, even though she was going to lose. Letting my weight push her further into the ground, she whined, and the sound went straight to my cock, already so hard it was painful.

"Never run in a straight line, sweetheart." I pinned her wrists to the damp sand. We were where the tide hadn't yet reached, beach flat and perfect except for where her struggles showed. "Didn't anyone ever tell you that?"

"Sorry, I didn't get instructions on how to run from a psycho." Her struggles were slowing, her energy useless in the face of my strength.

"Oh, you have no idea. Let me show you." I moved one of her wrists so I could grip them both, pushing up the frothy skirt so it bunched between us. Even further so it covered her face. Nothing but white panties underneath.

White, with a dark damp spot right over her pussy.

My growl echoed down the beach. "Wetter than the fucking sea already. Soaking through your panties because you want my cock so badly."

"*Never.*" Isolde bucked her hips, and I shoved them back down, knocking her legs wide and pinning them with my knees.

Ripping the fabric to the side, I slid a finger into her with no resistance and added another. Her arousal gushed onto my hand, the obscene sound of her being fucked by my fingers louder than the ocean behind me. "You're a bad liar, sweetheart."

"Fuck. You." Each word was a heaved breath.

I moved so fast, sinking deeper into instinct and need, spinning and pushing her legs up so she was nearly folded in half, her knees caught between mine. I sat on her chest, pinning her arms beneath my cock and balls. Now that my hands were free, I tore her panties, the cotton shredding beneath my fingers, fully baring her cunt to the air. I groaned at the wave of perfume circling me.

My hand came down on her clit, the stinging smack echoing across the beach. She gasped, arching and fighting, and entirely pinned the way I had her. My naughty little Omega wasn't going anywhere.

So I spanked her clit again.

And again, and again, watching her cunt get wetter with every slap. It glistened in the moonlight, a feast just for me.

"Please," she begged, arching and writhing. "Stop."

"You don't want me to make you come?"

"No." Half sob, half moan.

Isolde's scent was all sweetness and ease. No longer even a hint of fear. There was only desire. Her resistance was part of the game.

"Too bad I don't care what you want." I bent and covered her with my mouth, sucking hard, scraping her clit with my teeth and tasting her sweetness. A swirl of my tongue and she was moaning, cum flooding my tongue, hips rising to meet my mouth even though she fought me. With Isolde's struggle with pleasure, the immediate orgasm told me exactly how much she wanted this. My Omega fucking *loved it.*

"You monster *let. Me. GO.*" She bucked her body with feral strength, and it almost worked.

Almost.

"How does it feel?" I whispered the word against her bare thigh and savored her shiver. The chills that rose all over her skin. "Knowing I have you here, completely at my mercy, and able to turn your body against you. Make you come even though you claim not to want it."

I consumed her, fucking her with my tongue as deep as I could make it reach. Sealing my mouth over her and sucking hard enough to bruise. I teased her too, finding that little spot we had that first night that made her pussy surge with slick all over again.

"No, no, no, no." The soft chant of protest had no force behind it. Every part of her scent and the movements of her body spoke of enjoyment regardless.

"What's your safeword?" I growled.

"Banana."

"Using it?"

She laughed once. "You wish."

I moved again, abandoning her pussy and letting her free for a fraction of a second before I was on her again. "Fine. Then you'll come on my cock next, no matter what you fucking feel like."

Flipping her over, Isolde's feet collided with my chest and a brutal kick that pushed me off and to the ground. She saved all her strength for that, and that alone, and it worked.

My Omega was up and running before I could gain my feet, heading back the way we came, toward the caves.

I wiped her arousal from my mouth with the back of my hand. Her scent was even stronger now that she'd orgasmed and slick was running down her thighs. Even no longer running in a straight line, it painted a path right to her.

My senses sharpened again, ready to catch and *take*. "Run all you like, little Omega, you're still mine."

As soon as she disappeared into the caves, I followed.

## CHAPTER THIRTY-TWO

ISOLDE

My heaving breaths echoed loudly in the darkness of the cave. My legs burned from running on the sand—something I hadn't done since college and volleyball training—and the orgasm Vaughn ripped from me like it was nothing.

I splashed through the puddles on the rocky floor, shallow since the tide was out. It had been years since I was in these caves, but I still knew them well enough. The pitch black would help conceal me. Hopefully.

Lowering myself down on the ground, I spread some of the water on myself. I didn't have much time. Vaughn was fast, and he was probably already on his way, but the water might dampen the scent a little.

Outside the caves, I heard his voice in a singsong that gave me goosebumps. "Isolde."

I pushed forward, dragging my hands on the rock wall until I felt what I was looking for. A little passageway between two of the caves, small enough to fit through for some. I could, but I doubted Vaughn would fit.

Back deeper into the cave again before doubling back and crossing into the third and final one—the one closest to the mansion. A corner I'd used for hide and seek for *years* hid back here, within viewing distance of the entrance, but no one would be able to find you if you didn't already know where you were.

Or if they were hunting you.

Steps scraped on stone, a low purr echoing through. "Smart girl," he chuckled. His voice was louder. So he'd found the passage. "I'll still find you."

He would, but I wasn't going to make it easy. I waited until I couldn't hear him anymore before I backtracked. A wave of delicious orange and cream washed toward me from the entrance of the second cave. My heart kicked into high gear, and I pressed myself back through the crack in the stone. I only had seconds or he would find me. Quickly.

*Quickly.*

There. I breathed out in relief, pressing close to the crack and listening for the barest hint of a step on the other side.

"Nice try."

I screamed, turning and running straight into Vaughn's chest. "*Quiet.*" His mouth slammed over mine while he shoved me against the stone wall, tongue invading before I could stop him. So I bit him, making sure not to break the skin.

Vaughn jerked back, smiling. "Wanna make me bleed, sweetheart? Be my guest. It's not going to change anything."

Pure, sultry heat swept through me. Why did I like it when he said things like that? Why did I crave knowing he was going to take what he wanted no matter what?

Because I knew he would stop.

With one little word, this would end. It was all a choice, and I chose him. He hadn't taken my hands yet. "Fuck off."

A hand circled my throat, pushing me into the stone and stealing my air. "Sure that's the way you want to go? I can be nice to you. If you're nice to me." His lips brushed mine. "If you get on your knees and say you're sorry."

I couldn't breathe, air scraping through my throat where he squeezed. "The only way I'll ever kneel is if you make me."

All he did was smile. My stomach tumbled with want and the barest hint of fear. I loved the edge of it, making everything sharper.

"Careful what you wish for, sweetheart."

He didn't release my throat. I clawed at his hand, unable to move him, unable to focus on what he was doing. The sound of tearing fabric reached my ears, my skirt splitting, the damn ocean air hitting my legs once more. The sleeves torn off and discarded.

Everything blazed to life. The world poured back in along with my air. I coughed, dizzy and blind and not fighting back because I couldn't. Vaughn grabbed my hands and turned, pinning me against the wall of the cave with his back. He had my wrists and was tying them together with the ripped cloth.

I tried to pull my hands apart, but they wouldn't move. And now they were tied. *Around his body.*

Vaughn turned back with victory in his eyes. "Get on your knees, or I'm going to put you there."

I straightened to my full height. Hell, I went on my toes in defiance. He caught me, but I wouldn't go down that easily.

His hands landed on my shoulders, and with one push, his strength overcame mine. My legs, weak as they were from running, buckled, skin scraping on the stone, my hands still bound around his legs. He widened them too, making sure they couldn't move as he lazily undid his belt. All that was left of the skirt were filmy scraps clinging to my legs.

"I didn't have to make that pretty cunt come, you know." The words were dark. "I could have fucked you. Put your face in the sand and made you mine until you passed out. Serves me right for being nice."

He gripped my jaw, fingers forcing my mouth open. "No more."

I only caught the barest hint of his cock in the darkness, but I saw he was thick, and the moonlight glinted off a piercing. Then he was in my mouth, pushing deep. Metal studs grazed my tongue and the roof of my mouth before he hit the back, making me gag.

Vaughn gripped my hair with one hand, the other coming around my throat again as he pulled back and thrust in again, further. It was too much. My body rebelled against him, and at the same time, my nipples hardened and slick gathered between my legs.

Something in my mind clicked, sinking into a place of nothing more than obedience and submission. It yawned open in front of me, a delicious void of nothing but pleasure at his hands. I should fight back, but with his cock pressing at the entrance of my throat, his gaze burning hot, I didn't want to.

He felt the change, the air going tight between us.

Vaughn stopped holding back.

I didn't even know he had been, and suddenly he was fucking my mouth, pushing past it into my throat like it was a mold made for him. Rumbling growls filled the cave, the back of my head hitting the wall as he held me there. Ruthless. Relentless. Stroke after stroke getting deeper. His piercings were a marker, and one by one, he worked them into me.

When he wanted me to breathe, I did. When he didn't want that, I didn't. The whole world was hazy and soft at the edges, tinged with moonlit silver.

"Take it." His hand tightened in my hair. "Take it like your throat is your cunt. All the way."

Vaughn pushed deep, cock sliding into me until his hips met my mouth, whole body pinning me in place. "God fucking damn," he mumbled, rocking deeper. "I could knot you behind your teeth and keep you here."

The world went fuzzy again from the lack of air, but being this full of him felt good. Felt *right*. I wanted more.

Moving his hands to either side of my head, he gave me more. Vaughn took my throat like a heathen. Wild and barbaric, every thrust pushing in to the hilt, over and over again.

"I'm going to come." The words lingered in the darkness. "And you're going to swallow everything, Omega."

That hand cupped my jaw again, holding it open with a squeeze as he pulled back and came, pouring himself all over my tongue.

*Fuck me,* he tasted incredible. Like oranges and cream. Like the best ice cream ever. Like I wanted to drink him down and savor him like a gift. Never in my life had I wanted anything more than to swallow.

Which was why I locked eyes with him and spat his cum on the ground, knowing exactly what would happen. Wanting the feral savagery still locked inside him. I was fully gone into my instincts now, and they were in the driver's seat.

The Alpha looking at me was gone too, the righteous anger in his eyes searing me like a brand. I didn't wait to see what he would do, lunging, knocking him with the full force of my body. He was off balance, and I *pulled*, using my bound arms to trip him and make him fall.

*Freedom.*

I tore my hands from around his fallen legs and sprinted. His roar echoed out onto the beach. There was no way to outrun him, but I still had to try. Maybe I could lead him around the rocks.

The archway loomed in front of me, the first waves of the rising tide pooling around the base of the giant stones. There was a chance I could lose him here. A chance—

He pounced from the other side of the arch, already there, arms coming around me and taking me to the ground. I struggled and kicked, but there was no use. Vaughn wasn't just Vaughn, he was in his Alpha, strength beyond his own powering his body, eyes nearly black with it. He wasn't in rut, but he was damn close.

So much like the first time he caught me, he pinned me to the sand and knocked my legs apart. Unlike the first time, he thrust into me with one stroke.

Water swirled up and around our legs, pulling at us, our clothes, the sand, as he stared down at me, the predator. Vaughn's swollen knot from his first orgasm pushed against my entrance, both a promise and a threat.

"*Mine.*"

One hand pinned me to the ground by the throat, the other pushing my bound hands deeper into the damp sand above my head. Another wave enveloped us. More, because the tide was rising.

I smiled at him, saying the thing I knew would break him. "I'll never be yours."

Vaughn snapped.

He snarled, driving himself into me just like he had in the cave, but this time there was no resistance. My body was made to take him, and those fucking infernal piercings were heaven. Dragging against me on both top and bottom, pressing where I needed him. But I wasn't there. My clit felt like one brush would send me over. All that sensation coiled and ready to burst.

Something gave way deep inside me. A different kind of submission. Needed something so much more. Needed my *Alpha*. More than oxygen and more than life. Down in my bones, I surrendered. A delicious fracturing that would last longer than tonight.

"Please."

I wasn't teasing him this time. Not begging him to stop. I needed more.

My Alpha fucked me harder. Sweat dripped off his body, mixing with the wave now curling up and over my shoulders.

"Please, I need it."

His fingers jerked against my throat. "Say it."

I swallowed and watched his eyes grow blacker when he felt it. "No."

"I caught you, sweetheart." Vaughn leaned closer, never stopping, never slowing. "This cunt is *mine*. I earned it. And you're not coming unless you admit it."

My head shook back and forth. I couldn't do it. Not after fighting him so hard. Everything in me wanted to relent, but I also wanted to be strong enough not to.

He lowered even further, squeezing my throat as the water flowed over it and his hand. "Tell me who this pretty cunt belongs to, and I'll let you come. Tell me who *you* belong to."

"I can't." This felt like more than the game. It felt bigger, and there wasn't a way to stop it. "I can't."

The words were so soft, a gentle caress in contrast to the brutality of how he buried his cock in me, filling me to the point of pain. Perfect, beautiful, pleasure and fire and madness. "Tell me, Isolde."

"I'm yours."

Vaughn ground his hips downward on the next thrust, dragging over my clit, and I exploded. The wave came, washing over my head while my world went white. It didn't matter if I was underwater. I was already drowning in pleasure and in him. It didn't stop, carrying on while he took what he needed.

Finally, as he held me under another wave, he slammed his knot home, heat filling me, mixing with the salt of the sea.

His hand released my throat, and he hauled me upward, wrapping me around his body while he knelt in the sand. The Alpha who chased me was gone. I felt it. Our game was over, and I was knotted to Vaughn, who held me like I was the most precious thing he'd pulled from the sea.

"Fucking hell, sweetheart."

I laughed once.

"Are you all right?"

"Yeah."

Exhausted, pleasured out, and boneless. But I was fine. More than fine.

Pulling back so he could see me, he searched my face. "Did we cross any boundaries? Are you injured anywhere?"

I shook my head. "I'm good. I promise. Just..."

"Just?"

"Will you kiss me?"

Vaughn smiled. A real smile, and pulled my mouth to his. Soft and gentle. Grounding. Safe.

That's what I was. We'd just done something most people would consider crazy or wrong, and somehow, I'd never felt more safe than I did now.

"You guys good?" Cade's voice came from some distance away.

"We're good. Going to need something to cover us both on the way back," Vaughn said, standing in the shallow waves. "I'm going to take you back inside and we'll get you cleaned up, okay?"

"Okay." The swaying motion of his walking was lulling me into drowsy bliss. "Vaughn?"

"Yeah, sweetheart?"

"Thank you."

He tightened his hold on me and purred all the way back to the suite.

## CHAPTER THIRTY-THREE

ISOLDE

My eyelids felt heavy. But I was warm. Comforting darkness surrounding me, along with the sharp scent of citrus softened with cream.

I was awake while he got us into the shower and cleaned off all the sand and everything else. But awake and coherent were two different things. I'd used every ounce of energy, and I was happy to let him take care of me.

Vaughn's purr rumbled against my back. I had my head tucked under a blanket, unsure which one of us had put it there. But I liked the way he kept me close. I loved waking up tangled, like whoever it was wanted me close, even when neither of us were conscious.

It had started off that way with Beau, but it faded pretty quickly. I brushed it off as nothing more than being tired and busy.

Taking a deeper breath, I turned in Vaughn's arms, pressing my face to his bare chest and that relaxing vibration. "What day is it?"

He laughed quietly. "It's the morning after."

"Thought I'd sleep longer," I mumbled.

"You can still sleep if you want to. In fact, I think Joel wants to spend the day pampering you. Naps can definitely be part of that."

"Not you?"

Slowly, Vaughn pulled the blanket away from my head. I blinked against the sudden brightness. "I'll do whatever you want or need, sweetheart. But you haven't spent time with Joel yet, and you already know comfort is what he craves. That being said, if you want me, I'm yours."

"Right. You're opposites."

He smiled and brushed a kiss to my temple. "Kind of."

The lightness faded from his face, and he ran a hand through my hair. "How do you feel?"

"I feel good."

"You sure?"

I wiggled, tensing and stretching. There might be some scrapes on my knees, and some sensitivity from the sand, but nothing hurt. Not really. My instincts were still close to the surface, my Omega enjoying the warmth and closeness. I felt more like an Omega than I had in a long time. "Feels like I worked out really hard. I'm fine."

"Good." His hand kept stroking through my hair. "That was a lot, and I want to make sure you're fine with everything that happened. I know I asked you at the end, but it's different on the other side of sleep."

Closing my eyes, I snuggled closer. "It was intense, that's for sure. But I liked it. I didn't know I could even do something like that." My eyes flew open. "Are *you* okay? I tossed you onto the rocks in the cave."

"I'm fine, sweetheart." His purr grew stronger, and he laughed. "You took me by surprise there. Had my Alpha all riled up."

"I didn't even think about the fact that people could see us. Hear us."

"Everyone else was spaced out, making sure we weren't disturbed or interrupted. I wouldn't put you in that position, I promise."

"They helped?"

I felt him nod.

"That was nice of them."

Vaughn held me a little tighter. There was a hitch in his chest, like he might say something else, but he didn't.

Drifting for a while longer, I felt the mattress dip near us, and someone kissed my shoulder. "You awake?"

"Barely."

Joel pulled me so I looked up at him. "Want to take a bath with me?"

A bath did sound nice. I glanced at Vaughn and found him grinning. "I'll be just fine."

It felt weird to separate from him after the intensity of our night, but he wasn't wrong. I wanted a different kind of softness, and I wanted to know what Joel would do. So I looked back at him. "Yeah, I'd like that."

"Perfect. Stay here, and I'll start the water."

Vaughn rolled over me, pinning me to the bed and reminding me exactly what he'd done. "Thank you for letting me chase you," he breathed, kissing me.

"Thank you for doing it. I don't think I'll ever do anything like that again."

"I hope that's not true, sweetheart."

"Me too."

Easing off me, he helped me sit up and be at the edge of the bed when Joel came back for me. I blinked. "Shit. The bachelorette is tonight."

"You'll be more than ready by then," Joel said, lifting me up and carrying me into the bathroom. "And there's plenty of time."

"Are you going to the bachelor party?"

The giant tub was already filled with bubbles, water steaming. Joel helped me in before stripping his own clothes off to get in with me. I scooted forward, happy to let him get behind me.

"I don't think so. Warren is a good guy, but we're not his friends. And," he tugged me back against his chest, lifting up some water to drizzle it over my shoulders. "I don't think it's a good idea for any of us to be in the same room as Beau. Warren might lose his best man."

"You wouldn't really kill him."

Joel's arm came hard around my waist. "Don't be so sure about that. I get the feeling what you've told us and what we've seen is barely scratching the surface."

That same hand stroked down my body to the insides of my thighs. "But I don't want to talk about him. He's not worth your time. This might be, if you're not tired of being fucked."

"Does anyone get tired of that?" My body chose that second to yawn, making us both laugh.

"It's okay if you're tired."

"I am tired," I admitted. "But I also want you."

A warm kiss on the side of my neck followed by his hand lifting my leg to one side of his. "Only comfort, Isolde."

I leaned my head back on his shoulder. When he said it, it sounded easy. But lying here with him, even though it felt amazing, was hard. They were here for me, and while it was quiet, it was hard to just exist in my thoughts. I should be doing something.

"Can I ask you something?" Joel's voice was low and soothing, along with his tracing fingers, which hadn't touched me where I wanted him to. *Yet*.

"Sure."

"You were in a relationship for a long time where you weren't appreciated. Then you were on your own, making ends meet. Now you're here, and… you didn't want to let us help with the little things like the doors."

I pressed my lips together. My words came out harsher than I intended. "That's not a question."

"How long has it been since you actually allowed yourself to let go?" Joel kept speaking before I could. "And I don't mean when we've pushed you into it. We can guide you into relaxing or having a good time, but it won't help you if you don't allow it."

And how was I supposed to do that?

The words were on the tip of my tongue, ready to lash out and snap. But Joel hadn't said anything untrue, and the fact that I had such a strong reaction to them was on me.

But the question, without the hostility, rattled around in my head. How was I supposed to let go when I held my life together with both hands? At the end of the day, I was the one responsible for me. I was the one who would still be here after they left. I was alone. I couldn't afford to let go for longer than the space of time they helped me. Because if I did, everything would fall apart.

"I didn't mean to shut you down."

"It's not as simple as it seems," I told him. "I… can't do that."

"What if you could?"

I huffed a laugh. "Then it would be great. But I can't. I don't have anyone else, Joel. My family and my friends—" I broke off. "It's not the same. It's not like being someone's priority. And I miss that. Even more so when I realize I was *never* someone's priority, I only thought I was. After the wedding, when you all are back to your lives, I'll still be here, and no one's priority."

Joel's fingers stilled on my thigh, nothing but silence filling the surrounding air.

"Sorry." I scrubbed a hand over my face. "Must be more tired than I thought."

He sat up in the tub and took me with him, wrapping his body firmly around mine. His arms held mine against me in an embrace, his legs pressed against the outsides of mine. "Don't apologize. Please. Not for saying what you feel. I'm sorry for asking a question that took you there."

I sagged into his hold, trying to imagine this all the time. The ability to break and *know* someone would clean up the pieces. Tears pricked the back of my eyes at the thought.

"You are my priority," he whispered.

The tears grew.

"What's going on in here?" Cade stood in the doorway with a mischievous smile that dropped away when he saw me. "Isolde, what's wrong?"

"It's me," Joel leaned back with me again, keeping me close while spreading my legs with his. This time when he let his hand creep downward, he brushed my clit. "Asking Isolde questions instead of doing what I promised and making her feel good."

He touched me slowly, like a sensual massage. Not trying to make me come, but merely making my body *aware* of his and his moving fingers. It felt good, despite everything.

Cade smirked and came over to the tub. "If he's bothering you, princess, you can come with me and I'll take care of you. I've been wanting to show you my rope."

My eyes went wide, and Joel pulled me more firmly to him. "*Mine.*" But the word was playful.

I reached for Cade's hand. He crouched by the tub to take mine, smoothing his thumb along my wet skin. "I do want that. But after last night, I'm still really tired."

"After the bachelor parties then. If you want."

"I very much want."

Cade's eyes crinkled at the corners when he smiled, and the scruff on his jaw made him look even better than he already did. "Then it's a date. What's your favorite color?"

"Why?"

"It's a surprise."

I rolled my eyes, but smiled. "Emerald green."

"Like your party dress."

"Yeah. Rin knows how to pick things I can't resist. The one I'd picked was black."

He lifted my hand and kissed the back before standing. "I'm glad you wore the green. Now I'll let you get back to relaxing. Sorry I interrupted." Cade left with a wink.

Joel's fingers still moved slowly over me, barely brushing my entrance before retreating to my clit, over and over again. A gentle purr that kept me relaxed and limp. I hadn't even realized my eyes were closing until Joel moved, and I jerked awake.

"Sorry," he murmured into my hair. "I'm going to move us to the bed, okay?"

"Kay."

He dried me off, and I found myself in the center of the big bed, wrapped in a blanket so soft I had no idea where it came from. Then Joel was with me, curling me further into the blanket, arranging us together with his hand between my legs. "Before you fall asleep—"

"I'm not asleep."

Joel chuckled and kissed my cheek. "Well, before you are, little sleepy Omega, I'm sorry I brought up something that's hurting you. But you can always talk about it with us, okay?"

I frowned. "You'll let me call you just for that?"

He laughed again. "Of course. How does sleepy sex sound to you?"

Our conversation in front of Cream Dream came back to me. Waking up with sex. In my clouded mind, that sounded yummy. "Yes please."

"Rest. We'll make sure you're awake for the party."

I'd never fallen asleep so quickly.

## CHAPTER THIRTY-FOUR

JOEL

Isolde fell asleep, body softening against mine. Telling her everything had been right there. But I could wait one more day. Tomorrow. We would tell her tomorrow.

She *needed* to hear it.

The grief in her voice speaking about being alone tore me apart inside. But she would never be alone again. Not if she didn't want to be. We were so far gone for her, we barely wanted to let her out of our sight.

Every instinct told me she was ready. I only hoped she would believe it. Isolde had put herself so thoroughly inside a box in her own mind, she might second guess the truth.

Vaughn stepped in quietly, watching her. He looked happy and at peace. Thankfully. I hoped that me taking care of her now helped heal the wound I'd given him a long time ago. We'd moved past it, but things like that left a scar.

"Is she okay?"

I shook my head and shrugged. "Yes, and no. She's fine from last night, but it's deeper than that. She needs to know. Her Omega is so fucking tired, Vaughn. Like she's been treading water for the last five years without any rest. No wonder she crashes whenever she sleeps with us."

He looked as upset about it as I felt. One more day. We could make it one more day.

"Warren asked if we want to go to the party. I said we didn't want to intrude."

"Good."

The five of us, alcohol, and Isolde's ex all in one space, was a recipe for disaster, and not for us. I preferred not to go to jail when we'd just found our Omega.

"I thought so. He said we could use whatever. Including the gaming systems in their wing, if we wanted."

I smiled. That would be fun. I could kill some time there while waiting for Isolde to come back. Gaming was a hobby, but it was incredible how it faded to the background when someone like Isolde came into the picture. My priorities were different, and even though she didn't know it, she was number one.

Still, I'd relax while she was with her friends.

Vaughn nodded toward the beach. "Rowan's headed to the house to check on things, and I figured I'd head down to the water for a bit if you're good here."

"We're fine." I nodded. "Hell, I'd be fine forever having her here like this."

Vaughn huffed out a laugh. "Know the feeling."

Though she was asleep, I kept touching Isolde, moving my hands over her and watching her body relax where it naturally tensed without being touched. Time felt like it was passing so fucking fast. It was time to start waking her up for the party. And this way of waking her up was going to be my favorite.

My cock had been hard since we were in the bath, so it was easy to pull her to me, slipping into her from behind.

*Holy shit*. I closed my eyes, fighting the urge to come before she'd even woken. Her pussy gripped me like a vise. She was fucking made for me. It was the only reality and truth.

I rocked my hips deeper into her, slow and steady, kissing along her neck. "Time to wake up, Omega."

She whined quietly, stretching, squeezing down on me without even knowing she did it. "*Fuck*," I whispered. "You feel incredible."

Isolde froze, and she squeezed my cock again. I felt her come into alertness, realizing I was inside her. She smiled, pushing her hips back into me. "Sleepy sex?"

"It won't be so sleepy if you keep squeezing me like that."

She giggled. So fucking cute I couldn't stand it. Her eyes fluttered open, face turning to find mine. "It feels good."

I moved her, slipping out just long enough to roll her beneath me before pushing in again. I needed her face to face. Needed those beautiful green eyes on mine while I fucked her slowly and made her lose her breath.

"What's your favorite?" I asked.

Her teeth sank into her lower lip, neck arching. "Favorite what?"

I bit at that same lip, dragging her into a slow kiss. "Favorite way to be fucked. We might know *what* you like, but not *how* you like it."

Isolde dragged her hands up my arms and across my shoulders, holding onto my neck while I rolled my hips, keeping the movements so fucking slow and even I was going to go mad, even though this was my favorite.

"What if I don't know?"

"Then I'd love to help you figure it out." I shifted my hips so the thrusts were shallow. I was the shortest of my pack, but also the thickest. I could push a certain button more easily than they could. I just had to find it.

Her legs flew up around my hips, jerking me closer. "What was *that*?"

I smirked. "Found it."

"What?"

Not changing my angle at all, I thrust a little harder right there, loving the burst of wetness around my cock and the tantalizing swirl of perfume. "One of the places I can use to make you feel good, little Omega. Does it?"

"Yesss." A hissing breath. "So good."

"Harder?"

She nodded. I released myself, pushing harder into her, but not faster. Isolde's eyelids closed. She was still tired, and I loved it. I wanted to fuck her back to sleep every chance I could.

"I feel heavy," she said. "I'm sorry."

I nipped at her neck. "Feel heavy. Feel sleepy. It's what we both wanted, remember?"

Up close her eyes were so warm and open. Unguarded. "But if I actually fall asleep, I promise it's not cause I'm bored."

"If you fall asleep impaled on my cock, I'm fucking honored your Omega trusts me enough to let me use your beautiful body. And watching you wake up with my cum leaking out of you is going to make me come all over again."

Her needy little whine made my cock *ache*.

"Is this enough?" I asked. "To get you there?"

She shook her head with her eyes closed. "No, but it's close."

I was glad she couldn't see the smile on my face. Right now my goal wasn't making her come, it was making her feel *good*. And I was happy to keep her drowning in the delirious half-awake state of an almost orgasm for as long as I could.

Because she *was* my priority, and always would be.

Perfume exploded outward, so strong, her body growing wetter even as she slipped deeper, like her instincts were stronger as she dozed.

Just a little longer, and I'd wake her up for real. I didn't want her to be late, but I wanted my drowsy Omega full of everything first. Relaxation, comfort, and *me*.

I dropped my forehead to hers, inhaling that floral sweetness, and fucked her as gently as I could.

## CHAPTER THIRTY-FIVE

ISOLDE

Joel's rough groan brought me to the surface again, my body exquisitely weighted down by the bonds of sleep. I forgot how much I *loved* sleep, because these past weeks with them had been the best I'd had in years.

Dragging my eyes open, I found Joel braced above me, hand squeezing his cock as he milked the last of his orgasm from himself and into me. His knot was swollen at the base, but he hadn't locked us together. Probably because I was supposed to get ready right now.

He caught me watching and smiled before reaching between us, and he didn't look away as his fingers pushed leaking cum back inside. A flush rolled up my body. There was nothing to fear from this—I'd had the quick procedure to pinch off my tubes as soon as I realized I didn't want to be a mom. It was reversible if I ever changed my mind, but I doubted it.

All the same, the movement was fucking hot, and I had no idea why.

"You need to get ready," Joel said.

"And maybe take a shower."

A soft growl, and his mouth came down on mine. "If you want to, but I'd rather you didn't."

"You like the thought of your cum dripping out of me?" Why was my voice so breathy? Why didn't there feel like there was enough air between us?

"Like isn't a strong enough word. I *love* the thought of me dripping out of you. I love the thought of my scent mixing with your perfume while you dance tonight. I love the thought of you coming back and sitting on my face and letting me taste us both together."

"You're making staying home sound really good."

He smirked and kissed the tip of my nose. "I'm not going to be responsible for depriving your sister of you at her bachelorette party."

"Fine." I frowned. My perfume hovered in the air, and I wasn't perfuming right now. Which meant it had been while he fucked me. Asleep. "Can't believe I was perfuming while asleep."

"I enjoyed it." Joel helped me up off the bed. It didn't take me long to put on the clothes I was wearing. Just jeans and a green halter I liked. We were going to a club, thankfully, nothing too fancy.

Joel was dressed when I came back out, typing on his phone. I loved Ellie, and I was sure as soon as I got there it would be fun. But the idea of a night at the club with all of her friends wasn't my favorite thing. If Ocean and Rin were there? Sure. "What if I decide I want to come back early?"

"Call us. We'll be there."

"Just like that?"

"Of course." He stood and took me in slowly, lifting the hair off my shoulders and brushing it back. "We would never leave you stranded somewhere you didn't want to be, Isolde."

I nodded. They wouldn't. Nothing they'd done had made me think otherwise, but I still wanted the reassurance. Fuck Beau and the number he'd done on my brain. Every day it was becoming more clear that he'd damaged me more than I had allowed myself to admit.

"Just have fun." He took my face in his hands and kissed me softly. I knew exactly what he meant by comfort now. He'd given me all that comfort. Even when I was breaking apart, it hadn't felt uncomfortable with him there.

"What will you do?"

"Warren gave us free rein with his gaming systems, so we might go kick some ass. Vaughn is surfing and Rowan is home tending to his plants. And maybe making some candy for you, I'm guessing."

I startled. "Candy?"

"The man is amazing at making edibles. You'll have to have him make you his caramels, since I know you love that. But the lemon bars are my favorite."

"I could probably use one right about now."

"We'll make sure you try them." He kissed me one more time. "Don't be late."

I headed to meet Ellie, but I wanted to stay. Who was I turning into? Since when did a quiet night in ever top going out? Before I'd moved, a night at the club like this would have been at the top of my list no matter who was there. Society parties? No thank you. Club with the girls? Yes please.

Now, curling up with Joel while he played video games sounded really nice.

Maybe I was getting older and changing.

Or maybe it was just who they were.

Ellie stood in the foyer with Warren, in a white pair of jeans and a tank top with a sparkly *bride* blazoned across the front. "Embracing tradition I see."

She grinned. "Bet your ass. I only get one, so it's going to be all the tacky shit. Be ready."

"I think I am."

My sister looked at her fiancé. "Be good."

"You know if I wasn't banned from your party I'd rather be there with you." He only had eyes for her. "And if you change your mind, we're just down the street."

The guys were hanging out at a dark, smoky cigar bar down the street. Most guys would probably want the classic strip club experience, but Warren wasn't most guys. I'd been on the phone with her when she asked him if he wanted to go to a strip club for the party, and the horror on his face was hard to forget.

In the space it took me to remember that, they were making out in a way that wasn't going to get us out the door. "Get a room," I joked, grabbing Ellie's hand. "Or use the one you have later."

"You be good too," Warren called after us.

Ellie slid into the back of the SUV first. Her driver already knew where we were going. She snorted. "As if I wouldn't be good."

"Wouldn't be the first time someone got a little too rowdy before their wedding."

"Rowdy, yes. But there's a reason we're having the parties a week in advance. So we can get absolutely *blasted* and still have a fantastic wedding."

"And then Warren can take care of you."

Ellie grinned. "Exactly."

I reached out and took her hand. "Sorry I haven't seen you as much."

"I've been so busy I should be apologizing to you. With having a wedding planner and everything, I thought things would be calmer this close to it, but it feels like I've been going at full speed this whole time." She squeezed my hand. "I'm just glad you're here."

"I'm glad about that too."

"I bet you are. With a pack like that?" Ellie leaned back and shook her head. "I'm so fucking in love with Warren, but even I've got my eyes. And they can't take theirs off you, Iz."

"It's been... nice."

"You did not just say they're *nice*."

"What? It's true."

She burst out laughing. "*Isolde*. Those men worship the ground you walk on and one look at them tells me they know exactly what they're doing in bed. So please tell me it's better than fucking nice."

I turned as red as a strawberry. Or a tomato. Or my hair. Ellie grinned at me in victory. "I knew it."

What would everyone think after the wedding when they suddenly weren't around? What would *I* do? Every day that passed made me a little more comfortable with them and a little more afraid of what was going to happen when it was over. I didn't *want* it to be over.

My mouth went dry. It was the first time I'd let myself think it. I didn't want it to end with them, despite it being temporary.

Trinity had better be ready to pick me up off the floor because it was her idea.

"Hey," Ellie said. "Where'd you go?"

"Sorry. Just got lost in my thoughts."

"Of them? Do I need to kick their asses?"

"No," I said with a laugh. "You don't have to kick their asses."

"Good. That wasn't on my agenda for tonight."

We pulled up to the club, which wasn't too far from the house. Nothing was very far in Clarity. There was already a line outside though the sun wasn't quite set, and we walked right past it, our names already on the list.

Because of me getting ready and Ellie's make out session, we were a touch late, and the rest of the bridal party was already there. Including Angela. I groaned, and Ellie looped her arm through mine on the way up to VIP. "I know. The girls already know to make a barrier between the two of you. If everything goes well, you won't even have to talk to her."

"That's nice of you, but I'm a big girl. I can take care of it if I need to." Then I paused. "Wait, is she in the wedding?"

"No. She's just around because of Beau. And..." She winced. "Fuck, this probably isn't the best time to tell you this. Remember how you're the co-maid of honor?"

"Meaning you're too nice to me and let me get away with not coming to shit? Yeah, I remember."

"Yeah. Well, Tina's husband is in the wedding. One of them, anyway."

There was a sinking feeling in my stomach. "So that means..."

"You'll have to walk down the aisle with Beau. Are you going to be okay?"

I scrunched up my face. "It won't be the most comfortable thing I've ever done, but yeah, I'll be okay. Whether the guys will be is a different question. But as long as I don't have to sit with him too, we're good."

"Hell no. He's at the end of the head table with Angela. He wants her involved? He has to give up a good spot."

We finished walking up the stairs. "I knew I loved you."

"Because I'm amazing."

The rest of her friends saw her, and I lost her to screams and promises to buy the bride a drink. I turned and looked out at the club, trying to soak in the atmosphere. This used to be my world. It didn't feel like it much anymore, but there was a certain nostalgia to it.

But I couldn't say I missed it.

Ellie eventually dragged me away from the railing and shoved a drink in my hand. I didn't know her friends well, since they were all Ellie's age and a few years younger than me, but they were nice. Fun. And were so intent on getting wasted that they didn't notice I wasn't drinking much. Enough to feel good and loose. Not enough to black out. Okay, more than enough to feel loose, but I was still fine. Maybe.

"Let's dance!" My sister nearly tripped over herself—and everyone else—getting to me. "Come on. I wanna dance with my sister."

We both laughed on the way to the packed dance floor, ignoring the hoots and shouts from people who knew it was a bachelorette. I was drunk enough to pull out my phone and take a selfie to send to Joel. He wanted his scent mixed with mine? It was happening. Right now.

I sent it to him.

Isolde:
*Thinking of you.*

Then I put my phone away, ignored it completely, and just danced.

We danced until the whole rest of the bridal party joined us. We danced until I was parched and desperately needed a drink. I grabbed Ellie and shouted over the music. "*I need a drink.*"

The bar was packed, but I eventually got the bartender's attention for a water and another cosmo. Time to go back to VIP and take a break.

I barely managed to save my drink when I turned, knocking straight into someone.

Not just someone. *Angela*.

She looked at me with a look that could kill. "Watch it, bitch."

I rolled my eyes. "The hate is unnecessary, Angela. I'm not trying to get Beau back. I don't want him. I'm not trying to step on your toes. I just want to get through the wedding."

Stepping past her, I went to weave through the crowd until I heard her. "Sure. I really believe you." Something else was too low to hear, but it wasn't anything kind.

Too bad for Angela I'd had enough to drink that I didn't give a shit. I turned back to her. "What the hell is your problem? I haven't done anything to you except what you've made up in your head."

"Whatever."

"Yeah, whatever." I stomped across the club and back to our table, waving to Ellie when I saw her looking concerned.

A couple minutes later, I looked up to find Angela charging towards me. "You know what? Not whatever. I think what you're doing is gross and over the top, and you should be fucking ashamed of yourself."

"What are you talking about?"

"I mean the *pack* you brought to make Beau jealous."

My eyebrows flew into my hairline. "Excuse me?"

"It's obvious. You lost Beau, so you bring the kind of guys he can't stand to piss him off and make him jealous so you can steal him back."

I stood up. "Okay. How many times do I have to tell you I have no interest? I don't know what he told you, but he's the one who broke it off. So, I have no idea what you're talking about. This is a pointless conversation."

"Damn fucking right he broke it off. He should have done it so much sooner."

I rubbed my forehead, my brain fuzzy and not comprehending how we'd even gotten here. "What?"

"He told me everything. How you never gave him any space. How you were so fucking clingy, he had to sneak out in order to see his friends. How you were so possessive and jealous he thought he wouldn't ever get away from you, so he had to change the locks while you weren't home."

I blinked. "That's what he told you?"

"It's the truth. I was the one who had to throw away all your shit because he couldn't trust you to come get it. So I see what you're doing. You saw a chance to make him jealous, and you're taking it."

Suddenly I was tired. So fucking tired, and I wanted to be anywhere but here. "That's not what happened, Angela. I didn't bring them to make Beau jealous."

"As if you could."

"Are we done now?"

She tossed back what was left of her drink. "Not until you're not in the wedding. Because like hell am I going to let Beau walk down the aisle with you. He doesn't deserve that."

I pulled out my phone, ready to call the guys to come get me, and she smacked it out of my hand. "What the fuck?!"

"Do you have any idea what you threw away, Isolde? You threw away the best man and the kindest person on the planet to slum it with men who can barely afford a proper suit. The shit they wore to your parents' party was insulting, not to mention pawing at you in front of everyone like they were dogs in heat." She lifted her hands into quotes. "'Baby girl.' Are you serious right now? Figures the only people you could manage to hold on to are addicts. Do you help them get their next fix? Is that why they stay?"

Something inside my brain snapped, and my whole body went still. "What did you just say?"

Angela puffed up her shoulders. "You heard me. You're such a toxic bitch that the only guys you can attract are ones on drugs. You think I didn't see you at the bonfire? Smoking god knows what? What dumpster did you scrape them out of? I want to know so I can make sure they know where to go home to once they're free of *you*."

I tossed what was left of my drink straight in her face. She sputtered, teetering backward on her heels. I felt like I'd turned to ice. Totally calm and smooth, with anger burning straight to the core of me.

"Insult them again. I dare you."

Angela smiled, the move full of poison. "Trash you dragged in to make up for your personality, Isolde. You notice that no one in the bridal party talks to you? They don't want you here. No one fucking wants you here except the shit clinging to your shoes you call a pack."

The scream coming out of me was lost in the music. I lunged at Angela, taking her down to the floor. Dead. She was fucking dead. How *dare* she talk about them like she knew them?

It didn't even matter, because she had this coming.

I hit her, and she laughed. "See? Can't even take the truth."

"*It's not the truth*," I shrieked, right as an arm came around my waist and hauled me away from her. "Let me go. Let me *go*."

"I can't do that, sweetheart." Vaughn's voice cut through the noise of the club, but not my anger. "You can't do this."

"Yes I fucking can. She insulted you, and she *has it coming*."

Across from me, Angela got to her feet. Blood shone on her lip in the lights from the club. Good. Fucking bitch deserved it.

Suddenly I couldn't see her, Rowan stepping into the space between us and lifting my face, checking me. "Ellie called us. We got here as fast as we could."

I didn't recognize my own voice, rage building beneath my skin. "Get out of the way, Rowan."

"No." Alpha power rolled through the single word. "Back down, Isolde."

My Omega retreated in the face of his Alpha, anger giving way to grief and fear. Tears burned, and the lights blurred into a kaleidoscope in front of me.

A third voice reached me. Cade, speaking in my ear. "She's drunk and so are you, princess. She probably doesn't know half the things she's saying, and even if she does, they're not true. Let's go home, okay?"

Ellie was suddenly there, and I felt so much worse. "I'm sorry, El."

She raised an eyebrow. "I would have let you keep going, but I can't have my maid of honor getting arrested. But for the record, you have my permission to beat her ass at any time."

Across from me, Beau was there too, holding back Angela, who was still trying to get to me. His eyes were only on me and not on her at all. "Run away, bitch. Just proves what I'm saying. You're an Omega so desperate for love you'll do whatever it takes to keep people, no matter who you hurt in the process."

"Let's get out of here," Hawk growled, taking my hand and keeping it. Vaughn's arm was still around my waist, and they walked me out of the club under the watchful eyes of the bouncers.

What she said was true. At least that part of it. I was desperate for love, because I wanted it. Did that mean I hurt people? Was I holding onto these men too tightly because I didn't want them to leave? Was I as toxic as she claimed?

Maybe there was something I hadn't seen when Beau tried to kick me out. Was it me?

It echoed in my head.

Was it me?

Was it me?

We were back at the estate so quickly I barely remembered getting there. Still too buzzed, I let them get me into bed and dry the tears that didn't seem to stop coming, no matter what I did.

They spoke softly, held me tenderly, but I couldn't stop hearing those words and feeling them cut me open.

Was it me?

## CHAPTER THIRTY-SIX

### ISOLDE

Pain pounded through my skull. My mouth tasted like death, and I needed water. I was hot. Hot with shivers and chills. Sure, I had stuff to drink last night, but not enough to make me feel like this.

I wasn't perfect. I'd done my share of partying in college, before college, and even a bit after. I knew how much I had to drink to have a bad hangover, and last night I wasn't even close.

Didn't stop me from losing my cool though.

Fuck, I never should have gone after her like that. She was trying to piss me off, and it worked. But hearing her say things like that about them? I couldn't let it happen. The need to defend them against what she said hadn't been a choice. It was a necessity.

But her parting shot still stuck with me. Maybe I was someone who clung to people too hard and made them regret it. Maybe I was the one who was at fault somehow.

Maybe I was already doing it with this pack, even though they didn't belong to me.

Fear and grief lodged in my chest, curling around my heart. I shoved my face harder into the pillow I clung to, prepared to sit in the physical and emotional pain. Because ever since Vaughn and the beach, my instincts were higher, and it was so much harder to shut things out.

A gentle hand skimmed across my arm, smoothing all the way

down it and circling my wrist to try to make me let go of the pillow. I didn't. "Hey, baby girl."

No moving. If I didn't, it was possible I could make him think I'd fallen back asleep.

But of course that didn't work. He gently and insistently separated me from the pillow, rolling me back so he could see me, and I could see all of him. From his beautiful face to the tattoos that rolled down his chest. I couldn't meet his eyes.

"How do you feel?"

"Like shit," I whispered and cleared my throat. "I'm... pretty embarrassed right now, and I'd rather none of you see me like this, if you could give me some time."

Hawk frowned, nothing but concern in his eyes. "Why are you embarrassed?"

I still wasn't looking at him. "Because I made a fool of myself, and some of what she said about me is true. So, I'll just stay here until I don't feel like death warmed up."

Movement at the corner of my eye had me looking at Vaughn, who stood at the edge of the bed, eyes burning with anger. "Which things did she say that were true?"

My breath hiccuped, and I looked away, keeping the emotions in check. Barely. "I am desperate. And maybe that makes me do things I shouldn't. I probably held on too tightly. Maybe I do hold some of the blame."

His growl had my hair standing on end and chills running over my skin. He pulled me to the edge of the bed, still careful with me, but not giving me a choice either. He sat me on the edge, legs on either side of my knees so I had nowhere to go. My face was in his hands, and all I could think about was that he smelled so good, and I didn't want all of this to be ruined.

"I don't know what she said to you before we got there. When Ellie called us, I don't think we've ever moved so fast, and I'm grateful the club is close. But *nothing* I heard while I was there was remotely true. About you, us, or anyone else. Don't you dare let her into your head, Isolde. That's exactly what she wanted."

My lower lip trembled, and I focused on the little hollow at the base of his throat. "But what if it's true?"

"It's not. Because there's nothing wrong with wanting to be loved, sweetheart. And if the right people love you, they *want* you to hold on tight. Okay?"

Everything felt so close and so real. I couldn't manage to speak, but I nodded once.

Vaughn leaned down to kiss my forehead. "Why don't you go take a quick shower so you feel a little better? Then the five of us want to talk to you."

I looked up at him in panic, and he smiled. "It's not about last night at all, or anything bad. I promise."

"Still not reassuring," I muttered.

"I promise," he said again, helping me up off the bed.

The shower made me feel a little better, but I still felt rough, and it didn't make sense. Probably just me getting older and not being able to handle alcohol as much. Which was shitty, but also a reality.

I pulled on the biggest sweatshirt I brought, and some sleep shorts. Being comfortable was my biggest priority right now with my stomach in tangles because they wanted to talk to me.

All five of them sat on the couches in the living area when I came out of the closet. Fear so visceral ran through me I couldn't even take a step forward. Joel was the one who stood and came to me, pulling me against him. "Your scent right now makes my heart break, Isolde. You don't have anything to be afraid of."

"Usually needing to talk isn't a good thing," I said quietly.

"Well, it is this time."

I whined, but let him tug me to the couches to sit between him and Rowan. A sweatshirt was a bad choice. I was already too hot, sweating beneath it. My head pounded, nausea rising like a tide. I really needed to go back to bed.

Hawk leaned forward, elbows on knees, with his dark eyes on me. "We decided a couple of days ago we were going to talk to you, baby girl. We've wanted to, and we can't wait any longer."

Unnatural heat filled the back of my throat. "I'm sorry—"

I sprinted for the bathroom, dry heaving over the toilet when I got there. There was nothing to throw up. I'd barely eaten yesterday because I'd slept for most of it, and what was left of the alcohol was already gone. But everything swam. I felt hot, and I could smell the toothpaste I left open on the counter. The lingering scent of my bodywash from the shower. I felt like I could smell *everything*.

It was physically impossible for me to be pregnant, thank fuck, but whatever this was? I didn't like it.

A knock came on the door. "Isolde?" Rowan's concerned voice. "Are you okay?"

"Yeah." I opened the door, frowning. "I didn't throw up. I have no idea what's happening."

The scent of coconut slammed into me, followed by that trace of salt I couldn't get enough of. Rowan's familiar scent, but it had never smelled like this before. Sweeter and sharper and with a hundred different layers. It curved around me and melded to me and changed me. I would never be the same after scenting something this delicious. All I wanted to do was bury my face in his chest and inhale, so that's exactly what I did.

My fingers gripped his shirt, my nose in the fabric before I could take another breath and holy *fucking shit* he smelled so good. I never wanted him to take a step away from me again. I would glue him to my side because he was mine.

Dawning realization reached me.

Oh. Fuck.

He was *mine.*

I looked up at Rowan and saw the concern on his face. He brushed my hair back. "Isolde?"

"Is it all of you?" I whispered.

Before I could answer, I pushed past him into the room. All of their scents crashed over me in a wave. A mixture and medley of everything good in the world that told me the truth. They were mine. They were my Alphas. My pack.

My knees buckled, and Cade met me halfway, catching me before I could fully hit the floor. I heard their cries of distress from somewhere else, sinking into the depth of his soft sandalwood. His fingers brushed my head, and he went rigid. "She's burning up. I think she's going into heat."

Rowan wrapped around me from behind with a purr, lifting me up and turning me so I could hold him too. Tears streamed down my face. Everything moved so fast I didn't know if I was happy or shocked or angry.

*They were mine.*

No questions or wondering, no having to figure things out. They were mine, and they would have known this whole time.

My voice broke when I found it. "Why didn't you tell me?"

Rowan's hand held the back of my head. "We were about to. Just now. We'd agreed we couldn't wait any longer."

"But before. Why?"

"Because you wouldn't have believed us," he whispered. "You weren't ready."

Another set of arms came around me, and suddenly Vaughn held me. He nuzzled into my neck before speaking. "You told us you didn't want anything to do with us outside our arrangement. Not even sex. We knew the second we met that you were ours, but we weren't going to lose you because we moved too fast."

It was true. If they'd told me this when we first arrived, I would have panicked and ran. Maybe even sent them away. Part of me felt like I should be angry with them for not telling me, but I wasn't. They were right. I was too broken and I wouldn't have listened.

"But we never lied to you, baby girl." Hawk's voice came from behind us. "I need you to know that. We left this out, but we never lied. And we tried to tell you how much we wanted you without outright saying it."

*I'm not pretending with you.*

*You are my priority.*

*You're* mine.

Hawk's voice at the anniversary party. *My pack and I. She's our Omega.*

All the times they'd spoken of things that could come in the future. The quickly hidden flashes of hurt whenever I dismissed it. Because they'd already known they wanted me. And I missed it entirely.

I pressed my face into Vaughn's neck, breathing him in. He was fucking lickable. I loved his scent before and now I was obsessed. At the same time, I needed the others close to me so I could have theirs too because it was all incredible.

"Speaking of the arrangement," Joel said quietly. "We returned your money as soon as we arrived at the house. We didn't need to be paid to spend time with our Omega. And I hope—" He took a hitching breath that had me looking over at him. "We hope you know how much we want you. You're the last client we'll ever have, because you're ours. If you want us."

*If* I wanted them.

*If.*

Like it was even a question. The only reason I hadn't dived headlong into them was the knowledge that it wouldn't last and it was fake.

Somehow I was in Joel's lap and kissing him and I didn't remember moving. "Of course I want you. I wanted you even though I wasn't allowed to, and I was already planning on how I was going to survive when you left."

"We're not leaving you. Ever."

I whined, perfume exploding around us. That explained why I was perfuming even while asleep. "It's not time for my heat," I whispered. "I don't know why this is happening."

Cade laughed. "I don't care how. I'm glad it did."

"I'm guessing it was the beach," Vaughn said. "Your instincts were just as high as mine, and last night when you defended us to Angela, it pushed you over the edge. It can happen."

Omegas had at least one heat per year, but we could have more. He wasn't wrong. My Omega had been just below the surface for days. It wouldn't have taken much, and that bitch pushed exactly the right buttons.

A new wave of heat and nausea rolled over me, far stronger. No wonder I felt hungover. An unexpected heat like this could make you feel completely different, and it was coming on fast. Pain gripped my gut suddenly, constricting because I was empty and I needed to be filled with a knot. Right now.

My hands fluttered on Joel's shoulders. "It hurts. Please."

Rowan stood beside us. "We have a nest at our house. It's not far, but it will still take a little time to get there."

"I have one here," I managed, letting my head brace against Joel. "It's probably dusty as hell, but—"

No, that wasn't right. After I moved in with Beau, my mother asked if she could repurpose it because it had a good view and nice natural light. It was now her office. "No, I think it's gone now."

"Okay, baby girl." Hawk was already moving. "We'll get you to ours. I think your parents are in the breakfast room. I'll tell Ellie and your parents what's happening so they don't think we're kidnapping you. And I'll ask for some extra things for the nest."

No, he couldn't.

I struggled to my feet, nearly falling into his arms in the process. Panic ripped through me, made all the hotter by the burn writhing under my skin. He couldn't go. He couldn't leave. I couldn't take it again.

"Please," I begged. "Don't go."

Hawk leaned in and kissed my forehead. "I'm not going anywhere, baby girl. I promise. All I'm doing is going to get some things to make sure you're comfortable."

"*No.*" I barely recognized the strangled, high-pitched voice coming out of me. I clung to him. "Don't leave me, Alpha. Please.

Please don't go. I'll do whatever you want. Just please don't leave me."

"Isolde." Hawk stared at me, horror on his face. "Why would you—"

His face transformed into anger so sharp it stole my breath. "Did he leave you while you were in heat?"

Tears welled in my eyes, my hands fisting his shirt. I didn't like to think about it. It still hurt after all this time. "Don't go," I whispered.

"I'm going to fucking kill him."

Arms came around me and lifted me. Sandalwood and vanilla with a touch of deeper sex and sweat. Cade. He smelled so *good*. I turned into his hold, pressing my face into his neck.

"I'm not leaving you, baby girl," Hawk said. "Not even for a second. We're all going together. I'll take care of this, okay?"

I nodded into Cade's neck. Low words floated around me, but they were all here and I was *safe*. Cade was safe. They were here, and they were mine.

Voices echoing drew me back to the world through a swell of rising temperature and perfume. The waves were growing sharper.

I hadn't even noticed we were moving until I heard the door slam open ahead of us, and Hawk's voice slicing through the breakfast room. "You left her alone while she was *in heat*?"

Vaughn pushed open the door in time for me to see Hawk pull Beau out of his chair by his collar and hit him in the face. I cringed into Cade, the sound of the hit violent... and satisfying.

The table erupted, people moving to pull Hawk off Beau, but it barely worked. Hawk kept hitting him. "You fucking worthless excuse of an Alpha, leaving an Omega alone when she needed you." Another punch.

A whine slipped out of me. I wanted Hawk with me. Closer. I loved this, but it could come later.

"Elliot," Cade said, and it was the only thing that got through. Hawk's head whipped up, eyes finding mine. He was across the room to us in seconds, leaving Beau on the floor, groaning. Angela was screaming something, but I didn't care. I noticed it was the bridal party, but no one else. My parents, Ellie, and Warren weren't in sight.

My Alpha kissed me and we were moving out of the house and to their car.

"Are you sure?" Joel asked. "We can stay at the nest here if you like. Just use the bed in the suite."

"I'm sure." I didn't want to be in the same house as Beau and Angela. As anyone. All I wanted was to be alone with *my* pack. The nest being perfect didn't matter. I would have plenty of heats in my life to have a perfect nest. Right now I needed them and the truth of what was between us. Something I should have known the day I met them. I wish I'd known.

But they weren't wrong. I never would have believed them. Probably would have sent them away and tried to muddle through the last two weeks alone. Miserable and sad.

Cade arranged me over his legs in the back of the car, my feet ending up in Vaughn's lap. I closed my eyes and drifted, knowing they would take care of me.

# CHAPTER THIRTY-SEVEN

## ISOLDE

Rowan took me from Cade and carried me inside. It was too bright out here. I needed it to be dim and cozy and warm. Not bright. I shut my eyes. The sun warmed my already over-heated body too quickly.

Soon the coolness of the indoors soothed the burning under my skin. The air smelled like them. A tantalizing blend of everyone together.

And I was *theirs*.

Happiness bubbled up, trying to break free, but I couldn't move. All I needed was a knot. And a nest. I needed them.

The last time I had a heat, I was all by myself. Beau hadn't stayed. He said he was sorry, but he left. I could barely remember what a good heat was like. Even the ones before that had been... basic. Barely enough to get by.

Rowan stepped into a small hallway that was bright, like it had windows. "Almost there," he said.

Darkness opened in front of us.

There was no scent in here, like no one had used the nest before. My Omega preened, loving being the first and the fucking *only*. This was *my* nest. No one else's.

Cade stepped up beside me and picked up my hand. "Sorry there's no time to get it ready, princess. We'll make it up to you."

I looked around the space, and my jaw fell open.

A deep bowl of cushions and pillows, all in different shades of turquoise and blue. Like we were looking down on the ocean from above. One side of the space looked like it could slide open. Maybe to the windows? But right now it was blissfully dark, a couple of low lights rendering it cozy and safe. The ceiling and the walls that weren't lined with cushions were painted a dark navy like the summer beach sky, and I spotted little silvery constellations across it.

"What do you mean?" My voice rasped. "This is beautiful."

"You like it?" Rowan asked.

"Yeah."

He put me down, and I wandered into the nest, feeling the soft squish of the pillows. It was stunning. My Omega was already picking out things to tweak and change, but she had no problem with this. It reminded me of them. Open and free. Like relaxing on the beach with the wind in your hair.

I sank down into the cushy floor, need drizzling over me like someone was pouring hot honey over my skin. And yet, my Omega was settled and comfortable. With my Alphas and my Beta.

Tears burned in my eyes. I didn't know how to feel, because after so long, it wasn't real. It couldn't be real. They couldn't really be mine.

Somewhere along the way, I'd given up hope that I'd actually have anyone, or deserved anyone.

"Isolde?"

I looked over. All five of them were in the doorway in varying states of undress, and suddenly my mouth was watering. "What are you doing over there?"

Vaughn smiled. "It's your nest, sweetheart. Can we come in?"

All I could do was nod.

Joel reached me first, hitting his knees in front of me. "We're here, and we're not leaving you, okay? You're ours. We're going to take care of you."

They told me the first day that they would take care of me. But I had no idea how deeply they meant it. Every single action they'd taken had been for me. Making sure I was okay. Giving me pleasure. Drawing me out of my own head. And they did it all while thinking I might not want them.

It was too much.

I sobbed and reached for him.

"Not the reaction I was expecting," he laughed quietly.

"It's good. It's just so much. I don't even know what to do. I barely remember how to do this. I just—" I shuddered, desperation rattling to my core.

Joel took my face in his hands. "Do you trust us? That we'll help you? You can have as much power as you want, little Omega, but if you want to let go, you can. We've got you."

The last bit of tension slid from my spine. "I trust you."

"Good." Joel's blue gaze went darker than I thought possible. "Because shower or not, I can still smell myself on you, and I need to knot your pussy as much as I need to breathe."

He lifted the sweatshirt, and I helped him toss it away. The shorts were gone too. I wasn't sleepy this time, and something told me I was going to like regular sex with Joel just as much as the other kind.

Neither of us had any more patience.

Joel shoved my legs apart, lifted my hips, and slammed home, swallowing my cry with a ravenous kiss that lit me on fire. Whatever I'd been holding back was gone. I might as well have been in the middle of a volcano the way I felt now, like I was incandescent and glowing. Molten metal. Everything I touched would burn. And I would burn too. Every place where he touched me and kissed me was a bright, starry explosion, and Joel wasn't holding back.

Orgasms were easier when I was in heat, but they still weren't *easy*. Still, I wanted it. I needed the bright light my body chased with every driving stroke. But they were here in this too. I pulled Joel's face to mine. "I might not be fast enough for you. It's okay."

His growl shot straight to my clit, and the scraping of his teeth beneath my jaw made me crave the bite it promised. "You're mine, Isolde. You're my fucking Omega. I don't give a single shit if pleasure doesn't come easily to you. It's your heat, and a privilege to help you get there. No matter how long it takes."

Above both of us, I saw Hawk. The view straight up his body was delightfully obscene in the way the dim light highlighted his muscles and tattoos. His pierced cock. "And remember what I told you, baby girl. We're still learning you. We're going to have a lot of practice knowing exactly how to get you there."

Joel stole my mouth, shifting his hips, and suddenly he was hitting that same spot he had yesterday. That one move sent my body into overdrive. I moaned into his mouth. "How do you do that?"

He chuckled. "We're experimenting. So let's try this."

It was the opposite of soft, slow comfort. Joel fucked me hard and fast, plunging directly into the spot that made my vision sparkle. Heat built under my skin, and the normal resistance I had disappeared. They were *mine*.

Bright light flashed behind my eyes, pleasure cracking through me like I was a glow stick and Joel was the one to break me. He groaned in my ear, knot swelling and locking us together.

Nothing had ever felt as good as his knot, knowing he wasn't doing this as a favor or because there was money between us. It was because he belonged to me and he *wanted* to.

Joel rested his forehead against mine, our breath mingling. "I'm sorry what happened last night is what pushed you here, but *fuck*, I'm so glad it did, Isolde. Not being able to tell you was torture."

"It doesn't feel real," I admitted.

"It's very real. Hell, I was the one who broke the plan. We weren't supposed to tell you our real names, and then I scented you and I couldn't bear to do anything else. You were mine. I wasn't going to pretend to be someone else."

He rocked his hips, making me gasp, the heat pulling those tendrils of pleasure and amplifying them. Reminding me that I needed more. I felt like there was a gnawing hole in my chest and they were the only ones who could fill it.

I was insatiable.

"What were you going to tell me your name was?"

"Andrew."

A choked laugh came out of me. "You're not an Andrew."

"No?" One eyebrow raised. "I think I could be a good Andrew."

"Never."

"What if I told you it's my middle name?" I gasped, and he laughed before kissing me long and slow. "I'm kidding. But you're fun to tease."

Joel's knot loosened, freeing me for the next one, and I *wanted it.* All of them. More. Right now. Cade was there, rolling me over and fitting himself to me from behind. "I can't knot you, princess, but I can still give you what you need. There are knot sleeves I can get for next time."

He took my breath away, pulling me up against his chest with a hand at my throat. It reminded me of that first night with all of them, helping me get where I needed to go. "I don't need toys," I managed. "I just need you."

I knew even without looking at him it was something he needed to hear. That I didn't want him less because he wasn't an Alpha. On the contrary, Cade was the first one to tell me I was safe with them. He was everything, his scent driving me just as crazy.

Now I could scent the layers beneath it. Not just balmy vanilla and sandalwood. But the crispness of woodsmoke and that light, earthy scent of dry branches and burning bonfires. I wanted to taste him now that I knew.

All of them.

"You didn't get to tie me up."

"Don't worry, angel. I'm still going to tie you up. We'll have plenty of time for you in my ropes. And plenty of time for all of us to fuck you in them."

"I—" My brain was fuzzy and flighty with all the sensations and scents and the mental image he painted for me. So fucking hot I couldn't breathe. I wanted that. Could we do that right now?

I already knew the heat wasn't patient enough for me to be tied up and untied and all the things that came along with it. But there was something incredible about the idea of being entirely immobilized with nothing to do but enjoy while they played with me.

Hawk sprawled in front of me. "Don't stop, Cade. I'm finally going to have my taste." He sealed his lips over my clit, sucking deep and moaning when he did. "Fuck me, baby girl, it's a good thing I didn't know how good you taste. I would have needed you instead of the waffle."

Cade's cock driving up into me, his hand at my throat, Hawk's tongue teasing me was all too much. They sent me into a silent, shuddering orgasm. Cade pulled away so Hawk could consume me and the slick the orgasm gave me, finishing across my back.

I loved being painted with him. The scent of him lower and darker, like his cum on my skin could mark me deeper than they already had.

Pulling back, Hawk licked his lips with a grin. "Worth the wait."

"My turn." I lunged forward, wanting that sweetness all over my tongue. Hawk had been sweet before, and now he was pure sugar. I was going to get a sugar high just from licking his skin.

The metal of his piercing slid across the roof of my mouth, and he hissed, gathering my hair in his hands. "Shit, baby girl."

Rowan had told me I was good at this, and I chose to believe him. I took as much of Hawk's length as I could, but he was a bit longer than Rowan was, and I didn't make it all the way. He didn't seem to care. And I couldn't keep my focus because another body slid beneath mine and pulled me down onto a now-familiar pierced cock.

*Vaughn.*

*His* piercings made my vision disappear entirely, stroking where I was already sensitive. And he knew exactly how much I could take. Vaughn gripped my hips, fingers digging into my skin as he yanked me down onto him just as hard as he was thrusting up into me.

"Don't think that's all she can take, Hawk. I know for a fact she can fit your entire cock down her throat, and she likes when you make it."

Heat flushed across my face because it was true, and the tightening of Hawk's fingers in my hair had my mind and body opening and surrendering. That same falling sensation, into pleasure and safety and so much fucking more.

Vaughn reached up, his hand curling around my throat just as Hawk pushed deep. He felt so much bigger pushing against the force of Vaughn's hand, but he was all the way down, and it felt easy. Like I needed to be reminded I could trust them and my Omega reacted.

Wet heat circled one of my nipples, Vaughn pulling as much of my breast into his mouth as he could before doing the same to the other, squeezing my throat and fucking me like the world would end if he didn't.

"Even here, you have your safeword, sweetheart. Use it if you need it. Or tap out."

I loved having it at the same time I knew that—for the moment —I didn't need it.

"Take a big breath, Isolde," Hawk said through gritted teeth. I hauled in air, not fully comprehending anything because there was so much sensation. Everywhere. It was too much and it wasn't enough because an orgasm was building but it wasn't there yet and I *needed* it.

Hawk buried himself all the way in my throat and held me there. His hands gripped my hair, and that edge of pain cut through me along with his growl. "Good girl."

Pleasure cascaded over me, so fucking close.

I whimpered around his cock, wordlessly begging for a little more. Vaughn had me so close, every push helping the building brightness I was slowly being lowered into.

Hands smoothed over my ass, spreading me wide, a tongue exploring me there too. Shock morphed into heat and light.

I shattered.

There was pure, divine sweetness on my tongue and ecstasy flaring through my veins. My body was no longer mine to control, instead owned by the pleasure they overloaded me with. And they had done it because they wanted to. Because they wanted me.

Because I was theirs.

I went limp in the aftermath, all that sensation replaced with peace and safety. Sleep beckoned me, and I nearly groaned. I was so tired of being tired. But if we were going to get through this, I needed the rest. They would keep me safe while I slept in my nest.

My eyes couldn't stay open, but I was excited for the rest of the heat.

## CHAPTER THIRTY-EIGHT

HAWK

I could still taste her on my tongue.

My little Omega who was now sated and soft, trapped on Vaughn's knot beneath me. Happiness and so much more surged through my chest. She knew, and she wanted us. Nothing had ever felt so right as having her in our house and in our nest. *Her* nest.

As soon as possible, I wanted her here, making the nest into what she truly wanted. Making our space hers and showing us how we could shift our life to fit around her. Because she was ours.

I smirked. "Well, that wasn't really how I thought telling her would go."

The others laughed quietly too, and Rowan nodded. "No kidding."

Joel was the one who looked at me. "You have her phone, right?"

"Yeah."

"We need to call Ellie and her parents. They weren't there for the show in the breakfast room. I'm sure they know by now, but we still need to tell them."

I stepped carefully around Vaughn and Isolde. "I'll do it. I'm the one who punched the best man, and I can own that."

"Don't go too far," Vaughn whispered. "In case she wakes up."

No, I wouldn't. The panic and pain I saw earlier wasn't anything I ever wanted to see again, and the bruises on my knuckles weren't enough. Punching Beau had felt good, but it didn't compare to the pain he'd inflicted on Isolde. My baby girl.

I grit my teeth, trying to quell the anger, and grabbed her phone from where I'd left it. There were already texts and missed calls, so I chose Ellie and pulled up a video feed.

She was talking before she even looked at the camera. "Holy shit, where did you go? Everyone is freaking out, Iz." Ellie froze when she saw me. "Where's my sister?"

"Isolde went into heat this morning. We're at our house taking care of her."

"*Oh*, okay. That makes sense. Honestly, it all happened so fast, no one could really say what happened except for Beau having a black eye and you guys carrying what looked like an unconscious Isolde out of the house."

I winced. "That's on me, and I apologize for causing a disturbance, though I'll be honest, I'm not sorry for hitting him. Isolde panicked when I tried to leave the room because he *left her alone* during her last heat. And I lost it."

Ellie glanced around behind her. "You have no arguments from me. I don't like him. I've never liked him, and I have no problem with you hitting him." She snickered. "Can't say he's happy about it, though. He's still in with Warren, yelling."

Taking a deep breath, I kept my voice even. "Where is Warren in this?"

"He wants to talk to Isolde when she's back. He's bothered by what happened last night, and last week in the entryway. But it's hard when you've known someone for so long and you've never seen their bad behavior up close the way he has these past few days." Her sly smile gave me hope. "I'm pretty sure he's right on the edge. I looked in there, and he's pretty much just staring at Beau, pissed off. But Warren will never jump to a conclusion without all the information. So he needs to talk to you and Isolde. But he's pissed."

Not where I hoped he'd be, but we could work with that. Even Isolde would recognize the difficulty of changing your view of someone. She'd just become aware of how toxic some of his behaviors were while we'd known her. So as long as Warren wasn't taking his side, we were in an okay place.

"Still," I said. "I know I probably strode in there and caused all kinds of chaos. I'm sorry about that. Are your parents okay?"

"They're fine. Just want to know where Isolde is."

I nodded. "Will you tell them? I'm not sure how long her heats are, but everything should still be fine for the wedding."

Ellie waved a hand. "Do whatever you need to. If you guys need anything, let us know. We'll do it. After everything, we just want Isolde to be happy."

"I appreciate that, and I'm sure Isolde does too, even if she doesn't recognize it." I saw Warren approaching in the back of the frame. "I should get back to her."

"Keep us posted."

Leaning against the wall, I blew out a long, slow breath. I barely remembered getting to the breakfast room. My Alpha was in full control, only looking for the source of pain for my Omega. I remembered the shocked look on Beau's face and savoring the crunch of his jaw under my hand. His eye too.

I wasn't sure how many times I hit him, but it wasn't enough.

Cade turned the corner and saw me slumped against the wall. "Everything okay?"

"Seems to be for now. Warren wants to talk to us and Isolde once her heat is over. I think he wants to get a different side of the story than the one Beau has been feeding him."

"Fair enough. You okay with grabbing the blanket from your bed? We don't have nest blankets and stuff, so we thought something from each of us might make a good blend of scents before until we can buy them."

Hell yes, I was okay with that. I wanted Isolde wrapped in our scents for the rest of fucking time. "I'll help you grab them."

Walking into the nest again almost put me on my knees. Isolde's red hair spread out against the blue of the pillows, making it so much more vibrant. In the dimness here, she was like a fallen star, bright even in the darkness.

It was a good thing she knew she was ours now, because I was in love with her. There was no way *not* to love her. Every hesitant smile and worry that crossed her mind. Every time she trusted us enough to let go even though she was afraid. Each piece of herself she revealed was another piece that fit against me, completing a picture I hadn't even known was missing something before we met.

I dropped the two comforters I'd brought to the side, instead stretching out beside her and pulling just my blanket over the two of us. She let out a little sigh, shuddering and stretching into the new warmth like a cat.

Joel smiled at us from across the nest. "She's more relaxed. She still had tension at the estate. Here it's like she melted."

"Good," I murmured. "She needs a place where she doesn't have to have any walls."

It didn't matter how long it took for her to wake up, or how many days her heat drove all of us to fuck, knot, come, and start all over again, I wasn't leaving her.

I tucked my fingers around her hip and pulled her closer, my lips on her temple. The scent of magnolias and roses drowned me, and I was happy to drift away, but I couldn't close my eyes. Couldn't miss a single second. Because she was here, and she was *ours*.

## CHAPTER THIRTY-NINE

ISOLDE

I felt so warm. I never wanted to move. A second later there was a rumbling purr beneath my ear, and a hand stroking through my hair absently. Sunshine and coconuts, salt and sea. Rowan's big body beneath mine. This time with a blanket over both of us.

Stretching, I pulled myself further onto his body and placed my ear right over his heart so I could hear it beat along with his purr.

"My Omega is awake?"

"Kind of."

"If you're not, it's okay. I like having a soft Omega cuddling me."

I sighed. "You say such nice things."

Another stroke of his hand on my hair. "I'm not going to stop saying them. You're ours now, remember?"

He felt me smile into his skin, because he rolled us together so I was cushioned in blankets and pillows, pinned down by his body. "Hello there."

"Hi." I searched his eyes. "How does this work?"

"How does what work?"

I shook my head. "I don't even know. We're just together?" Hesitation flooded his gaze, and I hurried to keep talking. "Not that I don't want to be. I do. I just... it's so fast I can't wrap my head around it. This morning I thought I would have to spend several weeks sobbing on Trinity's floor because I wouldn't be able to handle you leaving, and now you're mine."

"We've been yours since you walked down that escalator toward us," Rowan whispered the words on my lips. "As for how it works, that's something we'll talk about. But basically? However we want. Right?"

"Right," four other responses, nearly in unison.

"When the heat is over we can give you a tour, but if you hate the house, we'll buy another one. The one thing none of us want is to be without you, Isolde." He bent to kiss the skin of my shoulder. "Now that we've found you, we don't want to let you go. If that's what you had wanted, we would have stepped away, but we're so fucking grateful you didn't."

Vulnerability crept up my spine, made so much more acute by the fact that I was in heat. "Even someone as broken as me?"

Rowan placed his cheek against mine, distracting me from the sounds of the others' protests. "Call yourself broken again, Isolde. See what happens."

"Maybe not broken, but I'm clearly still fucked up from everything. And I wish it would disappear just because you're mine, but it won't."

He kissed me slowly, deepening it until I couldn't breathe, and still deeper. We both panted when he broke away. "No, it won't. But I don't care about that. We have baggage too. Everyone does. Yours just happens to be on the surface right now. It won't always be so close to you."

"Baggage, huh? Any crazy past clients I need to worry about?" I didn't mean the question as anything more than a tease, and he knew.

Rowan laughed. "No, I don't think so."

I hissed, fire filling me up like someone dunked in a vat of lava. Arousal followed on so fast it made me dizzy. "So soon," I moaned. "My heats aren't like this. They're like lazy heats. Slower, less intense."

Lifting me and turning me so I was in the center of the nest, Rowan leaned over me. He took up all the space above me and made me feel small. Cherished. "Ready to surrender for a while?"

I nodded. *Yes*, please. "How long?"

"Until I'm satisfied." His words rocked a shudder through my body. "Hold her for me." He lifted my legs and pushed them up and out until they were caught by other hands. Hawk and Vaughn settled on either side of me, big hands behind my knees, holding me open for their packmate to drive his cock straight into me.

"Maybe your heat is responding to us differently, and that's why it's more intense." Vaughn whispered into my shoulder. "Maybe your Omega knows how much we fucking want you, and is giving us a chance. Or maybe," I felt his smile. "Your heat is so intense because you want *us*."

Rowan's cock stole my breath so I couldn't answer, but he wasn't wrong. I wanted them desperately. Even now I wasn't sure I believed it, but with each inhale of their scents, they were written more firmly on my soul.

Mine. Mine. *Mine*.

The word pulsed in my heartbeat and the rhythm of being fucked.

"Cade, get over here," Rowan growled. "Feed her your balls and see what she does with them."

My back arched off the pillows. "Rowan, you can't say things like that."

"And why not?" He drove into me harder, showing me without words that he owned me right now. I couldn't tell him that his words made me feel needy in a way nothing else did, and I didn't know how to respond. All I could do was take what he gave me.

Every part of me tightened in anticipation.

"Open your mouth, princess."

My eyes had closed. Now they were open and staring up at Cade, knees on either side of my head. I obeyed, melting into their hold and relishing the taste of Cade's skin.

His hand stroked his cock firmly as he slipped his balls into my mouth. I moaned around them, unexpected need surging. This was something I'd never done. I wasn't thinking about anyone else but them right now. But this was new, and I didn't know why I liked it.

It didn't actually matter why I liked it. I was an inferno at the center of four flames, growing brighter under their attention. Able to let go and be free like I couldn't with anyone else.

"Fuck her throat," Rowan ordered, and Cade slid into my mouth, cock dragging across my tongue before gliding into my throat in one go.

Hawk pulled my leg further open with a groan. "You look so pretty with a cock in your throat, baby girl."

"Mmm." Vaughn was with him, teasing me with hands on my skin, spreading me wider for Rowan. "We can see the outline of it every time he pushes in." Teeth grazed my shoulder. "I'm going to take a video of you taking *my* cock just like this, watching your throat bulge with it. Do you think we'll be able to see my piercings too?"

An orgasm broke over me, small but fierce. Their words painted images in my head, and they got me so close so fast.

Rowan moaned. He *moaned*, and I nearly came again. Hearing them undone for me and a sound like that was so fucking hot I couldn't breathe. "Our girl likes dirty talk," he said. "That made her so fucking wet I can barely stay inside her."

I could breathe again, Cade pulling away with a searing look at me. The others had backed away too at Rowan's silent signal. Now his weight held my legs where he wanted them, rocking into me like his life depended on it, taking what he needed.

He nearly lost control, giving me those moans in my ear while he came, filling my body with heat and a knot that made my entire body tingle. "I have so many plans for you. Not all of them can be during the heat."

"Yes, please."

"But I have plans for right now, too."

I managed a smile between the aftershocks of pleasure. "Not satisfied yet?"

"Not even close." Then he leaned in. "Do you remember what I asked you in the library?"

There wasn't anything about that day I didn't remember, but he would have to be more specific. "Which part?"

He drew his hand down my side. It felt like that touch sank beneath my skin and lit me up. I was bioluminescent, like the blooms we sometimes saw in the ocean. All the way down past my hip, where my legs now wrapped around his waist, and further still, until his fingers brushed my ass. "I asked you if you'd be willing to try again."

"I—"

Rowan's mouth covered mine, tongue delving deep. He tasted so good. I could live on their kisses. Among other things. "If you don't want it, tell me now. Otherwise, every hole you have is getting used, Omega. We're going to wring pleasure out of you until you can't take it anymore."

I squeezed down on his knot, slick gushing around his cock. He smiled in victory, and I was blushing. "Go pink all you want. Your cunt loves when we talk dirty." Nipping at my lips, he pressed into me, fucking me with his knot until I gasped for breath, right on the edge, my clit swollen and desperate.

"Can I make you come from words alone?"

He probably could, but I needed it now. One touch was all it would take, but I couldn't seem to lift my hands from his shoulders. I shook my head. "I don't think so."

"I think we could. Get your gorgeous mind so worked up it can't tell the difference between words and sensation. We'll have to practice, for sure, but I think we can do it."

"Rowan," I whined, trying to fuck him back, get my hips closer to the one touch I needed. "Please."

"We'll have Cade tie you up," he breathed, not moving closer, still thrusting just enough to keep me on the edge. "Have you on your knees while one of us takes your mouth, and another helps. Grips your hair and makes sure you're taking every inch of cock while they whisper dirty things in your ear. Over and over again until one of our voices sends you into oblivion."

He reached between us, pressing the pad of his thumb to my clit and circling. I came apart with a silent scream. No breath, no movement. The pleasure ravaged me and left me starving for more. My heat was a furnace. The more they made me come, the more they fed the fire.

Rowan's knot released. "Good girl. And taking your ass is the first step to taking three of us. Maybe more."

Still breathless, my eyes went wide. I'd seen those porn videos. Hell, they were the ones that got me off the fastest. But it didn't seem like it could be real. Or that *I* could do it.

I swallowed and twisted my head to look around at the rest of my pack, landing on Joel, whose fist wrapped around his swollen cock. It looked like he was about to come, but his gaze was so fixated on me, I didn't think he would until he touched me.

"I-if you really w-want me there," my breathlessness made me stutter. "Then yes."

Rowan lifted and arranged me so I was on my knees, and hands brushed down my back. Further. "Princess, your ass is a work of art," Cade brushed a kiss down my spine. "I want my cock so far inside it you'll feel me for days. And since I don't have a knot, it's probably best I go first."

One hand cupped my jaw, and another fisted my hair. "You're still mine," Rowan reminded me. "So clean me up while he takes your ass."

Chills ran over my whole body, nipples hardening and hair standing on end. Fuck. Me.

The flavor of Rowan mixed with *me* was a heady thing I couldn't comprehend. It felt wrong and dirty and delicious running my tongue over him and tasting myself. Cade's fingers dipped between my legs and drew wetness up to my ass. But it wasn't that. "Here."

Hawk was at the door to the nest, a bottle in his hand that he tossed to Cade. I hadn't even noticed him leave, but now that I'd seen him, I couldn't look away. He smirked, crossing his arms, not at all bothered by being naked and hard. "You finished cleaning him, baby girl?"

"Yeah." I sounded parched. "Oh, shit."

The sensation of cool liquid on my ass had me squirming. When I'd done this before it had been slow, awkward, and not a thing I wanted to repeat. Cade pushed a single lube-soaked finger into my ass, and I already knew it wouldn't be the same this time.

I vaguely registered Rowan moving before I stretched my arms out in front of me on the cushions, presenting. It felt *right*, and that fucking infernal finger felt so strange and so good. Two orgasms. I'd already had two orgasms during this session, and my body craved more. I wasn't one of those women who could orgasm endlessly, given it was already hard. But with them it was easier.

Cade's finger was replaced, and he was so much bigger than his finger. I giggled, my mind a bit delirious and laughing at the obvious comparison. A sharp smack on my ass had me moaning into the pillow. "Are you laughing at my cock, princess?"

"No, Sir."

His low intake of breath preceded shocked silence. Suddenly, his back lined up with mine, cock slowly easing into my ass. How did it feel this different from the first time? Why did it seem like Cade's cock turned my body into a lit stick of dynamite ready to blow?

"What's so funny then?" His breath tickled my ear and one hand skimmed around my body to toy with my clit. Slow and steady, just like the way he pushed into me. There was absolutely nothing funny about this. "You were just so much bigger than your finger, and that's so fucking obvious that I laughed."

They all laughed with me, but the laughter turned into moaning as he sank all the way into me. If I wasn't in heat it would have taken longer. My Omega was ready to be taken any way she could be, including this. "Your ass is so tight I'm not going to last long," Cade breathed, moving faster. "We'll talk about it later, but during the heat you can call me Sir, princess."

"You like that?"

"Understatement." He gritted out the word, unable to hold himself back, and taking me at full force. I wasn't close enough to come, and I didn't care. I loved floating in the in-between space, where pleasure never ended and hovered like a cloud around my mind.

If someone had asked me how long it took until I felt Cade shudder and come, adding another brand new sensation, I couldn't have said anything.

The wave of heat wasn't over. My body wanted more. *Needed* more. It wouldn't let me stop, though I was starting to tire again.

A little whimper fell out of me at Cade's absence. "We've got you, Isolde," Rowan said, one hand under my chest, lifting me back to hands and knees. "We've got you, and we'll take care of your greedy little cunt. Got it?"

Slick dripped down my thighs. Hell, they were right. Words were the key to my body. Depraved fantasies and raw language. *Yes*. Hawk's face appeared by mine. "You tired, baby girl?"

I nodded. "Yeah."

"Still need more?"

I nodded again, beyond words.

"It's gonna be hard and fast. I'm going to fill you up with my come and then make you sit on my face while I eat it out of you. And if you need more, someone else will take a turn."

My eyes rolled back in my head.

"Hard and fast is good," Joel said. "I think that's what we need." He knelt in front of me with his angry, swollen cock, already glistening at the tip. My mouth watered at the sight. The scent of him. He plunged into my mouth as Hawk buried himself balls deep.

I went blank. Scorching pleasure burned, white-hot, rendering me blind and unable to hear a fucking thing. Hawk's hands on my hips tugging me back onto his cock and pushing me forward onto Joel's. Back and forth, taken without mercy or hesitation. Somewhere I realized Vaughn's head was beneath me, sucking my nipples until so hard they nearly hurt.

*This* was what every heat should have been. Mindless, incredible fucking where I didn't have to think about anything except when to open my mouth or spread my legs. I loved it. And this was mine forever now.

It was that thought that pushed me over the edge. My cries were muffled by Joel's cock, my mouth stretched to wrap around him. He was easier to take with length, but he filled me to bursting, not holding back.

"There we go," he purred. "Coming between us like the good Omega you are. Open as wide as you can and breathe, Isolde."

I obeyed, only pure instinct driving my actions.

With one breath Joel pulled back, and another he surged forward, coming down my throat, knot swelling behind my teeth.

Panic swam behind my eyes before his hand stroked my hair. "I'm not all the way in your throat. You can breathe."

He was right. Barely. But the more I relaxed, the more I could breathe around him, even while Hawk's movements drove my lips against Joel's stomach. "You knotted her mouth?" Hawk asked, not bothering to slow. "Goddamn, baby girl, that's the hottest thing I've ever seen."

He did love to watch.

Hawk pulled back just enough not to knot me. I nearly cried around the knot in my mouth. I needed it. Needed to feel them swollen inside me, pressing into the secret places that set my brain on fire.

He didn't give me a chance to regret, moving and pulling my hips down onto his waiting mouth, following through on this promise.

I shook with the orgasm slamming down on me. His tongue fucked me, swirling and licking in places I didn't know I needed to feel him. Over my clit and back down again. Sucking harder than I thought possible. Consuming every bit of me and him together. Until I was shaking again, my body so far gone I wasn't sure it *could* come again without a break.

But if anyone were to prove me wrong, it would be Hawk and his tongue.

Joel's knot eased. He pulled back, leaving my limbs weak from all the pleasure, still held and ravaged by Hawk's mouth. "I don't think —" I gripped his hair. "I don't think I can."

The only thing I could see were his eyes, and they promised me I could. Determination and dark fire, fingers gripping my hips and pulling me more firmly onto his face.

"Yes you can." Vaughn's voice was close, and he smiled. "Let's try more words. You think you can't come again, but you're made for this, sweetheart. Made for us to pleasure until you think you can't take any more, and then give you more. We'll find a patch of woods where we can *all* chase you, and every time we catch you, our mouths will ruin that pretty pink cunt and leave it messy and satisfied. Now give your Alpha what he wants and let him drink your cum."

Hawk's tongue slid beneath my clit, finding where I needed him, and I broke apart with a cry. Vaughn caught me before I could collapse. I was utterly boneless, and still the wave wasn't finished. But I couldn't take any more. I couldn't.

"You taste so good, baby girl. I'm going to have to do that again."

"Not now," I said, chest heaving.

"No," he agreed, lifting me out of Vaughn's arms. "Not now. I think it's time for a shower. Get my Omega wet and soapy before we make her scream again."

Rowan laughed and followed close behind. "Can't wait to hear you echo off the walls. And you're going to smell even better in here, Isolde. If that's even possible."

I tucked my face into Hawk's chest, blushing at the compliment and enjoying the weightless feeling of being held. When this was over I was going to be exhausted, but it would, without a doubt, be the best heat I'd ever had.

## CHAPTER FORTY

ISOLDE

Fingers stroking my clit woke me. Just gentle movement. Enough to feel good, but not enough for more. Cade stretched out behind me, his clever fingers teasing me.

"Thought I'd try out Joel's tricks," he whispered, kissing my neck. "While everyone is asleep. Even you."

"Mmm. Not asleep anymore."

"Which is good for me."

I wasn't awake enough to register how I ended up with my legs over Cade's shoulders, one of his hands holding my wrists on the floor behind my back while he slowly licked me. Teasing and gentle, like he'd decided he wanted to explore every inch of my pussy with his tongue.

Familiar pleasure blossomed low in my gut. Like my body had accepted that they knew how to make me come and surrendered to it. I hoped this ease of pleasure would stay after the heat was over, but I doubted it. But I was sure it didn't matter. They didn't care how long it took to make me come.

The way Cade restrained me with nothing but his hands made me that much wetter. He groaned against my clit, doubling down with his tongue and not letting me go. Low fire pulsed in my gut. It was called forth from wherever it hid instead of creeping up on me.

That same fire caught the arousal spreading from Cade's tongue and turned it into an inferno. Impossibly fast. It was never this fucking fast. I wiggled, but the way he had me gave me no leverage, and as strange as it was, I loved it. I loved when they made me helpless, unable to do anything but feel. The way it short-circuited my overthinking was something I would never take for granted.

He shifted both of my wrists to one hand so he could use the other, pulling back just enough to add his finger to the equation. And by now they knew the invisible spots that made me see stars. He found it almost immediately.

No more staying quiet. A whimper and a whine fell out of me as I rocked my hips against his mouth, trying to get his tongue closer. "Please, Cade."

My Alphas stirred around the nest. Their attention came to me and the way I writhed and begged. Without even looking at them, their scents strengthened, and I felt the nest warm with renewed lust.

Cade smiled, slowing everything, tongue and finger slipping inside me together before he whispered. "Is that my name when I have you restrained and begging?" He locked eyes with me while he continued to consume my pussy like it kept him alive.

"Sir." The word shivered out of me. "Please make me come, Sir."

He did. Another finger and sealing his mouth over my clit had me coming apart with breathless pants, melting, shuddering, and shaking.

He laid me down and appeared over me with a grin. "I like watching you get lost in pleasure."

"I like getting lost in it."

His mouth shone with me. He made no effort to wipe it away before he pressed his forehead to mine. "You like being instructed? To call me that?"

"Definitely don't mind it."

The way his eyes lit up told me how he felt about it. "God, I can't wait to dive into all of this with you. When you don't have the heat burning you alive."

Like him saying it made it remember, I gasped with the temperature boiling in my veins. This was *sharp* and nearly violent. A need skimmed the surface of my mind, but it couldn't happen. I whined and grabbed Cade's face, hauling him closer. "I want all of you. I know it's crazy and impossible, but *fuck me,* I want all of you at once."

Rowan crawled next to us. "Why is that crazy and impossible?"

I strained to kiss him and he closed the distance. Too gentle for how I felt. "Because I'm not cheese."

A laugh burst out of Hawk. "Baby girl. Cheese?"

"You know the cheese with all the holes in it? I don't have enough holes."

"You have enough if you're creative." Rowan winked and rolled away. "Where's the lube?"

Joel found it and it passed from hand to hand, ending with Hawk. He smirked. "What are you thinking, Rowan?"

"I'm thinking our Omega wants all of us, and we're going to give her all of us. But—" He turned back to me and came close, kissing me again. "I want to blindfold you."

My whole body flushed at the idea. But I still asked. "Why?"

"You know exactly why."

So I didn't think too hard or worry about what they were going to do. So all I focused on was them and their mouths and cocks. So the only thing I could do was be an Omega in heat. *Their* Omega.

"Okay."

He winked again. "Good girl."

"I've got one," Cade said. "Be right back."

Across the nest, Hawk drizzled lube on his cock, fisting it slowly while he looked at me. I wanted to watch him do that forever. Yet, at the same time, I knew what came after that look, and I wanted that more than watching. But I was definitely starting to understand the appeal.

Need spiked in my gut. I leaned back, breathing out slowly. As soon as they touched me I would turn into a supernova, so I needed to go slow until they were ready. And once I was blindfolded. "Of course he has one."

"I heard that sass." He was already back, what looked like an eye mask in his hands. "I do have one. I have many. And I'll be using them on you again. Here." He slipped the mask over my eyes.

It was soft and had padding around the edge so no light came in, but it didn't crush my eyes. "I thought you would just use a tie or something."

"And risk you seeing halfway through? Never."

A kiss skimmed the skin of my shoulder. It might have been Cade, but I also wasn't sure with all their scents so close in here. And it didn't matter.

I erupted.

Desperation like lava roved in my body like a living thing. "Help," I gasped. "I need—"

"We've got you." Joel.

Strong hands lifted me and carried me across the nest. A hard chest hit my back just before my senses were overwhelmed with the scent of frosting and sugar. Hawk's hands held my thighs, his cock already pressing at my ass. "Relax for me, baby girl."

"But I need it." I found his hands with mine, urging him faster. "I need it."

A new hand circled my throat, freezing me. Hawk still spoke. "You'll get it. *Relax.*"

It wasn't a command to my emotions, but to my body. My mind went blank, obeying, muscles easing enough for his cock to enter me. Already, that piercing felt different than Cade had. Or Rowan or Joel. I hadn't taken a piercing back there yet.

He slid in almost too quickly. "Shit," he held me steady. The ache was incredible. I didn't love pain, but my heat didn't give a fuck. If a little, and in this case, yummy, pain got me closer to being knotted? Bring it on.

"I want it," I breathed. "All of it."

"Are you—"

"*Please.*"

Hawk lowered me the rest of the way. The hand fell away from my throat. I was so full. So *full*. I let my head fall back on his shoulder, my nails dig into his hands, and the fullness fueled my need. So wet I was dripping.

"You like my cock in your ass, baby girl?"

I had no words. They were gone. My body contracted, squeezing him, and he cursed under his breath. Dizziness took me for a second while he moved. We were flat now, and someone was in between my legs.

Oh.

*Oh.*

When I asked for all of them I knew, but I still didn't realize it. They would take me together just like Rowan had implied. My clit throbbed in time with my heart, waiting for that first touch and the feeling of the impossible.

Heat pain ripped through me with an urgency that made my whole body ache. Like that feeling of forgetting to eat the whole day and suddenly you were so ravenous you thought you might throw up. Except this was so much more. Craving and necessity and acute, sweltering heat. I needed them *now*.

"It hurts." I rocked back and forth. "It hurts. It hurts it hurts it *hurts*. Need a knot."

Different pain stole my breath. Someone's fingertips landing directly on my clit. And again. And again. Distraction. Delight. Devastation.

Another spank on my clit, and I cried out, opening my mouth.

It all happened at once. Driving into my pussy until I couldn't breathe. I thought I was full before—I was wrong. A hand turned my head, and someone slid into my mouth to the hilt. Hands on mine, making me push my breasts together. "Keep them right fucking there, princess." *Cade.*

The heady flavor of Rowan soaked my tongue. Yes. Please. But not enough. My head turned the other way and Vaughn pushed in, taking my throat with the roughness I craved.

Cold liquid on my skin before Cade fucked my tits, and not gently.

All of them. I had all of them. Just like I wanted. The pain morphed into bliss, and beneath the blindfold, my eyes slid closed.

Back and forth. They took turns in my mouth, which meant Joel was the one fucking me with Hawk. And they *fucked* me. Together and then opposite, their rhythms not quite matching. This was too much and not enough. I couldn't think about anything—couldn't even focus on one sensation long enough to think about pleasure. It was already there.

Brightness behind the darkness in my eyes and Joel slipping deeper because of my orgasm. Vaughn's piercings dragging across my tongue. The head of Cade's cock touching my chin and him pinching and pulling my nipples while I held my breasts for him like an offering.

Somehow, I came again. Which was impossible. But so was this. All of them together with me at once. Something intangible hovered in the spaces between us—a connection that needed no words and no bond to feel. Something *forged* by the heat and our need for each other.

Rowan slid deep and held me there, rocking between my lips. His cock jerked, filling me up and still holding me captive on his cock. "Swallow, Isolde."

I barely needed to, he was so deep in me, but then he wasn't, Vaughn holding my head with both hands. He didn't warn me and didn't go deep when he came, the sweetness of citrus and the subtleness of cream.

A growl morphed into a moan. "Don't you dare spit it out this time."

I had no desire to. All I wanted was him. Over and over again. I swirled my tongue around the head of his cock and was rewarded with more of his sweetness.

"Almost there, baby girl. We need you with us."

Joel thumbed my swollen clit, circling it in time with his thrusts. It was the gentleness compared to their driving force that sent me to the edge. Even if I wasn't blindfolded, I wouldn't be able to see. My senses rested in tatters on the floor. The only thing left was rapture.

Cade caught my jaw and held my mouth open. The tip of his cock touched my lip, and I heard the slick rhythm of him racing to the finish. The sound of him and his groan crashed into me and took me with it, over into an orgasm so deep and so wide I thought it might kill me.

They'd find me after having a heart attack because I'd come so hard.

Hawk's knot swelled in my ass, the sound of him lost in the middle of everything. Cade's cum filled my mouth while he held me there and Joel's knot burst into existence all at once. It pushed against Hawk's, stretching me in ways I didn't know I could go.

I swallowed and screamed, no longer in control of anything.

For a flash, I remembered the sea. When I'd been swept away and there were moments when I didn't know if I'd come back. Here, I hovered on that edge, tipping either way before falling towards them and into cool weariness.

Shivers ran over my skin, now cold with sweat. It was over.

The blindfold gently slid off my face. Joel stared down at me, checking me over like he thought I might be hurt. "I'm done," I told them. "It's over."

Rowan gently placed the back of his hand against my forehead and smiled. "You okay?"

"Yeah."

Beneath me, Hawk purred. Hell, all the Alphas purred, the nest filled with comforting sound. It made everything soft and lovely, my Omega knowing she was completely safe.

I'd had enough heats to know they could be rocky after. Emotions ran high with all the hormones, but I felt okay. Maybe there were so many negative emotions right before the heat that I got them out of my system. Maybe they'd come later.

Hawk's knot eased first, but he stayed until Joel's did, both of them pulling away together. I felt empty without them. We would be doing that again, that was for fucking sure.

"I hate the cold after." I shivered again.

Vaughn grabbed a blanket and wrapped it around my shoulders, but I made him stay and hold me.

"How many days did it last?" Time seemed to disappear during the heat. The only thing I cared about was the next knot inside me, so I had no idea how long we'd been locked in here, even with the brief breaks for showers and food.

"It's morning, day four," Hawk said. "Still a few days till the wedding."

"Okay, that's good." I needed to talk to my parents and Ellie. About the heat, but about everything else too. "Are we going back to the estate?"

Joel shrugged. "We can if you want to. We can also stay here. Either way is fine with us."

I didn't want to share them yet. It was different now, knowing they were mine. "I'll ask Ellie if she's okay with me staying here. It's her wedding, and I've already caused commotion, so whatever she wants, we'll do until after the wedding."

"And what are your plans?" Rowan asked softly. "For after the wedding?"

I tried not to chew on my lower lip and failed. Nerves jangled in my stomach, but not necessarily bad ones. "I don't know. All I know is that I was dreading the wedding because it meant the end of this, and I'm still basking in relief."

Vaughn rubbed a hand up and down my arm over the blanket. "Let's get a shower, and some food, and then we'll talk about it, okay? We have time."

My smile couldn't be contained, because he was right. Now we had time. "That sounds good."

He kissed me before helping me up and lifting me into his arms to walk the now familiar path to the shower. "You can put me down," I whispered.

Our foreheads bumped together, and he whispered back. "No, sweetheart, I can't."

## CHAPTER FORTY-ONE

### ISOLDE

We barely managed to keep our hands off each other in the shower, in spite of the festival of fucking we just had. But we did, if only because all of us were exhausted. I saw a nap in my near future. But first, I wanted to see more of the house.

I had no clothes with me, so Rowan's t-shirt was currently skimming my bare thighs as I crept back by the nest. The guys were getting dressed, and Vaughn had mentioned ordering food, so I was free to spy on everything.

The only rooms I'd really seen were the nest and its connecting bathroom, but I vaguely remembered a bright hallway before we got there. That was where I went, pushing open the door and blinking tears out of my eyes. I'd been in cozy dimness for days. The sun was a bit much, but when my eyes cleared and I saw out the windows, my jaw dropped.

There was a door. I stepped outside into balmy summer heat and a breeze that smelled like water and salt. It couldn't be, right?

But it was.

We were on the cliffs, magnolia trees dotting here and there. From here I could look down on the estate and see all of it laid out. The beach too. This was where I used to climb and sit, using the rickety switchback path. There was a gate in front of it now, but it was still there.

Holy. Fucking. Shit.

"Wondered when you'd find this. Guess sooner rather than later." Rowan stood by the door in soft jeans and a t-shirt that looked equally soft. The wind ruffled his hair, the sun glinted off his skin, and he was smiling at me. He looked so good it hit me in the chest. But I still couldn't comprehend this. "You live here?"

"We do."

"I can't believe this."

He chuckled and came to me. "Is that a good or bad statement?"

"It's fucking *great*. When we were driving from the airport, I saw someone had built a house up here and I was sad because I used to come up the path and sit up here all the time. This house wasn't here when I left."

"No," he said. "Sounds like you left right around the time we broke ground. We've lived in it for a few months now."

"But it's yours."

"Could be ours," he said. "If you want that."

Behind him the house rose two stories, a classic style that suited this place more than the glitzy and modern mansions that dotted most of the coast. I had barely seen the inside of it, but I knew it was beautiful. Because they had put so much time and effort into a nest that wasn't even being used. They would make the same effort with the rest of their home.

"Isolde?"

"I'm sorry. It still doesn't feel real to me. I know it is, but..." I huffed a breath. "You're sure?"

He stepped closer and cradled my face with both hands, letting them sink into my hair. "I've never been so sure of something in my life. You were dreading the wedding? So was I, because we didn't know what you would say when we told you. We didn't know if you would believe us without a heat to prove it. We just hoped we had enough time to prove we wanted you. *Needed* you."

I swallowed. "Wow."

Rowan laughed and kissed me. "Nothing is going to change our minds, Isolde. The only thing that could make us walk away is you telling us to. Otherwise, we're yours. Everything we have and everything we are. We'll go where you go. Whatever you want, we'll make it happen."

Holding onto his wrists, I searched his face. "What about you?"

"I want you. Nothing else matters."

I made a face. "You're allowed to want things besides me. And

I'm basically the reason your career is ending, so you're entitled to want something."

He took me by the shoulders and turned me so we both faced the ocean, holding me to him. "We all have things we do in our free time, and would be happy to continue doing or monetizing. You already know mine. I've wanted to set up a high-end specialty dispensary for a long time. Clarity is the perfect place for it, I just never had the time."

"I've been told to try your candy."

"You can absolutely try my candy. And I'll have to show you my grow room in the basement."

Leaning back against him, I smiled. "I want to see everything."

"Vaughn's ordering Italian food for everyone. That okay?"

My stomach growled in response. We'd eaten, but when you went that hard for so long, you needed more. I was starving. "That sounds amazing."

He kissed my hair. "I don't want to take you away from the view."

"That's okay. The view isn't going anywhere. Even if I'm annoyed you didn't tell me you live *right here*."

"I liked the look on your face though." Rowan kept his arm around me as we went back into the house and through the hallway I'd been distracted by. The main story of the house was large. The house sprawled rather than going vertical, which I understood.

A cozy, sunken living room centered around a fireplace with overstuffed couches and armchairs. There was a television too, but there were doors that could hide it so it wasn't the focal point of the room.

There were warm colors and half-walls making the space seem open while still having some division. Stairs led up to the second floor, and there was a hallway with branching rooms beyond the airy kitchen.

Hawk sat on one of the leather couches on his phone. Joel was pouring a drink in the kitchen, and the others weren't back yet.

"Isolde has thoughts about the house," Rowan announced.

I looked up at him and made a face. "I'm going to have words with whoever decided not to tell me you guys lived right here. I love this clifftop. I used to come up here every fucking day in the summer."

Hawk grinned, and I stepped down into the living room far

enough for him to drag me to him and across his lap. "Are you saying you'd have agreed to be ours earlier if we'd shown you the house?"

My clothes were still non-existent, so the sweatpants he had on were doing almost nothing to separate our bodies. I decided to tease him. "I guess we'll never know now, will we?"

"Does that mean you're staying, baby girl?"

I dropped my eyes, blushing. "I want to."

Pulling me closer, he didn't let me get away. Instead, he pressed his forehead to mine. "Why do I hear a 'but' in there?"

This was what post-heat was like, because all of a sudden emotions washed up out of nowhere and I choked back a sob.

Hawk held me tighter, crushing me to him. "Hey," his voice was soft. "If you don't have an answer, it's okay. I'm sorry."

I shook my head where it was buried in his neck. "It's silly."

He laughed softly, but he wasn't laughing at me. I felt his nerves in the way he held me. "I'm sure it's not silly, baby girl. Just talk to us."

Pushing back, I swiped at my face to get the tears away. Cade now leaned against the pillar leading to the living room, and Vaughn stood behind the half wall barring the kitchen. They were all here with me.

"I want you so much," I whispered. "So it doesn't make sense that I feel terrified. But I do and I hate it. It's like standing on the cliff outside *knowing* there's a net at the bottom and I'm still scared to jump."

Hawk just nodded. He didn't look offended or angry or anything like it. Instead, he lifted a hand and curled it around the back of my neck, thumb gently brushing back and forth along my jaw. "What are you scared of?"

My mouth opened and closed. Words didn't form. I didn't have any specifics, only this big, nameless *thing* inside me that was scared to move forward, because what if it fell apart?

"Are you scared of us?" He asked.

No. Never. I shook my head. Hawk smiled. "Then do you mind if I give it a go?"

I toyed with the collar of his t-shirt. "Okay."

"I think you loved Beau," he said quietly. "Maybe not at the end, but I think he swept you off your feet, and you had no reason not to love him. And then like the absolute piece of shit he is, he took advantage of your sweetness. Your kindness. And he taught you that being loved was accepting what you could get, being alone, and never being satisfied."

"But—"

He pulled me close and kissed me, silencing my protest with gentle insistence. "You didn't even know those things were happening. I know. You thought it was normal, and Beau's a good actor. No one thought anything was wrong. Not even you, which is why him breaking up with you, even if he claims it was a ploy to bring you closer, was so devastating.

"And all those years and all that history crumbled into dust in the space of a day. Being scared of it happening all over again isn't silly, it's natural."

I lifted my eyes to his, swimming in their darkness, and he smiled again. "But we have something he didn't."

"General human decency and the skill to actually bring me to orgasm?"

Laughs burst out through the room, including Hawk. "Those, yes. But we have the knowledge that you're perfect for us. And we're perfect for you."

While scent matches weren't rare in theory, they were rare in practice. With all the Alphas and Omegas in the world, how were you meant to run into the one person or pack who was yours? I knew a couple of scent matches, but they were few and far between. There were matchmaking services that could help you, but they were expensive as shit, and it didn't always work.

"And Isolde," Hawk said. I knew whatever came next was deadly serious because he used my name. "I'll do whatever you need to show you I mean it. Including bonding with you right fucking now if that's what you wanted."

The whole room went still. "You would do that?"

"Hell yes," Vaughn said. "I would."

Murmurs of agreement from the others.

I twisted to look at them. "And that doesn't scare you?"

"No," Joel said. "At least not in the way you're thinking. There are always nerves when you make big, life-altering decisions. But for me, for this, the nerves aren't about whether it's a good idea. It's the same kind of nerves you get when you're about to get news you're excited about. Or you're about to go on vacation. Anticipation and not questions or worry."

Melting off Hawk's lap onto the couch next to him, I stared up at the ceiling, realizing that here, the room went up two stories and there was a massive skylight letting in the sun.

I let my thoughts drift, and as I did, Hawk pulled my legs into his lap and stroked down my skin, the touch easy and warm. No one said anything, but it wasn't an uncomfortable silence.

The thought of going back to my shitty apartment across the country made my entire soul wilt. I didn't want that. My friends were here. My family was here. I liked the weather and the city better here. And they were here.

Why was this even a conversation? They were here. Was I scared? Yes. But like both Hawk and Joel had pointed out, it wasn't the same kind of fear. Fear because of prior experience. Fear because it was huge and irrevocable and any sane person would be nervous of it. But was there even a shred of a chance of me walking away from them?

No.

They were mine.

That's all there was to it.

"So you're okay with an Omega who's probably going to be skittish for a while, and really wants this but doesn't know how?"

Cade suddenly hovered above me, and he knelt beside the couch before kissing me. "I'm okay with you, princess. Everything you are."

I wrapped my arms around his neck and pulled him down on top of me. He just barely managed to keep himself from crushing me, and he whispered in my ear. "I'm so much more than *okay* with you, Isolde. I'm very much in love with you, and even if everyone in this pack isn't ready to say it, they are too. I might not be able to match with you by scent, but you're still mine."

Shock rolled through me. "You are my match, Cade. Your scent hits me just as hard as everyone else. Even if you can't feel it, I can."

Rowan sat down on the couch across from us and leaned forward on his elbows. "Does this mean you're staying?"

I bit my lip and nodded. "Yeah. I am."

They all closed in, pulling me into a tangle of limbs and kisses that lifted me off the couch. Off the ground.

"I always was," I finally whispered. "I'm sorry I let my head get in the way."

"Never apologize for making sure something is *right*, baby girl. But fuck me, I'm glad you're mine."

I let myself relax into their arms. "Me too."

Then my stomach interrupted again, loudly, breaking us all apart. Vaughn held up his phone and grinned. “Food’s almost here. Then we can stuff our faces, and most importantly, make plans.”

I didn’t think I’d ever been as excited about making plans.

## CHAPTER FORTY-TWO

### ISOLDE

There was food and exploration. The house was cleverly designed, and there was so much more space inside than it looked like. The basement, which was the size of the entire house, helped. It housed their gym, Rowan's growing space and industrial kitchen, Hawk's music room, and Cade's rope studio.

He winked and told me it was for more than *just* rope, but I couldn't take my eyes off the dark beams of wood and all the different colors of rope hanging on the wall.

They all had bedrooms, and there was an empty one for me. Joel had a room on the first floor where he'd worked on all their admin tasks for the escort business and played games.

But I was still tired from the heat, and I needed to get my clothes and everything else from my parents' house before I passed out again.

Cade gave me a pair of sweatpants to put on, and I smirked. "It's Clarity. I'm sure there have been more scandalous things than an Omega walking outside in nothing but a t-shirt."

I was teasing him. I didn't want to go outside half-naked, but I wanted his reaction. Cade didn't disappoint, stepping into me with that look that told me he wouldn't mind bending me over the nearest surface and reminding me who he was, Beta or not.

His voice was gentle in the quiet, but I still shivered. "I'm about to get possessive. Are you going to let me?"

It wasn't a question about this moment, but our boundaries together. I already knew they could change and shift. None of them gave me any doubt. Right now? I wanted them to own me.

So I bit my lip and nodded.

One hand pushed me against the wall, the other slipping between my bare thighs. He wasn't touching me where I so desperately needed him, instead grazing my skin so lightly I could barely hold myself still. Those rings he always wore added a shiver of cold.

"What's between these gorgeous legs of yours belongs to us now. Like hell am I going to let anyone else scent it because you're outside without panties, or worse, catch a glimpse of it." A smirk that made my stomach tumble. "So put the fucking pants on, princess, or I'll do it for you."

"Gonna tie me up while you do?"

He laughed. "No, I wouldn't need to. But I still want to tie you up, among other things. The heat didn't change that."

I ran my fingers over the scruff on his jaw. "I wouldn't have picked you for this."

"What do you mean?"

"You all have such different hobbies and things you like, but if I'd had to choose, I would have said you would be more like Joel than Rowan."

Cade leaned in and brushed his lips over my cheek. "That a problem?"

The silky darkness in his voice reminded me of the way he gripped my throat the first night they all pleasured me. "Definitely not."

"Good." The hand not currently between my legs found its way into my hair, making sure I didn't look away from him. Those infernal fucking fingers still teasing my skin and not giving me nearly enough. "Do you know what started it all?"

"No."

"I was always interested," he said. "But I'd never really explored it. Then I met someone who was like me and it opened up all the possibilities."

He was so close and smelled so good. Perfume filled the air in the hallway, betraying me. "Like you? What does that mean?"

Cade's hand tightened in my hair. "I'm a Beta." The words were a velvet whisper. "I can't knot you and keep you squirming exactly where I want you. I can't bark and expect you to obey. I have to earn that." He smiled then, lips brushing over mine. "And that makes it so much sweeter when you do."

"Who says I want to?"

"Only you can say that," he murmured. "But your heart is racing, your pupils are wide, you're perfuming and barely breathing. So you tell me, princess. Are you curious?"

I was tempted to tell him no. To pull away, put on the pants, and go out the door to the car. But I couldn't lie to him. We hadn't spent much time one on one yet, and I wanted to see what happened when he was unleashed. Because he was fucking right. Being a Beta meant absolutely fuck-all with the raw dominance dripping off him, and I wanted to *obey*. I already knew it would be different than what was between Joel and I. This would have more push and pull, but he would win.

Always.

I wanted him to win.

I wanted to *obey*.

He was right. I *was* curious. I always had been, and I'd never had a chance to experience it. Now the entire world was at my fingertips, including this.

"Yes." I wet my lips. "I'm curious."

"Then tomorrow, after we've both had more sleep, you're mine. I'm taking you down to the studio and having my way with you. Right?"

"Right." I shivered, though it was warm, the heat of the day spilling through the nearby windows.

Cade pulled back and released me, including the teasing between my thighs. "Now put the sweats on so I'm not half a second from making you come on my face or from decking the first man who looks at you."

The pants had fallen to the floor when he held me, but I put them on, unable to stop my smile. He and the guys were taking me down to the estate to get all our things. They didn't all need to come, but they claimed they didn't want to be apart, and neither did I.

When the sweatpants were rolled a couple of times so I could walk without tripping, I reached for Cade's hand. "You said you hadn't explored it until you met someone like you. What does that mean?"

One squeeze of my hand. "I always wanted to be an Alpha. Never really felt like a Beta. I had these instincts that felt out of place, and I still struggle with it sometimes." He shrugged, but he was looking away as he guided me to the SUV. I made him turn back to me, his expression a mix of shame and embarrassment.

"I'm the last person who's going to judge you for struggling with shit, Cade."

"I know. But I don't like the struggle. I enjoy who I am and this pack. You. So when it comes up, it's hard. But I'm getting better."

I pressed my body closer to his. "Does me obeying you make you feel more like an Alpha?"

"You obeying me makes you feel like you're *mine*. And that's all I need. Promise."

"Okay. Sir." I winked.

Cade hissed out a breath and kept me close. "You're going to be the death of me, princess. We're going to talk about what you call me tomorrow or we're never getting to the car."

I opened my mouth to tell him *yes, sir*, and he covered it like he knew he was coming. "Anyway," he said with a grin. "I had all these impulses that didn't make sense, and I didn't really think you could be dominant without being an Alpha. Then one of my friends invited me to a BDSM club. That was all it took to set me straight. There were Alphas on their knees for Betas. Betas dominating. Even Omegas taking charge.

"Just because something is true for *most* doesn't mean it's true for *all*. Kinky people are just kinky, no matter their designation. And I embraced what I wanted without feeling strange about being a Beta. Which makes that insecurity go away." He inclined his head. "Most of the time."

"So I'm kinky?"

All he did was raise a single eyebrow, making me dissolve into laughter. Yeah, there wasn't any question about that.

Hawk's arm came around my waist and pulled me away. "Let's get down there and get back. I want to take a nap with my naked Omega."

"Why do I think that a naked nap is going to turn into *not* a nap?"

"I'll try very very hard not to let it," he said, helping me into the car. "But shit happens."

"I have to sleep sometime." I laid my head on his shoulder. "Otherwise you'll have a zombie for an Omega."

Hawk buckled me in, and I didn't fight him on it. They wanted to be possessive and protective. They *wanted* to do things for me. It wasn't because of money or obligation, and I didn't mind it when I knew it was what they wanted. "Even if you were a zombie, you'd still be cute."

We all laughed. It didn't take long to get down to the house, the guards waving us by. Joel turned around from the front seat. "Do you want to pack your stuff or do you care if we do it?"

I paused, thinking through everything I had. It's not like it was a huge hardship if I left something here. We could just come get it. "I'd like to talk to my mom and Ellie if you could grab it for me."

"Sure thing."

Geoffrey opened the door for us. I smiled at him. "Is Mom in her office?"

"She is."

"Thanks."

The guys went towards the guest suite—not before Rowan kissed me hard enough that Geoffrey cleared his throat—and I went in the opposite direction. I knew the way by heart, because her office used to be my nest. I was up here all the time.

What she'd done to it was really beautiful. She'd opened the space up and made it light and airy, with peachy colors that made it seem like the transition from inside to outside was seamless. But still stark enough it could be a blank slate for her designing.

I rapped my knuckles on the doorframe. "Knock, knock."

Mom turned around and pulled her reading glasses off. She was dressed casually for her, in jeans and a t-shirt that probably cost as much as a week's paycheck from my bartending job.

She smiled. "Well, aren't you a sight for sore eyes. Were we expecting you?"

"No. Just finished the heat this morning, so we came to grab our things." I wandered in and curled up on the end of her couch. "Where's Ellie?"

"She's at her final fitting, actually. I wanted to go with her, but I have a deadline tomorrow."

"Oh. I can come back."

I went to stand, and she waved a hand. "Talking to my daughter for a few minutes isn't the same as taking two hours to go to a fitting. I'll be fine. How are *you*?"

My face flushed pink. My family had never been... *embarrassed* by sex, but it wasn't something we talked about openly. And they didn't know yet about the truth of the heat.

"I'm really good," I whispered. "They're my pack."

She laughed. "I would hope so."

"No, Mom. They're *my pack*. When my heat kicked in, so did the scent matches. They already knew, but hadn't told me because —" I cut myself off. The six of us hadn't talked about how we would break that particular news to my family. If we would be up front and honest about how we met or keep a white lie in place.

I didn't want to say anything more before I talked to them.

But mom stared at me in utter shock. She was quiet for so long I thought I might have broken her. But then she was standing, her eyes filled with tears as she sat beside me and pulled me into a hug. "Oh, Isolde, I'm so happy for you."

"Really?"

"*Yes.*" She swatted my arm. "I'm a bit sad someone's going to take you away from me again when you just got back, but you deserve this kind of happiness."

I really smiled then. "I'm not going far. You know that house up on the cliff?"

"Yes."

"It's their house."

"No it's not."

"It is. I came out of the heat haze and wandered outside and nearly lost my head."

Mom took one of my hands in both of hers. "That's such good news."

"Do you think Ellie will care if I don't stay here?"

"I think if your sister were here she'd be pushing you out of the house faster than I will. As long as you're here for the rehearsal on Friday, and you know, the actual wedding."

I huffed a laugh. "Don't worry, I wouldn't miss it. I'm glad the heat didn't happen later."

"Ellie would have understood."

"I still would have felt bad, though."

Mom stood and crossed to her desk, pressing a button to call one of the staff. "Where is your pack?"

"They're packing everything up in the suite."

"So you have time to talk for a bit? We haven't had a chance."

One of the staff stepped in and mom ordered a tea tray.

They wouldn't care if I spent time with my mom. I nearly rolled my eyes at the automatic thought. There had been times with Beau where spending time with my family had been an issue. That worry was long gone. "Yeah, I can do that."

"Good. I want to hear more, because I know my daughter, and even over those video calls, I know there's a lot you haven't told me."

I made an innocent face. "I have no idea what you're talking about."

"We'll see. But first, tell me more about *them*."

## CHAPTER FORTY-THREE

CADE

It didn't take us long to pack everything up and get it into the car. Not with all five of us here. Geoffrey told us Isolde was still with her mom, and that was fine with us.

"Do you guys want to take the stuff back?" I asked. "I can wait and call one of you when she's ready. Or one of you can bring the car back."

Rowan nodded. "I want to make something for her. It won't take long, but it's better if it's a surprise."

"I'll bring the car back," Joel said.

"I want to stay," Hawk said with a wince. "If Warren is here..."

I nodded. We knew Ellie and Warren wanted to talk to Isolde, but it might be good for Hawk to talk to him without her. "Yeah, let's find out."

The others left to go back to the house, and I spotted Geoffrey heading down the hall. "Geoffrey?"

He turned and smiled. "How can I help you, Mr. Barlowe?"

"Is Warren here?"

"I believe so. Miss Ellie is at her final dress fitting, but as far as I know he'll be in their suite."

"Thank you." We knew where that was. It was where we'd watched movies with them, and we spent a few hours utilizing Warren's massive television and gaming setup before the bachelor parties had gone to hell.

Hawk was with me, and he showed no signs of being nervous, but I felt it. He'd acted on raw instinct. There wasn't an apology needed for that. But as much as we hated Beau, we also didn't want to fuck up Isolde's relationship with her brother-in-law. We needed to have a relationship with him too now.

I knocked on the door.

"Coming," I heard from deeper inside.

Warren opened the door and took us in, surprise rolling over his face. "Hey."

"Can we come in?" Hawk asked.

"Yeah." He let us pass. "Good to see you guys are finally coming up for air."

I laughed as I sat down. "We're not complaining."

"No, I don't imagine so."

Hawk didn't sit down, watching Warren carefully before he spoke. "First, we live in that house up on the cliff. You and Ellie are welcome any time. I know you want to talk to Isolde about what happened. You can come up the path or drive. Either way is fine."

"Oh. Wow."

I hid my smile. There would be a lot of surprises for the family about us and Isolde. But she needed to be the one to share most of them.

"Would tonight be okay? I'd like to speak with her before the rehearsal dinner."

"That's fine," I told him.

Warren nodded and looked at Hawk. "From the looks of Beau's face, you got him good. But he won't say shit about it, so I've let him get away with that until I could talk to you and Isolde. From what I've overheard, even Angela isn't happy with him. I know what you said, because everyone else told me, but..." He spread his hands. "I'd like to hear it from your side."

"When Isolde was going into heat, I told her I was going to find you, Ellie, and her parents to tell them what was happening." Hawk sighed, and I knew him well enough to know even the memory was difficult. For me too. "She had an *immediate* panic attack and begged me not to leave. But not me, *Hawk*. Me, *Alpha*. And the way she said it there was no mistaking what she meant. She'd been left before by an Alpha in heat, and I saw red. You pretty much know what happened from there."

"Shit," Warren said, scrubbing a hand over his face. "Yeah, I don't blame you for that. I'll be honest, it's hard for me to reconcile the Beau I know with what Ellie has said about him. But we haven't been as close the past few years. I was working out of the country, and we grew apart. Then, a couple of years ago, when we came back and reconnected, I met Isolde, and through her, Ellie. But I've known him since we were kids. That's why I want to talk to Isolde.

"Beau's done a lot for me, but I don't want to be blinded by misplaced loyalty." Then he laughed nervously. "The looks you're giving me right now don't make me feel better."

"It's Isolde's story to tell," I said.

He stood. "We'll be over tonight to hear it."

"Sounds good."

Warren reached out and shook Hawk's hand. "No matter who it was you punched, I like Isolde. I don't know her that well, but I'm glad she has someone to stand up for her, regardless."

The tension in Hawk's shoulders eased. "Thanks. We're not going anywhere."

I texted Joel that we were finished talking to Warren while we said goodbye and went back to the foyer. I sat on the set of stairs to the second floor. "That went better than I expected, but also worse."

"As much as I hate to say, I understand it." Hawk paced slowly back and forth, arms crossed. "Isolde didn't know how badly she was being treated, and if she thought it was fine, everyone else probably did too. If you've known someone your whole life, it can take a lot to overcome that vision of them."

"Let's hope tonight is enough, then." Because I liked Warren. And Ellie. But I wouldn't be getting buddy buddy with someone who tolerated a man like Beau or his behavior. I wouldn't be able to keep my disdain in check. If Beau had pulled half the shit he had at any of the clubs or classes I went to, he would have been banned a long time ago. It didn't take much to respect someone.

The front door opened and Isolde's stepfather Henry came in, spotting us immediately. He smiled. "Didn't know when I would see any of you again. Is my daughter here?"

"She's speaking with your wife," I told him.

Henry stepped forward and shook Hawk's hand. "Remind me to buy you a drink at the wedding. You know why."

"I will, sir."

He chuckled. "I know I said I enjoyed it when you first got here, but don't call me sir. Don't get me wrong, I appreciate the respect. However, I get enough of that at work and it's exhausting."

I stood to shake his hand.

"Are all of you back?"

"No. Just the two of us and Isolde. We'll be staying at our home." Then I smiled. "We're actually neighbors."

"Yeah," Isolde's voice echoed through the foyer. "They live up on the cliff and didn't tell me." Her voice was sour, but she was smiling. Even dressed in Rowan's giant t-shirt and my sweats, she was fucking beautiful. More than that, there was light in her eyes that hadn't been there when we met her.

I was so busy staring at her, I missed what they were saying. Isolde hugged her stepfather, and they had a quiet conversation.

"We'll see you on Friday?" He finally asked.

"Yes, you will."

Henry looked over at the two of us with serious eyes. "Take care of her."

"We will," Hawk answered immediately.

Kissing Isolde on the head, Henry went in the direction she'd come from, loosening his tie as he went. She looked at the two of us, and Hawk held out a hand. "Ready, baby girl?"

"Yeah. Let's go home."

Fuck, I loved hearing those words come out of her mouth. Sweeping her off her feet and outside, I took my Omega home.

## CHAPTER FORTY-FOUR

ISOLDE

"Excuse me, *WHAT?*" Trinity screamed through our video call, making both Ocean I wince before laughing.

"Yeah. So, I owe you dinner and coffee and flowers for the rest of my fucking life," I said.

When I finally bothered to look at my phone, my friends were nearly feral. Ellie had told them I was in heat, but they wanted the details. Me calling and blurting out that they were my scent match hadn't been on their bingo card.

"So what does this mean?" Ocean asked. "Are you staying here? With them?"

I nodded, hiding my face in the collar of my hoodie. As much as I liked wearing the guys' clothes, it was nice to have my own again. "Yeah, I am. I honestly have no idea what's going to happen after the wedding. I'm kind of playing it by ear. Don't know where I'm going to work, don't know how long it'll take to get the rest of my stuff from the apartment, but I don't really care. We'll figure it out."

Trinity blew out a breath. "I think this is the best possible outcome of me breaking an NDA. Like I was already happy with you and them, and I was fully prepared to get sued. But this? What are the odds of that?"

"Not high. But then again, it can happen any time. Who knows. Maybe the two of you will be blindsided next."

Rowan stuck his head through the door of the room I sat in—

the empty one they told me would be my private bedroom. He smiled, and I smiled back. I still couldn't quite believe this was real.

"Who just walked in?" Rin asked.

"What do you mean?"

Ocean grinned. "Your entire face changed is what she means. I don't think I've seen you that happy..." She thought about it. "Nope. Not even the volleyball championship had you looking like that."

Rowan came over and sat next to me, leaning into the frame. "We're going to try to keep her that happy."

"Better be more than *try*," Rin muttered.

He had a little box with him. "What did you bring me?"

"Chocolate. Not the fun kind yet. Those can happen after your sister and Warren leave."

They were coming over to talk to me about Beau. I couldn't pretend I wasn't nervous. Beau wasn't what I wanted to talk about, but it needed to happen. If it did, maybe I wouldn't have to walk down the aisle with him.

"Did you make these?"

"I did. Don't get too excited, they're just plain chocolate. There wasn't time to make fancier ones."

He opened the box and slipped one into my mouth. It wasn't quite cool. "Wait, did you *just* make these?"

"While you were still at the house."

"Fucking hell," Trinity said. "Thank you, Rowan, for creating a standard that can never be reached."

He smirked. "You're welcome to have my chocolate any time, Trinity. We owe you one. Even if—"

"Yeah, yeah, yeah, I know." She waved a hand. "I must have a superpower or something, because I knew you guys would be good for her. Guess I'm just incredible that way."

I rolled my eyes, the chocolate still warm and sweet on my tongue. "This is really good."

"Thank you."

"*Ocean.*" A voice snapped through the phone. "Our guests are here. *Now.*"

She winced and looked at us. "Gotta go," she whispered. "Talk to you later."

Her video disappeared, leaving Trinity and I looking at each other in bewilderment. "What was that?"

She shook her head. "I've asked her, but she hasn't wanted to talk about that. I know she's had her hands full with flowers for the wedding, but there's something else going on."

Ocean lived with her aunt and uncle, who held power over her she couldn't legally break. Yet. We'd tried. She had some independence with her floral business, though she was still forced to rely on staff most of the time. But even though her family wasn't kind, I'd never heard them sound like that. "After the wedding, we need to figure it out."

"Yeah. Anyway, I should get back to this. I also have family dinner tonight, which... you know." Trinity sighed. "Dad says he has something he wants to tell me. So maybe he's going on his next adventure."

Trinity's biological father was a bit eccentric, always taking off to do things people would consider strange or impossible. His pack indulged him because he was a good guy, and more often than not, he came back with a new woman in tow who stuck around with them for a few months before things fell apart and the cycle repeated.

I shrugged. "Maybe he'll go to a volcano this time."

"Yeah, because what Dad needs is to play around with lava. Anyway, I'll let you know. But I hope you're about to have fun, and I hate you."

"Love you too."

She stuck her tongue out at me before ending the call.

Looking down at the box, I notice all the little chocolates are shaped like magnolias. "Oh my god. You really did make these for me."

Rowan laughed and leaned in to kiss my cheek. "Of course I did. Like I said, this wasn't hard, mostly melting the chocolate and putting it into the molds. When I have more time I'm going to make your favorite. And that's a little harder."

"What's my favorite?"

"Chocolate with caramel."

I rolled my eyes, remembering. "You guys have a whole guidebook to me with that questionnaire, and I still feel like I know nothing about you."

"Just because I cheated a little doesn't mean I don't want to get to know you the real way." He popped another little chocolate on my tongue. "And you'll get to know all of us. We have the time, little flower."

"True." I yawned, cuddling against him. I loved that nickname.

"Tired?"

Absolutely. I could sleep for a week. "Do I have time to take a nap before Warren and Ellie come over?"

"Yeah. But I think Hawk might be sad if you take one without him."

I flushed. "That's fine. I don't want to sleep alone." Even lower. "I don't think I'll want to sleep alone for a while."

Rowan closed the box of chocolate and handed it to me before helping me up off the floor where I'd been sitting. "It's going to take a while to let go of your old reactions, but I need to tell you this. We're not going to get angry at you for closeness or for wanting it. If we need space, we can find it, and we can ask for it without making you feel like a burden or like your request isn't important. Okay?"

A whine floated out of my chest. He'd seen the core of my reaction before I even realized it. My next instinct was to say sorry, but I already knew he wouldn't want that. I bit my lip. "Okay."

He kissed my forehead. "Hawk's in the living room."

I kept my box of chocolates with me, finding Hawk stretched out on the couch, scrolling on his phone. I put my phone and the chocolates on the coffee table before laying down and wiggling under his arm so I could snuggle near his chest.

His smile was in his voice. "Hi there."

"Hi."

"You sleepy, baby girl?"

I nodded, closed my eyes and listened to his heart beat under my ear. Relaxed into the sweet scent of sugar. Hawk shut his phone, turned toward me to cuddle me closer, and purred.

My eyes opened, and I knew it was later. The light in the living room had changed, and my body had that delicious heaviness that came after a really good nap. Like you could probably close your eyes and just float back down.

Hawk still purred, one hand slowly rubbing my back. I stretched, feeling like a cat in the sun. He was so warm and smelled so good, I could just stay here forever.

In a way I was, because I was staying with them forever. "How long was I asleep?"

"A few hours."

"Are you numb from me sleeping on you?"

He laughed quietly and kissed my hair. "No. But I think your sister might be here soon. I saw her name pop up a couple times on your phone."

"Right. That'll be a fun conversation."

"He's not mad at me at least. So I'm hoping he's open enough. I think he will be."

I reached for my phone. Now that my back was against Hawk's front, it was incredibly obvious how hard he was while pressed into my ass. "Are you hard because you took a nap and woke up?" I asked with a giggle.

"No, I'm hard because my Omega fell asleep on me and I haven't had nearly enough of her, if I ever will."

"Oh."

He kissed my neck. "Never underestimate how tempting you are, baby girl."

"I probably will. A lot."

"Then I'll be happy to remind you."

Unlocking my phone, I scrolled through Ellie's texts.

ELLIE

I just got back from my fitting and mom says you have shit to tell me.

Okay Warren says we're coming over there tonight to talk, but I want to knoooooow.

Iz?

Woman PICK UP THE PHONE.

I'm going to tell your pack embarrassing stories about you if you don't text me back.

For the love of god you're fucking again aren't you.

Fine. Not like I can be mad at you about that.

I laughed, and so did Hawk, reading over my shoulder.

ISOLDE

For your information, I was taking a nap, not fucking. Taking a nap BECAUSE of all the fucking.

Yeah, I do have stuff to tell you, but I'm waiting till you come over cause I need to see your face.

ELLIE

We're coming right now.

Rolling off the couch, I stumbled to my feet. "Do we need to get anything ready before they get here?"

"Nope."

I didn't care about what I was wearing, but I wanted to use the bathroom and splash some water on my face before this conversation. And I was glad Hawk couldn't see me stumble into the coat closet before I found the door to the bathroom.

Voices sounded while I was still inside, and when I came out, I was nearly tackled. "You *lucky. Bitch.*"

I turned and hugged Ellie. "I know. This house is incredible."

"No kidding. I think living up here is the only way I'd live so close to Mom and Dad."

"I'm sure they'll find a way to come up here," I said. But my parents, while they loved spending time with us, weren't overbearing. They had their own lives. It would be good to be close and still have distance.

Warren and the guys were already talking deeper inside, towards the living room, so Ellie pulled me toward the front door. "I'm literally foaming at the mouth. Tell me."

I pointed. "You are not."

She smacked my hand away. "*Iz,* I've been dying. Mom was practically dancing around her office, so what is it?"

"We're scent matched," I whispered.

Her eyes went wide. "Shut the fuck up."

Everyone turned and looked at us, and I started laughing. "I will not."

"You're serious?"

"Trust me. It's not something I'd joke about."

Ellie blew out a breath. "No fucking wonder he punched Beau in the face."

"Yeah." I swallowed, nerves popping up. "Hey, Warren."

He smiled warmly as he sat on the couch. "Hey. Thanks for talking with us."

Ellie swatted his arm. "Stop acting like a lawyer."

One eyebrow rose. "I *am* a lawyer."

"Well, this isn't a deposition, so chill."

The living room was packed full of all of us. I ended up between Joel and Rowan, Hawk choosing to stand just outside the space, like he was worried he would influence the way I spoke or what Warren thought of me.

"Okay," Warren said, leaning forward and pushing a hand through his hair. "I want to hear everything. But I'll tell you a little more than I told Cade and Hawk this afternoon. Beau's family and mine are friends. His parents are kind of like a second set to me. They'll be at the wedding too. So when we were kids it was that classic 'forced together cause our parents are close' friendship, and we were close all the way through high school. But I went to college on the east coast, and I worked out of the country until I moved back two years ago and met you and Ellie."

He looked over at my sister and smiled. It was that smile which had told me they were perfect for each other. He looked at her like she was the only thing in the world, and he'd done it from the moment he met her.

"But we honestly weren't close during those years. He's my oldest friend, but he's not my best friend." He laughed, wincing and taking Ellie's hand. "I don't make friends easily. Ellie's my best friend. The guys in the party are old friends too, but the closest friends I have still live overseas, and it's impractical for them to come for the wedding.

"I wanted to tell you that to explain a little. I chose Beau to be my best man because I've known him the longest, and he did a lot for me when we were younger. But I don't really know the man he is now."

I pressed my hands together between my knees. "I don't really know either," I admitted. "It's... there are a lot of things I didn't realize weren't normal that I'm now learning. But I'll do my best."

It took a while to walk through everything I'd learned about Beau, from the bracelet, to his telling me what he actually wanted from our breakup, to him leaving me alone during my last heat. The guys helped with subtle touches, and jumped in with examples I'd told them. Like leaving parties earlier or what he'd said about Angela after we broke up.

Warren listened with a straight face, but he didn't seem angry or outraged. Didn't break in to defend his friend, he just listened. When I was finally done, and completely tired of hearing my own voice, he sighed.

"Beau and I haven't talked a lot about you," he said. "But the little we have didn't sound like this. I dismissed what he said as hurt feelings and jealousy. But it seems like more than that. I'm sorry I didn't see it while you were with him."

I shrugged. "How would you have known if I didn't?"

"I'm going to talk to him. Because of our family connection, I'm not sure I can pull him out of the wedding."

The statement was met with growls, and I looked around at

them. Warren held out a hand. "I need to talk to him. Because he has a lot to answer for, and I want to see if he'll tell me the truth. I want to see if the Beau I know is anywhere still in there. I owe him that much."

"But nothing more," Ellie said. "Right?"

Warren shook his head. "No matter what happens on Saturday, I can't imagine us being close after this. But I'll still have to see him. Our families practically spend every holiday with each other." He looked at me. "And that's the only reason I'm trying to preserve any kind of peace. For my parents' sake."

"I get that." Family could be sticky at the best of times, and weddings were hard. I knew more than enough stories about weddings bringing out the worst in people.

"I'm sorry all the same."

Laughing, I relaxed into my Alphas. "You don't have to apologize, Warren. You've been nothing but great to Ellie. But remember what I told you."

He smiled then. "If I hurt your sister, you'll make sure my body disappears off the coast and is never found."

"Damn right."

My pack watched me with a mixture of horror and amusement. Hawk choked on a laugh. "I didn't know you were so vicious, baby girl."

"About the right things." I smiled.

Ellie stood and grabbed my hand, pulling me toward the back of the house like she'd been here before. "We won't stay in your hair," she called over her shoulder. "Just need a sister moment."

She found the door to the back of the house and yanked me through it. The sunset blazed across the sky, gorgeous. I lived here now. Holy fucking shit.

"You just wanted to come see the view, didn't you?" I asked.

"Maybe."

I shook my head. "Mom said it would be fine, but you're okay with me staying here and not down at the house, right?"

"Of course. Not like I couldn't find you if I needed you."

"Thank you."

"Isolde," she turned to me. "Whatever happens this weekend, I'm fine with it, okay?"

I frowned. "What do you mean?"

Ellie glanced toward the house before looking at me. "It means I know you, and I know you won't want to make waves or steal my thunder. So I'm telling you that whatever happens, even if it's making your scent match permanent, I won't mind. I'll be thrilled."

My eyebrows flew up into my hairline. "What?"

"Don't pretend you haven't thought about it."

I shook my head. "I honestly haven't. Not yet, anyway. Because it's so fast and I like... barely just got out of heat."

"And fast is a problem?"

Our conversation from this morning came back to me. I already agreed to be theirs. We were going to figure it out together. But my mind hadn't gone to bonding. Was that really that much of a step beyond committing to be together?

No, it really wasn't. With anything other than a scent match, this would sound absolutely crazy. Toxic. Red flags everywhere. But with a scent match? I already knew. There wasn't anything to wait for. They were mine.

"I guess not," I finally answered.

Ellie smirked. "If you want to wait and have a ceremony, I fully support you. If you want to have a ceremony later, I support that too. If all you want to do is bite each other and fuck it out?"

"Let me guess. You support me?"

She laughed and pulled me into a hug. "I'm just happy for you. After everything with Beau, you deserve it."

"Thank you."

"Don't forget we exist while you're up here, okay?" She sprinted back to the house and blew me a kiss before disappearing so fast I couldn't follow her.

I looked out at the ocean down below. This morning I told them it was like being out here and knowing there was a net at the bottom. But now? I thought I might be ready to jump.

## CHAPTER FORTY-FIVE

ISOLDE

Cade shut the door behind us in his studio, and I shook out my hands. "I'm nervous."

He grinned. "Why?"

"I don't know, I just am."

The room was cast in low lighting, warm and cozy. There was nothing frightening about it. I'd just never done anything like this before.

After Warren and Ellie left, we were all still tired, and we ended up in the nest, sleeping only. We needed it. And it gave me more time to think about what Ellie said, along with this.

Every single one of us slept late, and after a breakfast Joel made, Cade snagged me and pulled me to the basement while the others laughed.

Walking to me, he took my face in his hands and kissed me. "Don't be nervous, princess. The real secret to all of this? It only happens because you want to. The only reason I have any power—that any Dom has *any* power—is only because you give it to me."

I smirked up at him. "So I get to boss you around?"

"Maybe sometime. Today? Not a fucking chance."

We both laughed, but he was still holding my face and staring into my eyes with such heat I couldn't laugh anymore. "What happens now?"

Cade kissed me again. "As much as I wish we could dive in, we need to talk about a couple of things first."

"Like?"

"Like you calling me 'Sir.'"

"Oh." I pressed my lips together. "You liked it, right?"

His arms slid down and around me, locking me against his body. "I love it. But I think it means something different to me than it does to you."

I knew enough about the kinky lifestyle to know the basics, but here in the cozy warmth, I leaned my head on Cade's chest and enjoyed the sound of his voice when he spoke.

"I'd love it if you call me Sir, Isolde. But I'll ask that you keep it here. When we're playing together. If we ever go to a club or somewhere we'd do this, that's fine. Or," he paused. "If there's ever a time when you need me to step into that role. No matter when it is. This doesn't have to only be about sex."

Wrapping my arms around him, I pressed my forehead into his shirt. "So no teasing you?"

"I love when you tease," he whispered. "But I'd prefer you didn't do it with this."

"Okay."

Cade kissed the top of my head. "Thank you."

"Did I..." I winced and looked up at him. "I'm sorry for doing it before."

"Remember yesterday when you told Warren he didn't need to apologize because he didn't know?"

I nodded.

"It's the same. I'm not upset with you teasing me that way when you didn't know my preference. And," he pinned me with a stare, "if you still do it by accident, don't panic, please."

My heart fluttered. "I think eventually I'll unlearn the panic. And everything else."

"You will," he murmured. "We're going to help you."

We stood together, just breathing in the moment for a while before he spoke again. "I'll never cross any limits you set, Isolde. But when we play, when you hand over control, I own you. Your gorgeous body is mine to play with. Your cunt, ass, mouth, everything belongs to me."

"*Fuck.*" The word shook through me, barely a breath.

A ghost of a smile. "Problem?"

"No. No problems." I couldn't exactly tell him how I'd nearly blacked out from the sudden wave of arousal. Because holy *crap*.

"Now, as for what I have planned. There's about a million and one things I want to do to you and with you. But we'll start slow. Rope doesn't have to be naked. Do you want to be?"

Raising an eyebrow, I looked at him. "So you're not tying me up to fuck me?"

"I never said that." He smirked. "You're skipping ahead."

Taking the time to sort through my thoughts, I finally felt them. "I think I want to be. Though I can definitely see the appeal of having clothes sometimes." My mind filled with images of me wrapped in a blanket and tied up so I couldn't move. It would be cozy as shit.

"This is your first time with rope, right?"

"Right."

Cade ran his hands over my arms. "I don't want to do too much the first time. We want to make sure you like it."

"I'm going to."

I liked his smile. "I think you will too. But everyone has reactions, and sometimes you'll find something you didn't expect. So today, I want to restrain your arms and your legs."

"In the air?"

"No," he shook his head. "Not your first time."

That made sense. Suspending someone probably had more risks, and if he wanted to start slowly, the floor was the better choice.

"After I tie you up, I want to play with you."

"What does that mean?"

Turning away, Cade stripped his shirt over his head. "I really want to say 'whatever I want it to mean.'"

My heart kicked up faster. "But?"

"But again, not the first time." Slowly, he tugged on my shirt and pulled it over my head. "I want to touch you. With my mouth. With my fingers. I might want to use your mouth for my own dirty purposes. I'm not going to deny you today, but if you have to come, I still want you to ask permission."

"Why?"

"Because I want you to form the habit for when we play. And I want you to have a reminder of who owns you when we're inside this room."

The wink he threw my way had heat pooling between my legs. "And the fucking?"

Cade dropped his mouth to my shoulder, kissing across my skin as he took off my bra. "Today, this time, this is about you." He smiled. "Mostly about you. Believe me, I have plans to tie you open and fuck you until you don't know your own name. But we have plenty of time."

We were both naked from the waist up now. The rich scent of him was all around me, infused into this room from so much time here, and rolling off him. "Are you sure?"

"I am."

I shivered. The easy dominance rolling off him turned me on as much as it made me feel safe. "Then tell me what to do. Sir."

His eyes lit up, and he kissed me again, unable to help himself. "Good girl. Take the rest off and kneel."

He retreated to the wall covered in rope, and I obeyed, tossing my clothes to the edge of the room and kneeling. There were mats on the floor. Not quite soft, but not like kneeling on hardwood either.

"I asked you for your favorite color the other day because I wanted to make sure I had some ready for you." The bundles of rope he brought back were a rich, deep green. Not the silky kind of rope you often saw with pictures of people tied up. When Cade held it out for me to touch it felt like regular rope, but it was beautiful. "It's going to look stunning on you."

"Thank you."

Setting the rest of the rope on the floor along with some safety shears, Cade knelt behind me. "You don't have to be nervous. I've got you. And if you need to stop, we stop."

His hands lifted my hair off my neck, and he put it up, tying it out of the way. "Are you using rope for that too?"

"I can." He chuckled. "This time it's just a hair tie."

Cade touched me, stroking over my skin with slow intention. One wrist was pulled behind my back, and then the other. He arranged my arms against each other. "Keep these here."

Then there was the rope. A delicious blend of sensation, slowness, pressure, and occasionally the quick, sure movement. Cade wrapped the rope around my shoulders and ribs, the way it held my arms like a sudden hug. I barely noticed him tying my hands and weaving the rope between my breasts. It just felt *good*.

"You okay, princess?"

"I'm so good," I said, making him laugh.

"Good. I'm going to lay you down."

Giving him my weight and not being able to catch myself was strange, but he did it with ease, making sure I was comfortable. My whole body floated. Or that's what it felt like. Floating. Like I had in Vaughn's arms. I could just stay here. Nothing bad could happen while I floated like this.

Cade wound rope around my legs, binding my calves to my thighs. I didn't even realize how open I was until I was on my back, legs open to either side, Cade kneeling over me with satisfaction in his eyes. He ran his fingers under the ropes in a few places.

I whined, wanting him to touch me more. He was so warm and smelled so good. Why wasn't he closer?

His arms braced on either side of my head. "How do you feel?"

"I feel yummy."

"That's good. No pinching anywhere?"

"Nope." I popped the p. "I'm good. But you're not touching me."

Leaning close, he pressed a kiss to the center of my chest. "I will touch you," he said. "When and how I want. My Omega is all tied up for me, so you have to wait."

"But—"

"Quiet," the gentle word dropped on my lips before he kissed me. "You gave control to me, princess. Do you want to take it back?"

"No."

"No, what?"

My whole body shook, the sensation that much more intense because I couldn't move. "No, Sir."

"Good girl." He started to move his mouth down my body. "Unless you're telling me to stop or asking to come, those are the only words I want to hear from you. Yes?"

"Yes, Sir."

He chuckled into the curve of my waist before taking my breasts in his hands. "I loved fucking these during your heat. I want to tie them together so we can all have a turn. Make you a *mess* with all of our cum. What do you say to that?"

One cocked eyebrow dared me to break his rule, but I had zero objections to the image he painted. I was getting wet imagining it. "Yes, Sir."

That infernal mouth of his slid into a smirk that lit me from within, telling me he would catch me slipping up eventually. It was just a matter of time.

Palming my thighs between his ropes, Cade spread me open even further, lowering himself down so I could feel his heat but not yet feel him. The anticipation sank through me and sharpened everything, but I was still floating, breathless, dazed, happy.

"Look at this pretty little clit," Cade said. "It's swollen already and I haven't even touched it. Like it's begging me to suck it."

He did.

Cade consumed me like he was a dying man and I was his last meal. More than that. He licked my arousal off my skin where it had leaked onto my thighs. He drove his tongue inside with ruthless, carnal intent, and he did everything while groaning in pleasure.

"You taste so fucking sweet, princess. I'll never have enough of you."

The whimpering sound that came out of me was small and desperate. I needed him. There was no way to tell how long his mouth had been on me. Time didn't exist in this blissful space of hazy pleasure. But I needed more of him. I wanted—

"Please," I gasped.

Two fingers sank into me in the brief moments he pulled his mouth away. "Please what?"

"Fuck me."

He laughed. "Wrong question. Try again."

I wanted him inside me. But if I couldn't have that— "Please, may I come? Sir?"

"Yes." His mouth was on me, words muffled. "Drown me."

It only took seconds more for lightning to flash behind my eyes, the sharpness of my orgasm dragging through me, so much harder because I couldn't move. Nowhere to hide.

Pants open, Cade crawled up my body. His cock was at my lips, pressing into my gasping mouth. Dragging the heady taste of him across my tongue. "Imagine what I can do to you, princess, while you have to be still and *take it*."

He didn't stay in my mouth, pulling back and moving out of sight. Suddenly I was dizzy, moved up onto my knees, where my tied body couldn't balance. But I didn't tilt forward. Didn't fall.

Cade had me.

Strong body behind mine, holding me in place, Cade cradled me. His strength was mine. I was *safe*.

One hand stroked down my stomach and between my legs. He didn't tease me when I was already sensitive, didn't fuck me into another orgasm. He placed his hand over me. His other hand circled my throat as his teeth scraped over the skin of my neck and left chills in their wake.

"Who owns you, Isolde?" Low, dark, velvet words against my skin.

I whined, needing everything. Needing to tell him. "You do."

"And who am I?"

"Sir."

A long, slow kiss just beneath my jaw. "Good girl."

I shivered, my eyes closing. "Hold tight, okay?"

"Mmkay." I felt buttery and soft and so fucking good. Somewhere, I noticed I was down on the ground again. Cade's hands stroked and touched and held as he undid the ropes binding me. The last thing to come undone were my hands. But he didn't give them back.

He massaged them, making sure I moved my arms slowly. They were stiffer than I expected. Cade murmured words in my ear, but I couldn't focus on them. All I wanted was to cuddle up with Cade and let him hold me.

I took a breath in and realized I was on the soft couch in the back of the studio. A soft blanket curled around my body, and Cade around that. "Welcome back."

"Where did I go?"

He laughed quietly, nudging the side of my face with his own. "You got a little rope drunk. Some people would call it subspace, but everyone's different. Some people have different reactions to certain scenes, or don't go as deep as others."

"I liked it."

"I'm glad."

I pouted at him. "Why wouldn't you fuck me when I asked?"

"Because we hadn't agreed beforehand."

"But—"

Cade kissed my cheek. "Once you start to play, your endorphins and chemicals are all over the place. It's like being high on your own body. And as much as you wanted it, you can't consent when you're high. Remember the beach?"

They hadn't fucked me because I'd already smoked, waiting until later. "Yeah."

"Same thing."

I sighed. "All right. I understand it, even if I don't love it at the moment. You didn't get to come. Unless you want me to help with that now."

"You know I love your mouth, princess. Watching you make my cock disappear like a magic trick is one of the hottest things I've ever seen. But it's not a trade. It doesn't have to be even. You don't *owe* me an orgasm, and I never want you to think you have to make sure everything's equal all the time. Especially with five of us in the pack." He raked a hand through my hair, making my whole body tingle. "I'm more than happy to have you here like this. Watching you come apart in my ropes is going down as one of my favorite memories."

Everything in me warmed. I hadn't thought about it as transactional. At least not consciously. But I understood what he was saying. "The same goes both ways," I said. "I might want to make you feel good. Maybe wake you up the way you and Joel wake me up."

He groaned. "Fuck, princess. You absolutely have my permission to do that. I want to wake up with my balls in that sinful mouth of yours, roll you over and pin your throat to the bed with my cock and come before we've even said good morning."

My eyes nearly rolled back in my head, and I was suddenly perfuming enough to make Cade laugh. "Okay, I admit it. I do love it when you guys say dirty things like that."

"And you'll like it even more when we follow the words up with the real thing."

I sank into him, snuggling closer.

Around me, his hold tightened, and I knew without him saying that if he could purr, he would be doing it. Satisfaction and happiness gathered around him like a cloud. "I love the marks on you."

"Marks?"

Cade pulled the blanket away from me to show my legs. The imprints of his ropes zigzagged across my skin. "They won't last long, but fuck, these are sexy, princess. Mind if I take a picture?"

They *were* sexy. "Please do."

Easing away from me, Cade retrieved his phone and snapped a few pictures of my arms and legs covered in rope marks. They were... hot.

"I'll send them to you. But first." He tapped away on his phone before showing me the picture of my legs, nestled between the blankets with those rope impressions all over them, was now his lock screen.

"Cade." My eyes went wide.

"I'm going to want to look at it again. It's convenient this way."

Cade reached over onto the end table and grabbed a bottle of water, undoing it to help me take a sip. "You're probably thirsty."

The picture wasn't scandalous. It didn't show anything I'd be embarrassed of. The fact that he wanted it as his screen made me squirm with happiness inside. Taking the water bottle from him, I drank nearly half the bottle in one go. "Woah."

He grinned. "Yeah, that can happen." Then he crouched in front of me, more serious. "Anything you *didn't* like?"

I pulled him closer until he came back on the couch with me so I could lean on his shoulder and sink into him again. "No, that was incredible. Thank you."

"So you want more?"

"Yes please."

Cade tilted my chin up with one finger and kissed me. We didn't need words to understand what was said. He kissed three words onto my lips, and I kissed them right back.

## CHAPTER FORTY-SIX

ISOLDE

Cade's hoodie and a set of boy shorts weren't something I was in the habit of wearing around, but what the hell. I lived here now, and I wanted to be comfy and surrounded by scents I loved.

I wasn't loopy anymore. Just relaxed. Staring into the flickering flames of a fire pit I hadn't noticed when I was outside yesterday. Tucked into a camping chair, the sea breeze ruffled my hair as the sun began to set. This was...

Well, it was perfect. I couldn't quite wrap my head around it, or what Ellie said yesterday. The guys had cooked dinner, and I was pleasantly content. They talked about s'mores, but I would be happy just sitting here forever.

"I have a question," I announced.

Joel chuckled. "Hopefully we'll have an answer."

"Why did you pick St. James for a pack name?" I looked over at Rowan. "You have some kind of secret superpower I don't know about?"

"No." He smirked. "Honestly we just tried all our names, and we liked that one the best. We didn't want to pick something that *wasn't* one of our names. It didn't feel right."

I nodded. "Fair. I do like it, I was just curious."

"As the pack's newest member, I'm glad you like it. And I hope you like these too." Rowan put a box on my lap. "These are the *special* ones."

I grinned up at him and flipped open the lid, eyeing the little chocolate seashells. "Oooh, they're pretty. And how long do these take to kick in?"

"You won't feel a thing for at least two hours."

"Perfect." I popped one in my mouth that looked like a nautilus shell before giving him the box back. If I kept it, I would want more of his delicious chocolate. But if I ate more of these I would be so high I wouldn't know up from down. One was enough.

The door behind us shut loudly. "Baby girl, have I got something for you."

I tipped my face up to Hawk's as he appeared at my side. "Oh?"

Not saying a word, he handed me his phone, the screen already open to—

My whole body froze. It was me. In that first photo Janet had shown me. Back arched, eyes heated because I was watching Hawk watch *me*. It had been edited, the colors tweaked, an added softness overlaying the picture.

I scrolled through them, unable to believe I was the woman in the pictures. Because she was *hot*. When I got to the pictures of me and Hawk, perfume exploded outward around me. His smile while I curled around him on the end of the bed. The way he looked at the camera with such fucking sureness. Him knowing and being sure about me was written in every single frame.

The photos of us—tastefully—naked nearly put me on the floor. Hawk had an incredible ass, and I looked so taken with him...

And he'd told me even though I didn't understand it yet. About Alphas wanting to practice giving me orgasms. About taking pictures with everyone together. Exactly what he'd told me. No lies, and he'd already decided.

Hawk kissed below my ear. "You're fucking beautiful, you know that?"

"It barely looks like me. They're incredible."

"They look exactly like you. I'm gonna have some printed for the house."

My jaw dropped. "We can't hang those."

"We absolutely can. And when we do the next photoshoot with everyone, we'll make sure you have at least one picture with everyone."

Rowan raised an eyebrow, gaze bouncing between us. "Do we get to see?"

"I already sent the link to the gallery to the group chat. The new one."

I frowned. "New one?"

One side of his mouth pulled up into a grin. He pulled my phone out of his back pocket—must have found it wherever I left it—and handed it to me. "The new one with you in it, baby girl."

"Oh." I took the phone from him slowly. The little things were the ones that made this real. A group chat. For our pack.

The rest of the guys already had their phones out, looking at the photos wide eyed and with more than one obvious erection. But Hawk knelt in front of me and made me set my phone down before he took my hands.

His expression gave me butterflies, but I also couldn't tell what he would do, so I cleared my throat. "Is this the part where you tell me you're about to throw me over the cliff to my death?"

"No." He laughed. "Not off a cliff, and definitely not to your death. But I'm going to say something and it might freak you out."

"Then don't say it."

Hawk squeezed my hands. "I have to. Because I've been wanting to say it for days, and it's going to kill me if I don't."

My stomach twisted with nerves. "Okay."

He leaned forward and tugged me closer, voice quiet so it was just for us. "I love you. Am in love with you. You already know we want you, and I hope that it goes without saying that we love you. Cade already told you as much. But I need you to hear me say it. More than one of us has been waiting."

Mind starting to spin, he didn't let me think.

"And before that gorgeous mind of yours has time to come up with reasons for it not to be true, give me a chance to calm those fears. You are my Omega. Biology paired us together. But biology can't *force* love on people. It can help it go faster," he grinned. "But it's not as simple as that. You're beautiful. You're *kind*. You care so deeply about the people in your life that you'll put them first in almost everything. I haven't known you for long, and there's not a single thing about you that makes me hesitate or question. I am fucking in love with you, and I am with you. End of story."

Tears blurred the world in front of me faster than I could blink them back. I fumbled, reaching for him and needing him closer than he was. I couldn't see through my tears, but my lips found his anyway. Every single thing I felt but was terrified to say, I poured into the kiss. My soul was still damaged from the last time I let someone love it, but I *felt* the love from these men. All of them, even if they hadn't all said it yet, and neither had I.

Hawk pulled back, barely, lips still pressed against mine. "Do you believe me, baby girl?"

I nodded, still not finished kissing him.

But he moved out of reach, showing me what I hadn't noticed. The rest of them—my pack, my Alphas and my Beta—had converged while I was wrapped up in kisses and confessions.

Vaughn tugged me up out of my seat, phone falling by the wayside, and into his arms. "Hawk stole my thunder. I was gonna make you a s'more and tell you I loved you more than chocolate. But this will work too. I love you, sweetheart. I love you, and I'm not taking it back." He laughed, and I laughed with him. "And I'm going to teach you how to swim. My heart couldn't take it if you got swept away."

Choking on a laugh, I buried my face in his chest. "Only swept away by you?"

"Only by *us*."

Vaughn spun me away from him and into Rowan's waiting arms. The height difference between us made it nearly comical to stand side by side. Especially when I wasn't wearing heels, but the way he enveloped me felt safe. The way he held space for me to surrender made me feel protected. And everything else made me feel loved.

He smiled gently. "Do I need to make a speech, little flower? Because I will."

I shook my head. "Not a speech, no."

Rowan wasn't silent, but he was quieter than the rest of them. His words were always intentional. I didn't need words on words on words—I only wanted the ones he *needed* to give me.

Taking one hand, the other falling to the small of my back, Rowan held me as if we danced. "You're it for me, little flower," he bent down to whisper. "And I'll always be the place you can come to when you need to let go. I'll never let you fall."

"You guys are going to make me have a swollen face for tomorrow's rehearsal dinner," I sobbed into his shirt.

Rowan's purr roared to life inside his chest, soothing all my worries and every tense bone I had in my body. It was too much, and yet, it was everything I'd ever wanted.

Hands drifted up my arms, and Rowan released me to melt back into the scent of bourbon cooled with the freshness of cardamom. He was a drink I wanted to down over and over again.

He fully wrapped himself around me, burying his face in my hair. "You are my priority, Isolde."

I gasped, realizing what he'd said the other day. He'd told me he loved me without me knowing. They all had, in their own way.

"I love you too," I managed. "All of you."

How could I not? Everything they said about me was the same way I felt about them. They smoothed out the hard edges of my scars and filled in the empty spaces I'd never noticed. They cared for me effortlessly, and when I was with them, it was easier to breathe.

I was *never* going to change my mind.

The thought clanged through me like a silent bell.

I was never going to change my mind.

Ellie's words rang through me, winding their way down into my heart. We knew. Did we have to wait?

Using the sleeves on Cade's hoodie, I dried my eyes. He watched me carefully. They all did.

"What's that look on your face, princess?"

Vaughn laughed. "I didn't think your scent could get any sweeter, and you just proved me wrong."

Swallowing, I looked around at all of them. I was nervous. Not about the result, but whether they'd want this so soon. "I think I'm ready to jump."

Joel rocked me back and forth where he still held me. "What do you mean?"

"When Ellie brought me out here yesterday, she told me she was okay with whatever happened. No matter what. Even if we wanted to make things permanent. She wouldn't think I was stealing her thunder or anything."

The air went breathless and tight between the six of us, nothing but the rustle of the breeze and the low crackle of the fire.

They all stared in awe, but the silence was too much, so I kept going. "If you don't want to do it so quickly, I get that. We can do a big ceremony with it if you want. Or we can do it now with a ceremony later. I just know I'm not going to change my mind and I don't want to wait to feel you simply because some people might think it's too fast."

Hawk came to me so quickly he nearly stumbled, cupping my face and kissing me. He was purring. The air was suddenly filled with it. "I've never wanted anything more in my *life*," he said, pulling the hoodie over my head and glancing at me. "Do you want to go to the nest, or?"

I laughed, suddenly in the middle of a tangle of limbs as they touched me. Hugged me. Kissed me. The hoodie I'd been wearing ended up spread on the ground, a makeshift blanket of all our clothes.

"We'll do whatever you want, sweetheart." Vaughn rolled himself over me. "Ceremony. No ceremony. A ceremony every fucking weekend. But I'm not letting another day go by without you being mine." He searched my face. "Are you sure?"

"I'm sure."

His smile took my breath away. "Then we're going to bite you first, fuck you after, and I don't know if we'll ever want to stop."

"That's the whole point, right?" I smirked. "Forever?"

"Forever," he agreed. His mouth dropped to my skin, lips skating along my collarbone to the edge of my shoulder. I didn't have time to wonder what it would feel like. Vaughn bit down, and the pain made me arch, and then it was nothing because I was drowning in *Vaughn*. His wild playfulness and the dark, feral part of him that liked to chase and take. The love he spoke to me rang true, and more than anything else, feeling that told me this was right.

Perfect.

"Woah."

Vaughn's pupils were blown wide where he looked at me. "That's about the only word there is, huh?"

"Yeah."

Cade was in my line of vision. I reached for his hand and pulled him toward me. My gut knew he needed to be next—needed him to know he wasn't going to be last because he was a Beta. He wasn't a fucking afterthought. "Where?"

One hand came up to cradle my face, and I leaned into his touch. "Where what?"

"Where do you want me to bite you?"

He pulled my face to his with deliberate intention, taking my lips in a sinful kiss that had heat dropping through me and showed me exactly what I was in for later. "I'll wear your bite with pride no matter where you choose to put it, princess. I'm yours."

"Do you care if it shows?"

"I'd love that, actually."

I didn't second guess. My instinct drove me, and I bit where his neck met his shoulder, our bond springing into existence in the same way Vaughn's and mine had. But Cade felt different. He felt like *him*. Steady and controlled, and so deep I shuddered to feel all of him. The way he looked at me. Saw me. Loved me. I knew this was a moment where it was okay. "I love you, Sir."

Cade's eyes flared. Not with anger, but with desire. I felt how the words hit him and how they struck true. This wasn't a joke and it wasn't teasing. I loved the very heart of him.

He kissed me one more time. "Go get bitten by your other Alphas before I go get some rope to tie you down with."

I didn't have to go far. Hawk's arm circled my waist, pulling me back against him. "Any preference, baby girl?"

"No." All I wanted was him.

Teeth pierced my neck, nearly identical to where I'd bitten Cade. Hawk's sweetness filled my chest—settled next to the others. His teasing and the way he cared. The way he liked to watch me. Not only during sex, he liked me in his sights because I made him happy. He loved me. Holy shit. It was all so much.

How didn't I know?

"Because you weren't looking," he whispered quietly. "Now you never have to."

It was Joel's turn, hair bright as a flame in the dying sunlight. "I think part of me knew." He caught a stray piece of my hair flying in the wind. "When I answered the phone that night. People have found us before, and I never kept talking. Always hung up. With you, I couldn't. Some part of me knew you were ours before we even met you, Isolde. I felt with everything in me, that if I hung up the phone, I'd regret it forever. I'm so glad I was right."

"Me too."

My Alpha gave me a mark matching Vaughn's on my other shoulder. The easy, breathless comfort of him snapped into place through our bond. The Alpha who liked to fuck my body into pleasure when I couldn't even feel it, and make sure I was cared for no matter what. He kissed my forehead, and I got teary all over again.

The only one left was Rowan. He had me on my back in a second, body covering mine, giving me his warmth and his strength. "You're mine," he murmured against my lips. "Body and soul."

"And you're mine."

Rowan's bite was the twin to Hawk's on the other side of my neck. The *power* sinking through me into our connection stole what little I had left. There was no question of surrendering to him because he hadn't lied. He would never let me fall. It simply wasn't an option.

"Rowan."

"Hold on, little flower. We're about to show you everything."

Knocking my legs apart, he sank into me in one stroke. His pleasure echoed in me and mine echoed back, and oh *fuck* this would change everything. I was already climbing to the impossible peak of pleasure, and it would only get easier. Not just because they wanted to practice with me and shower me with orgasms like rain, but they could *feel* what I felt and what got me closer.

My first orgasm blew through me like a golden wave, and it wasn't the last. They didn't knot me, not able to wait for them to go down fast enough to suit them.

It didn't matter. Our pack was a tangle of pleasure. I tasted every one of them, got filled up over and over, was taken to the edge and over more times than I remembered ever being able to while not in heat.

We disappeared into each other, and by the time we were nearly finished, spent, panting, and satisfied, the sun had set, and I was floating for another reason too. Rowan's chocolate had me floating delightfully, and nothing in the world could be bad right now.

I was knotted on Joel's cock, sprawled on his chest, and Hawk was behind me, not quite finished. Joel turned to the side to help him as he fucked me, hand finding my clit, working it the way he could now feel drove me crazy. "One more, baby girl. Give me one more."

Exhaustion ran heavy in my veins. I whined before I spoke. "I don't know if I can."

"You can." He breathed the words into my neck. "Come on our cocks like the good girl you are."

Hawk licked over his mark on my neck, sending a new wave of heat rolling through me and carrying me with it. I writhed between them, my voice locked away behind the force of everything.

Groaning into my neck, Hawk came with me, knotting my ass. I moaned, the feeling of two knots still too much and just enough. Someone's hand stroked my ankle, reminding me we were all here. Tangled together. I felt all of them in me now, and nothing had ever been more *right*.

The fire still burned, and I drew patterns on Joel's skin with my fingers. My mind was high and drifty. "Can we have a fire on the beach?" I asked. "I've always wanted to."

“We absolutely can.”

I wasn’t even sure who said it, and I didn’t care.

Tomorrow was going to be a hell of a day. I giggled, thinking about the chaos this would cause. Everyone who mattered wouldn’t care, and those who might weren’t worth my time.

They felt the direction of my thoughts. Hawk rolled over from behind me and kissed my spine. The smile in his voice was obvious. “So who’s going to tell Beau?”

“Oh, I’m going to tell him,” I said, smiling at my plan. “And I won’t have to say a fucking word.”

# CHAPTER FORTY-SEVEN

## JOEL

"I know we live close, but we do need to go if we don't want to be late," I called back into the house.

Bonding right before Ellie's rehearsal dinner probably wasn't the best plan, if only because the six of us were so insatiable stopping to breathe was hard.

Other than the moments Isolde called her friends to tell them what happened—and the inevitable happy screaming that followed—one of us had been touching her. It was a need I couldn't describe, the feeling of wanting her close and safe. When she was in the center of the five of us it felt perfect. Like she was our sun, and we orbited around her.

The forecast for tomorrow and the wedding was perfect. Crystal clear and sunny—the ideal Clarity Coast summer day. But today? Clouds rolled in from over the ocean, painting the day in muted grays. Rain would fall before the day was over. Maybe even a thunderstorm. But quick storms were the norm here in the summer, and I was intrigued by the idea of my Omega in the rain.

*My* Omega.

It didn't seem real, but there she was. Her bright spark in the middle of my chest, surrounded by the echoes of the rest of our pack. It was strange being able to feel them for the first time as well, but I liked it. I already knew this would help our communication going forward.

Isolde was so sweet, like a hit of sugar I could keep with me at all times. Right now she was overwhelmingly happy, and we were all going to make sure she stayed that way. She more than deserved it.

"Let's go, St. James Pack, your chariot awaits."

Cade came around the corner, smirking. "Blame Vaughn."

"No, I won't take the blame here. I blame whoever created the dress she's wearing. I didn't know she would have to redo her lipstick entirely."

Isolde came around the corner, and any thought of blame slid out of my head. She wore a spring green dress that hugged her curves before ending in a flouncy skirt right above her knees. The off-the-shoulder neckline displayed all of our bites like they were jewelry. Her own necklace made of us. She didn't wear a necklace either, highlighting them. Instead, sparkly earrings dangled and drew even more attention to the bite marks on her neck.

I laughed. "Now I know why you said you won't have to tell him."

"Yup." Her eyes sparkled, and I felt her delight at the vicious bit of satisfaction she was about to have. "This wasn't what I had planned to wear, but I think it highlights things well enough."

"More than enough." I snagged her around the waist as she walked past, holding her against me. For all our sakes, I hoped the rehearsal and dinner didn't go too long. I needed my Omega underneath me again, my cock sinking into her perfect heat. And again once she was asleep, making sure her body had its fill. "You're perfect."

Isolde's cheeks turned pink in a flush, but I felt how much the compliment sank into her and made her feel so much more than loved. Along with her sensing my desperate need.

"Ready to rehearse?"

"Bet your ass. Especially since Beau is walking me down the aisle."

I couldn't stop my growl while I helped her up into the car. "Did we know about that?"

"Ellie dropped that particular bomb at the bachelorette, so probably not. We were busy. But now I can't wait, if only to rub it in his face."

Leaning in and kissing her shoulder where I marked it, I savored her shudder. "If he puts his hands on you anywhere other than where it's necessary to get you to the end of the aisle, I can't promise what I'll do."

"Try to keep his face intact. Five on one isn't a fair fight, even if he is an ass."

Cade buckled her seatbelt. "We never promised anything fair when it comes to you."

Our Omega didn't hate that idea. She hadn't been outwardly possessive yet, but I liked knowing she felt like she owned us just as much as we owned her. Any way she wanted to express that was fucking fine with me.

The drive only took a few minutes, and there were nearly as many cars here at the estate as the day we'd arrived.

Sudden nerves danced through my bond with Isolde. Nothing too bad, but I didn't blame her. Walking into your sister's wedding rehearsal, bonded, and not having told anyone, was a bold choice. I pushed confidence through to her.

"I need to get used to that," she muttered, waiting for Vaughn to open her door.

"What?"

"All of you feeling what I'm feeling and then making me feel better."

Hawk helped her down and made sure she was balanced on her hot-as-fuck high heels. "You do need to get used to it, cause we're not going to stop."

Geoffrey opened the door for us, and if I hadn't been looking for it, I wouldn't have noticed the slightest freeze when he saw Isolde and her still-healing bites. Then he smiled. "Nice to see you, Miss St. James."

Her small intake of breath hit me right in the gut. Damn, that sounded good. Isolde's legal name wouldn't change unless she wanted it to, it was Geoffrey's way of letting both her and us know he acknowledged the bond.

"Thank you, Geoffrey. I assume everyone is already outside?"

"They are."

"Thank you."

We went straight through the mansion out back. In the days we'd been locked away for the heat, the back of the Caruso estate had been transformed. A giant tent now dominated a large portion of the backyard. Lights were everywhere. Curled around the tent poles and along the walkways—new stone ones that had been laid just for the wedding.

Beyond that, an area down by the beach where the actual wedding would take place. It was clear there would be flowers and decorations here tomorrow, but because of the weather and wind, it was a little bare. The bridal party congregated there, waiting for everything to start. Isolde's parents too, along with Ellie and Warren.

Here we go.

Ellie spotted us and waved, coming over. We all stood back, watching when she got close enough to see.

The ungodly *shriek* Ellie released had Warren running and confused when he saw his fiancée hugging Isolde while jumping up and down.

Everyone else converged around her, people offering congratulations. Her parents. Everyone. She was full of joy and surrounded by joy.

Rowan chuckled. "I'm glad Ellie said what she did. Otherwise, I don't think she would have asked yesterday."

"No," I agreed. "Definitely not."

"I bet the five of you are fucking pleased with yourselves, aren't you?"

We knew who it was before we turned. Beau stood to the side, having circled around the chaos to get to us. I spotted Angela, still standing among the chairs, looking a bit lost. Beau's expression was pure poison.

"We are," Cade said. "Thank you for asking."

He shook his head, looking away. His eye looked better, the bruise Hawk left turning yellow and nearly healed. I wouldn't mind adding another one, but we wouldn't. For now.

The wedding planner started calling everyone forward. We would sit in the audience and watch. Wait.

"I guess I was right about her. A few weeks with you and she commits when she runs away from us after four years? What a fucking joke."

Shrugging, Vaughn looked at him. "When you know, you know." He didn't need to know we were scent matched. It wasn't his business.

But something nagged my brain.

People were paired off, and the planner searched for Beau. But the bridal party was still messing around while she made sure she had everyone.

"What do you mean you were right about her?" I asked.

The way Beau smiled, my stomach dropped. It was the face of someone who was about to do damage.

Beau sneered at the five of us. "You know who her family is, right? And you probably don't know mine, but let's just say we're equals."

I struggled with the urge not to roll my eyes. We knew *exactly* who Beau was. I'd done research on him as soon as I knew Isolde was hiring us to deal with an ex. Yeah, his family was powerful in their own right. Half the population of Clarity could say the same. He wasn't nearly as special as he believed.

"Beau," Warren called, tone harsh. "Get your ass over here. The faster we do this, the faster we can get to dinner."

Beau didn't move. He remained fixated on us.

"Us together?" He laughed. "I don't need to explain why that's a good idea. But her doing this? Choosing *you*? A pack of nobodies? After all the time I put into her, and still not willing to hear me out? It means I was right. Even with everything a match like ours could bring, she's not worth the trouble."

I saw red, my body tightening with the need to *defend* my Omega. But he just kept fucking going.

"Turns out those years I spent fucking people who actually *got off* during sex was time well spent." He snorted and looked at Rowan. "I have no problem pleasing a woman. Ask my fiancée. So enjoy dealing with a cold, broken Omega for the rest of your life."

"Does Isolde know?" I snarled at him. When we asked her if Beau had cheated she said no, but that had also been before she trusted us completely. I wanted him to confirm it, like the piece of shit he was.

Beau just smirked at me, his answer written all over his face. No. She didn't fucking know.

Without another word, he turned and went, adjusting the cuffs on his suit as he stepped into place beside Isolde.

Vaughn was ready to lunge. We all were. I placed a hand on his chest. We had to wait. "Fuck me, I want to hit him too, but she can't find out like this," I said. It was aimed at Vaughn, but they all heard me.

She deserved to know, and before he started spreading it around just to be an ass. But in the middle of the rehearsal when she was about to walk down the aisle with him wasn't the time to deliver that news.

"Later," I said. When we could hold her and comfort her in her grief.

Our Omega didn't care about her ex. But going from thinking he was an ordinary piece of shit to knowing he'd spent your entire relationship cheating on you wasn't something easy to hear. It would hurt, and he knew it. It was why he told us. One last parting shot.

Isolde looked over her shoulder and smiled, but even from here I could see her brow furrow. She didn't understand why we felt like this right now.

"Later," Hawk ground out.

We moved around the side to where we could sit out of the way. Sit and watch and plan the ways we could smother our Omega in love. And maybe a few ways to bury a body.

## CHAPTER FORTY-EIGHT

ISOLDE

Ellie screamed. She knocked into me so quickly I almost lost my balance in the heels. Frankly, I had no business wearing heels this high, but I wanted the complete look while delivering the best news of my life to my family and the worst news of his life to my ex.

"*Holy shit.*" My sister still jumped up and down. "You actually did it."

"It was because of you," I said. "I don't think I would have done it right away if you hadn't said you would be fine with it right now. And I have zero regrets."

"What's wrong?" Warren asked. He looked panicked, gaze bouncing between the two of us.

I laughed. "Sorry, Warren. I surprised her. Everything's okay."

Warren's eyes dropped to my bites, and his eyes widened. Then he smiled. "Congratulations."

"Thank you."

The rest of the bridal party was closing in to see what the fuss was about, and suddenly I was surrounded by people congratulating me and asking questions. Through the crowd, my parents filtered through. By the time they reached me, they knew, having gathered from listening, and Mom swept me into a hug.

"I'm so happy for you," she whispered. "I'm so happy."

"You're not mad we didn't do it like this?"

She laughed. "If you want a party, we'll plan a party. But I'm just happy you're happy."

"Don't suffocate her, Adelaide. Let me have a turn."

I smiled at my stepfather. "I assume Mom told you everything?"

"She did." He took me by the shoulders and looked at the bites before meeting my eyes. "And you're happy?"

"I don't think I've ever been happier," I admitted.

"Good. I'll be digging into them more anyway, but good."

More? He'd looked into them at all? Clearly he hadn't come up with anything if they were still here. We all laughed. "You don't have to. They'll tell you anything you want to know."

He nodded. "I'll be asking."

I met Ellie's eyes, and we rolled them together. Our father didn't have his ruthless reputation as a lawyer for nothing.

"Okay, everyone," the wedding planner called. "Let's get lined up and have everyone in place so we can start going over everything."

Mom grabbed my hand and squeezed, and I squeezed back before they went back to their places for the rehearsal. One benefit of announcing the bonding like this was just being able to enjoy it. Because of everything else, we didn't have time for a lot of questions. Those would come later, I was sure.

"Are you going to be okay during this?" Ellie asked, looking over.

Because I was about to line up next to Beau. "I am. I wore this dress on purpose."

"Fuck yes. That's my girl. And Beau has been a little shit, by the way. He's avoiding the conversation with Warren at any cost, and neither of us are happy about it."

"It's okay," I told her. "Truly. What can he do that hasn't already happened?"

She winced and smiled. "Yeah. Anyway, I want details later, okay?"

"Not too many."

"You're telling me absolutely everything."

I rolled my eyes, and suddenly I put a hand to my chest as *rage* surged through the bonds with my pack. I glanced back and found Beau standing in front of them. That would do it.

The wedding planner came down the line, making sure everyone was in place. "We need the best man?"

Warren turned. "Beau. Get your ass over here. The faster we do this, the faster we can get to dinner." His tone was as harsh as I'd ever heard it.

Beau waited a minute longer before coming over to me with a smile that was all satisfaction. Rage so bright it stole my breath was in my chest. "Beau," I greeted him.

"Isolde."

I glanced over my shoulder at them and found them watching me. They were angry, and I wasn't sure why, other than that I was standing next to the Alpha who hurt me, and that was unacceptable.

"I never thought you'd stoop this low," he said.

"Excuse me?"

One glance at me was all he spared. "There were other ways to hurt me if you wanted. You didn't need to *bond* with a pack that's clearly beneath you."

"Oh, please. This had nothing to do with you. I bonded my scent matched pack. Believe me, I didn't make a lifelong commitment just to spite *you*. Wearing a dress that showed it off? That was to spite you."

"Scent matched?" He scoffed. "Bullshit."

I said nothing.

In front of us, the wedding planner went through the order and how fast we were meant to walk. And thankfully, blissfully, Beau stayed silent.

"I'm surprised to see Angela here," I said.

"Why? She's my fiancée."

"Still? I thought after you admitted that you still wanted me, you might have tossed her aside the same way you did with me."

Beau huffed out a breath. "You really think that little of me? We had four good years, Isolde. Just because you misunderstood the end of them—"

"For fuck's sake," I said under my breath as the line moved forward. "I thought we had four good years. But the more time I spend away from you, the more I realize they weren't good for anyone but you. I didn't know enough to realize just how much you used me and took me for granted. I should really thank you, because in spite of all the pain, being dumped by you ended up being the best thing to ever happen to me."

In the corner of my eye, I saw his jaw working, like he was holding himself back from saying anything.

We were next to walk down the aisle. My pack was now sitting in the empty rows of white chairs. Their anger was muted by their intense focus on watching me and the Alpha beside me. They wouldn't let me fall.

Beau held out his arm for me to take.

Nope. Not today, satan.

"Tomorrow."

"What?"

"I'll take your arm for the aisle tomorrow," I told him. "Today, both for myself and my pack, I'm not touching you."

He looked over at me like he'd been struck. "What kind of shit have they been putting in your head? It's like you're a completely different person. You're not the Omega I fell in love with."

"I'm not a different person. I'm just a person who now knows how much better life is when someone isn't holding her back and making her feel like shit. The reason I'm not the Omega you fell in love with is because that person didn't exist. She was someone you molded, and not who I actually am."

True anger was in his voice now. On his face. I felt the pack's attention on us, and their caution as they saw Beau turn red. "You act like I fucking abused you or something. What the hell, Isolde? We were happy. We could have been happy again if you hadn't left so quickly. Whatever you think of me? You're being manipulated. If you don't see how all of this is your fault to begin with, I can't help you."

I laughed. Actually laughed. Thank god it was time to split and stand on either side of the altar, because I needed time to compose myself. It was either laugh like I'd lost my mind or cry because I was so fucking angry at myself for not being able to see through his bullshit. For making excuses over every little thing that hurt me. For letting the love and kindness he'd shown me at the *beginning* of our relationship feed my heart far longer than it lasted.

Ellie looked at me as she came down the aisle with an eyebrow raised. Was I okay? I shrugged with a smile. Yes. I was okay and I wasn't okay and despite everything working out for the best, I'd never not regret letting it go so far.

Across from me, Beau glared.

Had he truly been this way the whole time and I just didn't see it? That was hard for me to believe. Even with all the shitty things Beau did, which made him worse than I'd believed, I'd never seen this... poisonous side of him before. I wasn't sure which was worse—him being able to hide this part of himself, or turning into him at all.

We had to walk down the aisle a few more times to get it right, and we said nothing to each other as we did so. The ceremony part was easy to rehearse, as was the walk back up the center. For the time it took, I kept stealing glances at the pack. They felt better now that I wasn't next to Beau, but our bonds were still taut with something darker.

As soon as the wedding planner told us we were finished, we were all walking over to the reception area where the staff had already laid out food for everyone and it smelled *incredible*. Food hadn't been the highest need on our list this morning.

The guys met me there, Vaughn pulling me into a fierce hug. Harder than it needed to be, considering I hadn't left their sight. "What—"

"No, no, no," Ellie called. "Food first. You guys can be sappy later. You have your whole lives for it."

"Just a second," I said. I looked at the guys. "What's wrong?"

Joel gave me a tight smile. "Nothing that won't keep for an hour."

"I can feel it. You're all amped up, and as much as I know you hate my ex, he's barely said anything to me and hasn't touched me. So what did he do?"

They all shared a look, and I narrowed my eyes. "Do I need to stamp my foot? What? I can handle it."

Joel blew out a breath and scrubbed a hand over his face. "He told us he'd been cheating on you. No details, but it seemed like it was for most of your relationship."

I waited for the horror and devastation to hit me, but it didn't. After everything, nothing that came out about him surprised me. It still hurt, but not the way I expected. "I probably should have guessed that."

Hawk's shocked expression made me smile. He searched my face. "You seem remarkably okay with it."

"Okay with it? No. Unwilling to let someone who doesn't matter affect my life anymore? Yes. It's already happened and I have you. I'll be okay."

The relief from all of them was palpable.

Vaughn kissed my hair. "I love you."

"Love you too."

We'd only been away for two minutes, so Ellie didn't harass us when we sat down. It was all in good fun anyway, but it was a good thing I knew. They felt better not keeping it from me, and I felt better because they felt better.

I was seated near Ellie and Warren, the guys in a line next to me, and of course, Beau and Angela were across from us. Angela met my eyes and smiled for a moment before looking away. None of the anger or vitriol which had been there a few days ago.

Whatever. If I didn't have to deal with two people hating me, that was just fine.

But Beau? I looked at him and felt nothing. What a fucking *relief*.

I looked at my sister. "Are you nervous about tomorrow?"

"No." She took Warren's hand and laughed. "I'm as excited for it as I'm excited for it to be over. Then we can go have fun."

They were going on a northern cruise for their honeymoon. Where it was cold and they'd probably see icebergs. I questioned their sanity, but Ellie pointed out to me that she didn't need to *go* anywhere to hang out on the beach. She wanted something different, and they weren't going to spend a lot of time outside of their luxurious ship cabin anyway.

"Good."

"I can't wait to see the final flowers," she said. "Everything Ocean's shown me has been incredible."

"I'm sure they'll be perfect. And Ocean always hides hidden meanings in all her designs. Flower language."

Ellie laughed. "She told me. I asked her to put the meanings on little cards for everyone so they would know." Then she glanced over at Beau. "Well, maybe not for everyone."

Smothering my laugh, I leaned into Rowan next to me and put my head on his shoulder. His hand found my bare leg, squeezing gently. The bond between us was filled with that steady, all-encompassing calm and control I loved about him. And when Beau stared straight at us like he could set us on fire with his gaze, Rowan turned and kissed me without any other thoughts. A pure, luxurious kiss without any worry or care who watched. It calmed the need I hadn't even sensed, and I felt his amusement at my wonder.

Ellie stood. "I have to pee. Iz, time for your maid of honor duties to help hold my dress."

"Isn't that when you're in an actual wedding dress?"

"Come on." She wiggled her fingers at me, waiting until I grabbed her hand to pull me up and out of the chair and into the house.

The big guest bathroom had actual stalls, and she went in alone. "If you don't want me to hold your dress, why did you bring me?"

"I didn't want to come alone, and I wanted to check on you.

Because your pack keeps glaring daggers at Beau like they want to kill him."

"Apparently he was cheating on me," I said. "He threw it in their faces to hurt them, and me. Too bad for him. It means nothing to me now."

Ellie flushed and opened the door, looking me up and down. "Holy shit."

"I probably should have known. It tracks with everything else. I just... I never felt like he was being secretive, and he was never gone long enough for me to think he was cheating."

"I'm sorry." Ellie washed her hands, looking at the mirror.

I shrugged, crossing my arms. "Like I said, it is what it is. Nothing I can do about it now, and it doesn't matter. It makes me question how the hell I missed it."

"He clearly didn't want you to see."

"Yeah. And Warren?"

She sighed. "Honestly, he's ready for the wedding to be over so he doesn't have to deal with Beau anymore. He told his parents about everything—what he could share without violating your privacy—and they begged him not to change anything for the wedding and keep the peace. Which is what he's doing, but Beau's not going to be in the pictures, and I'm pretty sure he's getting thrown straight out of Warren's life the second we say 'I do.'

"I know you guys think he—"

I cut her off. "Like I told him the other day. If I didn't see him for who he was when I was living with him and fucking him, I can't blame anyone else for not knowing. Especially with Warren literally living out of the country for most of it. Now let's get back out there. I spotted some of the dessert and I want that way more than I want to talk about my shitty ex."

"Good point."

We ran into Mom on the way out. "You girls having fun?"

"You know it," I said.

Ellie looped her arm through mine on the way back to the table, which was full of laughter and conversation. It was the first time I'd really been away from them and out of sight since we bonded last night, and seeing them again? The way our connection surged and everything felt complete was perfect.

Spattering drops of rain began to fall. We needed to wrap dinner up soon or everyone would be soaked. The sooner the better, because the storm needed time to clear out before tomorrow.

Cade looked over and smiled. I smiled right back, loving the feeling of him reaching out, like fingers stroking down the bond between us.

"I love your smile around them," Ellie whispered.

"Me too."

I sat down, and as soon as I did, Beau surged to his feet. "It's time for a toast. We're doing toasts, right? The best man always gets to do one."

Warren chuckled and eyed the rest of the table. "Usually at the actual reception."

"Well, I have something I want to say right now." Beau picked up his fork and clinked it against his glass of champagne. Everyone quieted and all eyes turned toward him. "Of course, I want to congratulate the bride and groom for having us all here. But more than that, I want to congratulate Isolde Allen on her bonding. To a pack of male escorts, no less. I think we should all be very proud. Everyone give Isolde a round of applause."

My whole body went cold, and the silence that reigned was deafening. Nothing but the growing wind and the sound of the sea. I glanced over at Ellie and Warren, shock written on their faces. At the other end of the table, my parents watched us too. But with far less surprise than everyone else. The one thing I didn't see was horror or judgment.

I looked at Beau. "Thank you."

"Male escorts," he said again. "You bonded a pack of *male escorts*."

The anger roiling in my chest from my pack had nothing to do with their former profession and everything to do with Beau attempting to humiliate me.

"And?" I asked. "Yes. That's what they are. Or were before we met. Of all people, you shouldn't care, Beau. I hired them because I didn't want to face you at this wedding alone. So... try something else if you want to get anywhere with this. You look foolish."

"Fine. You want to play?"

I smacked my hands on the table and stood. "No. I don't. I'm sick of this. I'm sick of *us*, Beau. We're over. No matter what you think or believe or want, we are *long* done. So if you're going to try to make this about me, you can't." I looked out over the table, suddenly nervous about the amount of eyes on me.

Fingers gripped my hand. Ellie, telling me she was fine and to do what I needed. I didn't look at my pack—I didn't need to. Their pride sang strong through our bonds.

"You ended our relationship with an ultimatum that, *apparently*, you thought would make me stay instead of leave. You claimed you still wanted me despite now having a fiancée." I looked down at Angela. "That was right after the anniversary party, by the way. And I'm sorry, but all that jewelry he's bought you? He didn't buy it. It was mine, and I left it behind when I got away from him."

She had the grace to look embarrassed, and deeper than that, hurt. This whole dinner she'd barely said anything.

"And I just found out, like, right now, that Beau cheated on me through the entirety of our relationship. So, cheers to that, asshole." I lifted my glass and drank.

Beau laughed, but he wasn't looking at me. He looked at my sister. "Damn, Ellie. After all this time I didn't think you would be the one to tell her. I had my money on the escorts telling her. Guess I should take bathroom trips more seriously. Or I guess I saw your mom go, too." He looked down the table. "Was it you, Mrs. Caruso? Or both of you together?"

The blood flowed out of Mom's face, leaving her white as a sheet. My legs gave out and I fell into my chair. Ellie was as white as her dress, and she wouldn't look at me. She hadn't acted with shock in the bathroom when I told her he'd been cheating. And earlier, when I questioned what else Beau could do to me, she'd winced.

She really had known.

"Honestly," Beau said, refocusing on me. "I kind of thought Henry might tell you first. You've always been a daddy's girl even though he's not your real father. See, Isolde? Even the first man to know you left."

My father went to stand, but Warren was already there. "That is *enough*. Get the fuck off this property and don't come back, Beau. I was willing to hear your side of things, but that's not necessary now." Warren leaned on the table, sagging like the weight of the world rested on his shoulders. "I don't know what the fuck happened for you to turn from the Beau I knew, who had my back no matter what, into whatever you are now. Or maybe I'm as big of an idiot as the rest of the world and fell for the mask you put on. That's over now. Get out."

"Fine." Beau tossed back his champagne. "See you tomorrow."

"Not tomorrow, Beau. Not ever. Get the fuck out of this house and do not contact me, my wife, Isolde, her pack, or the Carusos ever again."

For the first time Beau looked shocked. I couldn't enjoy it. He really thought everything would be fine. That he wasn't the problem.

Of course not. He was the golden child. The golden boy, golden man, golden 'I get everything I want whenever I want it.' He was a spoiled child in a man's body, and this was the result.

"You heard him," Dad said from his place at the table. "Get off my property. And you can be sure you won't be allowed back."

Beau stuck out his hand to Angela, and she shrunk away from him and shook her head. "No," she whispered.

The rage on Beau's face matched the thunder that cracked overhead, the rain starting to fall in earnest as he went toward the house. No one spoke until he was out of sight, breathless and tense.

Him disappearing was like a piñata bursting and confetti made of despair raining down on me. I couldn't feel my body, and everything was cold.

Ellie turned and reached for me, eyes tearing. "Iz, I promise you it's not what it seems like."

I pulled away, staring at her. It was like looking at a stranger. This hurt so much worse than finding out about the cheating. Not just her...

"Please," she begged. "Just give us a chance to—"

Standing so quickly my chair fell over, I kicked off my heels and went into the rain. Voices called after me, but they were lost to the wind, rain, and waves.

And I did what I thought I'd never do again.

I ran.

## CHAPTER FORTY-NINE

### ROWAN

Isolde sprinted toward the beach, and we didn't follow. Our precious Omega needed some time and space. Now that she lived inside us too, we could know. She wasn't angry with us. She was devastated by her family.

"I'll watch her," Vaughn said, heading out into the rain.

I doubted Isolde was going to run straight into the ocean, but it was good to have someone with her.

"Did you know?" Hawk focused on Ellie. "Really?"

She shuddered. "Yes, I knew. But it's not like she thinks. I wasn't hiding it from her, it just—"

Cutting herself off, she looked at us with heat. "I need to tell her and not you."

When she stood, I stood too. "Don't go after her right now. I know you want to, but don't. She needs the space." Then I looked at Warren. "Any issues if we?" I let the words hang, my meaning clear.

"Be my guest."

The four of us moved as one, heading toward the house and the parking lot beyond. It would probably be better if Beau had already driven off the property. But if he hadn't, we had some words for him.

He was about to get in his car, and he saw us coming. "If you hit me again, I will press charges. I'm already leaving, so fuck off."

Hawk didn't fuck off. He shoved Beau back into the car, pinning him in place without hitting him, though I felt every seething breath of how much he wanted to. "Before you drive off and rid the rest of us of your presence, I just need to know one thing."

"What's that?" Beau tried to shove him off and got nowhere.

"Why?"

"Why what?" He snarled.

"Why do this?" It was me talking now. "Why humiliate her? Why come after us? Why alienate the man who was once your best friend? Why make your whole life implode for a relationship you already wrecked? You cheated on her the entire time you were together, so you clearly didn't care about her—"

This time when he shoved Hawk away, he got free. "I *loved her*," he roared.

"You don't cheat on people you love," Cade spit the words. "Either that, or you have a really shitty definition of love."

Beau rolled his eyes. "Like a pack of whores doesn't understand what it means to have needs. I'm sure you've fucked plenty of women with impotent partners who still love them and just need a little more. It's biology, nothing else."

Absolutely fucking untrue.

"I'm going to hit him if I don't go inside," Hawk said, stalking away.

"You know what I think happened?" I said. "After fucking everyone you could find behind Isolde's back, you found someone who got your dick wet just the way you like it. And you kept her around. But she got needy, and you weren't willing to lose her. So when she gave *you* an ultimatum, you gave Isolde one. And she left. And then you realized how much you'd actually lost and what a mistake it was.

"But you still had some good sex and a woman who came from a passable family. Someone to pass the time until you could get Isolde back. And then you realized you'd never get her back, so like the rabid dog you are, you attacked instead of learning your lesson and letting go. You tried to destroy our Omega because if you couldn't have her, you didn't want anyone else to either."

"She was mine *LONG* before she was yours." Lightning shattered the sky overhead, followed by the thunder, and I smiled. I hit a nerve. The asshole was like a dog with a toy it didn't want to share. He was willing to do anything to make his wounded ego feel better, even if every single problem stemmed from him.

The others knew and felt the same.

"Do you have any idea how lucky you were?" Joel asked. "You had people willing to go to bat for you even after you were a dick. Warren was waiting to talk to you out of respect for your friendship, even after he knew most of what you did. And you threw that away because your pride was hurt. Karma really is a glorious bitch, isn't she?"

Beau moved first. He swung for Joel, but I was already moving. My fist knocked directly into his jaw, hurling him backward into the car like a limp sack of potatoes. Fuck, that felt good. Pummeling him to the ground would feel even better, but I needed to resist that.

"I dare you to press charges when you swung first," I told him. The rain dissolved the blood on his lip where I'd split it. If looks could kill, we'd all be dead a hundred times over.

"This is the only time I'll say this." Cade stepped forward, back straight, every bit of Dom power he had on full display. "If you contact Isolde again. If you let her see you. If you do anything to even make her *think* about you, we'll be there to put your ass in the ground. You claim we're so much lower than you? Maybe we are. But remember that those of us who play in the dirt know how to dig. And six feet isn't that far. Understood?"

The coward said nothing, instead getting into his car and nearly burning the tires on his way out of the gravel drive. I clapped Cade on the shoulder. "Good job."

"I would have rather had the hit. A little jealous of that."

"Definitely worth the bruise."

Through the bonds in our chests, we all shuddered. The pain Isolde felt, the agony and betrayal... it nearly sent me to my knees. But we couldn't go to her yet. This was something she needed to bear alone. Not yet, but soon. The second we felt the tide turn, we would be there.

Just inside the entry, Henry stood waiting. From the look on his face, he'd seen everything that just happened between us and Beau. Right now, I didn't want to look at him either. He'd hurt Isolde, and that meant he needed to stand far the fuck away from me.

Isolde's father sighed and slid his hands into the pockets of his suit. "I guess we need to talk."

"Actually we don't," Cade said.

"Five minutes. No more than that. Let me explain. Then you can think of me what you will."

I grit my teeth. Listening to anyone justify their behavior when

Isolde felt like this was the last thing on my to-do list right now. But Joel stepped forward, eyes hard.

"You have five minutes. Start talking."

## CHAPTER FIFTY

ISOLDE

I didn't stop running until I'd reached the arch beneath the rocks. My legs and lungs burned, at odds with the cold from running through the rain.

In true Clarity Coast fashion, the storm hit hard and fast. It wouldn't last long, but while it did, it was fierce.

The tide was at its lowest point, exposing what felt like miles of sand and leaving behind treasures you couldn't find otherwise. Shells and seaglass, the occasional bottle. Left behind and abandoned.

Pain lanced through my chest, everything crashing down on me over again. They knew.

They knew.

They knew.

They knew.

They knew and didn't tell me.

My rational brain told me something wasn't right with this. Ellie had wanted to explain. And I knew Beau always twisted things. But my rational brain wasn't here right now. It left the building the second my sister went pale, confirming my worst fear: That I couldn't trust anyone. Not even those closest to me.

Lightning split the sky, striking the ocean far out in the distance, the thunder booming seconds later. I tilted my face back to the sky and let the rain hit me. I was already soaked through, and I didn't care. It felt good to be out here and ruined.

At the very least, the world mimicked the way I felt. Not another sunny Clarity day where everything was happy and perfect while I was breaking apart.

The only thing that was right was them. Steady in my chest. Not flooding me with love or trying to stop this. Letting me feel it because I needed to feel it. If I wanted them, I already knew they'd be there as fast as physically possible.

But I didn't want them here for this. I didn't want them to see me this broken.

A sob broke through, making me collapse in on myself. My chest *hurt*. The last time I felt like this, I ran away to the other side of the country and didn't come back. There wasn't anywhere to run this time. Not when the people meant to be on my side weren't.

The beach stretched out in front of me, nothing but rain and sand and distant waves looking as lonely as I felt.

Wind picked up, turning the rain sharp, and the thunder was louder. Black clouds swelled and the world darkened. Even the shallows churned with the sudden fierceness of the storm, and *fuck* it felt good.

I wanted to scream and not be the loudest thing. I wanted to feel insignificant in the face of this vast ocean, because if I was small, there was something bigger than *this*.

Waves brushed my toes. I hadn't even realized I'd walked forward, all the way down to the tidal break, where the waves rushed in around my ankles. Sucked the sand from beneath my feet. Called me with sinister whispers and pushed me away at the same time.

Sloshing deeper, I stopped when the water reached my knees. Lightning flashed again, and this time I knew it was coming. I waited for the thunder and screamed.

I screamed until I didn't have breath.

I screamed until it hurt.

I waited for the thunder to drown me out.

And then I didn't wait anymore. I screamed and sobbed, giving in to everything.

*Everything*.

Every time I'd had small tears and pushed them back. All those times I told myself it wasn't worth it to cry or give in to the pain. Each instance I'd teared up with my pack over the simple joy of being treated like a person.

This had been hovering on the edges for a long time now, and it was here. My storm overcoming me at the same time the storm crashed into the rest of us.

I couldn't stop it now, ragged sobs choking me, the sounds ugly and raw. Everything made the pain worse. It pulsed with my heart and shook me. Stole every bit of brightness I thought I had and smothered it.

No matter what happened, I would never forget feeling like someone slipped a knife between my ribs, reaching the part of me they'd promised to protect. Like the cliffs were crumbling beneath my feet and the net my pack had given me wasn't there. All that lay at the bottom was sand and the remnants of too many hopes.

Another rolling boom of thunder, so hard I felt it in my bones.

Like it had finally cracked the rest of me, everything flowed out. All the pain and rage. The betrayal. The whys. Everything drained out until I felt as flat as the rained-on sea, and left me tired.

I barely heard the splashing of steps before arms circled me from behind. Vaughn. Deep citrus infused the wet air, sharper than normal. Threads of rotten darkness—his anger at Beau and sadness for me. He hadn't come until I needed him.

I hadn't even realized I called, but I had.

Vaughn scooped me up and carried me out of the water without a word. We didn't go back to the mansion. He carried me straight up the path, weaving back and forth on the switchbacks until we broke over the top, and Rowan was already there unlocking the gate.

I was passed to Joel, and I closed my eyes, not willing to be anywhere at all. They brought me inside and I moved when they told me, helping them get me out of the dress and letting them towel me off. A blanket that was *warm* wrapped around me, and it was Hawk who carried me to the nest and into delicious darkness and safety.

He kissed my temple. "We've got you, baby girl."

They had me.

And they wouldn't let me fall, even when the cliffs crumbled.

At some point, I fell asleep.

When I woke, a low, rumbling purr vibrated beneath my ear and the scent of bourbon curled around me. Joel, who was now dry. I pulled my eyes open, though they were heavy. They were all here with me. Vaughn looked like he was sleeping, Rowan scribbled in a notebook, Hawk and Cade were on their phones. All dry now.

"I made you all get wet," I said.

Four pairs of eyes locked on me, and Joel's purr grew louder. Vaughn smiled, stretching from his nap too. "We don't mind, sweetheart."

Before, when I needed it, they'd kept their distance. Now that I was in their arms, our bonds were flooded with love and comfort and happiness that I was here with them. "That didn't go as planned, huh?"

Joel chuckled, interrupting his purr briefly. "No, I'd say not."

"Did you hit him?"

"Rowan did. Once. And only because he swung first."

I pulled my blanket more snugly around me. "That's too bad."

Amusement and pride in my chest from all of them.

Joel stroked a hand slowly over my hair. "Do you want to talk about it?"

"What is there left to say?"

Hawk sighed. "We talked to your dad."

My stomach twisted. "Did he say anything?"

"Not much. But enough that we think you should talk to them. All of them."

Tears came to my eyes, and I squeezed them closed. I didn't want to cry anymore. Now that I was awake my head hurt and I didn't want it anymore. "I'm not sure there's a point."

Slowly, Joel pulled me up his body and arranged me so I sat with my back to his chest and he could hold me better. Rowan leaned forward and caught my eyes. I felt him touch our bond with tenderness and control. "We'll never force you to do anything you don't want to, Isolde. But I want you to remember one thing."

"What's that?"

He sighed. "Beau was trying to hurt you. It was the reason he told the five of us he cheated, because he wanted that news, coming from us, to hurt you and drive a wedge between us. But it didn't. You announced it, and because he's a piece of shit, he retaliated by hurting you the last place he could, with the one thing he hadn't been able to touch."

"So you're saying they didn't know?"

"No, I'm not saying that. But from the little I know, you might want to hear them out. The truth might not be the way he made it look."

"Also," Hawk cleared his throat. I felt the way he didn't want to say whatever was coming next. He scratched the back of his neck. "Your family would like to know if you're still coming to the wedding tomorrow."

Panic clawed at my chest. The thought of not going broke me apart, but how could I go now? Everything was a mess and it all rose up like a tidal wave.

Rowan lunged forward and took my face in his hands. "*Breathe*, little flower. Take a big breath and hold it."

Command laced through his tone, giving my Omega no choice but to obey. I hauled in a breath and held it, getting lost in the warm brown of his gaze.

"Blow it out slowly."

I did.

"Now take another one."

When I obeyed, his thumbs moved back and forth over my jaw gently. "Good girl. Now don't panic, because we've got you, okay? No matter what you decide, everything's going to be okay." A whine slipped out, but he didn't stop talking. "We'll go little by little. Do you want to talk to your family about what happened?"

My lips trembled. Did I want to? No. Did I *need* to? "Yes."

"Okay. Do you want to talk to them tonight?"

I shook my head.

"In the morning?"

The wedding wasn't until the afternoon, so that would be fine. "That's fine."

"And do you want to go to the wedding?"

"Yeah." My voice shook, and a tear spilled over.

Rowan nodded slowly and pressed his forehead to mine. "And may we tell them all of that?"

Finally, I nodded.

"Thank you."

In the corner of my eye I saw Hawk typing on his phone, probably to send that exact message.

Joel smoothed his hands down my spine. "It's still rainy," he said quietly. "It might be a good time for a movie."

"That would be nice. But if you guys want to do your own thing, that's okay. I'll be fine."

Cade crawled over and pulled me to him. "We can feel you're not fine, princess, and it's okay to not be fine. You're not alone anymore. You don't have to hold everything in. We share it. Lift the burden together. It's one of the best things about having a pack."

Our bond shimmered with the truth of his statement.

"And I, for one, haven't had nearly enough time with my Omega yet. I don't think I will for a while. So whatever we're doing, we're doing as a family. Right?"

Affirmative answers all around.

I leaned against him, all the tension flowing out of me. "Thank you."

"Do you like popcorn?" Vaughn asked.

"Only if it's white cheddar."

He nodded. "I can make that happen."

I looked at Rowan. "Can I wear one of your hoodies? You're the biggest, so it'll be like a blanket."

"Of course you can." His smile crinkled his eyes at the corners, and I loved that. "I'll grab one."

Joel helped me to my feet, but he didn't let me go. Just as well, I felt unsteady on my feet. With Rowan's hoodie swallowing me whole, I curled up next to him on the couch. But I didn't stay there, moving from one to the other when my Omega needed them.

They held me until we were all falling asleep, the sun long set. Even after, they didn't let me go.

## CHAPTER FIFTY-ONE

ISOLDE

I hadn't bothered to really dress. If I were going to still be in the wedding, my hair and makeup would be done by the people Ellie hired, and if I weren't, I probably wouldn't be getting out of my sweats.

My hands were fully pulled inside the long sleeves of my t-shirt, a pure sign of nerves, and Hawk's hand rested on my knee as we pulled up to the estate.

"Do you want us to come with you?" Cade asked.

"Not to talk to her, but please don't leave."

"We won't," he promised.

When I picked up my phone this morning—the guys had brought it back with them yesterday—it was a mess of frantic texts from every person I knew. Ellie, begging to talk to me and promising it was okay. My parents. Rin and Ocean, having found out through the grapevine.

I read them, but barely absorbed them.

Hawk slid out and held the door for me. The storm left nothing but perfect weather behind. It would be a beautiful day. For an outdoor wedding, you couldn't ask for anything better.

That would be nice.

The guys were behind me, following me inside, but the rest of it I needed to do alone.

I didn't wait for Geoffrey to open the door. I knew the codes, and I let myself inside, heading straight for the suite where Ellie and Warren were staying.

He answered my soft knock with a grim expression. "Hey, Iz."

"Hi."

Sighing, he pushed the door wider to let me in. "I'm sorry about yesterday."

"And I'm sorry that my relationship has played such a big part in your wedding. I really am."

Warren smiled. "Even though Beau can go fuck himself, you dating him allowed me to meet Ellie."

"At least one good thing came out of it. Are your parents okay?"

"After hearing the shit he pulled? All of it? They're just fine. We'll see how they deal with Beau's parents later." He nodded toward their bedroom. "She's in there."

"She okay?"

"Okay isn't the word I'd use, no."

I nodded. "Then that makes two of us. Thanks."

"Are the guys here?"

"Yeah, though I don't know where they ended up."

Not waiting for more, I went to the bedroom door and opened it slowly. Ellie sat at the vanity in a white robe. Crumpled tissues covered the surface of it, and I heard her sniffle. What little I could see of her face was red and puffy. She looked like she'd been crying almost as much as I had.

"Hey," I said.

She jumped, turning to look. "Oh my god." She threw herself across the room at me and pulled me into a hug, sobbing. "I'm so sorry. I promise it's not like he made it sound. I wanted to go after you as soon as you ran but they wouldn't let me and—"

I hugged her, still feeling pretty blank. "Well, I'm here to listen. I said I'd do that."

"Yeah. Right." She pulled back and went to grab another tissue, dabbing at her face. "After everything happened with Beau. And I mean *right* after. You'd already booked a flight and were gone, but we didn't know that. No one had heard from you, and even Ocean and Trinity didn't have any idea where you were. We were panicked."

I winced. Not my finest moment. Mom cried in relief when I finally answered their call from my hastily-rented apartment.

"So I went to your house. Beau's house. I don't know if he didn't remember I had a key or if he just didn't care. But I walked in, shouting your name, because your car was there, and I found Beau fucking Angela on the kitchen island."

"God, I hope he sanitized if they were doing it in there the whole time."

We both laughed a little, the tension breaking.

Ellie wiped her nose and sank down onto the bed. "I handed his ass to him, obviously, and left. I'm pretty sure I threw the key at his head. Because to me, it seemed like you'd found him cheating and bolted. Then, when you told us what happened, and you didn't know..." Her eyes watered again. "You were in so much pain, and it was already over. So I said to myself that I'd tell you later. I told Mom, and she told Dad, and everyone agreed that we would tell you when you were a little better. But then you *didn't* get better. Or not much, and none of us wanted to be the one to re-break your heart all over again." Her voice drops to a whisper. "I'm sorry."

"Fuck." I scrubbed my hands over my face.

They were right. Beau had made it hurt as much as possible, lashing out where he knew my weakest point was, and I let him. Was I happy they'd kept it from me? No. But holding back on something they didn't know until after he'd already thrown a grenade into the middle of our relationship was worlds away from my whole family knowing Beau cheated on me—and *had* been cheating on me—and choosing not to tell me.

"God, he really is a dick, isn't he?" I burst out.

Ellie laughed. "Yes. Yes, he is."

But she wasn't smiling. Her face was filled with hope and fear, and I knew exactly how that combination felt. I'd lived with it almost daily. I went and sat on the bed, pulling her into a hug.

"I'm not happy about you keeping it from me," I told her. "No matter what I was feeling, I deserved to know. My feelings aren't your responsibility. They're not Mom's or Dad's either. So don't ever do it again, okay?"

All I got back was a sob, and I held her tighter. She managed, "I promise."

"But I'm sorry I ran away before I could listen. It hurt me where I had the least armor, and it felt like if I stayed I was going to unravel completely."

She sighed. "I could have prevented all of it if I'd just told you."

"No more secrets, okay?" I asked. "Sorry I didn't tell you they were escorts."

Ellie snorted. "Yeah, we already knew that."

"*What?*"

"Dad looked into them the second they walked through the door. It was crystal clear you guys didn't know each other. Sorry, you've never been that good of a liar. But the way they looked at you, and the way you lit up around them? There was no way *that* wasn't real. And we're not dicks. We don't care about them being escorts. Figured you'd tell us when you were ready."

"And here I was thinking I'd been stealthy."

"Not your strong suit, Iz."

We laughed together, and Ellie bit her lip. "So are you still my maid of honor?"

"I'm still your maid of honor."

She hugged me again, so tightly I couldn't quite breathe.

"And I'll say this to you as well. I already told Warren. I'm sorry my relationship with Beau has had such a big impact on your wedding. I hope it's not ruined."

"The only thing that would ruin my wedding is if you weren't in it," she said. "That, and Warren leaving me at the altar, but he won't. That man loves me."

"Yes, he does. The one good thing that came out of Beau."

"Right?" Ellie grabbed more tissues and dabbed her face. "I think Mom and Dad are still at breakfast. Do you want anything?"

I sighed. "I should talk to them too, if you'll give us a couple of minutes."

"Yeah, I ate already. So you're good to go. The girls will be here soon, and then the wedding hurricane can start."

"Don't invoke the weather gods," I told her, standing and heading for the door. "It's perfect out there."

"Good point. Isolde?" I turned. "I really am sorry."

I smiled. "I know. I'm sorry too."

We didn't need more words than that. The breakfast room looked the same as the moment when Hawk rushed in here and punched Beau, except that it was empty. Outside on the terrace, my parents sat at a table. Mom sketched and Dad read the paper. He still insisted on reading the physical version.

Opening the door, I let the sound of the waves rush in and comfort me before stepping all the way into view. "Hey, Mom. Dad."

Mom looked up and pulled off her sunglasses. "Oh, Isolde." She stood and pulled me to her. "I'm sorry, sweetheart."

I sighed and leaned into her. Mom smelled like lavender and

lemons, and right now, she smelled like comfort. "Ellie told me everything. I understand why, and I know I won't ever be in that situation again, but if it's my business, I want to know."

"We should have told you," she nodded into my hair. "Are you okay?"

"I am, actually. Turns out having a pack who actually cares about you is good for a lot of things." I pulled back. "I was going to apologize to you for not telling you the truth about the guys, but apparently you already knew."

Mom's sly smile made me laugh. "We did know, right, Henry?"

Dad stood behind me, and when I looked, he held out his arms. I stepped into them. "I looked into them because I wasn't going to let Beau happen again," he told me. "I felt guilty enough about not speaking up when he made me question. And after we found out he'd cheated... I wasn't going to let it happen."

"And you were fine with them?"

My parents laughed, and Mom spoke from behind me. "Iz, those men didn't take their eyes off you for a second. Like they could only breathe after you did. We don't care what they do, as long as they're good to you."

"And nothing bad came back on them," Dad said. "I meant what I said. I'll be digging further, because you can't be too careful, but I don't think there's anything to find."

I raised an eyebrow. "We're already bonded. I think it might be too late to dig."

Dad shrugged. "Guess we'll find out."

Smacking his arm, I took a step back. "Thank you for not being offended by it. As soon as they scented me they decided they were done, and they all have other things they do on the side. I'm still... I don't know what I'll do, but I'm okay taking some time to figure it out."

"We'll be glad to have you close by, and I expect you and your men to be here once in a while for family dinners. We want to get to know them, and not just as the men who you brought to the wedding, but as your pack."

I couldn't stop my smile at the thought. *My* pack. "I want that too."

Mom looked down at her phone. "Oh, the flowers are here. I need to help them be placed."

That meant Ocean was here too. "I'll go with you. See you soon, Dad?"

One of his arms was still around me, and he gave me a squeeze. "You bet. Have fun. And I'm sorry, Isolde. We'll do better for you."

The quick burst of emotion nearly caught me. I wasn't the only one who was hurting. I'd done plenty of my own damage when I ran away without a word and put them through hell watching me suffer. "Let's all do better for each other."

He nodded stiffly, turning to mask his own emotion. I touched him on the shoulder before following Mom. Ocean stood in the foyer, directing her employees, along with the woman who managed the flower business on her behalf.

Ocean did a lot of work for it, but because of her family, she hid a lot of it, pretending it was a hobby instead of something she'd carefully crafted and cultivated.

So many flowers were coming through the door it was like an entire shop, and Mom was already pointing them straight through to the venue in the backyard. She was in her element.

I bumped Ocean's shoulder. "Hey, you."

"Hi." She smiled, looking fully herself for the first time in forever. "You okay?"

"Yeah. It's... You, Rin, and I will have dinner and talk about everything, okay? I don't think I can go through it again today."

Ocean pointed to the side when a girl came in holding two paper bags full of plastic boxes. "The bouquets can go there, please. Boutonnieres too." She looked at me. "I totally get that, and yes, please. I need to get the hell out of my house, and I think we all have things to talk about."

"Are you okay? The last couple of weeks—"

She cut me off with a hand. "I can't do it today either, Iz, sorry."

It only made me more curious, but that was the thing about Ocean. She had to make sure she had a handle on everything herself before she told someone else. She would tell us when she was ready, even though I was dying to know. "That's okay. How can I help?"

"Do you know who's standing in for Beau?" She pulled a clear box out from one of the bags. The boutonniere was pretty, with some small white flowers, a petunia, and some pretty greens.

"I don't."

"I do," a new voice came, and my chest filled with love and affection as the guys appeared around the corner. Hawk was the one who spoke. "Since I was the one who punched Beau in the face the first time, Warren asked me to stand in. But it's okay, Ocean, I can just wear that one."

She looked horrified. "No, you absolutely cannot."

Hawk and the rest of my pack looked confused, but I just smiled. "What does it mean, Ocean?"

My friend pressed her lips together, fighting laughter. "It's petunia, basil, and hemlock. Or rather, anger and disdain, hatred, and death."

"Oh my god." I burst out laughing. "That's incredible."

"Remind me never to get on your bad side," Vaughn said.

Ocean smirked, but she looked at me. "I'll take a rose from your bouquet and put one together."

"Perfect."

Hawk tugged me away. "We need to go get ready. From everything I feel here," he pressed a palm to my heart, "you seem okay. Are you?"

"I am."

"Do you want to come back to the house with us?"

Leaning up on my tiptoes, I kissed him. "I should probably stay here. Gotta get all pretty."

"You're always pretty," he murmured against my lips.

It was a wave of love and touch as they passed, and by the time they got out the front door and slipped by the flower carriers, I was pink with it.

Ocean just stared. "Wow."

"I know."

She looked away too quickly and handed me one of the bags. "Will you take these to the bridal suite? They're all labeled."

"Sure." I waited, seeing if I should check on her, but the way she dove back into the organization told me no. Later, I'd get it out of her.

The bridal suite was already chaos. Clothes were everywhere, and about a hundred different bags and purses, hair tools, and make-up kits. Glowing stations like the one Rin had set up in my closet.

Ellie laughed and joked with the rest of her bridesmaids, and it was easy to fall into the camaraderie of the day. I felt so much better, and I could tell Ellie did too. This was the wedding day she was always meant to have.

A couple hours later, with makeup and hair done, dress in place, and all the chaos significantly lessened, I was closest to the door when someone knocked. Geoffrey stood there. "Hi."

"There's someone here, Miss Allen. And I'm not sure they should be."

"For the love of god, tell me Beau isn't trying to come to the wedding."

"No," Geoffrey said. "He's not here. But his fiancée is."

Ellie frowned. "Why? She can't think she's still invited."

"No, miss. She says she doesn't want to come to the ceremony." Then his eyes fixed on me. "She wants to talk to you."

## CHAPTER FIFTY-TWO

ISOLDE

"No fucking way," Ellie said.

I looked at Geoffrey. "Does she seem angry?"

"No, miss. It looks like she's been crying. Frankly, it's the most subdued I've seen her."

"Iz—"

Looking back at my sister, I shrugged. "You know what he can do, El. If she wants to talk, I'll give her one more chance. Don't worry, I'm not going to let her stay."

She looked unsure, but I followed Geoffrey out of the suite. "I put her in one of the sitting rooms so she was out of the way while the guests arrive."

"Thank you, Geoffrey."

He opened the door, and sure enough, Angela stood there. In a t-shirt and jeans, she definitely wasn't planning on coming to the wedding, which was a point in her favor. "Angela."

"Hi." She shifted her weight from foot to foot, clearly nervous. "I know I shouldn't be here, but I didn't have your phone number, and I wasn't going to ask Beau for it, so I needed to try."

"Try what?"

"To apologize. I've been a royal cunt to you, and it was because of all the things Beau said about you. Guess we were both taken in by versions of him that weren't real."

I was pretty sure my eyebrows had gone to visit heaven the way they were hiding in my hairline. Those were the last words I ever expected out of her mouth. "Oh. Wow."

She laughed once without humor. "Yeah. I'm not going to make you listen to what he said about you. There's no point, and it's clearly not true. I owe you an extra apology for the bachelorette. I was very *very* drunk, but it doesn't excuse the things I said. I was... god, I was so angry because he made me believe you had ruined his life and I was the one who had saved him from you. I really am sorry."

Before I could say anything, she continued. "And I'm not here for you to accept it. I don't deserve that. But I wanted you to hear the apology."

"I appreciate it. Really, I do." It wasn't easy to admit when you'd been wrong, especially when you went so far in one direction. If anything, I was impressed she was doing this. "We all do things for love, or what we think is love. You're not the first, and I'm not either. But I'm glad you have a clearer view of who he really is."

"Me too." The devious nature of her smile told me she wasn't done with Beau, and I didn't even want to imagine what she had planned for him. "Um, the jewelry. I didn't know. Would you like it back?"

"No." Even if I did, it was so steeped with all of this, I doubted I could even look at it. "When I left, I made sure I took everything I couldn't live without."

"Okay. I'll probably donate it somewhere then. I don't feel like I can keep it either..." she trailed off, lost in her own thoughts before she snapped back. "I appreciate you hearing me out. I know we're not friends, and I don't think we will be."

We both smiled, but I said. "Friends is probably a stretch."

"I'll settle for you not completely hating me."

"Done." I held out my hand for her to shake. "If only because most people wouldn't have been brave enough to come back."

Angela shook my hand. "Thank you. I hope the wedding goes well."

And then she left without another word.

I nearly crashed into Rowan's chest when I exited, stumbling when I see him standing there in a tuxedo. Holy. Shit.

The suits from my parents' anniversary party were one thing. Tuxedos? Whole new ball game. "Are all of you wearing those?"

"Yes." He chuckled. "Like what you see?"

I spread my hands over his chest and felt his heat beneath the clothes. "Almost as much as I like what's underneath." Then I paused. "How did you know I was in here?"

"Ellie sent up the alarm and said you might need backup. But considering you look absolutely perfect, I think you held your own." The heat in his eyes made me wish we had more time before the wedding, and in our bond I felt every word he didn't have to say aloud about how I looked.

Up in the suite one of the stylists did my hair in big waves before pulling it back and up into something elaborate, and I was in the dress she'd chosen—a purple rich enough not to wash me out.

"Thank you. I'll tell you about Angela later."

"Later, the five of us are going to be peeling this dress off you slowly and worshipping every inch of skin as it appears. So if you can tell us while we're doing that, feel free, little flower."

Arousal welled up in me, perfume filling the corner of the hallway. "You can't use your words against me like that. Not at my sister's wedding."

"Oh, but we absolutely can."

"Rowan."

He guided my body against his. "I'm not going to ruin your perfection... yet. But know this. Every single member of your pack loves you and loves the idea of you being wet for us when it's the least appropriate. So tell me if you want me to stop, otherwise..."

*Otherwise, every hole you have is getting used, Omega. We're going to wring pleasure out of you until you can't take it anymore.* His words from the heat echo in my head.

"Otherwise what?"

"Otherwise," he leaned down and whispered, "I will use my words against you so you're fucking dripping for *us* while walking down the aisle."

I should have told him to stop. I should have told him I couldn't risk a wet spot on the back of my dress when I sat down. I should have done a lot of things, and I did none of them.

The other bonds in my chest turned toward us with interest, feeling what Rowan was doing and how it was making me feel.

"When we get home I'm putting you on your knees in the living room," he whispered. "Right over Hawk's face, where he can push this skirt up past your hips and drink all that nectar you've been saving for us. Cade will tie your hands behind your back so you can't move them, and one by one, we'll take turns licking that needy clit of yours. Long enough for you to get warmed up, nice and slow, the way your body needs it. Maybe we'll make you suck your own taste off our tongues."

I moaned, unable to move, knowing it was working exactly the way he wanted it to.

"And finally, when we've eaten enough of your pussy to tide us over until our next meal. Then? That's when the fun begins."

My whole body shuddered, reacting to his words, growing wet, awareness shrinking down to him and the others in my chest. "You're evil."

"Not evil, little flower. Obsessed. Obsessed, in love, and eager. Now get back upstairs. Everything's about to start."

Rowan kissed me lightly so he didn't ruin my lipstick, smirking when I tried to make it deeper and he didn't let me. Bastard. He would pay for it later.

More likely I would be the one paying for it later. Deliciously. And now that we could all feel each other, they knew exactly how much I wanted to be the one to pay.

Ellie looked up when I came in, looking over my appearance like she expected me to have scratches from a catfight. "Everything's fine. She's gone."

"Just gone?"

"Yup. She wanted to apologize."

She looked as stunned as I'd felt. "Okay then."

The wedding planner came in. "It's time, ladies."

Our bouquets were made of roses, dahlias, and orange blossoms. Or, as Ocean had designed them, eternal love and commitment. They were beautiful.

Ellie and I were the last ones in the room. Her eyes shimmered with tears. "Are you okay?"

"Yeah. Promise. I'm just excited," she whispered. "It's finally here, you know? I can't wait to marry him."

I did know. More than she knew. "Let's go."

I helped her down the stairs to the foyer where everyone was waiting. Music already played, and the first pair headed outside to the aisle.

Seeing Hawk in a tuxedo had just as much impact as Rowan. "You are going to kill me."

"So dress in a tux whenever I need you to say yes to something? Noted, baby girl."

I rolled my eyes and straightened his jacket, noting the matching rose he wore. I loved that it was from my bouquet.

Just before we started walking, I looked back at Ellie and Dad. He hugged her gently, whispering something that made her nod. But their eyes were both filled with emotion. I had a feeling no one in our family was getting out of this with dry eyes.

"You okay to do this without rehearsing?" I teased.

"I think I can manage walking in a straight line," Hawk laughed softly.

My hand rested in the crook of his arm. "I don't know. Straight lines can be dangerous."

"Not nearly as dangerous as curves. Your curves specifically."

I had to stifle my laughter as we stepped into view of the guests. What he said was clever, and I was so glad to be walking with *him*.

The moment they saw me, I felt it. The awe, reverence, and intense desire. Rowan's words weren't the only thing making my body react. "It still doesn't feel real."

"What doesn't?"

"All of you. Us. Together."

"Better be real," he whispered. "If we're dreaming, let's not wake up."

We were almost at the altar. "Deal."

Hawk took my hand in his and kissed the back of it before we split to stand on either side of the officiant. I saw my guys, all staring at me, and all of them looked so *fucking good* in their tuxedos. I needed pictures. Lots and lots of pictures.

The music changed, and everyone turned to look. Ellie came down the aisle on Dad's arm, smiling so wide it had to hurt. She nearly walked too quickly in order to get to Warren, who wiped his eyes when he saw her.

I was right. All of us were teary, and there was no way to avoid it. Tears streamed down Dad's face as he gave Ellie away, which triggered my own happy tears.

The ceremony was simple and beautiful. They exchanged rings, vows, and a million secret smiles before they were pronounced man and wife to cheering and applause.

Hawk and I followed them out to the music, along with the rest of the bridal party, and I hugged Ellie. "You did it."

"I can't believe it."

"You'd better," I said. "After all this."

Ellie laughed. "Fair point. Let's get all the pictures done so we can party. And I want your whole pack in the family pictures, Iz. Not just Hawk."

"Really?"

"Wouldn't have it any other way."

Hawk hugged me close. "I guess we do need some pictures that *aren't* naughty too."

"You're insatiable."

"Janet's already on board with the group photoshoot, baby girl. It's happening."

I blushed, but said nothing, because I wanted the pictures. To feel that beautiful with all five of them in one room. "Let's start with the wedding photos and go from there."

Hawk kissed my hand again. "You already know, Isolde. We'll start anything with you."

## CHAPTER FIFTY-THREE

### VAUGHN

Isolde spun on the dance floor with Ellie and the other bridesmaids, laughing. The difference between the woman in front of us and the Omega who came down the escalator in the airport couldn't be overstated. Where she'd been timid and fearful before, and rightfully so, now she was vibrant and full of life.

Before her I'd heard stories about people who met their Omega and had their lives changed as quickly as this, but you could never understand the depth and totality of it without experiencing it firsthand.

I thought we were happy before, and we were, but it was nothing compared to what I felt now.

Cade stepped up beside me and nudged my arm. "Back."

"You got it?"

"Yup."

"She didn't notice you were gone."

He smirked. "Good."

Surprises were going to be much harder now that we were bonded. So covering the surprises with big emotions, like the wedding, was a good idea.

Across the tent, I saw Isolde's stepfather approaching our table with the others. I nodded to Cade. "Let's go."

It wasn't far, and we approached just in time to hear him start speaking. "Thank you for listening before, and for what you've done for her. Isolde hasn't been like this in... a very long time."

Rowan nodded, looking past him at our Omega. "It's our pleasure, sir. We love your daughter very much."

"My wife and I are looking forward to getting to know you better. Guess it shouldn't be too hard being just up the cliff."

"I hope not," I said.

"Well," he cleared his throat. "Besides that, I protect my family. You're a part of that now." Reaching out, he handed a card to Joel. "If you need anything, especially if Beau decides he hasn't had enough, you let me know. Or if you need help with the new careers."

Cade chuckled. "How much did you find?"

"My guys are still digging through it all. But, approximately? Everything."

We all laughed, and Henry pointed at Hawk. "We'll talk later about a manager for you. I represent several."

Hawk looked shocked, and for once, speechless. "Thank you."

"I won't keep you. I'm sure the last thing you want to do is talk to me when you could spend time with Isolde. But we're grateful to have you here."

"Is there anything—" I cut myself off, and Henry looked at me. "Is there anything we can do, legally, to make sure Beau stays gone?"

Rowan inclined his head. "Given most of this happened because of perceived damage to his ego, I don't trust him not to hurt Isolde again. Or us. Or you and Mrs. Caruso. He wasn't exactly pleased when he left."

The smile on Henry's face was exactly why he had the reputation he did. There was no kindness in that smile, only ruthlessness. "Don't worry about that. He won't be bothering any of us anymore."

There wasn't anything else to say after that. Henry slid his hands into his pockets and walked away.

Hawk blew out a breath. "I don't think I even want to *imagine* the shit Beau has coming for him."

I looked at them. "What do you guys think his real first reaction was when he found out about the escort thing?"

Joel shook his head. "I think that man is a vault, and we'll never know."

On the dance floor, the song changed, and Isolde was now dancing with Ocean and Trinity. Ocean checked her phone and said something. Suddenly they all stopped, Rin and Isolde staring at Ocean. The quieter Omega spoke again before hurrying off the dance floor and into the main house. It didn't look like she planned on coming back. A second later Trinity pulled her phone out of the top of her dress and spoke to Isolde, stepping off the dance floor.

So she looked at us.

Our Omega made her way to our table. Isolde's eyes were alight with happiness, skin glimmering with a sheen of sweat after dancing. "Hi."

"Ocean okay?"

She blinked. "Yeah. I think so. We're not really sure yet. But maybe?"

"That was... not an answer at all," Hawk said with a laugh.

"No, but it's all I've got at the moment."

Isolde grabbed a glass of water and downed it. I was tempted to ask her to just pour the water over herself, but that could come later. "Thirsty?"

"Dancing is thirsty work. You all should try it. Are you going to dance with me?"

"Hell yes," Cade said. "We will."

Out over the ocean, the sun sank toward the horizon, painting the sky in an almost violent display of pinks, purples, and golds. I glanced at the others, feeling the confirmation in our echoing bonds. "But first, want to take a walk on the beach with us?"

The sass in her expression made me want to kiss it off. "If I say yes, am I about to get chased and wet? Cause I'm not sure I'm done with the party yet, so any 'let's get dirty on the beach' ideas might have to wait."

Joel stood and came around the table. "No getting dirty on the beach. Right now, anyway. The sunset is beautiful, and we just want a second with you."

"I won't say no to that."

Ellie saw all of us going toward the beach and looked like she might come intercept us before I held out a hand. Her gaze fell on me and I winked. We would be back, along with our Omega. But first, we had to fix something.

We'd gone about a lot of our relationship backwards, and there was so much still in front of us. But we wanted every little thing with Isolde. To show her everything she'd missed and things she hadn't even begun to dream of.

Starting with showing her forever.

## CHAPTER FIFTY-FOUR

### ISOLDE

The reception was incredible. My lungs burned from dancing and it wasn't even dark yet. The freedom of knowing everything was good and going to be okay unlocked a part of me I thought was gone, and I wanted *fun*.

Ocean and Trinity found me after the ceremony, and they'd pulled me away from Ellie on the floor so we could dance together. I couldn't wait for us to do more ball gown bowling and dinners where we could talk for hours. All the things I missed when I was away, and while I was with Beau too, because I'd done those things less while he was around.

Ocean checked her phone and froze. "Shit."

"You okay?"

She smiled tightly. "I need to go. I'll call you guys soon."

"O, wait," Rin said. "Give us something, please. Because you're kind of freaking us out."

Ocean worried her lower lip between her teeth. "I'm getting married."

"*What?*" Rin and I spoke at the same time.

"When?" I asked.

Trinity followed up. "To who?"

Our friend stared at us and shook her head. "I have no idea."

Then she turned and left, nearly sprinting for the main house and leaving us both there in shock.

"What the fuck?" I asked.

"What the fuck indeed. There were a lot of things I guessed might come out of her mouth, and that was *not* it."

A phone rang, and Trinity pulled her phone out of her cleavage before I could even ask who it was. "Hello?" She paused. "No, I can't—hold on." Rin rolled her eyes as she pressed the phone to her shoulder. "I have to take this. I'll be back, though."

"I need a break anyway." I made my way over to my pack at our table. They all saw me coming, and I might have moved my hips a bit more just to feel the way they watched. "Hi."

"Ocean okay?" Vaughn asked.

I had no idea how to answer that, but I wasn't going to say anything until we knew what the hell was going on. "Yeah. I think so. We're not really sure yet. But maybe?"

"That was... not an answer at all," Hawk laughed.

"No, but it's all I've got at the moment." I grabbed a glass of water, downing it in one go.

"Thirsty?"

"Dancing is thirsty work. You all should try it. Are you going to dance with me?"

"Hell yes," Cade said, eyes full of fire. "We will."

Vaughn leaned closer. "But first, want to take a walk on the beach with us?"

I eyed him warily. "If I say yes, am I about to get chased and wet? Cause I'm not sure I'm done with the party yet, so any 'let's get dirty on the beach' ideas might have to wait."

Joel came around the table to me. "No getting dirty on the beach. Right now, anyway. The sunset is beautiful, and we just want a second with you."

It was beautiful. Fiery and neon. Clarity Coast had shown up for Ellie's wedding in her best colors. "I won't say no to that."

With his hand on the small of my back, Joel guided me out of the tent. Immediately everything was quieter, the music and conversation fading into the background and the soft rhythm of waves taking over. The temperature was milder in the breeze. Everything was perfect. We walked to the beach, passing the magnolia trees that were no longer blooming.

I paused at the edge of the sand in my heels.

"Leave them here. We'll come back for them."

Sand between my toes sounded great right about now, so I left my shoes on the grass, stretched out my hand, and laced my fingers with Vaughn's.

Closing my eyes, I inhaled the ocean air, sinking into that low, settling feeling I had when I was near the water. It was always there, even when I didn't look for it, but there were moments I *felt* it.

The ocean had always been my home. But now it was my second home. Because home was *them*. My pack. The men around me who'd already proven they would show up for me every time, no matter what.

Heat warmed my back and a kiss dropped on the top of my head. "What are you thinking about, baby girl?"

"Nothing." I smiled. "Everything."

Surrounded on three sides by them, I could stay here forever, looking out at the infinite water.

Vaughn looked over. "You really love the ocean. I didn't realize how much."

"I can't explain it."

"You don't have to," Cade murmured.

"I know it's just—it's always been there. No matter what is happening, it stays the same. It's always wild, always dangerous, always... endless. Always exactly what it is, despite everyone trying to tame it or use it or change it. It's just there. And it didn't matter where I was, it always felt like home. Until you."

Happy tears smudged the sky into a watercolor of nothing but light.

"You know," Vaughn said, "if we'd scented you on the street, or at a party, we would have done things differently."

I was about to ask how when Joel spoke low in my ear. "We would have courted you. We would have shown you who we were and what we wanted."

"We would have made plans and spoken to your family." That was Rowan.

Cade stepped closer in front of me. "And we would have declared our intentions."

To my right, Hawk stepped around where I could see him. "We have no regrets about any of it," he said. "The way we came together was meant to be, and I wouldn't change a second."

"But?" I looked at each of them.

"But we want you to have everything, Isolde," Vaughn whispered. "Everything you might have had or could ever want. Every detail and every tradition."

Cade reached into the inner pocket of his tuxedo and took a step backward, sinking down onto the sand. On one knee. "Cade what—"

He held a small box, and there was no mistaking what it was. Every one of their bonds surged with love at my recognition. The rest of them began to kneel, and I shook my head. "If all of you kneel I'll never get through this." My voice already shook.

"You asked us, and we said yes," Joel said. "And even though you're already ours, and we're already yours, we want to ask."

Rowan reached for my hand. I let him take it as Cade opened the box. *Green.* A gold band curled around an emerald with color so rich you could get lost in it. Simple and beautiful.

"Isolde Penelope Allen," Rowan said, taking the ring out of the box. "Will you be our Omega?"

The tears came so fast I could barely see, my chest bursting with both my happiness and theirs. "Yes. Of course I will."

He slid the ring on my finger and stood, bringing my lips to his. I couldn't kiss them fast enough. All of them. Addicted to this feeling of joy. I ended up held by Cade, trying to clear my skin of tears. "I've already cried so much today. I need to stop." Then I laughed. "I knew when you told me you wanted a walk on the beach it wasn't just that."

"Couldn't ruin the surprise." Cade kissed my cheek. "We love you."

"I love you so much it hurts," I told them, looking down at the ring. It sparkled in the last rays of light. "This is beautiful. How on earth did you get one that fits this well?"

"We measured your finger while you were passed out during the heat." Hawk grinned.

"Sneaky."

He bowed, proud of himself.

I couldn't stop smiling and held out the ring. "I love this. It's beautiful. But I hope you know I didn't *need* this. I wasn't expecting it."

"We know, but we wanted to," Cade said. "Better get used to it, because I'm not done giving you more than you ask for."

"Including dancing," Hawk said. "Let's go dance with our Omega."

"One more minute," I said, looking back at the ocean and the final moments of sunset. The way it flared before disappearing. One last hurrah. They gathered around me, enjoying the view.

Someone took my hand. Joel. "More than anything," he said, lifting my hand and kissing my new ring, "This is a reminder."

"Of what?"

They didn't have to say the words. If their love were an ocean, I would drown in it. I couldn't feel the edges. There were none. It stole my breath.

"A reminder of what?"

Joel smiled, and my pack stepped in, wrapping me in more than just their arms. "That the ocean isn't the only thing that's endless."

They held me until we could see the stars, and even then it was hard to leave. But when they pulled me onto the dance floor, twirling me until I was drunk and dizzy, it felt right. Everything felt right with them.

Swaying in a slow dance with Hawk, my head on his chest, feeling the rumble of his purr, I closed my eyes. They were mine, and I was the happiest I'd ever been.

## EPILOGUE

ISOLDE

**SIX MONTHS LATER**

"This is more complicated than I thought it would be," I said quietly, tired and trying not to make anyone laugh.

"Worth it." Vaughn snuck a kiss right over his bite mark, and I whined. "Sorry not sorry."

"We're going to have to finish this another time if you all keep sneaking touches like this."

The camera clicked, and Janet laughed. "Not a bad idea, actually. We've got plenty of good shots, but I'm tired, you're tired and... other things. We can always do this again. It was fun."

"Are you sure?"

"Absolutely. I love shooting you, Isolde. In the photographic sense only."

We laughed, but the guys didn't move, because I was bound in rope and absolutely *nothing* else. "I appreciate it."

Janet shouldered her bag and saluted us. "You know the drill, Hawk."

"Wash the sheets, lock the door," he called before the front closed.

"Thank fuck," Rowan said. His head dropped to my breasts, pushed out and up by the harness Cade put on me. He sucked one of my nipples into his mouth. "I'll happily do this again, little flower, but I need you to know, it's torture."

I laughed, breathless. "You think I don't know? There are *five of you* and you're all horny as fuck."

"And you're tied up at our mercy. Imagine everything we can do."

Oh, I had. This wasn't the first time I'd been tied up naked with the five of them. Not even close. If they had it their way I was tied up once a week. A few days ago Cade suspended me in his rope studio, murmuring words in my ear and keeping watch while the others took turns fucking me.

"I think I'm done with rope today," I whispered. "Please."

Cade kissed my shoulder and began untying the ropes in that way he had. Firm and deliberate, still making me feel held even though he was unraveling his work. "I'll compromise with you, princess."

"How?"

"I'll show you."

I sank onto the bed little by little as he untied me, sprawled between Rowan and Vaughn, Joel looking down at me, and Hawk across the room, watching. He stroked his cock, eyes full of fire.

"Gonna stay over there?"

He smirked. "Maybe. Maybe I'll fuck my own hand until I'm ready to give my baby girl exactly what she wants."

My limbs came free, and I stretched, feeling both blissful and horny at the same time. "And what's that?"

"A taste."

A film of need dropped over my eyes. Perfume filled the room so quickly that Hawk laughed in victory. He strode over, hand still on his cock. "I need one thing first." His fingers between my legs found the slick his words and hours of taking sexy photos of them had created. That wetness now coated his palm as he fucked his own hand.

"That has no right being that hot." I sat up and Cade met me, mischief in his eyes. "What were you saying?"

He held up a pair of handcuffs we'd used earlier in the shoot. "Compromise. No ropes, but no hands either."

"Why?"

Leaning down, he captured one wrist, slipping the metal around and locking it tight before kissing me. "Because you like it."

Fuck me, I did.

"And because being restrained makes our Omega's cunt even wetter, and we need it as wet as possible. We have another picture we want to take." Cade lifted me and turned me over, dropping me across Rowan's chest before trapping my hands behind my back and cuffing them in place.

No time was wasted. Rowan thrust into me almost too quickly because I was so wet. "What picture?" My voice was nothing more than a moan.

"You'll see." Cade came around the bed and took my face in his hands. "Do you trust us?"

"Yes."

Cool liquid on my ass followed my response. Vaughn slid his palm down my spine. "Gonna need a lot of this, sweetheart. But I think you're going to like it."

I couldn't even breathe. I knew what was coming, and the incredible stretch and pleasure of Vaughn pushing into my ass, one piercing at a time. We didn't do this as often, but I loved it when we did.

Joel appeared in front of me and I was already opening my mouth. Every part of me was stretched. My lips around Joel's cock, my arms where Vaughn pulled on the handcuffs. My pussy and ass from their cocks.

Time disappeared. It did when they fucked me like this, surrendering to the pleasure they could bring me. And they did. They didn't care how long it took for me to get off, they just cared that I did. To both their surprise and mine, once they took me past my first couple of orgasms, it was almost harder for me to *stop*.

A new sensation. Another thickness in my pussy along with more lube. I froze, realizing exactly what was happening.

Joel pulled out of my mouth and crouched down. "Are you okay with this?"

"Can I do it?" I honestly wasn't sure. Taking four of them like this added heat to the building fire in my body, but we'd never done *this*.

He smiled. "Yes, I think you can."

"I'll try."

Kissing my forehead, he breathed the words, "Good girl," before cupping my jaw and filling my mouth once more, no longer holding back. Rowan played with my tits, sucking and squeezing them while Joel took my throat, and the others...

Cade eased in, and in, and in, and holy fuck three of them were fucking me at one time. I couldn't move or breathe or even think. The only thing possible was to feel and take it.

Pleasure and emotion rose all at once, sweeping me away on the tide they'd been building since we walked into this studio. I loved them. So much. They were here with me, feeling my pleasure as much as I felt theirs, and it helped. Drove me higher and held me longer.

With Joel between my lips my only sounds were moans, but I did. There was no way to keep quiet with the way this felt.

Joel came first, filling my mouth with the flavor I craved. I had tried bourbon infused with cardamom now, and it still didn't compare to him. His knot pressed my lips as he pushed in one last time, groaning.

"Open, baby girl."

I did, just in time for sugar to hit my tongue. Hawk stroked himself as he came on my tongue, making sure I missed none of it. "Show me before you swallow."

The dark words had me lifting my eyes to his, and the phone pointed at me.

*We have another picture we want to take.*

Hawk took pictures of me impaled on the four of them. Oh *fuck*. I swallowed Hawk's orgasm while another of my own took me. I wasn't upright anymore, Rowan holding me to his chest.

Somewhere I felt Cade come, and then Vaughn. Rowan held me tight and fucked me hard after they pulled away, taking me the way he liked—with me boneless, at his mercy, and wanting every second of it.

His knot locked inside me, and my eyes closed, savoring the lingering bliss shivering through my veins. Cade unlocked my wrists, allowing me to cling to Rowan while the others cleaned up both themselves and the studio.

"Still breathing, little flower?"

"Barely."

He chuckled, purr starting beneath it. My body relaxed into his. More than just the purr, knowing I didn't *have* to move. They would have everything done by the time Rowan's knot released us.

Even then, I still wanted to be held. After sex so intense, I wanted to be with them, my Omega needing her pack. They knew. There was never a point when I wasn't touched, even on the ride home.

Vaughn brought me to the couch and collapsed there with me. I stretched and curled into his side sleepily. "I should work on commissions, but I need a nap first."

"You really have to work today?"

I snorted into his shirt. "I still have clients, even though some Alphas decided everyone should take the day off. No idea who."

Rowan sat down on my other side. "Open."

Chocolate and caramel seeped onto my tongue. "Mmm. Normal or fun?"

"Fun." He smirked, and I rolled my eyes.

That was one way to make sure I took the rest of the day off.

I hadn't wanted to go back to an office full time, but I didn't want to bartend either. Instead, I'd started designing freelance. So far it was going well. Everyone from my family to my pack pretended they weren't recommending me whenever they could, but I didn't mind. Those jobs were now bringing real word-of-mouth clients.

Hawk's phone rang in the kitchen, a ringtone all of us knew. "Don't answer it," we all said when we saw him reaching.

Dad helped Hawk get connected to the music industry in a way he'd never been before, but we'd had to put boundaries in place for his manager. So many people wanted to work with him, he would run himself ragged if we let him. So we didn't.

"Not until tomorrow." He made a show of putting his phone in the little bucket we made just for him.

"No fucking way." Vaughn stared at his phone.

"What?"

He turned the screen toward me. I gasped. Beau was on a video, being led out of what used to be our house, in handcuffs. "What the fuck?"

We passed the phone around. As soon as he saw it, Joel laughed. "At Ellie's wedding we asked your dad if we could help make sure Beau stayed gone. He said he had it handled. Looks like he did."

I read the story when the phone came back. Beau had been up to a lot more shady shit than just being an ass and ruining relationships. Most of it was financial, which made sense. If he could take the easy way to do something he would.

"Good riddance."

"Cheers to that," Cade called from the kitchen, lifting a beer in his hand.

I looked at Hawk. "Before you banish your phone entirely for the night, can I see them?"

"Absolutely."

Hawk wasn't the only one crowding around me to see his phone screen. And the pictures...

Holy fuck.

The lighting in the studio had still been set from our pictures with Janet, so it was dramatic and gorgeous where it could have been unflattering.

The pictures were obscene in the best way. I was stuffed with all of them, clearly so blissed out I didn't know my own name. And in the foreground, dimly lit, Hawk's hard cock slick with my arousal and his precum.

Even the picture of me looking up at him, mouth open, eyes dazed, was great. And these weren't even the ones Janet took. "Wow."

"Not bad, if I do say so myself."

"I love them," I said. "But we are *not* printing those."

"Aww," Vaughn pulled me into his lap. "What about for the nest?"

I rolled my eyes. "Yes, let's hang pictures in the room made of pillows."

"I vote we cover the hallway to the nest bathroom with naughty pictures." Hawk put his phone back in jail.

Cade nodded. "Seconded."

"And if people come over?" I asked.

Rowan smiled. "There are doors. With locks."

"Ugh, fine." I flopped back onto Vaughn dramatically, but I was smiling. They really were good pictures, and all the ones Janet took would be just as good, if not better. It would be fun to have a wall just for us that we could continue to update.

It was cold out, or as cold as it could get in Clarity, even in the winter. But since they were determined not to let me work...

"Can we have a fire outside?"

Joel stood, already moving. "A fire sounds good."

"With hot chocolate. The good kind."

"As if I would let the bad kind enter this house," Rowan acted like I'd stabbed him in the heart before heading to the kitchen.

In less than ten minutes we were outside, warming our hands with mugs and the growing flames.

The moment crept on me, the familiar feeling of peace and happiness I'd had since they became mine.

"What are you thinking about, baby girl?"

Hawk loved to ask me that since the wedding, and my answer was always the same. "Nothing. Everything."

They laughed, and I laughed with them.

Firelight glinted off my ring. Every time I saw it I was swept back, and I couldn't let it pass. "I love you."

The men I called home smiled. Rumbling purrs and the crackle of flames nearly drowned out the whispers of three perfect little words.

*The End*

There will be more in the Clarity Coast world soon!

Hello beautiful readers!

Diving into the world of Clarity Coast has been absolutely incredible. In no small part because the world of Clarity Coast is my love letter to the ocean. (Though it probably won't be the only one!) I've always loved the ocean, and it truly feels like I'm home whenever I'm near it, much the way Isolde feels.

I hope you loved your time on the beaches of Clarity and want to come back, because I can't wait to spend more time in this world!

In the meantime, I'd love to meet you! Sign up for my newsletter for updates and sneak peeks, and the occasional dessert recipe!

I also have a Facebook group where we share memes, I share snippets of works in progress, and everything in between. Come join the Delightful Deviants! I hope to see you there, and there will be more books very soon!

*Devyn Sinclair*

# PLAYLIST

This is a playlist of some of the songs I listened to while writing *Endless*.

You can listen to the playlist here, or scan the QR code below.

- **Airplanes** — Adam Ulanicki
- **Already Numb** — Dayseeker
- **Amar: Forgiveness** — Armand Amar, The City of Prague Philharmonic Orchestra
- **Amène-moi** — Gísli Gunnarsson
- **Amos sees Arieh** — Nicholas Britell
- **Arrival of the Birds** — The Cinematic Orchestra
- **Attention** — Sunsleep
- **Bad Timing** — Blindlove
- **Better Days** — Arman Cekin, Faydee, Kara
- **Better Off** — Sunsleep, Jonny Craig
- **Be with Me** — Ramen Djawadi

- **Black and Blue** — Hurtwave
- **Bleach** — Hurtwave
- **Blóðberg** — Sigur Ros
- **Break My Baby** — KALEO
- **Brightest Smile** — Thomas Bergen, Natalie Major
- **Can We Kiss Forever?** — Kina, Adriana Proenza
- **Can You Hear Me Now?** — Owsey
- **Catch You in My Arms** — Seion, dabl
- **Circles** — Greta Saab Bech, Ludovico Einaudi
- **A Cold Memory of You That's Beginning to Freeze Over** — Owsey
- **Contaminated** — BANKS
- **Crash And Burn** — Dayseeker
- **DECLINED** — Britton
- **DON'T LOOK DOWN (Feat. Lizzy Land)** — San Holo, Lizzy Land
- **Dreamstate** — Dayseeker
- **The Embers Glow** — Dayseeker
- **Fever** — Sunsleep
- **Fever Dream** — Hurtwave
- **Fill The Void (with Lily Rose Depp, Ramsey)** — The Weeknd, Lily Rose Depp, Ramsey
- **Find You** — Nick Jonas
- **Floating** — Borrtex
- **f.o.o.l.** — Ni/Co
- **For Granted** — Lauren Spencer Smith
- **For Me** — Lo Nightly
- **glad you're settling** — Jessica Baio
- **Goodbye** — Ramsey
- **Gris, Pt. 1** — Berlinist
- **Hard to Forget** Jane XØ
- **HAUNTED** — Britton
- **High For This** — The Weeknd
- **How Dare You** — Rachel Grae
- **Hundreds** — Lissom
- **If I Had an Airplane** — SayWeCanFly
- **if this is goodbye**— Britton
- **I'll Be Good** — Jaymes Young
- **Into The Light** — Brand X Music
- **Into Your Arms (feat. Ava Max)** — Witt Lowry, Ava Max

- **In Your Eyes** — The Weeknd
- **Lenitivo** Jeanelle Bolduc
- **Liberated** — Britton
- **Moncage** — Berlinist
- **Mór** — Sigur Ros
- **Our Funeral** — Always Never
- **Please Don't Go** — Barcelona
- **Quicksand** — Dayseeker, Spencer Stewart
- **Renegade (slowed to perfection) - TikTok Remix** — TommyMuzzic, ZeddMusique
- **Sacrifice** — Junkie XL, Ellie Goulding
- **Salvation** — Gabrielle Aplin
- **Sarah's Summer Wasteland** — Owsey
- **Sever** — Hurtwave
- **Shallow** — Tommy Profitt, Fleurie
- **She Will** — Lil Wayne, Drake
- **Signs - Dreamchaser Remix** — Caskets, Dreamchaser
- **Silent Prey** — Glasslands
- **Sleeptalk** — Dayseeker
- **Some Say** — Adam Ulanicki
- **Spin** — Axedia
- **Starving To Be Empty** — Dayseeker
- **Stolen Crown** — Sunsleep, Rory Rodriguez
- **Suffocate** — Nathan Wagner
- **This City is a Graveyard** — Baby Storme
- **Tides** — Crywolf, Skrux
- **tolerate it** — Taylor Swift
- **To My Younger Self** — Britton
- **Trust Issues** — SABAI, Adam Pearce, Zack Gray
- **Way down We Go** — KALEO
- **What if I took it off for you?** — Nemahsis
- **Without Me** — Dayseeker
- **Wrapped In Your Arms** — Fireflight
- **You Are a Memory** — Message To Bears
- **you broke me first** — Tate McRae
- **Your Guardian Angel** — The Red Jumpsuit Apparatus

# ABOUT THE AUTHOR

Devyn Sinclair writes steamy Reverse Harem romances for your wildest fantasies. Every sexy story is packed with the right amount of steam, hot men, and delicious happy endings.

She lives in the wilds of Montana in a small red house with a crazy orange cat. When Devyn's not writing, she spends time outside in big sky country, continues her quest to find the best lemon pastry there is, and buys too many books. (Of course!)

*To connect with Devyn:*

# ALSO BY DEVYN SINCLAIR

**For a complete list of Devyn's books, content warnings, bonuses and extras, please visit her website.**

https://www.devynsinclair.com/

Printed in Dunstable, United Kingdom

63629186R00231